FAERY REVENGE

Book Three in
The War Faery Trilogy

D1104691

Lush Publications
PERTH

Acknowledgements

I would like to take this opportunity to thank all of my loyal fans for your emails, tweets and Facebook messages. Your kind words make the late nights and hard work worth it.

Thanks also go to my editor, Felicity Kay, for her tireless work, her in-depth grammar lessons and her sparkling company; my cover designer, Derek Murphy, for another amazing cover; and to my dogs Chloe and Xena for putting up with late dinners and non-standard walking times.

I want to thank my Mum and Dad for always being there for me. I love you both with my whole heart.

And, last but not least, I would like to thank you for buying *Faery Revenge*. I truly hope you enjoy it.

Previously in

The War Faery Trilogy...

In Book One of the War Faery Trilogy, Isadora Scrumpleton (Izzy) is finally found by her familiar. The only problem is that he is a dog, an unprecedented event in the witching world. But even though his presence gives her access to her magic, she is unable to control her powers.

When the Faery Queen, Eloise, comes knocking on her door, Izzy learns that not only is she half-witch, half-faery, but that she is a dream-walker who roams the dreamland Trillania while she sleeps. In Trillania, she has been dating the scrumptious Aethan, a Faery Prince, and son of Eloise.

Unlike other faery dream-walkers, she has no memory of this because her witch-half, which is dominant in her waking hours, allows for no memory of these night-time dalliances.

After goblins crash her eighteenth birthday party, she joins the faery Border Guard and starts officially courting Aethan. Galanta, the evil goblin Queen, takes a personal interest in her and her relationship with Aethan. Izzy eventually realises that Aethan has been trapped into courting her by his Border Guard binding, a spell that prevents them from talking to others about Trillania.

Humiliated, Izzy runs away from him during an expedition into Trillania and calls Emerald, a dragon, to her. She rides Emerald into battle against the goblins, but is overcome and captured. Galanta tortures her, but an unexpected effect of the torture enables her to access her powers and escape.

After she has healed, Aethan reveals his true feelings for her, but is immediately kidnapped by Galanta. Izzy rides with the Border Guard to the Black Mountains in their bid to save him. There, they encounter a barrier that only she and her arch-nemesis, Isgranelda, are able to pass.

She and Isgranelda traverse the mountain and find Aethan unconscious, but alive. Isgranelda sheds her shape-shifting guise to reveal she has been Galanta all along. A vicious battle erupts between the two, but Galanta escapes before Izzy can kill her.

Izzy drips blood onto the rock where Aethan sleeps, releasing him from Galanta's spell. The rock splits in two and, as a strange wind blows around her, her two sides merge and her memories of Aethan return. He wakes as she kisses him, but when he opens his eyes and looks at her he has no memory of *her*.

The rest of the Border Guard arrives as goblin drums begin beating. They all flee down the mountain and back to Isilvitania. Izzy returns to her home, quickly falling asleep so that she can access Trillania to see what Galanta is up to. She is horrified to see Galanta weaving a spell over the rock on which Aethan lay.

While Izzy watches, Galanta sacrifices a little girl, releasing her blood onto the rock. A shape begins to emerge, flowing out of the rock until a man has formed. As the man speaks, Izzy is horrified to realise that Galanta has released Santanas Gabrielle, the mad War Faery, from the stone he was imprisoned in 12 years ago.

The story continues in *Faery Forged* when Orion asks Aethan to forge an alliance with the dark faeries by traveling to their land and bringing him home a bride.

Aethan chooses a small force to travel with him, and even though he still has no memories of her, Izzy finds herself a part of it.

Disaster strikes when they are discovered while trying to cross goblin lands. They are forced to flee but are separated when they jump into the river dividing the goblins' lands from the giants'.

Izzy ends up with Isla and Aethan, but they find that the rest of their band has been captured by giants. With the help of a friendly giant, they are able to rescue their friends and continue onto the home of the night faeries to carry out their mission. They are surprised when King Arracon offers up his own daughter and heir to the throne, Princess Ebony, to be Orion's bride.

With Santanas's power growing, their return trip proves to be even more treacherous. They are pursued by monsters as they race to take Ebony to Orion. Samuel, Ebony's personal slave, leads them to a safe place, but Wilfred is attacked and dies as they arrive.

Samuel has led them to an ancient place of worship and, while Isla weeps for her lost love, he prays to the Goddess Ulandes. She emerges from a statue and brings Wilfred back to life. The payment for this is that Wilfred and Samuel must reside with her in her land.

They continue to Isilvitania without Wilfred. Shortly after they arrive, Izzy overhears a conversation between Grams, Aethan and Rako in which she discovers that she is not what she seems. Before she can find out exactly what she is, goblins attack.

When Izzy risks her life to save Orion, Aethan declares his love for her. And although they are able to save Orion, they are horrified when they realise his good friend Legas has been taken to be sacrificed in a black magic ritual.

Orion insists on coming with them as they ride to save Legas. They follow the goblins to The Henge, arriving as the sun is about to rise.

Orion and Izzy fight their way to Legas, but when they get there, she finds it is not Legas strapped to the rock, but Orion himself. The Orion they have been traveling with is none other than Galanta, the shape-shifting Queen of the goblins.

With the use of Izzy's blood, Galanta is able to perform the spell that bonds Santanas into Orion's body. Izzy and the newly-resurrected Orion fight, and with her new-found knowledge that she is a War Faery, and the help of the narathymia, Mia, Izzy is able to maim Orion enough to allow them to escape.

They return to Isilvitania where Queen Eloise takes her pain from losing her son out on Isla. As the faeries prepare to seal the veil for a thirty day mourning period, Izzy takes Isla home with her. The last thing they see before the veil is shut, is Ebony being presented as a bride to Aethan, the new heir to the throne.

Now, read on to see what happens next...

Chapter One

Down the Rabbit Hole

E *merald. Down to the left.* The wind whipped my hair, lashing it out behind me like a cat o' nine tails as Emerald banked towards our prey.

Goblins. A *lot* of goblins.

Lightning bolts flew from my fingers as fire roared from Emerald's mouth. We skimmed over the top of the goblin horde, leaving death and destruction in our wake.

I glanced over my shoulder as we rose back into the sky and saw Isla leap from the cover of the trees. Almost too fast for my eyes to see, she pulled an arrow from the small quiver on her back, fitted it to her bow string, and released it into the nearest warrior. I saw Mia launch herself from Isla's shoulder, her claws extended as she sailed towards the nearest goblin.

A laugh burst from me as Scruffy darted out of the forest with Grams hot on his heels. She wore camouflage pants and a khaki t-shirt, and had a black balaclava pulled over her face. A heavy pair of military boots completed her outfit. She seemed to be enjoying herself immensely as she drew her sword and ran at the nearest goblin.

Shall we go down? Emerald asked.

In answer, I tightened my heels on her flank and bent down low over her neck. With one powerful stroke of her wings we were racing towards the ground. She pulled her wings flat against her body and straightened herself out like a spear, and I felt our speed increase.

'Wooooohooooo,' I screamed as the wind tore at my hair.

Just as quickly as it had begun, it stopped. She thrust her wings out to either side and pushed her legs forwards. I slammed into her neck, gravity holding me a prisoner until my acceleration matched hers.

As she touched down, I leapt from her back, pulled my sword from my scabbard, and raced towards the fight.

I leapt over a goblin, turning a full somersault in the air, and as I landed in a crouch I swept my blade out at his legs. Muscle and sinew and bone parted like butter and he toppled to the ground.

'Take that,' Grams shouted.

I spun to face a goblin behind me, thrusting my blade up under his ribcage and out through his back. Mia landed lightly on my head before propelling herself back into the air.

Scruffy appeared by my side, his lips pulled back to expose his fangs as he attacked the ankle of a goblin.

Isla leapt into the air and fired arrows into three luckless goblins, before landing on the back of the fourth. She pulled a dagger from her belt and thrust it into the side of his head.

Emerald batted at a goblin like a cat at a mouse. It flew into the air and landed about thirty metres away.

'**Isadora Scrumpleton**.' My mother's voice bellowed around the meadow behind our house. It froze me in the act of breaking a goblin's neck. 'Stop this right this instance.'

My blood lust and adrenaline faded away as I looked around at the field, seeing it for what it really was.

Goblins made of straw and sticks lay on their sides. Chopped into little pieces or still burning from Emerald's and my initial attack. It had taken us all morning to make enough of them so that all of us could have some fun. I resented having to stop.

What was the point of being a War Faery if you still had to do what your Mum said?

'**ISADORA.**' If I had thought she'd been angry before, it was nothing compared with now. When she got like that, it wasn't worth defying her.

'Phooey.' Grams pulled off her balaclava and threw it onto the ground.

Isla sighed and unstrung her bow. She pulled an arrow out of the straw man closest to her and slipped it back into her quiver.

Emerald lay down where she was and put a wing over her face.

Emerald. Disappointment tinged my thoughts.

She shrugged a shoulder and mumbled into my mind, *Last time we got in trouble she wouldn't roast me any meat.*

You have fire for breath. You can roast your own meat. I walked over to her and shoved her flank.

*Yes, but when **I** do it, it's all burnt on the outside. When your Mum does it...* She stopped thinking in words and, instead, a picture of a roast, so tender it was falling off the bone, popped into my head.

I sighed. Mum's roasts were almost worth being good for. *Almost.* And that was part of my problem. I hadn't found anything worth being good for since I had come back through the veil.

'Oh come on,' I said to Isla and Grams. 'We'd better get up there before she has an apoplectic fit.'

The two of them followed me as I traipsed from the field. It was only the fact that they were behind me that stopped me from kicking my feet in childish rebellion.

Mum was waiting for us in the kitchen. Her crossed arms and her tapping foot made it clear her mood had not improved in the last few minutes. Sabby stood next to her in an identical posture, but I knew her foot was tapping for a different reason. I hadn't invited her to our little 'party' because I hadn't wanted to distract her from her study for her first year exams. I could see now that *that* had been a mistake.

'Sit.' Mum pointed at the kitchen table. My former teacher, Radismus, was already there.

Scruffy's bottom hit the floor and he sat to attention. Isla and Grams slid meekly into their seats. I pulled mine out and flipped it around one hundred and eighty degrees before straddling it. My elbows rested on the top of the chair back while I investigated my nails.

I saw Sabby shake her head, a small smile quirking the corners of her mouth as she took the chair next to me. Mia let out a little mew and scampered over the table to Sabby. She hissed down at Sabby's familiar, Phantom, and then climbed up Sabby's arm to her neck. Sabby winced as Mia's paws started running through her hair. I pulled a face in sympathy. Mia's grooming, while sweet, was normally very painful.

Radismus stood and crossed to Mum's side. He pulled her stiff body into his arms, whispered something into her ear, and then planted a kiss on her lips. I was still getting over the shock of finding out that the two of them had become an item.

'I'll be off,' he said, looking around at the rest of us. The smile he was trying to hide was starting to break through. No doubt he wanted to get out of there before Mum turned her bad mood onto him as well.

Mum waited till he had left before she began. 'What in the Great Dark Sky did you think you were doing?'

I stared at her in sullen silence. I mean, it had been pretty obvious what we'd been doing.

Grams raised one hand in the air and, when Mum looked at her, said, 'We were having some good, old-fashioned fun.'

I felt a smile part my lips but Mum was not amused. She raised her eyebrows at Grams and turned her gaze to Isla.

'Ummm, generating a huge amount of noise and generally causing the villagers to panic.'

Mum's foot stopped its tapping and her expression softened. She had taken one look at Isla that awful morning we had come home and had easily slipped into the role of mother hen.

'That's right, Isla.' Mum reached behind her and picked up a plate of cupcakes. 'You can have one of these.'

Isla smiled and leaned over to take one of the cakes. From the smell of them they were still warm.

'Double-chocolate, choc chip?' Grams licked her lips.

Mum nodded as she offered the plate to Sabby.

'Yes, well, I'm awfully sorry about the racket. I can see now, in retrospect, how it could have caused quite a kerfuffle on the main street.' Grams's eyes were glued to the cakes. 'It's not every day that a dragon performs a full attack on your village.'

Mum still held the plate out of Gram's reach.

'I don't see why it was such a shock,' I said. 'Emerald's been here for a fortnight.' Our minds had collided as soon as I'd come back through the veil. Her arrival, an hour later, had created quite a ruckus. 'You'd think they'd be used to her by now.'

'Oh, I don't think it was *her* they were worried about,' Mum said, giving me a meaningful look.

I shifted on the chair. It always looked so cool when other people sat like this, but the hard edge of the wooden back was beginning to dig into my forearms. 'It was just a little lightning.' Oh great, now I had something stuck in my eye as well. It was going to look like I was trying not to cry. And I wasn't. I mean, I *really* wasn't.

Mum crossed to my side as the tears escaped, rolling down my cheeks. I pulled back from her for a second before giving into the crushing warmth of her embrace.

She had broken me again. Every time the pressing force built inside me, tearing and clawing and ripping until I couldn't handle the rawness of the pain, she would let it out. And for a few, short, blissful minutes I would be whole again.

I sighed and pulled back from her, wiping my face on the back of my arm. 'Sorry,' I croaked. I let my body relax as I enjoyed the emptiness inside me. It wouldn't be long before the despair found me again.

'Here.' She held the plate of cakes out to me, waiting till I had taken one before offering them to Grams.

I took a bite of the cake, chewed a few times and then swallowed. 'How bad was it?' I asked.

'Well, I only know what happened at the Cupcake Café.' I couldn't be sure, but it looked like Mum was fighting a smile. 'Agnes Hedge was entertaining her friends from London. Two of them jumped up and ran away, shrieking as if they were being chased by goblins, and the third slid clean off her chair.'

'Dead?' Grams broke a bit off her cake and popped it into her mouth.

'Fainted,' Mum said. 'Colonel Smith waved his cane in the air and started regaling stories about the Great Faery War.'

'He'll be going on about that for days,' Grams said. 'Remind me not to go up to the Toasted Toadstool tonight.'

'Deidre Rutherspoon got such a fright she dropped a tray of coffee cups.'

Isla grimaced. She was always more contrite than I.

'It's all right, Dear.' Mum patted her on the arm. 'I was able to repair them. Then there was Lindsey Nettle.'

Grams stopped eating and looked up at Mum.

'She fell backwards over a hedge and showed her underwear to the patrons of the Cupcake Café.' Now she *was* smiling. 'Big. White. Bloomers.'

'Ha.' Grams let out a satisfied snort. 'That'll teach her for making a play for Lionel.'

'I was just coming out of the library,' Sabby said. 'Old Tom was sitting out the front. He jumped up and drew a flip knife out of his pocket. Then he screamed something about goblins and took off.'

'He'll be halfway to London by now.' Grams shook her head. 'We told them all that the veil had been sealed. A goblin attack will be impossible for at least another two weeks.'

Two weeks. Only two more weeks till the veil was penetrable again. I felt a small hard knot start up in my gut. It was both too close and too far away.

'I'd better go and see if Emerald is okay.' I stood and flipped the chair back around, seating it back in at the table. I'm sure the fact that I didn't need to go and *see* Emerald to know she was okay wasn't lost on any of them.

'Here.' Mum opened the fridge and pulled out a haunch of meat. 'Tell her I'll cook her something tonight.'

I took the meat from Mum and headed for the front door. *Got you some meat.*

Stop. Emerald's mind screeched into mine. *Don't come down here.*

Her words had the opposite effect on me to what she had intended. I dropped the meat, yanked open the door and started sprinting for the field. It didn't take long for Scruffy to match my speed and I could hear Isla right behind me.

Emerald was in trouble, from *what* I couldn't begin to imagine, but there was no *way* I was leaving her to fend for herself.

I raced through the trees down the hill to the meadow, running faster and faster as I felt her mounting panic.

I'm coming.

Oh no. No, no, no, no, no.

It took far too long before Isla and I burst out of the trees and onto the flat. I raised my arm ready to throw lightning and…stopped.

I told you not to come, Emerald wailed in anguish.

An enormous black dragon loomed in front of her. The sun flashed off his scales, turning him from black to brilliant scarlet for the briefest of seconds. Steam curled out of his nostrils as he pawed at the ground. His talons tore up huge chunks of dirt and hurled them into the air.

He was, to put it quite plainly, magnificent.

As I watched, Emerald bowed her head and lowered herself to the ground in a posture of submission.

Isla let out a hiss, re-strung her bow and notched an arrow. It was only then that I saw the man standing beside the dragon.

Easily seven foot tall, he was sheathed in black armour that mimicked the colour-shifting tendency of his dragon, flashing from black to ruby as he turned to observe us. A helmet covered his head and masked his eyes, leaving only his mouth visible.

He lifted one hand in our direction and called out, 'I come in peace.'

Yeah, right. Emerald may have appeared submissive, but there was anger evident in her thoughts. Anger, and a tinge of something else. Embarrassment?

'My name is Turos, and I have come to take Silvanta home.'

Silvanta? It took me a moment to realise he was talking about Emerald.

'She *is* home,' I yelled back.

He shook his head. 'Your dragon does not belong here. It is time for her to come home and face her consequences.'

Emerald pressed herself further into the dirt and if I hadn't known that she was a big, tough dragon, I would have said she was quivering.

'What consequences?'

'All actions pay a price.'

'What actions? What price?' His refusal to answer my questions was really starting to cheese me off.

He tilted his head to the side while he considered my question, and his dragon swung its head around, observing us with cold, glittering eyes. The beast let out a steam-filled snort and Turos nodded his head as if agreeing with something.

I was betting that whatever conversation had just gone on had been less than complimentary about Isla and me. The whole dragon in the head thing was pretty cool when it was me doing it, but in this context it sucked big time.

'Put away the bow,' I murmured to Isla. Maybe he would answer my questions if we weren't physically threatening him.

Turos's body language remained alert as we walked towards him. I stopped far enough away that we wouldn't be forced to look up at him. 'Who are you?'

He clenched his hand and placed it on his chest, bending his head as he said, 'I am Turos, son of Bladimir, Head Dragon Rider of….'

I held a hand up to interrupt him. 'Sorry, is it you, or your father that's the Head Dragon Rider? Cause the way you phrased that sentence left me unsure?'

If I hadn't been looking for it, I mightn't have noticed the tightening of his lips that showed his annoyance. Emerald snickered in my mind and I suppressed my own smile. It was a petty triumph I knew, but a triumph none the less.

'My father, Bladimir, is the Head Dragon Rider.' He raised an eyebrow in the air and paused as if waiting for me to ask another question.

I waved a hand at him. 'Do go on.' My bad mood was definitely returning.

'Head Dragon Rider of Millenia.'

Isla let out a gasp. 'But, Millenia does not exist.'

'And yet, here I stand before you.' His smirk made my hands clench into fists.

I turned to Isla. 'What's Millenia?'

'An ancient city. A mythical city.' She shrugged one shoulder. 'Its existence has always been a source of much debate. Like your Atlantis.'

As I turned back to Turos, light crackled across the sky. The black dragon threw its head in the air and snorted.

'Yes,' Turos said, 'we must go. Come Silvanta.'

Emerald's misery was tangible inside my mind.

'She's not going anywhere without me,' I said.

'Without *us*,' Isla corrected me.

I looked over at her.

'Don't think you're going to have an adventure like *that* without me.'

'Now see here....' Turos stopped speaking as the sky did that weird flicky thing again. He glanced at the black dragon and then said, 'We are running out of time.'

I was pretty sure that wasn't what he had been going to say. 'We'll just go pack some things.'

'There's no time.' The sky flickered again. 'You come now or you don't come at all.' His dragon lifted a leg and Turos jumped onto it, pulling himself up onto a leather harness that sat around the dragon's neck.

'Isadora,' Mum called from the top of the hill. 'What's going on down there?'

I looked at Isla. Mum was going to kill us if we took off without an explanation, and there were no *words* for what Sabby would do to us.

'I'm *coming*,' Isla said, reading my mind.

The sky flickered again.

'Quickly,' Turos said.

'Mum,' I yelled as I clambered onto Emerald's back. 'Isla and I are going for a ride.'

'What?' Her voice was getting closer.

'Wait,' I heard Sabby yell out. 'I'm coming too.'

Isla handed Scruffy up to me and I tucked him against my chest with my arms nestled on each side of him. 'We may be gone for a few days,' I yelled. 'You'll miss your exams.'

'Isadora Scrumpleton.'

I looked over my shoulder and pulled a face as Isla climbed on behind me. That had been Mum's angry voice.

She broke from the trees onto the meadow with Sabby right behind her as Turos took flight. Their mouths gaped as they stared at the gigantic dragon. He had looked big on the ground, but in full flight the magnitude of his size became apparent. He was easily twice as big as Emerald.

Lance, Emerald thought at me. *His name is Lance.*

Turos and Lance circled the field, gaining height as Emerald took a few lurching steps and leapt into the air.

'Izzy,' Mum yelled. 'Where are you going?'

That was a *really* good question.

'Don't you dare have another adventure without me,' Sabby shrieked. Mia clambered up onto Sabby's head and spread her limbs, but we were already too far above her for her to be able to glide to us. I felt a pang, but knew she would be safer with Sabby than us.

'I'll tell you all about it when we get back,' I hollered down to them. I wasn't sure if they heard me or not.

I passed the leather straps tied around Emerald's neck back to Isla. She grabbed them and, as she pulled back, the leather webbing we had constructed for Scruffy opened up. I tucked him into it and crossed a second set of straps over the top of it. He stuck his head out of the top of his safety harness, a broad doggy grin on his face.

'They're not going to be very happy,' Isla yelled into my ear.

That was probably the understatement of the year.

Emerald stretched out her neck and sped after Lance. The sky flickered again, but this time, it didn't stop. Tiny licks of lightning danced around us. I held out a hand, watching as they prickled over the surface of my skin.

Faster and faster they swirled, growing in size as well as number until all I could see were the lights.

Hang on,' Emerald told me.

'Hold tight,' I yelled over my shoulder as I wrapped the leather around my wrists.

And then the lights coalesced into a huge ball of light in front of us. I could see the silhouette of Turos hunching over Lance's neck. The ball pulsed once, twice and as it pulsed the third time, Emerald let out a roar. The ball exploded, light rolling away like a shockwave from a hole rent in the sky.

Tendrils of icy air licked my face as we raced towards the black void. The blue of our sky disappeared and black encased us. Cold pressed in on all sides and I fought to breathe. I heard Isla's choked breath behind me and Scruffy let out a whine.

Before I could panic there was a second explosion and a blue slice appeared. Light blazed, illuminating us in its radiance. Two more strokes of Emerald's wings and we were through.

I sucked in air and looked behind to check Isla was all right.

Her eyes sparkled with excitement as she gave me a huge smile. 'I can't believe you tried to make me stay behind. I mean, *that* was *awesome.'*

Blue water stretched to the horizon below us. Lance banked to the left at the same time as Emerald did. She at least knew where we were going.

Where are we?

Millenia. Her thoughts held the feel of a shoulder shrug. I imagined if she had been a teenager she might have added a, 'Duh,' at the end.

I sighed. When she got all sullen it wasn't worth trying to converse with her.

Scruffy looked up at me, his tongue hanging out in a doggy smile. He nestled down into his riding bag and closed his eyes.

'There.' Isla leant forwards and pointed straight ahead.

I squinted at the horizon but it took me another minute before I could see what *she* already had. Smoke. Lots of it.

A few minutes later I could make out the shape of mountains pushing into the sky. A soft orange glow was visible on the tip of the highest mountain. The smoke came from this.

A volcano? Oh, that was just great.

'At least we'll be warm,' Isla yelled into my ear.

I turned to look at her. 'Have you not heard of Pompeii?'

She flashed me a grin. 'What's a little ash?'

The volcano never erupts. It was the first thing Emerald had said voluntarily since we had got there.

It's always never till the first time.

She let out a little snort of amusement.

I took that as a good sign. *So…do I need to start calling you Silvanta?*

There was a pause before she said, *I never really did like that name much. Admittedly, it was better than 'Dragon'.*

That's what Santanas used to call you?

She shook her head up and down. *I would appreciate it if you would continue to call me Emerald. It will remind me of happier times.*

I thought a question mark at her but she ignored me.

The mountains stretched higher and higher as we soared towards them, till they towered above. As we got closer I could make out structures on the highest mountain. Graceful buildings, linked by arched bridges.

Steeples and towers rose into the air like delicate pieces of lacework.

Each building had a large platform at its front, and as I watched, a dragon emerged from an enormous entry way and strode to the middle of the platform. A person, dressed in an outfit similar to Turos's, jumped lithely up onto the dragon's neck. A second later they were airborne.

I could feel Emerald's distress radiating into my mind and I rubbed a hand over her scales. As we headed for the largest of the buildings her anguish increased, tears built in my eyes as I shared her emotions.

We swooped down towards a platform where a group of men, covered in full-length, black capes waited. They were still as they watched our approach.

Emerald flared her wings and took a few running steps before she came to a stop. Isla dismounted and I untied Scruffy and handed him down to her, before sliding down.

Turos approached the group and bowed low over the offered hand of the man in the lead. 'Father,' he said. 'I have returned.'

I let out a snort. I mean I would have thought that that part at *least* was obvious.

Bladimir turned to observe us. 'You successfully managed to capture her?'

'She came willingly with Silvanta.'

Emerald's low moan filled my mind.

'And the other one?'

'A faery Princess.'

Bladimir nodded his head. 'She will be of use to us.' He clapped Turos on the shoulder and said, 'You have done well, my boy.'

Turos pulled his helmet off his head and ran his hand through bleached-white hair. His smile, when he turned to look at us was full of smug arrogance.

I took two quick steps towards him, leapt into the air, and smacked my fist into his face as hard as I could.

The rest of the men surged towards me, pulling weapons from underneath their cloaks.

'Don't hurt her,' Bladimir roared. 'We need her alive.'

Don't fight them. Emerald's panicked thought echoed around my head.

I ignored her as I turned to face the pack, ready to kill them all if I had to.

Where normal men would have still been a few paces away, the leader was already on me. He moved with such speed as he whipped a wooden baton at my head that I only just managed to deflect it. And even then the tip of it struck the side of my skull.

'Izzy.' I heard Isla shout my name, saw her struggling beside me.

My head rocked to the side and I collapsed to my knees. I raised a hand to my hair and stared incoherently at my red-stained fingers. The last thing I saw before I lost consciousness was blood running from Turos's nose. I felt a smile stretch my lips as my vision faded, and then all I heard was white noise.

Chapter Two

Order in the Court

I opened my eyelids to find Isla sitting cross-legged beside me. Her eyes were closed and her lips were moving but either I had lost my hearing or no sound was coming out.

I let out a little groan as I lifted my head off the mattress. Her eyes flew open and she leaned over, pressing a hand to my forehead as her beautiful blue eyes stared into mine. I could feel a heavy weight on my stomach and lifted a hand to feel Scruffy's body nestled there.

'Well,' Isla said, taking her hand off my forehead. 'That went well.'

'You think?' I let out a groan, sat up on the edge of the bed, and looked around. We were in a small, dark room, with a door made of metal bars, and one tiny window.

'We're still alive.'

'I wish I wasn't.' I moved Scruffy to the mattress beside me so that I could bend forwards and put my head in my hands. It hurt like a bastard.

'You say that, but I know you, and if you were dead you'd be really, really annoyed.'

I let out a laugh which quickly changed to a groan.

'Shame we didn't bring Sabby,' Isla said. 'She'd have had you fixed up in no time.'

I looked up at her through my fingers. 'I'm pretty glad we *didn't* bring her. In fact I'm wishing *we* hadn't come.'

She waved a hand in the air and sat back down on the end of the mattress, curling her legs up underneath her in one graceful movement. 'It's just like school camp. The first day all the kids are boo-hooing and wanting to go home, but by day three they're all having a lovely time.'

I shook my head. 'I don't remember ever having been concussed then locked in a prison cell while on school camp.'

'Oh,' she said, 'you just haven't lived then.'

I stretched out my mind feeling for Emerald. She wasn't there.

Sitting bolt upright on the bed, I tried again. Still nothing.

'Oh no,' I said.

'What?' Isla tilted her head, her face taking on a serious expression.

'Emerald's gone. What if they've killed her?' Tears welled in my eyes. Why hadn't we taken a stance back at the meadow when there was only Lance and Turos? We may have had a chance then.

Because you were looking for a reason to get out of there. A reason to leave.

The ugly little voice in my head had seen what I hadn't. I'd been so keen to come with Emerald, not for her sake, but for mine. I was selfish, and mean, and....

'She's alive,' Isla said. 'They said they were going to put you both on trial. They wouldn't have killed her if they were going to do that.'

'You think?'

She nodded.

I was silent while I contemplated her words. 'What are we being tried for?'

'She's being done for deserting, and you're being done for dragon theft, amongst some other things. There was rather a long list.' She smiled at me. 'You've been pretty busy.'

'I haven't...I didn't...I...what in the Great Dark Sky? They told you that?'

'They came and read out your charges while you were unconscious.'

'Did you tell them it wasn't me?'

'Oh yes, that would have sorted it all out. Silly me, what was I thinking.' She tapped a finger against her chin.

'You don't seem very worried.'

'These things normally sort themselves out. No use worrying until I have to.'

I refrained from mentioning that barely a month ago things hadn't worked out so well. She had lost her brother and I had lost my...pain slammed into me.

Aethan, Oh Dark Sky, *Aethan.*

By now he would be married to Ebony. By now he would be enjoying her lush body. By now he would have forgotten about me.

'Stop thinking about him.' Isla slapped my arm.

With difficulty, I stopped the Aethan and Ebony slideshow that was playing in my mind. 'How did you know?'

'You had that look on your face. You know, the one where you're about to throw up.'

I pushed Aethan back to the corner of my mind where I kept him, and refortified the walls I had placed around my heart. The pain only eased a little, but it was enough to let me breathe again.

'What are we going to do?'

'Well, I was thinking I might have a nap. I didn't sleep well last night. I could hear Scruffy snoring through the wall.'

I looked over at my little, white familiar, curled up on the end of the bed. 'He was farting too,' I added.

He opened one eye, yawned and then turned around-and-around while he kneaded the hard mattress with his front paws. Finally he let out a contented grunt and lay back down. A few seconds later a foul smell wafted over us.

Isla coughed and shuffled along the bed away from him. 'He never used to fart in front of me,' she said.

I shrugged. 'You live with us now.'

A second wave washed over us.

'I liked it better when he was trying to impress me,' Isla said through her fingers.

'Count yourself lucky. I never got a grace period.'

'If he doesn't stop this it'll be our dead bodies they put on trial.'

'You're on trial too?' I turned to face her fully.

'Oh yes.' Her voice sounded like she was trying not to laugh. 'I'm being tried for aiding and abetting a criminal.'

'Scruffy?'

She shook her head, 'Although, if they could smell this they'd have him up for crimes against humanity.'

She tensed and a few moments later I could hear footsteps echoing down the passageway outside our door.

'It's show time,' she said, standing.

Two guards appeared in the doorway.

'Only two?' Isla's voice had a teasing edge to it and I was guessing it had taken more than two to get her there.

'We have orders to kill the hound if you resist.'

Her face took on an ominous look, which I was guessing made us look more like sisters, because I was sure I had an identical one on mine.

I resisted the urge to hurl insults at him and instead picked Scruffy up, holding him close to my chest. He opened his eyes, looked around, and then promptly went back to sleep.

One of the guards let out a low laugh.

'What?' I snarled.

'He's just funny.' He shrugged his shoulders, pulled a key out of his pocket and unlocked our door. 'It would be a damn shame to have to kill him.'

'Nice eye make-up,' Isla said as she strode out of the cell in front of me.

His facial expression darkened and I noticed a purple bruise under one of his eyes. His mate let out a chortle and elbowed him in the ribs.

I let out a laugh of my own and followed Isla down the hall. I was guessing she had given him that bruise on the way in.

Two more guards were waiting at the far end. As we approached, they turned and took a corridor running off to the left. We followed.

Enough turns later that I couldn't have found my way back to the prison cell even if I had wanted to, we arrived at a large hall.

Stairs the full width of the right side of the hall ascended till I could see the blue of the sky. Two enormous wooden doors dominated the far wall of the room. They stood open, allowing me to see a crowd. The united rumble of their voices was a low murmur to my ears.

Isla elbowed me and nodded her head to the right. I looked up to see Emerald trying to negotiate the stairs. A metal hood covered her head. It was connected by chains to metal rings on her legs which were making it difficult for her to walk. Black liquid stained the scales beneath the rings. Blood.

I gasped and started to move towards her but one of the guards drew a sword and looked pointedly at Scruffy. Tears of frustration stung my eyes and I couldn't help but feel that I had betrayed her as I watched her stumble.

If only we hadn't brought Scruffy. I was pretty sure Isla and I could take the four guards easily, then we just had to free Emerald and get back up the stairs and then....

The harsh reality of our situation crashed into me. Because then we would be pursued by other dragons and their riders, and even if we out-manoeuvred them we would still be stuck in a different world with no idea how to get back to our own.

Our only choice was to behave ourselves and hope that they let us go back home. That *really* grated.

So, instead of fighting, I watched my friend be led down the stairs and into the room. The voices in the courtroom hushed as she entered. Our guards led us to the opposite side of the room from where Emerald stood on a dragon-sized platform.

I was guessing it was the metal hood that was making communication between us impossible and I didn't like it one bit. Her eyes were sad as she rolled them towards me.

'All rise for his Majesty, King Bladimir,' a voice intoned.

Chairs creaked and scraped along the floor as the silent congregation stood and bowed their heads.

Bladimir swept into the room, his long, black cape open to reveal a red velvet shirt and black pants. He strode to the front where a bench sat high on a platform, climbed the stairs to it, and sat down. Turos followed closely behind him. I gritted my teeth as the smug bastard took up the position on the King's right.

'There is not enough room in here for Lance,' Bladimir said. 'He will give his witness statement from the hall.'

There was a snort and then the enormous head of the black dragon appeared in the doorway. He looked over at Emerald and snorted again. She met his gaze for a few seconds before lowering her eyes again. Without having access to her thoughts I couldn't be sure, but if I had to give a name to the emotion in her eyes I would have said shame.

For the first time since the whole saga had begun, I began to wonder if perhaps Emerald *had* done something wrong.

'Be seated,' Bladimir said.

I positioned Scruffy on my lap as I slumped into a chair. Isla remained standing.

'Your Lordship.' When Bladimir looked at her, Isla curtsied; a feat I would have found impossible in the black, leather pants we were wearing. 'It seems that we have no legal representation. I bid permission to act on our behalf.'

If I hadn't known that underneath Isla's ditsy, happy-go-lucky personality there was a political mind that could rival the best, I would have broken out in a cold sweat.

Luckily he didn't know what I did. 'Of course, Princess.' He gave her a condescending smile and she fluttered her eyelashes and blushed.

I still couldn't work out how she could do that on a whim, but it sure had come in handy over the last couple of weeks. All Isla had to do was blush when Mum roused on us for our latest skulduggery (Mum's word) and Mum's face would soften and before you knew it we were getting fed lemon cake.

I sighed. Dark Sky, if we got out of this alive I'd take as many tongue lashings from Mum as she wanted to give us.

Bladimir picked up a piece of paper and read from it. 'We are here today to bear witness to the testament of Silvanta Dragontears, Isadora Gabrielle and Isla Gabrielle.'

I looked at Isla and raised my eyebrows.

'Well you *are* a Gabrielle,' she said. 'Besides, it can't hurt to use your Royal name in your hour of need.'

Bladimir cleared his throat and stopped talking. He stared at us until Isla blushed again, and I squirmed in my seat. I felt like I was back at school.

'Silvanta Dragontears, you are charged with deserting your country. How do you plead to this charge?'

Emerald snorted and shook her head.

'I'll take that as a guilty,' he said, writing something onto his piece of paper.

'I object.' Isla jumped to her feet and strode to the front of the room.

Bladimir looked up with a startled look on his face.

'As Silvanta is capable of communicating her thoughts, there is no need to guess what she is trying to tell us. Unless you remove her hood so that she can talk, this trial will be nothing but a farce.'

'To the other defendant?' Bladimir flicked a hand in my direction. 'She is a criminal. How could we trust what she tells us?'

'I'm sure that Silvanta is quite capable of confirming the accuracy of the translation with a simple nod of her head.'

Bladimir stared at Isla for a second, his mouth working as he tried to come up with a good reason not to allow it. Finally he nodded his head and said, 'Very well. Remove Silvanta's hood.'

Two of the guards came forward and unlocked the rings from her legs. I winced as I looked at her torn flesh. One of the scales was half hanging off, and another was missing entirely. She bent her head as they lifted the metal hood and staggered to the side with it. It must have weighed a tonne.

As soon as it was clear of her head, her thoughts rushed into mine.

I'm sorry.

Are you okay?

She looked down at her legs and then back up at me. *I've had worse.*

Emerald, what did you do?

'How does she plead?' Bladimir's voice interrupted before she could answer my question.

'Not guilty,' I said.

'And to the charge of deserting her mate?'

Emerald's head hung low and her misery seeped into my mind.

Emerald?

I just wanted to be something more.

More than what?

She shook her head. *More than just a female.*

Is that such a bad thing?

Female dragons live in the mountain, lay eggs and raise the hatchlings. They do not fly so high into the sky that air becomes thin and exhilaration fills them. They do not carry riders, or fly into battle, or hunt for fresh meat. They do not swim in the ocean or burnish their scales on the sand. But most importantly…they are not allowed to bond. Her words, which had been impassioned, now had a feel of resignation about them. As if by admitting all of that, she had sealed her own fate.

I took a deep breath. *There is nothing wrong with wanting to have more than what you did. To be more than what you are.*

Maybe not in your world.

'If you are quite finished.' Bladimir's voice had a bored edge.

'She pleads not guilty to that as well, your Lordship,' I said.

'Is this true, Silvanta?'

You didn't desert him. I said the words urgently before she could shake her head. *He deserted you by not allowing you to be what you want.*

You don't understand.

Yes I do. You couldn't have been happy with him the way things were. You had to spread your wings and find yourself so that you could come back to him.

She chuckled in my head. *You humans spend so much time thinking about emotions. But, strangely, I find I can relate to that.*

She looked over at Bladimir and nodded her head.

Lance let out a bellow of displeasure from the doorway.

What's up with him? I asked her.

You never asked who my mate was.

I looked over at him. *Lance? Big, bad Lance was your mate?*

She flickered her eyelids a few times and looked at him sideways, a small look of satisfaction on her face. *He could have had any of the females, but he chose me.*

So what happened?

Santanas came. He wooed me with tales of adventure and when he left, I went too.

So I'm guessing Lance wasn't very happy with that.

She shot him a look again. *I hadn't seen him again till this morning.*

I was suddenly struck with how lonely she must have been for all those years. Tricked into slavery by Santanas and then unable to return to her home.

Have you tried to explain to him?

His mind is blocked to me. She gave her head a little shake and her gigantic eyes shone with wetness. *Santanas told me I would only be gone a few weeks. That was thirty years ago.*

You still love him. It wasn't a question. I could see it on her face and feel it radiating into my body.

What you feel for your man. That is what I felt for Lance.

He's not my man any more.

'If you two have quite finished your discussion,' Bladimir's voice dripped with sarcasm, 'it would be good to proceed.'

'What did she say?' Isla managed to get her mouth to stay still as she whispered to me.

'Lance was her mate. She still loves him.' I garbled it under my breath while keeping an eye on Bladimir to see if he noticed.

'So Silvanta, when you left, was it your intention to bring back a faery horde to enslave us?'

I let out a laugh. The man was so far from the truth it didn't bear thinking about. 'She was bored,' I said.

Lance let out a snarl.

'Not with you.' I held my hands up to placate him. 'With where her life as a female was leading. She didn't want to be stuck in a hill, popping out babies.'

Lance's eyes narrowed, but I could tell he was listening.

'Come on,' I directed my words at him, 'you *knew* she was different. That's what attracted you to her in the first place. But then you expected her to give up the very thing that made you fall in love with her.'

'That's not true.' The look on Turos's face was almost comical as the words burst from him. 'I mean, she never talked to me about it.'

'Oh,' I said to Turos, 'and you didn't notice anything? Like maybe she got a bit depressed just before she left.' I was guessing now. I mean did dragons even get depressed?

'I thought it was the pregnancy.'

My eyebrows rode up my face as I turned to look at Emerald. *You were pregnant?*

He said a couple of weeks.

What happened to the baby?

She shifted uncomfortably, but didn't answer.

'Santanas offered her an adventure. She saw it as her last opportunity to have some fun before she settled into a life of mediocrity.'

'You mean *you* offered her an adventure,' Bladimir said. 'You are the rider bonded to her. It must be you who took her.'

'I'm eighteen,' I said. 'I wasn't even a twinkle in my mother's eye when Emerald, urr, I mean Silvanta left.'

'That's impossible.' Turos slammed his fist down on the table and leapt to his feet. He towered over us as he glared at us from the platform. 'Now you tell falsehoods.'

'Angry much?' Isla muttered.

His eyes flashed as red flushed his cheeks.

'It's not him,' I said. I had a feeling that a very, angry dragon was living in his head. I looked over at Lance. 'If you would just talk to her, this whole mess could be sorted out.'

Little flames shot out of his nostrils with a puff of smoke. If he didn't gain control of his emotions we were all going to be barbequed.

'Maybe it's a little soon,' I amended.

'He wants custody,' Turos said.

'Of what?' Isla asked.

'Of their child, after it hatches.'

'That was thirty years ago, how would....'

Turos held his hand up to stop me. 'Dragon females can incubate eggs in their bodies for as long as they need to until they deem it safe to give birth.'

'Elephants can do that,' Isla said. 'Well, not the egg part.'

'We do not know what this ephelant is,' Turos said.

Isla opened her mouth but I nudged her with my elbow. Now was probably *not* the time to correct his English.

'And frankly we do not care. We want custody of the egg once it has been laid.'

Tears filled Emerald's eyes as she bowed her head in agreement.

'Well, now *that* has been settled, we can set punishment for Silvanta for her desertion.' Bladimir rubbed his hands together.

'Don't you think she's being punished enough?' Isla asked.

'She was told she would only be away for a couple of weeks,' I added. 'She's spent the last thirty years mourning the loss of her land, her friends and her mate.'

'And now you are making her give up something she treasured enough to harbour in her body all this time. A lesser female would have given birth for the company alone. But she chose to keep the child safe.' Isla slapped her hand onto the table to emphasise her words.

Bladimir's face turned purple. 'I don't see how this is any of your....'

'It is enough.' Turos looked at Lance and I was sure by the look on his face he was asking him if he were sure.

Lance nodded his head once and Turos repeated himself. 'It is enough.'

'One down, two to go,' Isla muttered.

It wasn't much of a win though.

Emerald closed her eyes and lay down. Even if I wasn't feeling it in my head I would have known she was miserable. Every line of her posture shouted it.

She had finally got what she had wished for most, she had come home, but she felt even more alone than before. Having Lance so close to her, and how their time apart had affected him...she was torn between the agony of her own loss, and her knowledge of what she had done to him.

I had an urge to claw at my insides to purge the desperate darkness, and if it hadn't been a mirror to my own emotions over the last month, the despair would have brought me to my knees.

Isla reached out and took my hand and I realised that tears tracked down my face. I sniffed and wiped my free arm across my cheeks. Then I glared up at Turos, daring him to say something. But the expression on his face was thoughtful, not vindictive. Which was a real shame, because I was looking for an excuse to break his nose again.

'Well,' Bladimir waved a hand at me, 'I think this is proof enough that these two are fully bonded. Guards, take her away and ready her for execution.'

Isla let out a hiss and Emerald's head came up as her tail lashed from side-to-side. She let out a roar as steam oozed out of her nose.

I jumped up, backing away with Scruffy clutched to my chest. Just let them try it. I'd show them what I was capable of.

'Wait,' Turos yelled over the shrieks of the audience. 'There is another way we can be sure.' He turned to his father. 'If Lance were to read Silvanta's mind he could bear witness to the events of that day. He could verify if this is the person who stole her away.'

I looked over at Lance. He didn't appear very happy about the suggestion but he wasn't breathing out fire, so I guessed that was a yes.

'That's if you're okay with it?' I didn't realise Turos was speaking to me until Isla nudged me.

'Okay with the one idea which may save my life?' I shrugged my shoulders. 'Oh, why not?'

A small smile touched the corners of his mouth and for the first time I noticed how attractive he was. White-blond hair spiked over a face that held the most extraordinary iceberg-blue eyes. His bronzed skin only added to the effect of the colour combination. He moved with the ease and grace of a fighter, and I was betting that all seven foot of him was corded with muscle.

I didn't have to be told to know he was dangerous, and I suspected I had only landed that blow on him because he had let me.

He let his gaze wander down and then up my body, lingering on my chest before returning to my face, and then he winked. Annoyingly, I found myself blushing. It seemed Lance wasn't the only bad boy in the room.

'How do we do it?' I forced my shoulders back and looked him in the face.

He shrugged. 'Lance and Silvanta need to link.'

Emerald and Lance looked at each other, staring into each other's eyes, and then all of a sudden it wasn't just

Emerald in my head. I could feel a large male presence that I assumed was Lance. Turos's touch was much lighter.

Careful Lance, Turos said, *the faery isn't used to this.*

The heavy presence withdrew slightly and suddenly I had thoughts of my own again.

I, ahhhh, it was funny hearing my voice echoing in three other heads, *I didn't realise we would all be able to hear each other.*

Handy during battle. Turos directed his next thought at Emerald. *What happened that day?*

There was a pause while Emerald composed herself. Her emotions concerning her mental link with Lance were convoluted. Finally, she began.

You were away, Lance. I could feel the egg building inside of me, so when the other females came for me, I went to the mountains. She was in a cavern inside the mountain. Steam swirled and rose from patches of larva. Dragons lay in groups around stones...no...eggs. I was looking at the dragon hatching ground.

I wasn't ready. She directed the next thought more fully at Lance. *To never fly with you as we used to. To never skim over the tops of the clouds, or plunge into the ocean.* Suddenly I was with her as she and Lance played in the sky. They chased each other, snapping at each other's tails and they raced each other, skimming across the surface of the water as salt spray coated their scales. Then, as the sun set, they walked along a deserted beach, their tails wrapped as one. *I wasn't ready to give that up.*

Lance was silent in my mind, but I felt his anger ebb.

So I told them I would come back, and I left to wait for you, to say goodbye. Her pain was palpable. *On my way back down the mountain a man appeared before me.*

My teeth gritted together as Santanas, my grandfather, became visible.

He said he had a mission for me. That it was vitally important. My chance to make a difference. I told him I was waiting for you to come back but he promised me I would be back before you did. She was silent for a moment. *So I let him hop on my back, and when he opened the gate to the other world I took him through. But it was all a lie, and he never did bring me home.*

My throat was thick with unshed tears. If I had thought her present pain was bad, it was nothing compared with what she had experienced when she had realised that Santanas had tricked her. She had fought him but he had won, and once he had broken her spirit and her mind he had forced the bond. She had touched the mind of a mad man, thirsty for revenge and blood. I was surprised she was still sane.

How did you end up bonded with Isadora? Turos asked.

After Santanas was trapped, I wandered lost for many years. Then one night she found me in her dreams. She reached out a hand and she touched me, and I could feel she was good and kind. I didn't want to be alone anymore, so when she opened her mind to me I bonded. She was only ten at the time.

I smiled at the memory.

I've never heard of such a thing. A dragon binding twice in a lifetime.

Perhaps, it was the first thing that Lance had said, *it is because the first bond was forced on her.*

I'm so sorry Lance.

You didn't mean to leave me?

I love you. She did a dragon version of an embarrassed cough. *I mean I loved you.*

I felt them drawing off into a far corner of my mind and turned my attention to Turos to give them some privacy.

Why did you do it? I asked.

Do what?

Help me?

He let out a chuckle. *It's quite simple really. If I don't save your life, I'll never get to do this to you.*

I was overwhelmed with pictures of him kissing me, his hands roaming over me as he shed my clothes from my body. It was frightening in the clarity of the detail, but the look on his face as he stared into my eyes made it even more terrifying.

I felt my breath catch in my throat as he ravaged me with his thoughts. I snatched my mind away, staring at him with a look that I was sure was laden with shock. I was stunned by the suddenness of the mental assault, but more stunned by the fact that I hadn't been totally opposed to it.

A tiny part of me had enjoyed watching it. Had loved the feeling of power that came with the knowledge he desired me. That part would have gone with him right then and there and let him play out that wild fantasy.

'So now you know the truth,' I said, amazed at how steady my voice was.

'More importantly,' Turos said, 'now *you* know the truth.'

'She is innocent?' Bladimir asked.

Turos broke his gaze with me and turned towards his father. 'Innocent for now.' His grin spoke of other things.

After this trial I was going to get Emerald, and she, Isla, Scruffy and I were heading straight back through that hole in the sky.

'So,' I said, 'can we all go home now?'

'We will need to find a dragon willing to carry you home.' Bladimir shifted uncomfortably.

'If Silvanta is not welcome here she will be coming home with us.'

'You forget one thing.' Turos was wearing that insufferable little smile again. 'First she must lay and hatch Lance's egg.'

Damn it. I had forgotten about that. 'How long will that take?'

'Oh, a week or two. Maybe three.' His little smile stretched into a broad smug one. 'Just long enough for us to get to know each other better.'

Chapter Three

Birthing Pains

'I told you it would all work out.' Isla peered out of one of the windows of the gigantic suite we had been taken to after the trial.

I crossed to stand next to her.

Brilliant, green mountains towered on either side of us. They curved slowly, creating a crown with us, the jewel in the centre. I could see the sun setting over the ocean between two of the peaks opposite us.

Beneath us, the side of the mountain sheered away in a steep cliff, disappearing down to a shadow-filled valley which stretched across the distance to the mountains on the other side. It was breathtaking, and if I hadn't been so annoyed, I would have been enjoying it.

'So,' Isla said, 'that Turos certainly has it going on.'

'What do you mean?' My voice was far too defensive. Damn the man. I hadn't done anything wrong and he had me jumping around like a guilty rabbit.

'Oh puulllease.' She rolled her eyes. 'Don't tell me you didn't notice what a hunk he was.' She crossed over to one of the large, comfortable lounge chairs and sank into it. 'I didn't notice while you were assaulting him. I mean he seemed like a bit of a wuss then.' She examined her nails for a second and then stretched her arms above her head. 'What time do you think dinner is?'

'How can you think about food at a time like this?' I plonked myself onto the chair opposite her, sitting on the edge and tapping one foot on the ground.

'Well, it *is* dinner time.'

I shook my head. 'We're trapped here for at least another two weeks, while at home anything could be happening. And Mum will be going out of her mind, and Grams and Sabby will be....' I stopped talking and shifted back onto the couch so I could lay my head back. I could still see the look on Sabby's face when we'd left without her.

'Ahhhh. At home. Let's see. Well, no doubt both the witch and human Prime Ministers still have their heads stuck in the sand as they continue to ignore our warning about Santanas.' She shook her head at their idiocy. 'And if they do come to their senses, Grams and Lionel will be extremely capable of filling in for us. Lionel has far more credibility with them than I do anyway. Sabby is sitting her exams, secretly pleased that she did not miss them. Your Mum will have had her temper soothed by Radismus's hands and mouth.'

'Urghhhh. Can we please not talk about them like that.' I put my hands over my eyes hoping it would block the mental image of Mum and Radismus doing the horizontal tango.

'Why not?'

I dropped my hands and looked over at Isla with what I hoped was an incredulous look on my face.

Isla raised one delicate shoulder. 'I think it's beautiful.'

'Oh, and you're totally comfortable thinking about your Mum and Dad doing the wild….' My voice trailed off at the look on Isla's face. 'Sorry.' We still hadn't spoken about her Mother.

Before she could respond there was a knock at the door. Isla leapt lightly to her feet and floated across the room. She opened it to reveal a small woman holding a large, lit candle in one hand.

'I am Deidre. I've come to light your candles and see what you require for your comfort.' She looked down at Scruffy, who was taking an avid interest in her ankles. He finished sniffing, ruffed once, and then trotted back to the mat on the floor he had claimed as his own.

'You're not a faery?' I stood and crossed the room to peer at her. The gathering shadows made it hard to see her features.

She move over to a low table and used her already lit candle to light the ones sitting there.

'A have some small amount of faery blood in me,' she said as she moved to the next table.

I watched her as she went, trying to scratch my mental itch. Finally it came to me. 'You're Ubanty.'

Deidre paused in the process of lighting a candle. 'Now that's a name I haven't heard for a while.' She straightened and turned to me. I could see her smile in the soft glow of the candles. 'Once we were Ubanty. Once we were slaves. Now we are all Milleniums.'

'They set you free?'

'The night faeries who came here were the dragon keepers. When the magic makers began taking the baby dragons to force their souls into other beings they rebelled.'

'Hagons?' Isla said.

Deidre nodded. 'They found one among the magic makers who sympathised and they planned their escape. All the dragons, and as many of the Ubanty that could escape without notice, came with them. Here they set us free to find our place among them. Now we are all one people.' She turned and continued lighting the candles around the room. 'Shall I have your supper sent up?'

'Please,' Isla said. 'We seemed to have missed a meal today. We also need clothes.'

'Of course.' Deidre nodded. 'You will find toiletries already in your bathroom.' She crossed back to the still-open door, smiled at us again and then pulled the door shut behind her.

'So *that's* what happened to the dragons.' Isla had a gigantic smile on her face. 'According to folk-lore, one day they were there, the next gone. No wonder the night faeries failed to inform the world of what really happened. They must have been livid.'

I wasn't sure now if her smile was for the mystery solved, or for the fact that someone had gazumped the night faeries. I was going to go with both.

'And then Emerald showed up during the Great Faery War and turned the tide of battle. We all just assumed some disease had wiped the rest of them out.' She sat back down on the couch and stared off into space.

She didn't seem to notice the knock at the door as she worked her way through the historic sequence of events. I opened it to find Turos standing there.

'You look disappointed to see me.' He moved to lean up against the door frame before I could slam the door on him.

'I thought you were dinner.'

'I can *be* your dinner if you want.' He leaned in closer to me and I took an involuntary step back. 'And you can be my dessert.'

'Never going to happen.' I grabbed the edge of the door. If I slammed it hard enough, I might just be able to close it.

'What's never going to happen?' Isla asked.

Turos pushed past me till he could see Isla. 'Fair lady, I was just explaining to Isadora that dinner was on its way.'

'Coward,' I muttered under my breath.

'Oh fantastic.' She clapped her hands together. 'I'm famished. Will you be joining us?'

'Alas, no. My father requests the pleasure of my company tonight, but perhaps tomorrow night.' He gave me a look that spoke of other sorts of pleasure to be had.

Two other Milleniums, both holding a tray with food piled onto it, appeared in the doorway. I moved to the side so they could enter the room.

I had been too angry to be hungry, but now my stomach rumbled in response to the aroma that washed over me. Some sort of roasted meat – chicken? – a pile of vegetables, and a pudding of some kind. I was suddenly as aware as Isla that we had missed a meal that day.

'One day you will look at me like that,' Turos murmured.

I hadn't realised how close to me he was. 'Like what?'

I moved to step backwards, but he seized my arm and pulled me towards him instead. The musky smell of him replaced that of the food, and I could feel the heat radiating from his skin. 'Like you want to devour me and come back for seconds.' He rubbed a finger up and down

'I find coffee useful for that.'

He tilted his head and frowned.

'You don't have coffee?' I sighed. 'Oh well, I'm more of a tea drinker myself.'

Lance circled above the platform in lazy circles. Each one taking us closer to where Isla waited. She was bouncing up and down on her toes and I wasn't sure if she was excited or annoyed.

'My turn,' she said when Lance touched down.

Ahhh, of course. Excited.

'Where's Emerald?' I asked as I slid down to the ground.

Turos pointed along the platform and I noticed for the first time a row of rectangular openings partly filled with a door. Each door had a dragon head poking over the top.

Dragon stables.

The third head along was a deep, glossy green. I reached out towards Emerald's mind and she pivoted so she was looking at me and not Lance. One of her giant eyelids closed in a wink as her awareness rushed into me.

Isn't he marvellous?

He's a suicidal, egomaniac.

She snorted again. *Not Turos. Lance.* Her thoughts held the emotion of a love-struck teenager.

I looked back at the gigantic beast. The sun glinted off his scales, and red highlights shimmered as he moved.

He is something.

Isla let out a shriek of delight as Turos grabbed her hand and pulled her off the platform with him. I could hear her laugh disappearing into the distance.

Ummmm. Shouldn't he be going after them?

Just wait.

Lance moved to the edge of the platform so that his front claws were locked onto the edge. He rocked forwards and, with a thrust of his wings, propelled himself off the edge. With his body held like an arrow being fired towards the ground, and his wings making short sharp movements, he easily caught them before they were even halfway to the bottom of the valley.

I heard the breath I hadn't known I had been holding leave my lungs as they landed safely.

I walked over to Emerald and reached up so that I could place my hand on her neck. Even then, she had to bow her head to allow me to reach. *How are you?*

Scared, happy, sad, excited. Her thoughts paused for a moment. *No, make that happy, sad, scared, excited.*

Did you want to go for a ride?

She shook her head. *I couldn't carry you at the moment. My body is getting ready to lay the egg.*

Does it hurt?

Not so much pain as discomfort. The egg is shifting inside me and the shell is hardening. Soon I will have to go.

Is there anything I can do to help?

She bent her neck further and brushed the tip of her gigantic nose against my forehead. *Will you be there with me when it's time?*

Of course.

She rubbed her snout against me. *Good. Isla too.*

I'd have to knock her out and tie her up to stop her, and even then she'd find a way to be there.

Wind whirled around me as Lance's enormous wings lowered them back to the platform.

'Again,' Isla shrieked, jumping off Lance's neck and throwing herself off the platform.

Turos let out a laugh and raced after her.

Can he handle three? I asked Emerald.

He has caught up to nine riders before. And that was before I left.

Excellent.

I ran towards the edge, let out a whoop of excitement and dived head first off the platform.

***

'It's official,' Isla jumped onto the edge of my bed and pulled her legs up under her. 'Dragon diving is my all-time favourite sport.'

Our tour of the city had transpired into a couple of hours of dragon diving and then a lazy brunch. After that Turos had taken us on an aerial tour of the grand city. It had ended when a grim-faced courier carrying a message from the king had found us. We had been escorted back to our suite while Turos went to see his father.

'Admit it,' Isla said.

'Admit what?'

'You had fun.'

'What's not fun about dragon diving?'

'No.' She sat up straighter. 'You had fun with *Turos*.'

'We *both* had fun with him.' I hopped onto the bed next to her, shuffling backwards till my head reached the pillow. Scruffy jumped up next to me and turned around so that his back was snuggled into my side. I took that as a sign that he had missed me.

'You going to tell me what he did to make you so mad?'

'You going to leave it alone and stop asking me?'

She gave me her best butter-wouldn't-melt-in-my-mouth smile.

I sighed. 'I didn't think so.' I wiggled around until I was totally comfortable. Now that my adrenaline had returned to normal levels, the hours of lost sleep from the night before were making themselves known. 'He....' Dark Sky. How best to put it? 'Forced himself on me.'

'What? When?' Her normal whimsical expression had been replaced with one of anger and I immediately felt guilty.

'Not like that. Not like with you and.....' I swallowed the words King Arracon before they came out of my mouth. I know she had told me, but it still didn't feel right to bring it up. 'At the trial. When we were in each other's heads. He showed me what he wanted to do with me. To me.' I squirmed as I thought about it.

'Ahhhhh.' Isla nodded. 'And that would be repugnant to you at the moment. What with you being in mourning.'

I sat back up. 'I'm not in mourning. Well, I mean, I'm horrified by what happened to Orion. But, and no offence here, I didn't really know him well enough to be in full mourning.'

Good grief. Could that have sounded any worse?

She shook her head. 'No. You're mourning your loss of Aethan.'

'I haven't lost him. Yet.'

'Izzy.' Dark Sky I hated it when she actually got serious. 'He *will* be married to Ebony.'

I shifted uncomfortably. He was mine. I wasn't ready to let go of that yet. 'You don't know that.'

'There is a Great War coming. The union between the faeries of the dark and the light must happen if we are to have any chance of survival.'

'But he doesn't love her.'

'It is immaterial. He is the heir. And the heir does what must be done. We all do what must be done.'

'But, maybe…after the war…if we win…'

That was when I realised that the only thing worse than Isla looking serious was Isla looking sympathetic. She stared at me, her large eyes liquid with unspoken emotion as she said, 'We are not like witches and humans. Faeries marry forever.'

Pain lanced through me. I clutched at my chest, certain it was about to explode as I struggled to remember how to breathe.

He was gone. I had lost him.

Memories danced in my head. The tender feel of his hand in mine. The passionate fire of his embrace. The languid comfort of lying in his arms. Gone. All gone. Never to return.

Isla wrapped herself around me as the tears came. Deep, racking, sobs that tore at me and consumed me.

She held me like that as the despair flowed over me, dragging me down, down, down into a dark and starless night.

***

It was night when I woke. My head ached and my throat was raw. Scruffy was curled up next to my feet and Isla lay beside me, her hand still holding mine as she had been when I had finally drifted off to sleep.

A tapping noise. That was what had woken me.

I shifted my head away from the pillow and turned so that an ear was in the air.

Tap, tap, tap.

There, it was coming from the window.

Isla stirred as I slid my hand from hers. I sat up and made my way toward the window. Light from the main room illuminated mine enough that I was able to navigate around the furniture. Deirdre must have lit the candles while we slept.

'What is it?' Isla's voice was still full of sleep.

'I'm not sure.'

This time the tapping was more insistent. I pulled opened a window and looked out.

Turos's head moved up and down in time with the strokes of Lance's wings. 'It's time,' he said.

I reached out towards Emerald but she wasn't there. 'She's gone,' I gasped.

'We've hooded her,' he said. 'You wouldn't be able to block her pain.'

'What is it?' Isla asked.

'It's Emerald.'

She nodded once and then hopped off the bed. Pulling her hair back and braiding it deftly as she walked towards me. Scruffy followed her, jumping into my arms as I bent towards him.

'Give him to me,' Turos said, holding out his arms for Scruffy.

I shook my head. 'I'll hold him.'

'No,' he said. 'You'll be holding me. It's a tight flight in, and Lance is going to have to manoeuvre sharply. You can't do both.'

I stared into his eyes, unwilling to give up Scruffy. If anything happened to my little familiar I would be...just like I had been that afternoon. Just like I still was.

Lost.

'Promise me,' I said, desperation making my voice tight. 'Promise me nothing will happen to him.'

'He will be safe with me.' It was the first serious thing he had said since we got to Millenia.

Scruffy barked and wiggled in my arms, reaching towards Turos.

'Fine. But I'm not happy about this.'

'I apologise. I should have stopped for the basket you use to transport him but Lance is insistent we hurry.'

Lance threw his head from side-to-side and fire curled out of his nostrils.

I scrambled up onto the window ledge and leapt across onto Lance's head, timing it with a downward stroke of his wings. Turos reached forward, holding out his arms. He took Scruffy and then helped me step down onto Lance's neck to sit behind him. I slid back to make room for Isla.

'Hang on,' Turos yelled over his shoulder.

I was about to make a smart-arse reply about how I had been riding a dragon for years when Lance launched himself forwards. I felt myself rock backwards and just managed to grasp Isla's waist. I let out a gasp as I grabbed onto the leather straps in front of me.

Sure, I had ridden a dragon for years, but this was something else. Lance was fast. Much faster than he had been on our trip here. Much faster than Emerald, and I found myself wondering if she had been holding out on me.

We screamed through the sky, the glow of the volcano growing rapidly in front of us. I expected Lance to land on the plateau below the rim of the crater but instead he aimed for the solid mountain below, and to the side of it. I dug my nails into my palms around the leather straps as a dark hole became visible.

A tunnel. And while I was still contemplating the fact that there was no way that tunnel could be wide enough for a flying dragon, Lance gave one more mighty beat of his wings and then tucked them in by his sides.

We shot into that tunnel like a rabbit down a hole as darkness closed around us. A silent scream filled my lungs as Lance twisted through a corkscrew and then navigated a hairpin bend. Then we were heading straight down into the bowels of the earth.

It felt like forever that we fell through the darkness, but it was probably only moments before Lance whipped through another bend and straightened out. Soft light illuminated our path as the tunnel widened enough for Lance to spread his wings. And then the tunnel widened further until it was a vast cavern.

Crystal stalactites glistened like chandeliers as they reflected the light cast by small pools of lava. Warmth rolled over me in a wave and sweat broke out all over my body.

Dragons, lying lazily beside large eggs, were scattered across the floor of the cabin. Lance flew over all of them till we reached the far end of the cavern, then he back flew with his wings till we landed gently beside Emerald.

She lay on her side, curled into a ball and she wore the metal helmet she had had on at the trial.

'Help me get it off her.' I slid down one of Lance's legs and trotted towards her. She rolled a huge eye at me and then squeezed it shut tight as her whole body spasmed.

'You won't be able to take the pain.' Turos shook his head.

I stalked towards him and grabbed the front of his shirt with both hands, twisting my fists into the fabric. 'Take. It. Off,' I hissed, staring into his eyes.

He must have seen the violence brewing because he tugged my hands free and said, 'Don't say I didn't warn you.'

As soon as the helmet left her head her agony became mine. A whimper left my lips and Turos lifted the helmet back into the air.

'Don't you dare,' I rasped as I staggered towards her.

Another spasm wracked her, the flesh of her abdomen rolling like an enormous wave toward her tail. I dropped to my knees and clutched my stomach, waiting for the worst of it to pass before I crawled the last few metres to her. I placed a hand on her stomach and rubbed in a circle. Her mind calmed its chaotic wailing at my touch.

Izzy?

I'm here.

It hurts.

I know. Oh boy did I know. *We will get through this.*

Scruffy pushed up against her on the other side of me and Isla took up station at Emerald's head. Lance settled beside her and placed a wing over her.

Waves of agony crashed over me, each one lifting me up and depositing me a little further from my sanity. I lay on the ground next to her and concentrated all my energy on the movement of my hand on her stomach.

Sweat beaded on my body as the spasms increased in length and intensity, coming closer and closer together.

For a moment I thought maybe Turos was right. Maybe I couldn't do this. But the thought of putting that heavy helmet on her, of making her go through this alone stopped me from calling out to Turos. I couldn't do that to her.

'How long?' I gasped. I looked up at him through sweat-drenched hair.

'A few hours. Maybe more, maybe less. This is an unprecedented case. No dragon has held onto an egg for as long as this before.'

I closed my eyes and let out a moan in time with Emerald. I knew that whatever I was going through, had to have been ten times worse for her. It was her body that was contorting and bucking as it moved the egg closer to its release. I was just feeling a shadow of her pain.

I felt movement behind me and then Turos lay down behind me. He slipped an arm around me pulling me against his chest as he ran his other hand through my hair, smoothing the damp tendrils back off my face. He reached past me and laid his hand beside mine on Emerald.

'Easy there my beauty,' he whispered, his lips moving the hair away from my ear. 'We'll get through this yet.'

Blackness pressed in from all sides. Pain became my world. It was all I knew. All I had ever known. It felt like I had lived my whole life in that cavern, floating in a world of pain. I had no knowledge of my name, no knowledge of anything other than the feel of something tearing out through my flesh and bones.

I felt it building. The end was coming I knew. I just didn't know how it would be. Didn't know if I would still exist outside of this.

One last push. One last spasm. A great cracking and popping. Emerald's bellow blocked out my shattering scream, and then it was over. Instead of pain there was nothing.

I stared up at the cavern ceiling, trying to work out why there were stars there, and then I closed my eyes and sank inside my head.

Chapter Four

The Chosen

oft murmurs woke me. I lay beside Emerald, my hand still pressed to her side. Scruffy lay curled up against my chest, but the feel of Turos behind me was gone. For one guilty second I wished he was still there. Then I shook myself and sat up.

Emerald lifted her head and gazed at me with sleep-laden eyes. *There it is*, she said, nodding her head toward where her tail wrapped around an enormous egg.

Great Dark Sky. That came out of you?

I could feel her amusement in my mind.

I sat up further and Isla looked over at me from where she sat cross-legged next to the egg. 'I can see it,' she said. 'I mean him or her.' She pulled a face and turned her gaze back to the egg.

I peered back through the muted glow of the cabin to where the nearest Queen lay with her tail wrapped around her egg.

'Is it my imagination, or is this egg bigger than the others?'

'Not your imagination,' Isla said. 'Turos said it was at least twice the size of the largest egg he had ever seen.'

I could feel Emerald's contented pride at Isla's words.

'Where is Turos?' I said. 'And where is everybody else?'

'He's gone to inform the Dragon Masters of the successful laying of the egg. And apparently this,' she waved a hand between Emerald and me, 'is not normal. Queens are not allowed to bond for this very reason. Well that, and the fact that once a Queen starts breeding she lives here, helping the others with their eggs. She only leaves to mate.'

That's what Emerald had meant at the trial when she had said she wasn't ready to give up her freedom.

'But Emerald did bond. So she can't stay.' I wasn't letting them keep my dragon trapped here. Not if she didn't want to be.

Isla only pulled a face which made me worry about what else had been said while I was asleep.

I stood slowly, stretching out crinkled muscles before walking towards the egg. Isla was right. The egg shell was translucent in the light of the cavern. Inside the egg a little shadow moved. As I watched, it did a full somersault, waving its little wings around to stop.

Emerald let out a rumble. *He is going to take after his father.*

You know it's a boy?

The first egg is always a boy.

'It's a boy,' I said to Isla.

'Ooooooh,' she cooed to the egg. 'Aunty Isla can't wait to meet you, little man.'

How long till he hatches?

A week. Give or take a day.

I settled down across from Isla to stare in awe at the acrobatics of the baby dragon.

Turos and Lance returned a couple of hours later. 'Sorry we took so long,' he said as he slid off Lance with a basket in one hand. 'I brought food.'

I waited as patiently as I could while Turos pulled out a loaf of bread, a block of cheese, and a knife. He handed me a flask of water while he cut the bread and cheese into chunks.

I grabbed some bread before he could hand it to me and bit into its soft flesh, letting out a groan as I did. It was still warm.

Lance's jaw was wedged open with an enormous chunk of meat. He placed it gingerly in front of Emerald and nudged it toward her with his snout. She let out a pleased rumble and grasped it with her front claws while she tore a chunk off of it. She chewed twice, swallowed, and then ripped another chunk off.

Turos handed me a piece of cheese and said, 'The first riders will arrive soon.'

I shoved the cheese into my mouth and angled my head to the side waiting for him to elaborate.

'They will try and bond with the egg.'

I swallowed, opened my mouth to ask a question but decided instead to shove more bread in. I was still too hungry to not be chewing.

'So soon?' Isla was making a much daintier meal of her bread and cheese.

'It is normal for the males to be bonded from birth.'

'How does it work?'

'They will come in order of seniority and take turns touching the shell. The dragon will choose its rider.'

'That simple?' I swallowed the last of my bread and held my hand out for more.

'That easy.' Turos carved another chunk off the loaf and handed it to me.

We had barely finished our meals before the first of the hopeful riders turned up. A dragon so blue I was reminded of bright summer days, swept towards us with a number of riders on his back. He waited for them to dismount and then he and his rider immediately departed.

Turos nodded as the men approached the shell. 'Ritto,' he said. 'Dragons' luck to you.'

Ritto nodded back and then stopped in front of the egg, staring reverently at the little creature inside. Then he reached out a hand and rested his palm against the shell.

I wasn't sure if anything was meant to happen, but if it was, then Ritto wasn't the chosen one.

He held his hand there for a minute before bowing his head and stepping backwards. Disappointment etched his features.

In that short period of time another dragon had deposited more riders. They formed a loose line, according to their rank, and one-by-one they approached the egg.

More dragons came and more men queued and the afternoon turned into night. Well I guessed it did by the fact that my stomach started rumbling again and Turos dished out more bread and cheese. Lance returned with more meat for Emerald when they were down to the last few candidates. These didn't look old enough to be shaving.

The dragon masters stood in a half circle off to the side, observing the proceedings. As the queue shortened and the number of boys dwindled I could hear them muttering amongst themselves.

The last applicant approached Emerald's egg, a look of glee on his face. He stretched his hand out confidently as he claimed the egg for himself. His palm came into contact with the shell and I waited for something, anything that would tell me a bond had been formed.

A minute later he dropped his hand and stepped back, looking over toward the Masters. 'It's a dud,' he said, his face screwing up in disgust. 'A stupid, useless dud.'

He drew back his foot as if to kick the egg and everything happened at once. A snarling growl came out of Lance's mouth as the boy's foot headed towards the egg.

Stop him, Emerald screamed in my head.

Turos and I threw ourselves towards him, trying to stop him before he shattered the shell, but we were too far away.

Isla, however, had been sitting on the other side of the egg. She threw herself over the top of it, landing just in time to prevent his foot from connecting with it. Instead, it buried itself deep into her abdomen.

She let out an, 'Oooff,' as she wrapped around his foot like a rag doll, soaking up the blow that was meant for the egg.

I howled in rage and threw my hand out at the boy. He flew into the air, tumbling over-and-over before landing at the feet of the Masters. They seemed surprised to see him there, blinking around in the gloomy light as if trying to work out where he had come from.

Lance snorted, flames shooting out of his nose as he fixed angry eyes on the now trembling child. He pulled himself up so he towered above the boy, opening his mouth to roar.

'Easy, Lance.' Turos placed his hand in the air. 'No harm was done.'

It occurred to me that he was talking out loud for the sake of the Dragon Masters. I wondered what conversation he was really having with Lance.

'There, there,' Isla cooed. She knelt beside the dragon egg, her arms wrapped around her middle and tears tracking down her face. 'It's okay now.'

As we watched, she let go of her stomach and reached a hand out towards the shell. 'Aunty Isla won't let anything happen to you.'

The instant her palm came into contact with the egg, a million streams of light shot out of the shell. They raced across the cavern, bouncing off stalactites and chasing away the shadows.

Isla closed her eyes, a blissful smile on her face as her body swayed from side-to-side. The light returned from the far end of the cavern, forming one gigantic beam as it raced towards Isla.

I thought it would burn her when it made contact with her skin, but instead, it lit her up from the inside out till she glowed like the setting sun. She threw her head back as the light swirled around her and the egg. And then, just as suddenly as it had started, it stopped. The light sucked back into the egg and Isla sagged beside it.

'Hello Arthur,' she said to the egg, and then she collapsed onto the ground, one hand still pressed against the shell.

***

'You could have warned me.' I looked up at Turos from where I knelt beside Isla.

'Warned you about?'

'What was going to happen.'

'Believe me, if I'd have known, I would have warned you.'

'Then this,' I gestured between the egg and Isla, 'is not the norm?' That would explain the hissed conversation amongst the Dragon Masters and their rapid departure.

He shook his head and sat down beside me. 'The biggest reaction we've had before this was a bubble of light.' He looked at Emerald and then back to where Isla still touched the egg.

We could see the shadow of the baby dragon, the tip of one wing pressed up against the inside of the shell where Isla's hand rested.

'But then none of this is normal.' He let out a sigh and scratched the side of his nose. 'It makes me wonder if anything will ever be normal again.'

I quirked my head to the side and frowned. It didn't seem like the events of today, or indeed the past two days, were enough to illicit that reaction. 'Something else has happened?' It was the only possible conclusion.

He pulled a face. 'I'm tired and over reacting.'

'And keeping secrets.'

'Pot, kettle, black.' Turos pointed a finger at me. 'I nearly died of fright when you blasted that boy out of the way.' He shook his head as he muttered, 'Luckily no one else seemed to have noticed.'

'It's okay Arthur, I'm here,' Isla murmured. Her fingertips stayed glued to the shell as she rolled over. The little shadow mimicked her movement.

I smiled as I turned back to Turos. 'Is *that* normal?'

He put his hands on his hips and glared at me. 'Stop changing the subject.'

'Oh fine.' I let out a huff. 'I have a tenuous hold on some magical powers. Sometimes they do what I want them to.'

'Is that why you don't use it much?'

'I spent most of my life without it,' I said. 'So I guess that's part of it. But mostly it's because when I do use it, things tend to blow up.' I remembered my conversation with Deidre from the night before. She had said they had found a magic maker to help them. 'None of you have any magic?' I didn't mean for it to sound as incredulous as it did. Even though I hadn't had access to my own powers till just under a year ago, I had been immersed in a magical world my whole life.

He shook his head. 'Our bond with the dragons is the closest thing to magic that we've got.'

'But…' I shook my head. 'When I punched you.'

'Oh this?' He laughed and waved a hand at his nose. 'Good use of herbs.'

'No, not that. Your warriors. They moved so swiftly.'

'Oh *that*. No magic there. I could teach you how to do that.'

'You could?' My mind started to race. If I could take that sort of technique home with me then maybe this trip wasn't a total waste. Our chances against the goblins would dramatically improve if we could move that swiftly. I put my hand on his arm. 'Will you?'

'Sure.' He shrugged. 'Got nothing else I need to be doing. We can start right now.'

I heard a dragon roar from the other side of the cavern.

Turos tilted his head so that an ear was facing in that direction. 'Sounds like another egg on its way.'

The sound of dragon's wings, came to me over the next roar. I looked up to see the sky-blue dragon winging its way towards us. A single rider sat on its neck, his eyes fixed on Turos.

The dragon fluttered his wings backwards, bringing himself to a soft landing about ten metres from where we were sitting. The rider didn't dismount, instead beckoning to Turos with one hand while holding out a piece of paper with the other.

'Maybe not right now,' Turos muttered as he hopped up. He strode towards the rider, took the message from him and opened it. I watched as his eyes scanned down the page. He folded it back up and looked back toward me.

'I have to go talk to father. I'll return with food.'

He looked over to where Lance lay with his snout pressed up against Emerald's, shook his head and then walked back to the other dragon. He leapt lightly onto the dragon's front thigh and scrambled up till he was sitting behind the other rider. Within seconds they were winging their way back across the cavern.

'Is it just me,' Isla mumbled, 'or is it hot in here?'

'It's hot.' I reached out for a water bottle and handed it to her, helping her sit up so she could drink it.

She took it with her free hand and tipped the contents into her mouth and then over her head. 'That feels good.' She dropped the bottle and raked her hand through her hair.

'How long are you going to hang onto the egg?'

'As long as it takes.' She stared at the egg with a gooey look on her face. 'Can you believe he chose me?'

'*I* can believe it. The Dragon Masters weren't too happy.'

'You think they'll try to take him off me?' Worry marred her voice.

'I think it's a bit of a done deal,' I said. 'Bonding is for life.'

We were silent for a few moments while we contemplated the real meaning of my words.

'They're not going to let me leave, are they?' she finally whispered.

'They have to.' My voice held more conviction than I felt.

We were alone, in another world. If they decided we weren't going home then there was nothing we could do about it.

We sat like that, our silence joining us, until Turos returned with food.

***

'I don't see how this is *anything* to do with making me move faster.' I opened my eyes and stared at Turos.

'It has *everything* to do with it.'

I narrowed my eyes, searching for a hint of a smile on his face. There was none.

'Just do as he says, Izzy.' Isla sat with her back against the egg, her head resting against its long sweeping curve.

I could see Arthur's shadow as his fluttering wings spun him round-and-round. Watching him made me dizzy. Although in the last few days the loops had become slower as he grew within the confines of his shell. Turos advised us that it wouldn't be too much longer until he hatched.

'Fine.' I let out a huff and closed my eyes, sneaking one open again immediately to check out Turos's face. He still wasn't smiling.

'Take a deep breath in,' he intoned, 'and clear your mind of everything.'

I took a breath, filling up my lungs until I could feel them swelling inside me.

'Remove all your thoughts. One-by-one. Examine them and then discard them.'

I thought about Mum and Sabby and how annoyed they would be. It had been a week since we had left with

Lance and Turos. Then I took that thought, along with the emotions it evoked, and I pushed it from my mind.

I thought about Scruffy lying on his back against Emerald, his loud snores echoing in the cavern.

'You hear nothing, see nothing, smell nothing.'

I opened my eyes. 'How am I meant to clear my head of all sound with you yabbering at me continuously?'

This time a small smile did curl up the corners of his mouth, but his ice-blue eyes remained serious. 'Stop arguing and do it.'

I let out a huff and closed my eyes again, noting though, that he'd stopped talking. For now. Turos never stopped talking for long.

I sifted through my mind. Mum and Radismus. Grams and Lionel. The frustration over trying to get the government to realise the imminent danger we were in. Those things were easy to neutralise. But there were far too many other things in my head. Things too painful to examine. Things I didn't want to put aside.

'Now put your hands behind your back and open your eyes.' Turos kept his voice low.

When I complied, his clenched fist was in front of my face. I kept my hands where they were until his opened. The small stone housed within tumbled towards the ground. I snapped my hands round as fast as I could, just catching it before it landed. It was a small improvement on my last effort in which I hadn't caught it at all.

'*You* do it,' I said.

I held my hand in front of his face while he closed his eyes, waiting for him to open them again before letting go of the stone. His hand moved so fast I hardly even saw it. One moment it was behind his back, the next in front of his face, holding the stone.

'Impressive,' Isla said. It was the first time we had practised in front of her. While she had remained in the cavern with Emerald and Arthur, I had come and gone as cabin fever set in.

'I still don't see how it works.' I could feel my lower lip pushing out into a pout.

'Thoughts cause friction in our actions. If they are there at the forefront of our mind, they take up time and energy.'

'But, I'm not aware of them.'

'It makes no difference. Your subconscious brain is a fickle thing. It flicks between thoughts and reality like a butterfly as it analyses everything you are doing, comparing it to the past and present. Those hidden emotions affect your actions. Clear them away and there is nothing stopping you, nothing slowing you. You are focused and of purpose and unstoppable.'

He knows what he is talking about. Emerald's mind held a tinge of amusement. At least one of us was enjoying this.

Isla sat up straighter. She stretched her head to one side and then the other, pushing her arms above her head. 'I feel so cramped,' she said. 'Like I need to stretch or something.'

'Well you have been sitting in the one spot for a week.' She had only left Arthur's side for toilet breaks, and even they had been speedy.

She shook her head. 'Not like that. Like….'

A crackling noise stopped her from finishing her sentence.

'Oh.' Her eyes went round and she spun toward the egg. Small cracks had appeared on the surface nearest her.

It's time. Emerald removed her tail and turned so that she was facing the egg. She pressed her snout gently against the side and snorted. *He is so eager to be out.*

I could see the little dragon, the tips of his wings pushing out on the egg as he strained to break the shell.

'Come on Arthur.' Isla stood and placed both her palms against it. 'You can do it.'

With his wings still pressed against either side, he wedged his back and feet up onto opposite sides of the egg. His whole body strained as he threw his little head backwards with the effort of pushing.

'Ahhhhh, Isla,' I said.

'Shhhh. He's almost here.'

'You may want to step back a little.'

The words were just out of my mouth when, with a cracking snap, the shell shattered. A wave of fluid poured out of the egg and all over Isla. Arthur rode the wave like a professional surfer, bowling into Isla and carrying her to the ground.

When the liquid cleared, Isla lay flat on her back. Arthur sat on her chest, his brilliant, orange scales sparkling in the light of the lava. He blinked his eyes, shook his head, and then leant forward and pressed his snout to her face.

'Oh Arthur.' Isla let out a laugh and then wrapped her arms around him, still managing, even though she was covered in dragon embryotic fluid, to look beautiful.

Emerald and Lance crowded in on either side as Emerald's triumphant voice echoed in my head. *He's perfect. He's beautiful.*

'Is that a common colour?' I asked Turos. None of the dragons I had seen had even come close to Arthur's colouring.

He shook his head, his mouth partly open as he stared at the little dragon. 'He's magnificent,' he finally said. 'I've never seen anything like him.'

And even though I was overjoyed at Arthur's safe arrival, a tiny fear crept into the front of my mind.

If Arthur was such a rarity, there was no way they were going to let him go. And since there was no way I was leaving here without Isla, and no way she was leaving without him, that meant only one thing.

Things were going to get ugly.

Chapter Five

Stranger Danger

'He seems to be growing much faster than the others. I mean, I know he started off much bigger, but the gap seems to be widening.'

As I spoke, Arthur jumped onto another hatchling with a fierce growl and wrestled him to the ground. The two of them rolled around for a second, but Arthur emerged from the tussle on top. He wrapped his jaws around his opponent's throat and pinned him to the ground. In no *way* was it a fair fight. Arthur may have been several weeks the younger, but he was easily twice as big.

I could feel smug satisfaction emanating from Emerald, and Isla had a look on her face that was even more puke-worthy. It wasn't that I didn't share their adoration of Arthur, but having it constantly mentally imposed on me by Emerald was beginning to be a strain.

I looked over at Turos. He had a look on his face that I suspected might mimic mine. Pride tinged with a hint of boredom. I mean there was only so long I could watch Arthur play before cabin fever broke out again. Call me a bad Aunt if you will, it's just the way it was.

Arthur gave the little dragon one more little shake and then sat up. The magnificence of his orange scales was offset by his tongue lolling out of the side of his mouth and for a second I was reminded of old Raymond, the Eynsford Village idiot. Emerald let out a loud huff and I banished that thought from my mind.

'Want to get out of here?' I jumped as Turos whispered in my ear.

'Who's going to take us?'

Lance was lazing beside Emerald, his tail entwined with hers. I doubted very much he would be impressed if we asked him to get us out of there while the offspring of his loins was playing so magnificently.

'There's another way. We can go on foot.'

I didn't ask how long it would take us. I didn't really care. I was hot and tired and in need of some fresh air, and I could tell by the way Scruffy was staring up at me with pleading eyes that he was too. 'Lead away,' I said.

Turos led us to the edge of the cavern and then along the wall for what must have been half of its length before we came across an opening in the stone. I peered into the hole, waiting for my eyes to adjust to the lack of light. They didn't.

'Do you think you could…you know?' Turos flourished his hand through the air.

'Cave in the cavern? Blow up the tunnel?' I tilted my head to the side and gave him my most whimsical smile.

'Forget I mentioned it,' he said. 'We'll have to do it the old-fashioned way. Hold onto the back of my shirt.'

I bent and scooped Scruffy up, holding him close to my body. He wiggled around in my arm and, as I grabbed onto the back of Turos's shirt, let out a loud wavering fart.

Turos looked over his shoulder at me. 'Was…that…you?'

I let out a giggle. 'It was Scruffy. He needs more exercise.'

'Convenient,' he said. 'Blame it on the dog.' He waved a hand in front of his face. 'Let's get going.'

We plunged into a column of darkness. The floor felt smooth under foot, and I was guessing by how easily we moved down the tunnel that the walls were as well.

'What is this?' I asked.

'It's a lava tube.'

My laugh was cut short as I stumbled in the dark. When I had regained my footing I said, 'Is that your special name for it?'

He snorted. 'A lava tube is created by a river of fast flowing lava.' He stopped walking and I heard him sniff a few times.

'It wasn't me,' I said.

He laughed. 'I'm looking for the exit.' He shuffled forward another few steps and sniffed another couple of times.

'What are you trying to smell?'

'The ocean.' He repeated the procedure another couple of times before he said, 'Ahh, there it is.' He took a sharp right turn and started to move again, but this time his steps were faster.

'Hey,' I said as my foot caught another lump of rock. 'Blind back here.'

'Your senses don't seem to be very good for a faery.'

'I'm part witch.'

I felt him move as if nodding his head. 'That explains the farting dog.'

'He's not always that bad. I think it's all the gas from the volcano affecting him.'

'I think he produced most of it.'

'Don't you listen to him boy,' I said.

The inky blackness of the tunnel started to lighten ahead of us and suddenly I could make out Turos's outline. It took another five minutes till we made it to the end of the lava tube. We paused on the lip, staring out not into the valley, as I had expected, but over the vast blue of the ocean. A broken path started at the edge of the rock and meandered off down the slope of the mountain.

'It's steep in parts,' Turos said, 'but there's a beach down there.'

'We can swim? In the ocean?' I had swum in the ocean only a couple of times before and both had been at beaches made of pebbles, not sand, where you'd had to walk out forever just to get the water to reach to your knees. This water promised to be different.

'Of course. If you're game.'

I had been living in a virtual sauna for the last week. Even though we had taken sponge baths and changed our clothes, I felt like sweat encrusted my body and clothes. I didn't care what it was that Turos was eluding to, I was going for a swim.

'Come on boy,' I said putting Scruffy down. 'Last one in's a rotten egg.'

We didn't so much race down the mountain as carefully clamber. Occasionally the path disappeared altogether and we were left to navigate our way through loose boulders as we looked for the start of it again.

I caught a glimpse of snowy white sands and increased my pace, trotting down the path ahead of Turos. I could already imagine the feel of the sea closing over me, its cool waters washing away a week of sweat, grime and frustration.

The ground around us began to change. Rock giving way to soil, and grasses to shrubs and then trees. I lost sight of the beach as we plunged down through a stand of palm trees.

Scruffy ran ahead, sniffing at the palms, his tongue hanging out in a happy dog grin. He disappeared into the trees ahead of us, letting out the occasional happy bark.

By the time we made it to the beach, he was already sopping wet and rolling in the powdery sand.

I stopped and pulled my boots off, leaving them on a rock at the edge of the beach. After a moment of contemplation I pulled my trousers off and left them there as well. My shirt hung half way down my thighs and would cover enough to protect my modesty.

I turned to see Turos pulling his shirt off over his head. His olive skin rippled in the sun and his muscles flexed as he scrubbed his large hands through his spiky, white hair.

I peeled my eyes away from his chest and stomach. It wouldn't do to let him catch me perving at him. But then he unbuttoned his trousers and I found myself blushing and fleeing towards the water, needing to cool off for a totally different reason than before.

I plunged into the crystalline water, its blue-green depths embracing me with cool arms. It felt as good as, if not better than, I had imagined. A few kicks and some quick strokes and I left the shore behind, swimming out till the sandy floor was no longer within my reach. I undid my braid and slid back under the water, watching my hair floating like a million tiny tentacles around my head. A bright fish flashed in front of me, its orange and blue stripes glinting in the sun.

It was no use though. I couldn't shake the image of Turos out of my head.

I pushed back up out of the water and watched him from the corner of my eye as he strode to the water's edge, wading in mid-thigh before raising his arms above his head, looking for all the world like an Olympic gymnast as he dived into the water.

He wasn't naked as I had first feared, but his undergarments left nothing to the imagination and I felt myself breaking out into a fresh round of blushes.

I splashed the water onto my cheeks in an attempt to cool them off, suddenly feeling I was in over my head in more ways than one. I'd only ever kissed one man before the incident in the hallway.

Those thoughts opened the door I'd jammed shut the night Emerald had gone into labour, and thoughts of Aethan flooded in.

I sighed and sunk back under the water. What was he doing right now? Was he so wrapped up in the perfection of Ebony that he had forgotten all about me?

I missed the sight of him. I missed the touch of him. I missed the feel of him. It had been so long since things were simple between us. And now they never would be again. I let the agony in my gut compete with my lungs as they started to burn for air.

Finally, when the need for oxygen overwhelmed my misery, I stroked upwards, taking a breath as my head broke the water. Scruffy was a little white spot in the distance as he inspected the palm trees at the edge of the beach.

I trod water as I turned slowly, scanning the ocean for Turos. There was nothing but blue water stretching into the distance. He hadn't returned to the beach, and he appeared to have been a strong swimmer. I couldn't imagine anything happening to the huge warrior.

And then, as my concern was beginning to bloom, something grabbed my ankle.

My shriek echoed through the water, visions of sharks filling my mind. Bubbles blinded me as the surface of the ocean disappeared above my head. I tried to stroke upwards but the creature grabbed my other leg, scaling up my body like a monkey up a ladder till strong arms pinned mine to my sides and Turos's smiling face appeared before me. He kicked upwards, carrying me with him till our heads broke the water.

I took a deep, gasping breath. 'Let go.'

He shook his head, that infuriating smile still gracing his face. 'I know what's going to happen.'

'What's that?'

'As soon as I let you go, you're going to punch me.'

My anger ebbed and a small smile tugged at the corners of my mouth. 'Well, no-one could accuse you of being a slow learner.'

He trod water as he held me and suddenly I was aware of the movement of his skin brushing over mine. I could feel myself blushing furiously as I looked away.

'I won't punch you.' My voice was soft, but he must have heard me because he loosened his grasp.

'Promise? Because you punch like a man.'

I let out a snort and nodded my head, still unable to look at him.

My physical reaction to him confused me. I had never felt like this with anyone but Aethan. And even though I knew the theory of why I had to let Aethan go, I was having trouble with the practical part of it. I was still hanging onto a maybe. A what if. But when Turos was this close to me, I had trouble remembering why.

I pushed away from him, treading water as I finally met his eyes. 'You stopped trying.'

He shrugged one shoulder. 'I got warned off.'

'By whom? Isla?'

He smiled. 'By Lance. He said your heart belonged to someone else.'

I blinked tears out of my eyes and stared towards the shore. 'It did. I mean it does.' I sighed. 'It's complicated.'

'Love should never be complicated. It's the simplest thing in life.'

A laugh escaped my lips and I splashed some water at him. 'A romantic. I would never have guessed.'

'There's some romantic in all of us.' He waved his hand in the air in a dramatic flourish and then dipped it back into the ocean to splash me back. 'So this complicated man, is he waiting for you back home?'

I shook my head. 'If his mother gets his way he'll be married by now.'

'His mother gets to say who he will marry? Sounds like a wuss.'

'It's a long story. And it's....'

'Complicated?'

'See. You *are* a fast learner.'

A swishing, splashing noise reached us across the ocean. Turos froze and put his hand in the air in a warning motion. Then, as the black prow of a sailing vessel broke the water around the closest point, he dragged me back under.

This time I didn't struggle. Instead I followed him as he swam beneath the surface of the water towards the side of the bay. We came up amongst the boulders as the ship sailed fully into view. Sails flapped and sailors scampered over the deck and up the mast.

I didn't need Turos's warning finger against his lips to stay silent. A quick glance at the beach eased my fears. Scruffy was almost invisible against the white sand. If I hadn't known he was there, I doubt I would have noticed him.

'Who are they?' I whispered into Turos's ear.

'We don't know.'

My mind raced as I thought. Messengers from his father. Strained looks on his face whenever he returned from seeing Bladimir. 'This isn't the first time they've been here.' It wasn't a question.

'They've never approached this closely.'

Voices called out in a foreign language and sailors leapt to obey.

'Friendly?'

He shrugged and then pulled me closer to him behind a boulder. 'They're stopping.'

It takes a while for a ship that size to come to a stop, and by the time they had, they were across the bay and at the other point. If we stayed very still, I doubted they would notice us from there. I saw Scruffy skulk from his position in the shade up into the protection of the trees.

We watched as a boat was lowered over the side and a rope ladder unfurled. Then sailors scampered down the ladder, all of them with swords strapped to their waists and bows over their shoulder.

Turos let out a hiss as I said, 'Pirates?'

He shook his head. 'A few of these ships have been spotted. So unless it's a group of pirates working together, no.'

Once the boat was full, a bundle of material was thrown to the men below. Oars struck the water and the boat flowed swiftly towards the shore. It was there within minutes and all of the men except the oarsmen jumped into the knee-deep water.

Then the boat returned to the ship and the whole procedure was repeated, until it appeared that only one man remained on board.

'What's with the material?' I whispered.

'It's a net.' Turos spoke through clenched teeth.

'Surely they don't think they can catch a dragon with those nets?' I shook my head. A dragon was far too large for a net held by a dozen men to control them.

'They aren't after dragons,' Turos hissed. 'They're after hatchlings.'

My mind flashed back to the cavern. At least a dozen hatchlings had been playing with Arthur when we had left. From what I had seen as we'd flown in and out there was easily another dozen down the other end of the cavern. And while it would be impossible to steal a single hatchling from their mother, in the confusion of a fight, a hatchling could be smuggled out through the lava tubes.

'Arthur,' I said, starting to stroke towards the shore.

He grabbed me and pulled me back. 'They'll see us if we go now.'

I looked at him and smiled as I said, 'Good.'

'Good? We have no weapons. How can that be good?'

'Watch and learn, big boy.' There was no way I was letting them anywhere near Arthur. I reached out to Emerald and showed her what we were seeing, sure that Turos was doing the same with Lance. Then I stripped off my shirt, handed it to Turos, and swam to shore.

The sailors had made their way along the point to the sandy beach when they spotted me. I was sitting on a boulder as I combed out my hair with my fingers. I looked up at them, fluttering my eyelids as I waved.

The ones in front stopped. I stifled a smirk as the ones behind ran into the back of them, too busy staring to note the change in pace. They weren't faeries. But then I didn't know why I would have expected them to be. We were in a different world and probably the only faeries here were those that had come through with the dragons.

Well, whatever they were they certainly recognised a female form when they saw it. If the situation hadn't been so dire, I would have been amused by their sudden change of posture. Shoulders went back and chests stuck out and a few of them started shoving each other.

I stood, stretching languidly as I tried to look sexy, but I felt ridiculous standing there in my bra and underpants. They didn't seem to think I was ridiculous as more shoving broke out. The nets lay forgotten on the ground. And then one man pushed his way to the front and turned on the others, a low feral growl breaking out in his throat.

The others dropped back and no-one contested him as he walked towards me.

Eeeeeeeeeeeeep.

I mean I know that had been the whole point of the exercise. Divide and conquer and all that, but I had never fought before wearing only my underwear, and I was seriously regretting leaving my shirt with Turos.

Holding my hand out to the sailor, I shot a quick glance out to sea. Turos was still where I had told him to stay but the look on his face told me I only had a few seconds before he came to my aid.

I shot him a warning glance and then turned back to the sailor. Bristly, black hair covered his head and his face, flowing down his neck and under his shirt. I was guessing it covered his whole body, but I wasn't going to let him show me.

He stopped a few metres from me and said something in a gruff voice. I wiggled my fingers at him and smiled suggestively and then I turned and sashayed my way up the beach towards the palms. A quick glance over my shoulder showed he was following.

I quickened my stride as I approached the trees, widening the gap between us. I looked at him over my shoulder, fluttering my eyelids and giggling, before darting into the stand of palms. He seemed to like the challenge, letting out a roar as he chased me.

I was waiting for him, just not where he had expected. He stopped and looked around, confusion on his face. And then I dropped from the trunk of a palm onto his shoulders, wrapping my legs around his neck and twisting to the side.

He threw himself to the side in the direction I had twisted and we fell to the ground. The back of my head cracked against a rock as he rolled, pinning me down with his weight. His eyes were bright with excitement as he lifted back his fist and drove it towards my face. I shifted my head at the last second and his hand ploughed into the rock.

He let out an almighty roar of pain and I grabbed his head and threw him sideways, smacking his head against a boulder with enough force that the fight immediately left him. He slumped to the ground, his eyes unfocused as he stared at the sky.

Scruffy appeared from amongst the palms, rushing over to me and licking my hands as I dragged the sailor off the path. 'One down,' I said to him, 'nineteen to go.'

Was there any chance that they hadn't heard the noise of our fight?

I could see Turos as I stuck my head back out onto the beach. He had approached as close as he could while remaining unseen. The wait must have been killing him.

A smile crept over my lips at the thought and I used that smile as I messed up my hair and sauntered back to the sailors. The ones at the front knocked arrows to their bows while the ones at the rear drew their swords, and then they spread out, moving as a group up the beach.

Uhhh Ohhh. I guess that was a *yes* to the question of whether or not they had heard me.

I backed up into the trees, grabbing my pants off the rock as I did. They wouldn't give me any protection from arrows or swords but I would feel a lot better fighting if I wasn't worried about flashing certain bits of my anatomy at them.

It only took me a few seconds to slip into them but the first of the attackers rounded the corner as I was doing up the top button. Scruffy growled and lunged at the man's ankles, and without thinking, I wrapped Scruffy up in an air bubble and tossed him into the air.

The man stared up, a stunned look on his face as he watched Scruffy floating just beyond reach. I ball-kicked him in the face before he could recover, and followed it up with a hook. His head flew to the side and his sword dropped out of his hand as he collapsed to the ground. His eyes were rolling around in his head as I scooped up his sword and stepped over him.

The rest of the group were waiting, spread out across the entrance to the beach. I held my weapon up in a guard position and eyed them. A few of them seemed to know how to hold their swords, and the ones with the bows actually appeared to know how to shoot.

There was a blur of motion behind them and then Turos was upon them. He moved so swiftly I almost didn't see him as he downed the first archer with one mighty blow of his hammer-like fist. He had taken out two more before they even realised they were being attacked from behind.

Half the group turned towards him at the same time as the rest of them charged me. An arrow flicked towards me, rebounding off the shield I threw into place. I left it there long enough to let the men in the front smack into it.

One of them let out a gurgle and blood flowed out of his mouth as he looked down at the tip of the sword protruding from his chest. The man whose sword it was, let out a snarl, yelling what I was sure were obscenities as he pulled the sword free. His comrade's body slid sideways down the invisible shield, leaving a smear of blood floating in mid-air.

I shut down the shield and attacked. Leaping over them in a somersault as I swept downwards twice with my sword. My first stroke took an arm off, while my second lodged in the side of one of the men's neck.

I landed on the far side of the group, grabbed another sword off the ground, and turned to face the closest attacker.

'Izzy.' Another sword flew through the air, appearing point first out of my opponent's chest.

'Thanks,' I yelled back as the man collapsed forwards. I stepped onto his back, pulled out the sword and turned to face the rest of the group, a sword twirling from each hand. There were still eleven men standing. They held their weapons and eyed Turos and me warily. 'Five each?' I asked.

'What about the last one?'

'We can toss for him.'

Coming.

I could tell by the way Turos's head jerked that he had gotten the same message from Lance.

'Now where's the fun in that? Winner takes all.'

Before I could clarify exactly what 'all' the winner was going to take, he launched his attack. His swords were blurs as he leapt and struck, and before I could get my mouth shut again, two of his five were bleeding out on the sand.

Dark Sky. The only way I was going to match him would be to cheat. I slammed a barrier down the middle of the beach, separating him and the three men he was in the process of dealing with, from me and the rest of the sailors.

'Right,' I said, 'who's next?'

I was pretty sure they couldn't understand me, but they rushed me anyway. I slid my swords into the fastest of them, dodging to the side as his momentum carried him past me. I grabbed him, and swung him around and back into his comrades, plucking my swords back from his chest as he crashed into them. Then I leapt over him, flicking my swords through the carotid arteries of two of the remaining five.

'Hey.'

I felt Turos banging on my shield but managed to avoid looking at him, even though I *really* wanted to see the look on his face. That would be a rookie's mistake which could end up with me dead.

'Not fair,' he hollered again.

I spat a piece of hair out of my mouth and beckoned to the three remaining men. They looked at each other and then turned and sprinted towards the boat lying on the shoreline. I waited till they were pushing it into the water before I lowered the shield.

'You're letting them get away?' Turos was beside me in a flash.

'I'm thinking about it.' I pushed my wet hair back over my shoulders.

'But why?'

I turned to look up at Turos. His light-blue eyes blazed into mine. 'To send a warning?'

He shook his head and raked a frustrated hand through his hair. 'We've already given them fair warning. They keep coming though. And now we know what they want.'

'Dragons?'

He nodded.

'Well, okay then.'

A low rumble began behind us, growing in intensity until I could feel it vibrating through my chest. Two dragons soared into view. One sparkled green while the other looked like a piece of night in the brilliant sun-filled sky.

Emerald and Lance, flames shooting out of their mouths, roared as they swept overhead. They were magnificent and scary as all hell, and I would have been peeing myself if they weren't on my side.

The sailors in the little boat increased the pace of their rowing as they threw fearful glances upwards. I could see the one lone sailor on the ship up the front near the prow. He was fussing around a long metal barrel while shooting fearful glances up into the sky.

'Well,' Turos said, 'I guess that's that.'

I squeaked as he grabbed my shoulders and backed me up against one of the palms. '*What's that?*'

Emerald dived down upon the ship, grasping the mast with her front legs. The man let go of the barrel and lunged to the deck. The mast snapped like a twig and she threw it into the ocean before unleashing her fire upon the deck.

'I win,' he whispered as he leaned in close, the air from his breath tickling my ear. The tone of his voice left me in no doubt as to what exactly he'd meant by 'winner takes all'. And then he leaned in even closer, the length of his body pushing into mine and as he leaned down and nipped my ear.

I stiffened against him, my need for him to continue, warring with my need for him to stop. His lips nuzzled along my ear and then I felt the tip of his tongue graze the soft skin there. It took every ounce of self-restraint I had to push him away.

'Like hell you win.' I lifted a hand and a bolt of lightning flew out, crackling into the little rowboat and exploding it into tiny pieces. I watched just long enough to make sure there were no survivors.

Lance and Emerald were in the process of finishing off the ship. Tearing it to pieces and barbequing it at the same time.

I looked back at Turos. '*I* win.'

He stared at me with his mouth open wide.

'Oh what?' I said. '*Now* you're speechless?'

He swallowed a couple of times. 'I'm not speechless. I'm just not sure what to say.'

'That's fine,' I said, grasping his wet shirt in my fists, 'because I've got something else I'd prefer you to do with your mouth.' I pulled his head down.

I had a moment to admire the beauty of his ice-blue eyes, staring at me with an unnerving intensity, and then his lips were upon me. He licked my neck and nipped my ear, teasing me with his hands and his mouth as they made their way over my body. I squirmed against him, wanting more, needing more.

He moaned and arched against me as my hands slipped over the hardness of his chest. He lifted me up, pushing me back against the palm as I wrapped my legs around him and then his mouth finally found mine. I lost myself within his kiss, my mind arcing up into the sky as fireworks exploded inside my skull.

***

Erhherm. It was the equivalent of a dragon mentally clearing its throat.

Turos's lips left mine but he didn't release his hold on me. He looked into my eyes, pinning me against that tree with his gaze as much as his body. And then he shifted back, letting me slide to the ground. Regret and desire fought for dominance in his stare.

I licked my lips and broke the eye contact, looking over to the beach where Emerald and Lance were sitting. Scruffy floated next to them, his tongue hanging out in a doggy grin.

You brought us down here to do your dirty work so you could make out?

I blushed. *We killed the ones on shore.*

Emerald snorted and shook her head.

'What's she saying?' Turos asked.

'She's expressing her displeasure. Lance?'

'Just gave me a mental high five.'

'Oh.' I looked over at him. The urge to take up the kiss where it had left off was almost overwhelming but I had a feeling I would regret it later. I was still totally confused where he was involved, and it wasn't fair of me to start kissing anyone until I had my emotions sorted out. I was going to blame that one on the adrenaline. 'We'd better get back.'

He nodded. 'Isla will be worried.'

Scooping up my shirt from where he had dropped it, I dragged the heavy, wet material over my head. Then I watched out of the corner of my eye as he struggled into his clothing. Dark Sky, his body was perfect. My fingers itched to explore it.

I pushed all thoughts of kissing him out of my mind and walked over to Emerald. The tip of the ship jutted above the waterline, wisps of smoke curling off it. I climbed onto Emerald's neck, grabbing Scruffy out of the air and tucking him safely in front of me.

We were silent as we flew up the side of the mountain. We breached the top, the two dragons tucking in tight to race each other down the other side into the valley. For a brief moment I set my worries aside - Santanas, Galanta, Aethan, the invaders, being stuck in a foreign land, my confusion over my feelings toward Turos – I forgot all about them, revelling instead in the feel of the wind whipping by as the ground rushed past at break-neck speed.

We pulled out of the dive and headed straight up to circle over the city. Turos waved an arm at me and then he and Lance headed towards the buildings while Emerald turned toward the entry to the breeding cavern.

Isla was standing with her hands on her hips when we returned. I was guessing by the smooth path amongst the rock-strewn ground that she had been pacing. 'What happened? Where's Lance and Turos?'

'I'm guessing they've gone to report to King Bladimir. And we got attacked.' I slid off Emerald's neck and set Scruffy down on the ground.

'You're okay?' Her gaze swept over me, searching for injuries.

'Oh *please*.' I said. 'There was only, what, twenty of them.'

'One of these days your cockiness is going to get knocked right out of you.'

'Well, today was not that day.'

She closed the gap between us and grasped my chin in her hand, turning my head from side-to-side as she stared at it. 'What happened to your face? If I didn't know differently I'd say you got very thoroughly kissed.'

'Ahhh.' I squirmed and pulled my head out of her grip.

'Izzy?' Her voice was full of delighted shock.

'What?'

'Did Turos finally get around to kissing you?'

'Look,' I said, struggling to maintain a self-important voice. 'That's not important. What is important is that we were attacked. By dragon hunters. And it's not the first time they've come sniffing around.' Where was my cockiness when I needed it the most?

'He did.' She clapped her hands together and jumped up and down. 'Dark Sky, was it good? Cause he looks like he knows how to kiss a girl senseless. And with those big hands of his....' She stopped talking and took a deep sigh. Her eyes had a far off look as she said, 'I love a man with big hands.'

'It's not important right now.' I was floundering for ways to change the subject.

'Oh...Yes...It...Is.' She poked me in the chest in time with each word. 'It can't always be about saving the world. Sometimes it has to be about us.'

'Really? 'Cause I thought....' My mouth flopped open and shut while I thought about that, because as far as I was concerned I was in this highfaluting emotional mess exactly because we had to save the world and not think about personal matters.

I let out a huff and decided to braid my hair. It was easier than thinking about everything else.

She joined me on the cavern floor a few minutes later. Arthur was fast asleep in an orange pile of scales, his little rumbles a cross between cute and annoying. Scruffy joined him, turning circles a few times before pressing his back against the hatchling.

Without easing his snores, one of Arthur's wings popped out and scooped Scruffy in closer, till he was hugged against Arthur's chest like a teddy bear. As Scruffy closed his eyes and snuggled in even closer to the little dragon, I decided Arthur's snores were far more cute than annoying.

'Aren't they adorable,' Isla sighed. She pulled her knees up to her chest as she watched them. 'I keep thinking I couldn't love the little fella anymore and then he does something like that.'

'What kid doesn't want a little dog?'

'To eat?' A smile flashed over her face and she slapped my leg. 'Just kidding. Believe me, he has no intentions of eating Scruffy.'

I let out my breath and took up braiding my hair again. The water and fighting had put some serious snarls into it.

'Do you think this is what it feels like?'

I looked over at her. 'You're going to have to give me more information than that.'

'To, you know...have a baby? This love, it's more intense than I could ever have imagined.'

I was going to tell her that I was only eighteen, and what would I know about having a baby, but the look on her face stopped me.

Crystalline tears stood poised in her eyes and her face was absolutely still. I could feel sadness radiating off her, and I reminded myself that although she only ever showed us the surface, her emotional pool was rich and deep.

She had wanted more than she had. She had wanted a husband and children, but fate and circumstance had stripped that all away.

So instead, I reached over and took her hand. 'I'm sure this is exactly what it feels like,' I said.

Chapter Six

Stories

It felt like forever before Turos and Lance returned. In reality it probably wasn't that long, but it was enough time for my hair and shirt to dry in the warmth of the cavern.

His face was sombre as he dismounted from Lance, which wasn't a great sign, but I must admit I was more interested in the food he'd brought with him at that immediate moment than why he looked so serious.

'Hey Stud.' Isla uncurled from her position next to Arthur and danced over to take the heavy cooking pot from him.

It smelt like a lamb casserole. Or maybe beef. It didn't matter which it was, they were both delicious. I really needed to visit the kitchen before I left to find out what the delicate blend of spices they were using was.

'I thought you might be hungry,' Turos said, tossing me a bundle of fresh clothing. 'I know I was.'

'Kissing can do that,' Isla said.

I groaned and covered my face with my hands.

'Yes it can,' he agreed, a smile in his voice. 'Of course fighting can do that too. Although I'd rather work up an appetite through kissing.

'Oh, you're a lover not a fighter. I like that in a man. Wilfred is a lover.'

I let out a snort.

'What?' She peered at me and tilted her head to the side.

'Oh nothing. Just that he's a pretty good fighter.' I shook the shirt out of the bundle Turos had given me. It was the same colour as my eyes.

'Of course he is. Do you think I'd settle for a wimp? But he has these ginormous hands. The things he can do with those hands.' She paused for a moment, no doubt contemplating what those hands could do. 'And his mouth.' She let out a little moan. 'I really miss his mouth.'

'And *there* goes my *appetite*.' I moved till I was behind Emerald before stripping off my salt-stiffened shirt.

When I returned in my clean clothing, Isla had thankfully stopped her reminiscing. Instead, she delicately sank a piece of bread into her stew before placing it into her mouth.

I picked up the bowl she had filled for me and took a seat next to her. 'So what's going on?' I asked Turos.

He spread his arms and leant back against a boulder. 'What do you mean?'

I stopped with my spoon halfway to my mouth and stared at him. 'What do you mean, what do you mean?'

'I'm not sure I know this game,' Isla said. 'If I say *what do you mean*, three times in a row, am I winning?'

I had an urge to smack Turos hard enough to make sure his smile would dislodge. I couldn't believe I had let the smug bastard kiss me. 'I demand to know what is going on.' I felt strongly enough about it that I put my bowl and spoon down and advanced on him.

'Lover, not a fighter,' Isla crooned.

'Don't care,' I spat from between clenched teeth.

He stood up and flexed his head from side-to-side while shaking out his limbs.

'You know he's going to beat you,' Isla said. 'He's a trillion times faster than you.'

I was going to take offence at her use of the word trillion after I had whipped his butt. 'It's not all about speed.'

'Normally I would say not. But these guys take speed to a whole new level.'

I put my hands on my hips and spun to face her. 'Whose side are you on? I know you want to know what's going on as well.'

'I'm on yours. Which is why I am stopping you from getting hurt.'

'You don't know he'll win. I do have strengths he doesn't.'

'You willing to blow him up?' She met me stare-for-stare.

Damn it. It wasn't a risk I was willing to take. While I was betting it would feel really good for the second it took to do it, I knew I would regret it as soon as his body parts had finished hitting the ground. Well, perhaps regret wasn't a big enough word to cover what I would feel. 'No.' I took my hands off my hips and stalked back to my bowl.

You know anything? I asked Emerald.

They've been hiding things from me as well. Her thoughts bubbled with angst.

I took pleasure in the thought that she would be giving Lance a mental tongue-lashing as I ate the rest of my meal in silence.

When I had finished, I placed my bowl on top of Isla's and faked a yawn. Then I cleared an area and lay down with my old bundle of clothes under my head. I was suddenly overwhelmed with home sickness. I mean I know I had Isla, Emerald and Scruffy, but I missed Grams and Sabby and Mia. And I missed my room and my bed, but most of all, I missed my Mum.

I squeezed my eyes tight; partly to block out the light, but mostly to keep in the tears. It wasn't long before my fake tiredness became real and sleep took me from the cavern.

***

Well, when I say sleep took me from the cavern, that wasn't entirely true. I was still in the cavern, but in a twilight that would never naturally reach the innards of the giant volcano.

Trillania. I was in Trillania. The thirty days were over.

Would I be able to reach my home from where I was? Or was I trapped in the Millenia version?

The thought had barely flashed across my mind and I was standing in the field below my house.

Well, I never. So even though I was in a totally different world, we still shared the same dreamland. I couldn't wait to tell Wolfgang. And Radismus. No doubt when all of this was over, the two of them would secrete themselves in a library for a few months while they nutted out all the possible metaphysical probabilities that the knowledge brought.

So now that I was here, what was I going to do?

The most logical thing would be to try and make contact with someone. Mum would be beside herself by now and I would like to let her know we were safe. The problem with that was that the only other person I regularly met in Trillania was Aethan. He was the only other dreamwalker I knew. And I wasn't willing to run into him. Not yet. My tongue got stuck to the roof of my mouth whenever I thought about what I would say when I saw him again.

My best bet was with one of the Border Guards on patrol in Trillania. Or even better yet, Rako.

I propelled myself to Isilvitania, to the castle. There were always Border Guards there. The place was empty except for a couple of dreaming faeries chasing each other through the gardens. The female was obviously dragging her heels, hoping to get caught. I listened to her bell-like laugh as her lover caught her, sweeping her up into his arms and his embrace. That looked like a nice dream to be having.

'Izzy?'

I gasped and spun around, a dagger becoming solid in my hand. It dissolved again when I saw who was there, and it took all my being, all my pride to keep my voice steady as I said, 'Hello Aethan.'

'What are you...?' He shook his head and stared at me. 'How are you? I've missed you.'

A lump formed in my throat. 'I've missed you too,' I whispered. I was proud of the fact that I didn't reach for him as the words left my mouth. 'Where is everyone?'

He looked around. 'It's only mid-afternoon.'

My mouth made a soundless 'O'. I guess it *had* only been afternoon. The lack of sunlight in the cavern made it hard to keep track of time. 'So what are you...forget it,' I said. He was probably sleeping in with his new bride.

'I had the night shift.' His face held confusion as he stared at me. 'Want to go for a walk?'

I thought about all the other things I should be doing – watching an adorably overgrown hatchling play, putting up with Turos's smug smile, working out how in the Great Dark Sky we were going to get home.

'Sure,' I said, turning away from the ardent lovers.

We walked in awkward silence. He didn't remember a time when our hands were used to touching each other. But I did. I remembered it too well. It felt weird to let mine hang uselessly by my side.

'How have you been?' I was hoping he didn't get all doe-eyed and lovey-dovey on me, telling me all about the joys of marriage cause I might be forced to accidentally stab him.

'We've had a reprieve from goblin attacks.'

'Oh.' Not the answer I had been expecting, but a good answer anyway.

'We've managed to get a few scouts through and it appears that Santanas is still gravely wounded.' He turned towards me. 'Because of you.'

I shook my head. 'I failed. I didn't kill him.'

'No-one can kill him.'

'Then what are we doing? What are we trying to achieve? Do we just let him have the lands?'

'That wouldn't stop him Izzy?'

I shook my head. 'But if we use your logic, we can't win.'

'We can always win. We just need to find a way.'

We stared at each other while I tried to work out if we were still talking about Santanas. I wrenched my eyes away from his and continued our walk. 'What does he want?'

'Who?'

'Santanas? What does he want?'

'I don't know Izzy. I'm not sure he wants anything in particular. The only thing I know for sure is that he is crazy.'

I shuddered at the memory of Orion's peaceful face wearing the mask of a man crazed with grief and power.

'Aethan, I….' I stopped.

'What is it Izzy?'

'I'm scared,' I whispered. There was really no word big enough to describe the hard core of blackness that lived inside me.

He turned back to me, this time reaching out to me and pulling me into his arms. I know it was what he would have done for Isla, his sister, but I let him do it, imagining that the motion meant more to him than it did. I nestled my face into his chest and I breathed him in, knowing the whole time that it would probably be the last time I did.

When I pulled away I was crying and I hated myself for it.

'Hey.' He lifted a hand and brushed away a tear. 'What's this for?'

The last thing I wanted was him feeling sorry for me. 'No, it's not…I don't…I want…Oh Dark Sky, I feel….' I stopped and sniffed. 'I'm not explaining this well at all.'

He rubbed a finger across my cheek as he stared down into my eyes. 'The only thing that you need to know is….'

Before he could finish the sentence, I was jerked back into my own body.

'Oops, sorry,' I heard Turos say. 'I was trying to make you more comfortable.'

I put my fingers on the back of my head, feeling for blood. 'By braining me?'

'I tried to make your pillow bigger. It didn't work.'

I sat up and rubbed at my head. I had been with Aethan, and now I was here with Turos. I didn't know if I was going to survive the emotional onslaught.

I wiggled backwards till my bottom hit a boulder, then I leaned back. 'I don't know how much longer I can stay.'

'The cavern does get claustrophobic doesn't it? And might I just reiterate that's the reason we don't let female dragons bond?'

'Sure you can reiterate it,' I said, 'if you want to be a total bastard.'

He let out a low chuckle.

'But I wasn't talking about the cavern.' I let out a sigh. 'I am needed at home. Isla is needed at home.'

He was silent for a while as he threw pebbles at a much larger rock. 'You know we can't let you go,' he said, finally.

'Why not?'

He waved a hand at Emerald and Arthur. 'They belong here.'

I pushed my fists into my eyes while I tried to come up with logic he would get. 'When I say I am needed, I *really* mean needed. In an end-of-the-world-type scenario.'

He stopped his pebble throwing and looked at me. 'You tell me yours and I'll tell you mine.'

'Really?' I leaned over and peered up into his face to see if he was sincere. 'You're going to brief me without Daddy's permission?'

'You *really* know how to push my buttons, don't you?'

'It's a talent.' I paused for a second and then said, 'Well, are you?'

He let out a low laugh and shook his head. 'Yes. I will brief you without my father's permission.'

'Well, okay then.' I took a deep breath and then thought about where to start.

'The beginning,' Isla's soft voice echoed through the cavern. 'Always start at the beginning.'

'Yes, but whose beginning?'

I heard the noise of her boots scraping on rock and then she appeared before me. She dropped into a seated position with her legs crossed beneath her. 'Good point. I guess from Santanas's beginning.'

'Not where I would have thought.'

She cocked her head and looked at me. 'He is the one consistent player in the drama. This is his story. We are all just bit players.'

'Will you tell it? I mean, *his* story?'

'He is your grandfather. It is yours to tell.'

I shifted a little uncomfortably. 'I don't know it. Well, not the detail.' I was suddenly sure though, that that detail was important. Because maybe his story would give me the answer I had asked Aethan earlier. Maybe it would give me a clue to what Santanas wanted?

Isla began her tale in a serious voice. 'From the very beginning it was clear that Santanas was going to be a mighty warrior.'

I let out a snort. 'What? From when he was a baby?'

Isla paused to stare at me. 'Do you want to tell this story?'

'Dark Sky, no. I don't *know* this story.'

She nodded her head. 'I forget that you did not know him before.'

'And you did?'

'I used to rock his cradle.'

I kept forgetting how old Isla was. 'Sorry,' I said. 'Please continue.'

She rolled her eyes but took up where she had left off. 'He was faster, taller, more powerful than all the other boys his age. But he was also humble and kind. He grew into a fine young man and fell in love with Littiana. She felt for him as he did for her and they were married a year after they were initially betrothed. It wasn't apparent at this time that he was a War Faery.'

Turos sucked in a breath.

'That didn't become clear until the orcs' attacks began later on that next year. Perhaps if we had realised we could have helped him more. But one with that power had not been born for a couple of centuries. Although in retrospect, he was of the same lineage as Tralador. We should have been more diligent.'

'What are you talking about?' It wasn't like her to jump around so much.

'Tralador was the last born War Faery before Santanas. Which means you are also of his line.'

I shifted uncomfortably. I didn't really want to talk about me.

'One summer's day the orcs attacked closer to the capital than ever before. They were upon the outlying villagers before we even knew they were there. Santanas was at the castle with the troops, but Littiana had stayed at home that day. She was pregnant with twins. An almost unheard of event. She was alone in their cottage in the forest. He left the guard and fought his way single-handedly to their home, but it was too late.' She paused for a moment and tears swum in her eyes as she took a deep breath. 'They had torn the young from her womb and eaten them. Well, that is what we guess happened from the remnants that were left.'

I pressed a hand to my stomach as my dinner thought about performing an encore.

'His grief maddened him, breaking down the mental barriers he had erected to protect others from his wild, untamed power. He became a vigilante, hunting down bands of orcs till none would come into our lands. I think he was hoping they would kill him, but when they didn't, and there were none left to kill, he retired to his cottage and became a hermit.'

She sighed and rubbed at her eyes with her hands. 'We should have kept a better eye on him. Wolfgang tried for a few years, but eventually Santanas drove him away and even he gave up.'

'What do you mean by 'even he' gave up?'

She blinked at me a couple of times. 'Littiana was Wolfgang's only child. His wife died in childbirth and he never took another.'

Realisation drove into me like a hammer. That was what Ulandes had meant. *Do not let the dark swallow your broken heart. It will be made whole again.* He was still grieving the loss of his daughter as well as the loss of his grandchildren and son-in-law.

'So what happened then?' Turos's voice broke across my memory.

'Well,' Isla continued, 'for a time it appeared that he had recovered. He never came back to the capital to live, but he set up a training camp on the edge of the goblin lands and Father allowed it. Santanas had rid our land of orcs and we thought having him there would be a deterrent to the goblins.'

'When did you realise he had teamed up with Galanta?' I managed to say her name without spitting.

'Who's Galanta?' Turos asked.

'The Queen of the goblins.' My fists clenched as I said her name and Turos looked at me, his eyebrows raised as he tilted his head to the side. 'I have a score or two to settle with her,' I said.

'A month or two went by without us hearing from the camp and then rumours of black magic started filtering back to us. We successfully managed to infiltrate an agent, but before she could report, she disappeared.'

'Grams?'

She nodded her head at me. 'And then the goblin attacks began.' She leant back against a rock and sighed. 'I often wonder at which point he was beyond the point of no return.'

'What have you come up with?' Turos asked.

'I think it was finding Littiana. I think his mind was broken with the grief, and then the black magic drove him mad.' She looked at me and said, 'Perhaps I should be nicer to you.'

I threw a pebble at her. 'You're the least of my problems.'

She peered at me and smiled. 'I'd say your worst problem at the moment is a serious case of pash rash.'

'What?' My hands flew to my face. My chin felt tender under palpation. 'Oh, no!' I turned and punched Turos. 'You gave me pash rash.'

His face broke into a broad smile. 'You were most enthusiastic. But next time, I'll try to be gentler.'

My stomach lurched at the thought of a next time. Would there be a next time? Tendrils of guilt had already begun to wrap around the memory, and seeing Aethan had only made that worse.

'So what happened next?' I forced my mind away from the thought of what Turos kissing me gently would feel like, and back to Isla's story.

'Their army forced us through the veil. Even teamed with the witches and humans we were no match for them, for Santanas.' Her attention zeroed in on me again. 'He can do things you can't.'

'Duurrrrr,' I said. 'He's more powerful.'

She shook her head. 'It's not that. He is using both light and dark magic. You can only use the light.'

Or risk going crazy myself, was the unspoken part of that sentence.

Turos looked between Isla and me but before he could say anything she continued. 'It didn't take us long to see we would all be destroyed if we didn't surrender. But we knew they would destroy us even then.'

'So you tricked him?'

She nodded. 'We wove a spell into the paper the treaty was signed on. When he added his signature, the spell was triggered and his soul was trapped in that stone.'

'So what's the life-and-death situation you were talking about?' Turos shifted out of his cross-legged position. I tried not to admire his legs as he stretched them out in front. 'Sounds like the situation is under control.'

'He's back,' I said. 'And he's pissed off.'

'I'd be pissed off too if you'd burnt me to a charred cinder.' There was a teasing pride in Isla's voice.

'Is there something I should know? About you, I mean?' Turos pointed a finger at me.

'She's our only hope.' She laughed at the sceptical look on his face. 'It's true. She's the only one amongst us with enough power to go head-to-head with him.'

'I must admit that my knowledge of our time before we came here is a bit rusty, but aren't War Faeries incredibly powerful?'

'Unbelievably so.'

'Then why would Izzy be able to....' He stopped and stared at me. 'You're one too. But *you* can't control your powers.'

'Bingo,' I said. 'Give the man a balloon.'

'Sometimes I have no idea what you're talking about.'

'She means that you are correct, but her jovial way of saying it means she does not wish to discuss it.'

'Oh.' I could tell he was dying to ask me a question. He was probably brimming up and about to overflow with them but he just shut his mouth and took a deep breath.

It was a good time to change the subject. 'I saw Aethan,' I said to Isla.

'Oh.' She clasped her hands to her face. 'How is he?'

'Good. As far as I could tell. We didn't really talk about how he was 'cause, you know....' I shrugged a shoulder. 'Anyway, apparently the attacks have ceased and from what they can tell, Santanas is still recovering.'

'Did you tell him where we were?'

'Didn't get a chance before numb-nuts here woke me up.' I poked my thumb toward Turos. 'No doubt I'll see someone else tonight.'

'So the veil is accessible again.' She nodded her head. 'Let the games begin. Speaking of games,' she turned toward Turos, 'it's your turn.'

He muttered something about War Faery dream-walkers, cleared his throat and said, 'Yes, my turn. My story also begins long ago. There were a few amongst us who were alive when we fled Emstillia. They tell us that we came through the portal on dragonback and searched the seas for somewhere to land. This was the first land we found. It is also the only land we've found. But since it had everything we needed - fertile grounds, built-in protection and a suitable area for the dragons to lay, we were not concerned.

A few weeks after we arrived, strangers appeared. They came in boats, and from what is remembered, resembled the sailors we fought today. We hid deep in the caverns while they searched the island, and when they found nothing, they departed. Now they are back.'

'Surely we can handle a few ships,' I said. 'We made short work of that one today, and that was just two dragons. How many dragons are there?'

'The numbers have increased to five hundred strong. Half of which are males.'

Emerald let out a snort. *As if only the males amongst us would fight if our young were in danger.*

'Easy-peasy Japanesey,' I said, but Turos didn't look so certain.

'I've got a bad feeling about this.' He shook his upper body as if trying to shake it out of his head.

'Why do you think they came back now?' Isla asked. 'I mean you've been here for hundreds of years and the only two times they turn up are just after you arrive and then just after we do.'

As usual, she had seen something none of the rest of us had.

'Which means,' she said, following her train of thought, 'that the most probable conclusion is that they felt the opening between the worlds.'

'Which means,' I finished it for her, 'that they can use magic.'

I wasn't feeling so cocky now.

***

'Quiet. Quiet.' King Bladimir rapped on the long table with his knuckles and, immediately, the rumble of voices dropped to a whisper and then silence.

I stayed very silent where I was, at the far, far end of the very long table, seated next to Isla, with Scruffy at my feet. It seemed that she and I were at the bottom of dragon-rider pecking order and I wasn't going to push my luck by talking out of turn. Bladimir hadn't looked so happy when

Turos had arrived with us, and would probably use any excuse to kick us out.

'Turos,' Bladimir waved a hand at him. 'Report.'

Turos stood and swaggered to the front of the room. I listened as he accounted in brief, accurate sentences what had happened on the beach the day before. I was pretty happy when he left out the part about me blowing up the boat, and also the bit about the kiss. Nobody needed to know about those.

When he had finished he sat back down and Bladimir barked, 'Rand.'

Another rider stood and moved to the front of the room. 'I had this morning's patrol to the north,' he said. 'We did not sight any ships during the time we were sweeping the area.'

He sat back down and another rider hopped up.

'I had the morning's patrol to the east,' he said. 'There were no sightings of the enemy.'

Another rider hopped up. He had been to the south and also had nothing to report. I could feel the tight ball of concern that had started winding in my chest the night before, starting to unravel.

See. There was nothing to worry about. Just a few ships, and we had no doubt scared them off when we had so easily destroyed that one yesterday.

I was so busy feeling relieved that I didn't realise no other rider had hopped up until Bladimir said, 'Who had the west?'

'Landorn.' Turos's voice was tight.

'Well, go and see if he's back.' He waved an impatient arm at the door, and, as if he had willed it, it sprung open.

A dragon rider stood in the doorway. His tunic was ripped and dried blood covered his face. An arrow shaft protruded from his stomach. He grasped the edge of the door frame and leant over, placing his hand around the arrow, as if considering removing it. He let it go, and, with a perplexed look on his face, stared at the blood on his fingers. 'They're coming,' he said. 'From the west.' He slid to his knees, and then slumped to his side.

'Izzy.' Isla grabbed my shirt and yanked me up. 'You need to heal him, or he'll die.'

'I've only ever done it that once,' I protested as she dragged me towards Landorn. 'And Wolfgang helped me.'

'You're his only hope.'

I wanted to help him, I really did. But I had no real idea how to start.

Isla pushed me ahead of her into the crowd.

'Excuse me,' I said. 'Coming through.' I arrived at Landorn's side and knelt beside him. Isla joined me a second later.

'What do you think you're doing?' Bladimir grabbed my shoulder.

'Father,' Turos said. 'Let her be.' He gave me a smile that I would have liked to return but I couldn't. I was far too scared to smile.

'We're going to have to remove the arrow as you heal him,' Isla said.

'Give them room,' Turos yelled. 'Move back.'

I placed a hand on Landorn's shoulder. He was still breathing, just. Isla was right. If I didn't do something soon it would be too late. I closed my eyes and tried to remember what I had done the day I had healed Wolfgang.

I emptied my mind and reached out towards Landorn and suddenly I was flowing out of my body and slithering into his, with just a tenuous strand of soul to lead me back to my own.

His head was damaged but the most pressing concern was the arrow. It had been fired from below and the angle it had entered had allowed it to perforate intestine, liver and lung. More blood was leaking out inside his body than had been out of the wound, and his lung was slowly filling up.

'Cut the fletching off the arrow.' My voice sounded wooden to my ears.

I urged some of the blood vessels to knit back together and most of the internal bleeding stopped. 'Now pull it through.'

He bucked in agony as they did it, but I couldn't waste any time stopping his pain. The arrow had been acting as a plug to many blood vessels and as it was removed, a dam of red burst within him. I heard yelling from the rest of the riders as he choked on blood, but I ignored it.

Gently, so gently, I moved through the tissue, encouraging it to move back to where it had been. To repair. To rebuild. Tissue re-knit and blood vessels healed. The hole in the liver sucked back together, but the lung was a little more tricky. Such delicate membranes all torn and shredded. I looked at his healthy lung, and then imagined the damaged one as a mirror image. The membranes fluttered back into position and the bleeding stopped.

Everything in his abdomen seemed to be in working order but there was swelling on his brain and a break in the skull and the bones of his face. I took the fluid building up in his skull and forced it out through the break, through the tissue and into his sinuses. It started to drain out of his nose and I returned to the brain, repairing the damage before encouraging the bone to re-join back the way it had once been.

When his heart beat had stabilised and his breathing normalised I flowed out of him and back into my body.

'He still has blood in his lungs.' I opened my eyes. 'It's going to take a little while for the body to remove it. So we want to make sure he doesn't get any sort of infection during that time. Apart from that, he is whole again.'

I rocked back onto my feet and stood, stretching my arms above my head. Any minute now they were going to start singing my praise. I was thinking, next meeting, Isla and I might be at the *head* of the table.

I turned to look at King Bladimir. His face had gone red and there seemed to be some sort of froth coming out of his mouth.

'Arrest her,' he screamed, jabbing a finger toward me. 'Arrest her.'

'Oh Dark Sky,' I said, 'what have I done now?'

'Witchcraft,' Turos said from beside me. 'Sorry, should have mentioned it was illegal.'

'Mentioned?' I said. 'Should have mentioned?' He backed away with his hands in front of him while I advanced. 'Yeah. Next time a little warning might be in order.'

Scruffy let out a warning bark and then something heavy collided with the back of my head. Landorn looked up at me with confusion in his eyes as I sank to my knees beside him.

The room started to spin, dispersing into a million fleeing stars, and then darkness came.

Chapter Seven

Assassin

I was in the conference room, but I was suddenly all alone. It took me a second to realise I was in Trillania.

'Oh phooey,' I said out loud. 'I'm unconscious. Again.'

Seriously, if they didn't stop hitting me over the head they were going to do some permanent damage.

I shrugged a shoulder. Oh well. Not much I could do about it at the moment. I may as well make the most of my time. If my calculations were correct it should be early morning in Isilvitania. Hopefully someone would still be on duty.

I concentrated on the castle and a second later was standing outside of it.

'Izzy. You're alive.'

I turned to find Rako striding towards me.

'What made you think otherwise?'

'One hysterical mother and a semi-hysterical grandmother reporting you've been missing for a couple of weeks.'

'Oh,' I said. 'That ought to do it.'

'Is the Princess safe?'

'Safer than me. I'm unconscious.' I put a hand up to forestall his outburst. 'Yes, she's safe. Well, she was when I got hit over the head.'

'Izzy. You're not making this sound any better.'

'I suppose I'm not.' I sighed. 'It's as good as it can be.'

'Great Dark Sky girl.' He rubbed at the scar running down his cheek. 'Where are you?'

'We're in Millenia.'

'But...'

'Yes, yes. I know. Mythical city. It's where Emerald's from.'

He nodded. 'That would explain the enormous, black dragon.'

I filled him in on everything that had happened since we'd been gone. When I had finished he said, 'And it's not magical?'

'What?'

'Their ability to move so fast?'

'I tell you I've just been knocked unconscious and probably thrown back in prison and that's what you're hanging on to?'

A sheepish smile graced his lips for just a second. 'Well...is it?'

I sighed and shook my head. 'Not magical. It's a mind trick. Turos is teaching me. Now, what's been going on here?'

'The Prime Ministers have finally cleared their very important schedules enough to meet with King Arwyn and Aethan.'

'Well, that's progress.'

He pulled a face. 'Maybe. Maybe not.'

'Anything else?'

'Queen Eloise hasn't recovered from Orion's death.'

It was my turn to pull a face. She wasn't my favourite person but I wouldn't ask for that sort of pain for anybody.

'She has locked herself in the tower and the only person she will let wait on her is Princess Ebony.'

Totally different face pulling for that bit of news.

'Listen Izzy,' Rako put a hand on my shoulder, 'about Ebony and Aethan.'

'Yes, I worked it out,' I said.

'You did?'

'He's the heir now. Of course he is going to marry her.' I managed to keep my voice fairly steady. Only a little crack at the very end of the sentence betrayed me.

'Well actually, what I was going to tell you was….'

He disappeared from view and, suddenly, I was blinking up at the ceiling of the same prison cell I'd been in when we had first arrived.

Isla sat on the end of my bed and Scruffy lay on my chest.

'De ja vu,' I said.

'Oh goody, you're awake.' Isla leaned over and peered into my face.

'You under arrest as well?'

'Nah.' She shook her head. 'They let me come with you.'

I grabbed her hand and squeezed it.

'Don't go getting all gooey on me,' she said. 'It's just boring without you. That's all.' She softened her words by squeezing back.

There was a clanging noise and then footsteps approached. A few seconds later Turos appeared at the cell door.

'You okay?' he asked.

I turned my head away from him and said, 'I'm not talking to you. You let me save him knowing what would happen to me.'

'I didn't know you could heal.' He scuffed a foot along the stone floor. 'But I must admit, I was hoping you could. I'd heard stories about it, when I was a kid.'

'So you sacrificed me for a friend.' I remembered I wasn't talking to him and crossed my arms across my chest. 'Isla, tell him how mad I am about that.'

She put both hands in the air. 'I'm not getting in the middle of your lovers' tiff.'

I sat up and shoved her shoulder. 'We are not, *lovers*.'

'Tell that to your chin the next time you look in the mirror.'

'Urghhhhh.' I threw my arms up. 'You're unbelievable.'

'Thank you.' She smiled beatifically at me.

A look at Turos showed that he was smiling as well.

'You,' I said, hopping up and walking over to the bars, 'do *not* get to smile.'

He danced back out of arm's reach. 'What are you going to do about it?'

'Really?' I said. 'You did see what I did to that boat, didn't you?'

'Good point.' He put his hand over his mouth and wiped his smile away. 'Anyway I came to tell you that we are making ground getting you out of here.'

'Who's we?' Isla asked.

'Pretty much every dragon rider that saw you heal Landorn. Oh, and Landorn himself.'

'He should be in bed.'

'He is, he is.' He sat cross-legged beside the bars. 'Now, shall we continue your training?'

I looked around the cell and shrugged a shoulder, letting out a sigh as I realised there was nothing better to do. Rako was going to whip my butt if I came home without the secret to their speed. 'Sure, why not.'

An hour later I was wishing I hadn't bothered. My head throbbed and I was even further from finding the mental stillness that Turos was describing.

'I need a break.' I pushed up off the floor and stretched.

'But you were doing so well.'

'Really?' I let out a laugh.

'Actually,' Isla said from behind me, 'you were much faster that last time. The stone only made it half way before you caught it.'

'It's still not fast enough.' I sat on the edge of the bed and bent forwards, stretching out my legs. 'So what's happening out there?'

'A band of riders has flown west to see if what Landorn reported was true.'

'You're going to need me if it is,' I said.

He nodded. 'I know that. And I suspect father does too. He's just a little stubborn sometimes.'

'Pot, kettle, black,' I said.

He opened his mouth, no doubt to ask me what I was talking about, then slammed it shut as we heard another set of boots racing in our direction.

'Turos.' The rider stopped outside the cell. 'You must come.'

'Jaldor. How bad is it?' Turos asked.

'Bad. Very bad.' The young rider bobbed his head at us. 'Many ships come from the west. We are readying for battle.'

'How far away are they?' Turos asked.

'Two and a half hours flying when we left. Perhaps two hours now.'

'Has father?' He looked at us but Jaldor shook his head. 'You will be safe here,' he said. 'I will return with news when I can.' He turned and hurried off after Jaldor.

'Sure we'll be safe.' Isla plonked back down on the bed. 'Until the raiders take control of the city.'

'I'll blow us a way out of here if they do. Then we can get Emerald and Arthur and get the hell out of here.'

'Where?' she said. 'You heard Turos. There was no other land that they could find.'

'We'll go back home. We just need to work out how they did it.'

'It has to be the dragons,' Isla said. 'I've been thinking about it. No-one that came here had magic, and it's outlawed. The only way that Lance and Turos could have gotten to us was if Lance opened up the gateway.'

'Dragons are the only creatures that can willingly go through the veil and also into Trillania,' I said. It made sense that they could open up gateways between worlds. 'I don't think Emerald knows how to do it. Otherwise she would have come home by herself.'

'Oh.' Isla clicked her fingers and pointed at me. 'Remember what she said at the trial? Santanas came to her. He came here. That means….'

'That *he* can open gateways.'

'Which means?' She looked at me with a triumphant look on her face.

'That you think that I can do it too. But I *can't* Isla. I can't open a gateway. How would I even start? And how would I know *where* to open it to, even if I worked out *how* to open one?'

'I have total faith that when you do it, it will be like everything else you do. Instinctual.'

'I like your use of the word *when*, not *if*.'

'It's all about visualisation Izzy. You should try it some time. Now, if you don't mind, I have some visualisation of my own to do.'

She pulled her legs up underneath herself and closed her eyes. A few seconds later her lips started moving. I sat down beside her and leant my head back against the wall.

***

Darkness came and went and light again shone through the barred window of our prison before Turos returned. His footsteps were hurried, but uneven, and there was blood on his pants.

'You're hurt.' I reached a hand through the bars and pulled at the fabric trying to see how bad his wound was.

'It's just a cut,' he said. 'But we need your help. There's a lot of others far worse than I am.'

I felt my eyebrows ride up my head. 'So let me get this straight,' I said, 'you've come to my prison cell to ask me to do the very thing that caused me to be here?'

He shrugged a shoulder. 'Come on Izzy. You know it's not my fault you're in here.'

'That's not the point. What would your father say?'

'Well,' he pulled a face, 'I'm actually here on his orders.'

'Huh.' I backed away from him and then crossed my arms as I tapped a foot. 'So now he wants my help?'

'Come on, Izzy.' Isla shoved me from behind. 'There are people wounded far worse than your pride.'

'Fine.' I stopped tapping and walked back to the cell door. 'But you and I will be talking about this later.'

'As long as it doesn't end with you breaking my nose, again.' He shot me a devastating smile and then pulled a key out of his pocket and unlocked the door.

'So what happened?' I asked him as he led us through the windy passages of the castle. 'Did you destroy them?'

He nodded his head. 'But we took heavy losses.' He stopped and pushed a heavy door open; holding it so Isla, Scruffy and I could pass through. 'I've never seen anything like the weapons they had. Metal tubes that hurled balls at us, and others that cast out nets. And there were these other…things,' he spat out the word, 'that fired tiny chunks of metal at us. They were so fast we couldn't see them, and they chewed us up.'

I noticed blood drop off his leg to the ground and looked behind us. A tiny trail of blood showed our path through the halls.

'Stop.' I put a hand on his arm. 'We can't afford for you to lose too much blood.'

He didn't fight me, instead sliding down the wall to sit with his leg stretched out in front of him. I pulled up the leg of his pants and examined him. There was a small hole on each side of his calf. Blood oozed out in a constant trickle.

Isla moved her head so she could examine the wound from both sides. 'It looks like something went all the way through.'

'It did.' He reached into his pocket and pulled out a tiny lump of metal. 'One of these.' He dropped it into her outstretched hand.

I put a hand onto his bare skin and flowed into him, noticing as I did how much easier it was becoming. Then I scanned him from top to bottom for other damage. A few bruises and scrapes but the only real damage was the tunnel through his flesh. The bleeding was coming from a vein that had been nicked. It only took a few seconds to seal it up and knit the flesh back together.

I opened my eyes and took my hand off Turos's leg. He wiggled his foot from side-to-side, flashed me a quick grin, and jumped back to his feet.

'Come on,' he said. 'We'd better hurry.'

He increased his pace and we followed him at a trot as he led us down to the large hall outside the room in which we had had our initial trial. Men lay on the cold stone floor as women moved between them, some offering water, others performing first aid.

When we entered, one of them looked up and bustled toward us. She grabbed Turos's hand and dragged him with her. 'Oh thank the Dark Sky.' She cast me a look over her shoulder. 'The worst of them are over here.'

Men's moans echoed off the stone walls. Some of them cried and others just lay, staring straight up as if their minds were elsewhere. A few women knelt with their heads bowed, praying, I guessed, and still others sobbed in hopeless frustration as they applied pressure to wounds that wouldn't stop bleeding.

We passed a column of men whose wounds no longer bled. Their lax limbs and calm faces belied the damage I could see on their bodies. The metal had torn through them, turning them into mangled masses of twisted, torn tissue. No-one could have faced that sort of destruction and survived.

Turos was right. He had gotten off lightly.

'What about the dragons?' I heard the horror in my voice. If this had happened to the men, what had happened to their much larger mounts?

'We lost fifty.' Turos's voice was cold. 'The metal tore holes through their wings and they didn't make it back. Many more are badly wounded.' He looked over at me.

'But you got them?' Isla asked.

He nodded. 'There were more than two hundred ships. But we got them. Down to the last one.'

They had also lost ten percent of their dragon population doing it.

The woman stopped and let go of Turos's hand to kneel by the side of a man. His face was pasty white and sweating, and his teeth were clenched in pain. 'Bel,' he said, grabbing onto her.

I dropped down beside Bel and placed my hand on his arm. I flowed into him, almost pulling back out when I saw the damage there. Ripped muscle, smashed bones, a bleeding kidney, perforated intestines, and one of the vessels near the heart was straining to the point of breaking. I started there, strengthening the vessel. Then I flowed out through him, not so much concentrating on one thing, but running ribbons of power through him as I encouraged everything to return to where it should be. To begin to function as it should. Pieces of metal started popping out of his body, tinkering onto the stone around him as the wounds welded shut.

He sucked in a big breath of air, and then another one as I flowed back to my body.

'My pain…it's gone.' He stared down, patting at his armour which was riddled with holes and stained with blood.

'Rufos?' He reached out a hand to Turos. 'I can feel him.'

'He's alive,' Turos said.

'Come on.' Bel's eyes were wide as she led me to the next man.

'I'm going to help the other women,' Isla said.

I nodded as I followed Bel, watching as Scruffy trotted off after Isla. A long line of wounded men stretched out in front of me and Scruffy had correctly ascertained that his best bet of getting fed would be where Isla was.

Minutes flowed into hours as I moved from man to man. The healing became instinctual, and even though each one became easier, faster, I could feel my energy drying up. But there were still so many wounded, and I hadn't even *looked* at the dragons yet.

I stood up from my last patient, wobbling as I moved to the next one. The moaning had decreased and most of the men I had healed were now helping care for the ones I hadn't yet gotten to.

'Stop.' Turos put a hand on my arm. 'That's enough for now.'

'But....' I waved a hand at the long rows of wounded, looking to Bel for support. She wasn't there.

'Where's Bel?' My words were slurred.

He shook his head as he took my arm, guiding me to the side of the room. I let him push me down so that I was sitting against the wall.

'She left a couple of hours ago. She was exhausted. You're exhausted.' He squatted down in front of me and pushed my hair back behind my ears. 'You've been going for ten hours.'

'I have?' I looked around the room. Isla was walking towards me, Scruffy trotting by her side as he looked up hopefully at the bowl she was carrying. Steam rolled off the top of it and the scent of lamb stew punched into my nose. I was suddenly so hungry I felt sick.

'Here.' She handed it to me with a fork. 'I'll get you some water.'

I ladled the food into my mouth, moaning as the flavours danced across my taste buds. 'What about you?' I said to Turos between mouthfuls.

'I ate a couple of hours ago.'

Isla handed me a mug of water and a chunk of warm bread and slid onto the floor next to me.

'I need to keep going,' I said as I wiped the bottom of the bowl with my bread.

'Not at the moment you don't.' Isla rolled her head from side-to-side and stretched her arms behind her back. 'You finished with the life-threatening wounded a couple of hours ago. The rest can wait. Or heal naturally.'

'What about the dragons?'

'Can you work on dragons?' Turos scratched at his left cheek.

'I guess so. I don't have any knowledge of anatomy. I kind of just encourage the tissue to go back to where it came from. Don't see why that wouldn't work for a dragon.'

'They're pretty hardy,' he said. 'But there are a few that may not make it without help.'

'Lance?'

'He's hurting. But he's not bad. Took most of it on one flank. His wings are fine.'

'I'll get to him.' I patted Turos on the leg. 'Come on. I feel much better.'

He stood up and extended a hand down to me. I wasn't lying about feeling better, but I wasn't about to knock back his help either. I let him pull me up and followed him as he walked through the room.

Several of the women we passed stopped and bowed their heads, and a couple of men knelt.

'I keep forgetting how important you are.' I laughed as I punched him on the shoulder.

He looked at me for a second before understanding bloomed in his eyes. 'That wasn't for me,' he said. 'That was for you.'

'You've created a great number of awed fans,' Isla said.

I tried not to think about that as we approached the dragons. I'd never been comfortable with other people's awe.

The first dragon Turos took me to was a huge, red beast. He let out an angry snort as he raised his head to look at us and fire trickled out of his nostrils. I recognised the man standing next to him. It was the first man I had healed.

'Rufos?'

The beast opened his eyes again at the sound of his name, staring at me with cold, black eyes.

'He won't hurt you,' the man said, 'will you, boy.' He shoved at the dragon as he said the last words and the injured animal turned to sniff at his handler.

I held my hands out as I walked closer. His body was riddled with tiny puncture wounds.

'Hey boy,' I said. 'I'm not going to hurt you. I helped your rider. I want to do the same for you.'

Rufus stared at me while he considered whether or not to barbecue me for his evening snack. Then he snorted and lowered his head back to the ground. But he continued to watch me as I approached till I was close enough to lay a hand on the side of his neck.

It was much the same as healing a human but on a much larger scale. I heard metal plinking onto stone as I swept through him, encouraging his tissue to knit back together. It sucked the same amount of energy out of me as if I had healed ten men, but when I opened my eyes, and

Rufos reached out his head and nuzzled the side of my face, it was worth it.

I had to stop for breaks every couple of dragons or so, depending on how badly wounded they had been. And at one point, Turos made me lie down on a make-shift bed of blankets to sleep. But by the time the sun had risen, all of the badly-wounded dragons were healed.

'Come on,' Isla said. 'We need to get you to bed.'

I was too tired to talk, let alone fight with her about it, so I let her take my hand as we followed Turos back to the hall.

A man raced through the hall towards us. 'King Bladimir requests your presence,' he said to Turos. 'And that of Isadora Gabrielle.'

'Well, he's going to have to wait,' Turos said. 'She needs sleep.'

The man's mouth opened and closed a few times before he nodded and raced back the way he had come.

'He's not going to be happy about that,' Isla said.

'I don't really care.'

I stared at Turos as his head split into two faces; both of them staring at me with concern.

I felt Isla's arm wrap around me. 'Izzy?' Her voice seemed to be coming from the other side of the room.

'Come on.' Turos swept me up into his arms and I let my head loll against his shoulder. He felt so nice and strong and warm. It occurred to me that I wouldn't mind kissing him again sometime, and then I was fast asleep.

***

I shook my head, disorientated from having been totally exhausted one minute to now finding myself in Trillania. It made me wish I'd had time to grab my dream catcher before we'd left.

But I was here now so I may as well put it to good use.

I flicked to the castle to see if anyone was around. A couple of guards stood in front of the castle, their hands resting idly on their sword pommels. They tensed as they saw me, and one of them was instantly holding a bow.

'It's Izzy,' I called, waving a hand at them.

They remained alert, the nocked arrow trained on me.

I recognised the one with the bow. He had been at Stonehenge with us. 'Don't make me hurt you Boron,' I yelled out.

The bow disappeared back into thin air and he put a hand on the other guard's shoulder and said something. I approached slowly, letting them see my hands at all times.

'Izzy,' Boron said as I got closer. 'How have you been?'

'As good as I can be,' I said. 'Any news?'

He pulled a face. 'The goblins are on the move again. They've begun attacking villages both here and through the veil.'

'That's not the worst of it,' the other man said. 'We think they've begun to marshal an army.'

I felt the little energy I had left start to seep out of my body. It was replaced with a fear which slithered through my veins and lodged in my bones. All of a sudden, I wanted nothing more than to be an innocent 17 year old whose worst problem was finding a familiar. I'd had it much better then than I'd realised.

'Is Rako here?'

Boron shook his head. 'He was here earlier with Prince Aethan, but now he's off duty.'

I couldn't help but take note of the honorific. Before, Aethan had been one of them. Now he was the heir to the throne. I knew he would hate that. And since he was the heir to the throne…

I smiled as realisation hit me like a lightning bolt. There was no *way* Rako would risk him coming here by himself. He would have to let him come, or risk Aethan eventually going mad. But I was betting the times he was allowed to come, he would be under heavy guard, and for the minimal amount of time necessary.

Ha. Which meant when I had seen him the last time, he'd been here without permission. He was such a hypocrite.

'Well,' I said, still smiling. 'When you see Rako, tell him I'm working on getting home.'

They both had confused smiles on their faces but I didn't bother elaborating. I closed my eyes and thought about Aethan, my smile growing even broader when I realised he was in the dream world.

'Got to go,' I said. 'Things to do, people to scare the crap out of.'

I pictured Aethan again and flicked to where he was, making sure I arrived a few hundred metres from his position. He didn't hear me arrive and I didn't make a sound as I watched.

He knelt as he ran his fingers through the grass. I saw him straighten a bent blade of grass and then stand back up. He was tracking someone, and I didn't need to be a genius to know who that someone might be.

'She's not here,' I said.

He swore and spun towards me as he pulled his sword from its scabbard.

'Jumpy or what?' I said as I walked towards him. 'In my experience people are only that jumpy when they're doing something they shouldn't be.'

'Well,' his sword disappeared from his hand and reappeared at his side, 'you would know.' He shook his head as he looked at me. 'How do you do that?'

'Do what?'

'Find me.'

'I....' I stopped talking as I stared at him. I always knew where someone was in Trillania if I concentrated on them. Galanta could find me purely from our blood bond, but I could have found her anyway. I'd just never stopped to think about it. 'I don't know,' I whispered.

'It makes sense.'

'What does?' I was sorting back through my earliest memories. We'd always agreed where to meet the next night, but I could have found him anyway.

'That time you, Wilfred and I spied on Galanta, and Santanas knew you were there. It has to be a War Faery thing.'

'You think?' I couldn't believe I'd never thought about it before.

'Sure.' He shrugged his shoulders like it was the most normal thing in the world. 'You're special.'

I resisted the urge to throw something at him. Instead, I smiled. 'So...I'm guessing you're sound asleep with a fake dream catcher hanging above your head.'

 Guilt flicked over his face. 'Did you come to taunt me or to help me?'

'Help you, of course. But a girl can get a little taunt in at the same time can't she?'

It was his turn to smile. 'Is she here?'

'You know she'll be able feel me too, right?'

He nodded. 'We have to at least try.'

'Do you think the goblins will stop following Santanas if we kill her?'

'I don't know. That's not why I want her.' He walked over till he was standing right in front of me. 'She's taken too many things from me for it to be allowed to go unpunished. My memory, my brother.' He stepped even closer. 'My future.' He reached a hand toward me and brushed his fingers against mine for a fraction of a second.

I took his hand and laid it against the side of my face, closing my eyes as I concentrated on the warmth of his skin against mine. 'You're right,' I said, opening my eyes and staring into his deep-blue ones. 'We will find her, and then we will kill her.'

'Thank you.' He paused for a second.

I lowered his hand and let it go, gritting my teeth against the pain that came with the knowledge it might be the last time I would be able to touch him.

'Why do you think she comes here when it is so easy for you to find her?' he asked.

'I have a couple of theories.' I added a strapped dagger to each bicep, and moved my sword so that it was held across my back. I knew I could conjure them up at will as I needed, but I felt better with the feel of the steel against my body. 'Firstly, I don't think she was scared of me before.'

'Do you think she is now?'

'I hope not. It will make things easier.'

He nodded thoughtfully as he looked around. 'And what's the second theory?' he asked as his eyes returned to mine.

'I don't think she has a choice. I think she's like us.'

He sucked in a breath. 'A shape-shifter *and* a dream-walker?'

'It would make sense,' I said. 'They have to have them as well. Otherwise they wouldn't know about Trillania.'

'Santanas could have told them. He could have given them one of the armbands to copy.'

'That makes sense as well,' I said. 'But I know she doesn't wear one.'

'It could be concealed under her clothes.'

I smiled at him. 'When she freed Santanas's spirit from the stone, she was totally naked. As I said, I *know* she doesn't wear one.'

He cocked his head to the side. 'Perhaps that's where they met.'

I didn't even need to ask to know that Santanas was also a dream walker. 'Bereft and half-crazed, wandering Trillania by himself at night.' I nodded my head. 'He would have been lonely. He also would have been vulnerable. And if he was already toying with black magic he would have welcomed her company.' I was silent while I thought about it. 'Can the goblins use magic other than black?' I finally asked.

He shook his head. 'It's why they can't heal.' He scuffed the dirt with the tip of a boot.

I was procrastinating, and I knew it. I really wanted to kill Galanta. I wanted that so badly I tasted metal in my mouth whenever I thought about it. But there was one thing holding me back. 'What if *he's* with her?' I blurted it out.

'He can't come here any more.'

'Why not?'

'Wolfgang told me. It's something to do with the spell used to resurrect him and the fact that his soul doesn't belong in...in....' His face screwed up into a mask of pain. I waited while he took deep breaths and ran his hands through his hair. When he had his emotions back under control he said, 'If he comes here, his soul will be pulled back out and they'll have to go through the whole spell again.'

'Well,' I said, relief flowing through me, 'want to go kill some goblins?'

'And you're not going to give me the whole you're-far-too-important-to-go-gallivanting-around-in-Trillania speech?'

'I should,' I said. 'I should smack you on the bottom and send you home to Rako. I mean you *are* the heir to the throne.'

'And you're not going to because...?'

'You're a big boy,' I said. 'And besides, I miss hunting with you.' I held my little finger out towards him. 'Pinky promise.'

He hooked my little finger with his and said, 'I won't tell if you won't.'

We stayed like that while I closed my eyes and sent my senses out to Galanta. 'Ready?' I asked when I had her pinpointed.

'I was born ready.'

I let out a snort and then propelled us to where she was.

Dark smoke swirled from a fire; the light from the flames causing the shadows of the surrounding trees to dance and twirl.

'Damn it,' I said. 'She's already gone.'

'Yes,' Aethan said, staring over my shoulder. 'But she left us a present.'

I spun around in time to see a couple of goblin warriors break from the shadows and race towards us.

'Yippee,' I said drawing my sword.

Aethan pulled a bow out of thin air and fired off two arrows. They sank into the goblins' chests until only the fletching was visible. As one, the warriors sank to their knees and fell to the ground.

'Hey.' I turned towards him. 'Not fair. You have to share them.'

One side of his mouth pulled up and his little dimple appeared there. 'That's two to me.'

'So *that's* how it's going to be.' I turned back to scour the trees, hoping there was another couple hiding there I could take out before Aethan realised. I knew from experience that if I let him get too far ahead on the score card, he would be impossible to catch. But the area was clear of goblins. Bummer.

I could tell by the fact that Aethan's smile now touched both sides of his mouth that he knew what I had been thinking, but I stiffened my spine and threw my braid back over my shoulder. 'Ready?' I held my hand out to him.

He took it as I concentrated on Galanta's next position. I knew we wouldn't catch her. Not tonight. She knew we were after her and because of our blood bond she could feel me coming. But it had been far too long since I'd kicked some goblin butt and I knew we would at least get to do that. And, if it made things inconvenient for her, well that was good too.

***

The sun was streaming through the windows in my room when I woke. I could feel the weight of Scruffy's body on one of my feet.

I smiled as I stretched my arms above my head. We had only caught sight of Galanta once the whole time we had been there, but we had killed an awful lot of goblins trying.

'I thought you were always grumpy first thing in the morning.'

I started and turned towards the door. Turos leant against the door frame looking deliciously rumpled. 'How long was I asleep?'

'Twenty-four hours.' He raked his hands through his white, spiky tufts, and then stretched his arms above his head; flexing his body from side-to-side as he did.

I tried not to watch, but I could see his muscles flexing through his clothing. 'Isla?'

'She was fretting so I took her up to Arthur.'

'Your father?' The last thing I remembered was a summons to see him.

Turos's white teeth shone as he grinned. 'He's being very patient.'

I swung my legs off the bed and sat up. Scruffy jumped off the bed and trotted over to Turos. He scratched at his foot with a paw.

'You know what you need to do,' Turos said.

Scruffy immediately sat on his hind legs and lifted his front ones in the air. Turos reached down and handed him a scrap of meat.

'You taught him to beg?' I stopped in the process of unbraiding my hair.

'That's not the best thing. Watch.' Turos looked back down at Scruffy, lowered his hand to the floor and said, 'Lie down.'

Scruffy dropped onto his side.

'Roll over,' Turos said as he flipped his hand over.

Scruffy did a barrel roll and jumped back to his feet.

'Play dead.'

Scruffy collapsed in a heap.

Turos smiled at me. 'It hardly took me any time at all to train him. I can show you how if you want.'

I laughed as I continued to work on my hair. When I had finished undoing it I said, 'Scruffy, would you mind going into the bathroom and getting my brush?'

He woofed, trotted from the room and came back a moment later with my brush in his mouth.

'Actually,' I said, 'I need a new hair tie as well.'

He dropped the brush on my bed and disappeared, coming back with a hair elastic.

'Thanks boy.' I ruffled the hair on his head and looked over at Turos.

'You understand English?' he said to Scruffy.

Scruffy tilted his head to the side and hung out his tongue in a doggy smile.

'Unbelievable. I fed him most of my dinner last night training him to do that.'

'Sucker.' I tied the elastic around the end of my braid and stood up. 'Got to tell you though, if that's what it takes to get fed around here, I'm ready to beg.' My stomach growled as if to highlight my words.

'Right,' Turos said. 'Breakfast. Come on.' He gave Scruffy one more shake of his head and then turned and led me from the room.

'You want to come boy?' I asked.

'He ate his body weight in lamb about three hours ago,' Turos said.

Scruffy looked towards the door and then turned and jumped back up onto the bed, turning around a few times before snuggling into the cover.

It took us far too long to get down to the dining hall but only a few minutes more till I was ploughing my way through bacon and eggs on top of a pile of pancakes covered in some sort of sweet sauce.

'I don't know how you can eat your savoury with your sweet,' Turos said. He had opted for just the bacon and eggs.

'Don't knock it till you try it. Here.' I held my fork out to him. It held the perfect proportion of pancake, egg, bacon and sauce.

He screwed up his face as he took it from me and popped it into his mouth. I watched in amusement as his expression changed from disgust to delight. He swallowed and said, 'Why does that taste so good?'

'It's the whole sweet, savoury thing. You know, like salted caramel.'

He reached his fork towards my plate and hooked half a pancake off it. 'Salted caramel?'

'You guys haven't invented salted caramel yet? Oh boy. I'm going to have to talk to your head chef.'

'We haven't even invented this caramel thing yet.'

'You don't have caramel?' I could feel my eyebrows riding high on my brow.

'What's in it?'

'Butter, brown sugar and cream. I think. Mum does the cooking in our house.'

'We don't have sugar here,' he said. 'We use the leaf of another plant that we brought through with us. It thrives on the east side of the island.'

'Well.' I placed another bite of pancake into my mouth, chewing and swallowing before I finished the sentence. 'When we get home I'll get Mum to make you some.'

He stiffened, his fun face immediately shifting to his serious one.

I groaned and put my fork down. 'Are we going to fight about this?'

'We can't let you go.' He pushed some egg around his plate with his fork.

'Who says?'

'Father.'

'Yes, well your father also locked me up and threw away the key a couple of days ago.'

A wry smile touched his lips.

'Look.' I put my cutlery down and leaned across the table toward him. 'I am needed. The goblins are mustering an army.'

He shrugged one shoulder and leaned back in his chair, but he didn't meet my eyes. 'We left those sorts of problems behind us a long time ago.'

'Yes, well, now you have your own enemies, but you don't see me writing them off.'

He shifted in his seat and had the grace to look uncomfortable. 'We dealt with them.'

'And if it wasn't for me you'd be down half your army.' It was a tiny bit of an exaggeration.

'It's not up to me. If it was, I'd go with you.' He looked up, his eyes finally meeting mine. 'I'd follow you anywhere. You should know that.'

My breath caught in my throat at the intensity of his words. His eyes held mine captive as I drowned in the ice-blue waters within.

'Well then.' I cleared my throat. 'That's always good to know.' If I hadn't spent the night with Aethan, my response might have been different. 'Should we go see your father now?' I pushed my seat out from the long table and stood.

He also stood and I followed him out, trying not to notice how all other conversation stopped as we passed, how heads bent and hands reached towards me.

'I wish they wouldn't,' I mumbled under my breath.

'They love you,' Turos said.

'They don't even know me.'

'Well, when they do get to know you, they'll love you even more.'

I looked at him sideways but his expression was calm as he held the door open for me. I walked through and turned back to face him, waiting as he held the door for another man to exit the hall.

The man saw me standing there, and I held my hand up as he moved as if to bow. His attack was so unexpected that even if he hadn't been moving with the swiftness of one of the trained Millenia warriors I would have had trouble defending myself.

He was on me within a millisecond, and if he'd had a knife, I would have been dead for sure. Instead, he threw me up against the wall, grabbing my hair and smacking my head back against the hard stone.

'Witch,' he snarled as he pulled my head forward and started to ram it backwards again.

It took me all of that time, just to get my hands up between us. I could see Turos, charging the man from behind. He would get there before the man had a chance to break my skull open, but I didn't need his help.

'Get back,' I screamed. And then I unleashed a lightning bolt straight into the man's chest. He flew backwards across the hall, smacking into the far wall and sliding down to lie in a crumpled heap. A black hole was charred deep into his chest and all of his fingers had the tips blown off. An acrid smell hung in the air. Burned flesh.

'See.' I looked over at Turos. He was staring at the man with his mouth wide open. 'Not *everybody* loves me.'

'I think,' he stared down at the body, 'that those who don't, will put up a much better pretence from now on.'

People had started to crowd into the doorway. They all stared at the man with horror on their faces.

'Thor.' Turos pointed at one of them. 'Go tell Braydon there's been an assassination attempt. And organise to get this cleaned up.' He grasped my arm and started to pull me down the hall.

'Where are we going?'

'To see father.'

'Oh.' I don't know why I thought our destination would have changed.

A few minutes later we reached the start of a curving staircase. A single guard stood at the entrance. He clasped a fist to his chest when he saw Turos, but his eyes widened when he saw me and he bowed his head. I kept my distance, just in case. Let it not be said that I do not learn from my experiences.

I may have climbed the winding staircase more slowly than was strictly necessary. I wasn't at all looking forward to talking to King Bladimir.

There was a guard at the top of the stairwell as well. He clamped his fist to his heart and opened the door. 'Sire,' he said, 'the Prince is here.'

'Has he brought the witch with him?'

I elbowed Turos. 'Witch?'

'Well, technically, you *are* a witch.' He gave me a broad grin.

'I'm more faery than witch.' Huh. At some point during the last year I had actually begun to believe that. I mean I know it was true, but for the first almost eighteen years of my life I had believed I was pure witch. Isla was obviously rubbing off on me.

King Bladimir was at his desk, staring out a wide window into the valley. Dragons soared like gliders below us, weaving around each other as they swooped and dived. The faint hollers of their riders echoed up to us.

He turned and then stood as we entered, brushing his hands down the front of his ruby-red robes as if to smooth them.

'Son.' He clasped Turos's hand before turning to me. 'Young lady,' he said, 'it seems I must apologise for my hasty treatment of you the other day. You have my heartfelt thanks for the service you did my people yesterday.'

Turos let out a chuckle which I assume was due to the look on my face. The whole way there I had been readying myself for a tongue lashing.

'Urrrr,' I stammered, 'that's okay. Anyone would have done the same.'

He shook his head and clasped his hands behind his back. 'That's where you are wrong I fear.' He rocked back-and-forth on the balls of his feet.

'So, ummm, you're not going to punish me for using magic?' I wasn't sure if I was pushing it or not, but it would be good to know where I stood.

'As long as you only use your power for good, I don't see why not.'

'Oh boy.' I sat down on one of the seats lined up against the wall. 'Do you want to tell him or should I?' I crossed an ankle up over my other knee.

'What is she talking about?' The hard-arse was back in the King's voice.

'There was an attempt on my life,' Turos said. 'A few minutes ago.'

'Attempt on your....' The look Turos shot over his shoulder at me shut me up.

'We were attacked on our way here. Izzy used her power to save my life.'

'I see.' The King started rocking on his feet again. 'And you feel that if she had not intervened that you would not have survived the attack?'

'I may have,' Turos said. 'I mean I'm pretty good.' He let out a quick laugh. 'But you never can be sure in these situations.'

'That is true.' King Bladimir nodded his head. 'Very well then. We will not speak of the matter again. But,' his eyebrows lowered and his eyes took on a stormy look, 'do not let me hear of you using your powers in such a way to harm an innocent, or things will be very different.'

'Of course not Sire.' I stood and bowed as I backed towards the door, knowing a dismissal when I heard one.

'Well,' Turos said as we walked back down the stairwell. 'That went better than expected.'

I was about to make a snarky reply when Emerald's voice sounded in my head.

Come quick. Come quick.

I grabbed Turos's arm. 'Emerald needs us.' It hadn't been outright panic in her voice but after yesterday, I wasn't taking any chances.

Turos's eyes focused on nothing for a second, then he grabbed my hand as we ran down the stairs. I tried not to notice how nice it felt with his large hand wrapped around mine. I failed miserably and for a second I had an urge to force him up against the stone of the stairwell and take his mouth with mine. Instead, I concentrated on the urgency that had been in Emerald's voice. There was no time for making out. Not now, anyway.

'This way.' Turos dragged me through a side door and onto a broad balcony. He held my hand tight as he ran straight at the edge. We hurdled the top of the balustrading together, and I let out a whoop as we plunged into the ravine below us.

Then Lance was there, levelling out underneath us. Turos grasped my waist with his hands and positioned me in front of him for the landing onto Lance's neck.

He placed both arms around me and onto the piece of leather that hung from Lance's scaly throat. 'Sorry,' he murmured into my ear. 'I need to hang on to something.' I shivered and resisted the urge to turn around as his lips brushed my earlobe.

I didn't want to confuse the situation any more than it already was. I mean yes, I wanted to make out with him. Yes, I craved the feel of his lips on mine. But I didn't know what it meant beyond that. I knew that the lust that was in his eyes was probably mirrored in my own. But if you took the lust away, it you removed my crazy teenage hormones from the equation, what would be left?

With Aethan I had had it all. The rip your clothes off, smash your mouths together, can't get enough of each other, lust. But beyond that was an enduring love, a trust, and a friendship. I didn't have those with Turos, and that only made me yearn for Aethan more.

I pushed all of it from my head and concentrated on keeping my seat as Lance negotiated the tight bends into the breeding cavern. I kept an eye out for trouble as we soared through the cavern. Everything seemed as it should.

Lance fluttered to a standstill and landed next to Emerald.

'What's going on?' I said to Isla.

'Look. Look.' She pointed at Arthur.

The fat, little dragon leant forwards and then ran towards us, fluttering his wings as he did. He lifted a couple of inches into the air before crashing back down.

Emerald let out a huff of pleasure and wrapped her tail around Lance's.

'Yay.' Isla ran towards him with her hand held high in the air.

His tongue lolled out of the corner of his mouth as he reached down with the tip of his wing and tapped it against her hand. Then he let out a gurgly laugh and collapsed onto his back. Isla jumped up on top of his belly and scratched his arm pits. His laugh became a shriek as he waved his legs. She jiggled up-and-down with his motion before finally sliding back off him.

'He can fly,' she exclaimed running towards me. 'None of the other hatchlings can fly yet.'

I tickled the bottom of one of his feet and he let out another shriek. 'Yes, but we've already ascertained that he's far more advanced than any of his peers.'

'He's special.' Isla nodded.

I looked at him lying there, giggling and squirming with his tongue still hanging out of his mouth. 'He certainly is that.'

'Stop it.' She punched me on the shoulder.

Arthur stopped giggling and sat back up. He pushed himself up onto his feet and then started his sprint. His wings fluttered and flapped and then suddenly he rose into the air. He sailed for a hundred metres while Isla, Turos and I chased him, cheering and whooping.

'Now *that*,' I said, 'was *flying*.'

He reached his head down and pushed his snout to Isla's cheek.

She reached up and patted his neck. 'I know boy,' she said. 'It won't be long till we're flying together.'

'How long?' I said to Turos.

'Well normally,' he said, 'hatchlings don't start flying till they're at least six months old. And they can't support the weight of their riders till they're at least a year. With Arthur?' he shrugged his shoulders. 'Who knows?'

'Again,' Isla squealed.

Arthur turned and sprinted back towards Emerald and Lance. He took off, gliding higher into the air than he had before.

My little genius, Emerald murmured into my mind.

You could carry him couldn't you? If we had to leave? He might be a genius but I doubt he'd be able to fly far enough in the next couple of weeks for what we needed to do.

What's going on? She shifted her body and stared at me with huge unblinking eyes.

Santanas has begun to muster an army.

A small puff of smoke rolled out of her nostrils but she didn't respond.

I wanted to tell her that she didn't belong here, that we had to go home. But the problem was that I could see that she did. She may have been in my world for the majority of her life, but she had never belonged.

And now I was going to ask her to leave this all behind and take me back, for what? So we could defeat the man that had initially tricked her into leaving.

I suddenly didn't know if that was going to be enough.

Chapter Eight

A Choice of Two Worlds

'Behind you.' Aethan spun toward me, releasing an arrow over my head as I ducked.

I jumped into the air, turning head over heels to land behind the goblins that had just ambushed us.

'That's ten,' Aethan yelled.

I twirled a sword in each hand, sweeping the tips down through the Achilles tendons of two goblins. They screeched and fell backwards and I plunged a sword into each of their chests. I spun and conjured up a crossbow, releasing a bolt into another goblin. 'Hah. Twelve,' I called out, sighting another goblin down my next shaft.

Before I could release it, Aethan plunged a spear through the warrior's back. The goblin fell to his knees, clutching the tip of the spear with both hands as blood ran out of his mouth. Aethan put his foot on the warrior's back and wrenched the spear out. I had time to admire his form as he hurled it into the air. I followed its flight with my eyes, groaning as it lodged into a goblin still hiding in the trees.

'Thirteen.' Aethan dusted his hands together.

'This isn't working.'

'You're right. You're never going to beat me.'

I gave his shoulder a shove. 'That's not what I'm talking about.'

He gave me his cheekiest grin and said, 'Well what else do you suggest we do?'

'We need to shift as soon as she does. We're giving her too much of a head start.' Too much time to set up traps for us.

'It'll be dangerous while we're being attacked.'

'You'll have to cover for us. I'll just grab you as soon as I feel her go.'

He nodded. 'It could work.'

'It could mean that it's just us against her if we do it fast enough.'

I had begun using Isla's blood to mark my pulse points the way Wolfgang had showed me. It meant Galanta could no longer feel me through our blood bond.

'Ready?' I laid a hand on his arm and, when he nodded, moved us to where I could feel Galanta.

As soon as we landed we dived apart. I rolled back to my feet and shot an arrow off into the nearest goblin. Galanta stood in the middle of a circle of warriors. They had been facing out, ready for us, and now they attacked.

Galanta's lips pulled back to reveal her pointed teeth in a cross between a snarl and a smile. And then she disappeared.

I dived through the legs of a goblin, batted another's sword out of the way with my own, and then leapt high into the air, sweeping over the head of the next one. I came down in a crouch behind Aethan and grabbed onto his ankle as he thrust a sword through the chest of a warrior.

The forest clearing disappeared from view and Galanta appeared before us. A look of shock flashed across her face and then she was gone. I let her blood drag me as I followed, still holding onto Aethan's ankle.

We were on a beach, then back in the forest, then on a mountain top, then in the middle of a herd of fire-breathing buffos. Galanta kept shifting. As soon as she landed she was gone again. We were just as fast, but it soon became apparent that this tactic wasn't working any better than the last one had.

I stopped, let go of Aethan's ankle, and stood up.

He looked at me with unfocused eyes, wobbling as he shook his head. 'I feel a little unbalanced.'

I snorted. He looked far more than a *little* unbalanced. He looked ready to puke. 'We need to rethink this.'

He pulled a face. 'Actually, I have to go. Someone's trying to wake me.'

'Oh. Okay.' I managed to keep my voice neutral, even though I immediately had a vision of Ebony, breathtakingly lovely in a slinky nightie as she shook his shoulder. Possibly she was doing more than just shaking his shoulder to wake him up. And possibly she wasn't wearing anything.

'*You* don't look so good?' He put a hand on my shoulder and peered into my face. 'Are you dizzy?'

'Something like that.' I stepped backwards out of his reach. 'Well, you'd better get going.' I turned away from him and concentrated on my room back in Millenia.

'Izzy,' he said. 'What's the matter?'

I looked over my shoulder, forcing a fake smile onto my face as I said, 'Nothing. Everything is peachy.'

Even without all his memories of me he knew me well enough to know that I only used the word peachy when everything was as far from peachy as possible.

'No, really.' He grabbed my hand and spun me back towards him. 'You've been so distant lately. What's on your mind?'

I had a vision of Ebony straddling him, her full breasts pressed against him as she kissed his neck. I shook my head, trying to dislodge the image.

'Really?' I said. 'You have no idea what might be wrong with me?'

He shrugged. 'I know things have been pretty stressful. And you must feel that we are all depending on you.'

Well, that was true.

'And, you're stuck in another world.' He paused, looking thoughtful as he cocked his head to the side. 'Have you met someone else?' he finally asked.

'What?' I coughed out a laugh. 'Have *I* met someone else?'

He reached out and grabbed my hand again. 'What do you mean?'

'Oh please.' I snatched my hand away. 'I mean I know you didn't have a say in it but, really.' I put my clenched fists onto my hips.

His mouth opened-and-closed a few times and then he said, 'Izzy. I have no idea what you are talking about.'

'Really?' My voice went up a couple of octaves. 'So it's not *Ebony* there trying to wake you?'

Realisation dawned on his face. 'You think...you think I'm with Ebony?'

'Well, aren't you? I mean you must be married by now.'

'What ever gave you that idea?'

'I saw it.' I could feel my face flushing red. 'I saw it as we were leaving. They presented Ebony to you, as the new heir.' I looked down and shuffled my feet, starting to feel foolish. 'It's important to keep the night faeries on our side. I understand. It's okay.'

He took a step closer, grabbing my hand and pulling me toward him. 'So *that's* what's got your knickers in a knot?' He reached out his free hand and tucked a loose piece of hair behind my ear. 'You know, you're even *more* beautiful when you're jealous.'

'So you're *not* marrying Ebony?'

He pulled a face. 'I'm not *married* to her.'

'Ah hah.' I snatched my hand away and shoved him in the chest. 'So you're *betrothed* to her.'

He pulled a face. 'Well, if you're going to get technical about it. But honestly Izzy, I'm trying not to think about it.'

'Oh, a fat lot of good that's going to do me.' I stomped a foot. 'Honestly, Aethan.'

'Honestly, Izzy?' He stepped toward me as I took a corresponding step back. 'Lately, the only thing that gets me through the days is the knowledge that I get to be here, with you, at night.'

This time when he stepped forward I didn't move. He placed his hands on either side of my face and tilted my face back so that I was staring up into his glorious eyes.

His thumb traced a line across my lower lip as he said, 'I don't remember what it was that we used to do here together, back before all this started, but I'm guessing it was a little less like what we've been doing, and a little more like this.'

He closed the gap between us, lowering his mouth to mine. And for a few seconds I let myself forget about Ebony, instead concentrating on the overwhelming sense of Aethan.

The familiar scent of him; the feel of his lips moving against mine; the sensation of his fingers trailing over the bare skin of my arms. I gave myself over to those things.

To things that made my toes curl up and not those that made my hair stand on end.

But all too soon reality forced its way back to the front of my mind. He may not be married to Ebony yet, but he was going to be. He was no longer mine.

I put my hands on his chest and pulled away. Tears welled in my eyes as I looked up at him.

'Don't,' he whispered. 'Don't cry.' He wiped at my eyes with his thumbs. 'I love *you*, Izzy. Only you.'

'I wish that was enough,' I said. 'I wish we were just two normal people.' I shook my head and stepped back, relinquishing contact with him. 'But we're not Aethan. We're *not* normal. And whether we like it or not, the world needs us to do what's right.'

'Maybe,' he said. 'But if this all ends sooner than it should. If we win before I am married, then this will all go away.'

'No it won't.' I could hear tears of frustration in my voice. 'Do you think your parents would let you slight the night faeries like that? We would be exchanging one war for another.' I stepped backwards. 'I love you,' I said. 'But I can't let you do that.' I took another step backwards from him, both physically and mentally. The tears were running freely now. 'I'm sorry,' I said, 'but it's over.' And then I willed myself away.

***

I went to where I knew I would be safe. Where I knew he wouldn't think to follow - because he couldn't remember. Because Galanta had stolen that from us as well as so many other things. And as I lay on the soft bed of grass in the flower-filled meadow and cried myself out, I renewed my pledge to find the goblin Queen and kill her.

If it wasn't for her, I wouldn't be in this emotional mess. If it wasn't for her, I wouldn't have had to walk away from the man I loved more than life itself. If it wasn't for her, and he had his memories still, I knew he wouldn't have let me go.

I also knew that in the big scheme of things, one part-faery's feelings were immaterial. There were far bigger, far more important matters being decided, but I was sick of putting my emotional needs second to that of the universe. I wanted to wallow in my misery for a few minutes, or hours, or however long it took for me to regain the strength to get up and go on.

And so I lay there, and I cried, until my head ached and my nose was blocked, and only then, when I had no more tears to cry, no more agony to give, did I let myself go home.

***

'Did you get her?' Isla looked up from the book she was reading as I sat up in bed.

'No.' I looked guiltily at the white bandage bound around her wrist. 'But we were close.' I sighed. 'It's not working though, even when we get her alone we can't get her to stay still long enough to kill her.'

She let out a tinkly laugh. 'Did you expect her to make it easy for you?'

'Of course not.' I rubbed Scruffy on the head just behind the ears the way I knew he liked it. He let out a huffing noise of pleasure and collapsed onto his back with his paws in the air. 'I thought you'd be back up at the cavern by now.'

Isla's face lit up. 'I was,' she said. 'But guess who made it out of the cavern?'

'He flew out?'

She nodded. 'And Turos said we can start rider training tomorrow.'

'But, he's only a month old.'

'Oh, we won't be trying to fly yet. But we are going to practice riding positions and getting him used to the feel of the bridle. Turos is having a special one made up.'

'All this happened while I was asleep?'

'It's nearly lunch time.'

'Really?' I hopped out of bed and walked over to the open window. The sun was positioned high over the mountains. I had cried for longer than I'd thought.

'Turos said to meet him for training this afternoon.'

I pulled a face. The last few training sessions had ended with me throwing a tantrum and stalking out.

'You're getting better at it,' she said.

I snorted. 'I don't call continually getting my butt whipped an improvement.'

'Turos told me he's impressed with your progress.' Her voice floated back from the lounge area.

'The only one whose progress is impressive is Arthur,' I said.

She reappeared holding a covered tray which she placed on the corner of my bed. 'Are you having any progress with the other thing you've been trying?'

She was talking about my attempts to open a pathway home.

I rolled my eyes and sat back down, lifting the cover off the food. 'Of course not.'

'We have to get home,' she said. 'The goblins are gaining momentum. It won't be long before they start marching their army on Isilvitania.'

'I know. I know.' Of course I knew. I had given her that information. 'I just have no idea what I am meant to be doing.'

You'll work it out.' She sat down beside me and patted me on the hand. 'When we're ready, you'll know what to do.'

I blew out an unhappy sigh. Her blind faith in me was disconcerting. 'I'm not sure about Emerald,' I said. 'It seems unfair to ask her to return. She's so happy here.'

Isla sighed and sat down. 'I know. Perhaps you could hold the gateway open for her to return.'

'I can't promise that. And it's not fair to lie to her. And what about Arthur? Do you think she would leave him?'

'No.' Her long hair swished across her shoulders as she shook her head. 'And I can't go without him.' She flashed me a smile. 'It will all work out. You'll see.'

I snorted. 'The last person who said that to me was Wilfred. And look how well that worked out.' I froze in the process of moving a fork towards my mouth.

'It did work out.' Her smile was radiant. 'He is alive and serving a higher purpose. And he's doing well.'

'How can you possibly know that?'

She shrugged elegantly. 'I have faith. You should too.'

I put the fork into my mouth, chewing and swallowing before saying, 'You're going to have to have enough faith for both of us I'm afraid.'

'Consider it done.' She laughed and clapped her hands. 'Now finish your breakfast so we can get to training.' She jumped off the end of my bed and danced towards the door.

'You're going to train as well?'

She nodded. 'I consider it wise that at least one of us perfect the mind control necessary.'

I grabbed one of the many pillows on my bed and threw it at her. Her tinkly laugh floated back to me as she disappeared from my room.

***

'You don't get a stick today.' Turos grasped the end of the fake, wooden sword I was holding and twisted it out of my hands. 'I, however, get to use this.' He hefted a long fighting pole in his right hand.

I rolled my eyes. Oh Great. 'How am I meant to defend myself?'

'Dodge, weave, duck. Do whatever you need to prevent me from getting you.'

'Or what?'

'Or it's going to really, really hurt.' His eyes twinkled merrily.

'You're enjoying this, aren't you?'

'Just remind me, is it two or three times you've broken my nose?'

I ignored that. I didn't want him remembering it was four.

Isla sat off to the side with Scruffy lying next to her. Her eyes were shut and her hands were behind her back. Chanda, one of the other Millenium warriors, sat in front of her. His hand floated in front of her face, a stone nestled within. As I watched, she opened her eyes. His fingers opened and her hands whipped around from behind her back to snatch the stone out of the air.

I let out a groan. She was already better at it than I was.

I closed my eyes and cleared my mind, pushing thoughts of Aethan away. I pulled up Galanta and Santanas and tossed them aside. I rid myself of all of them and a peaceful void formed in my mind.

I couldn't do anything about any of them at that precise moment in time, so why had I been giving them so much energy? Why had I been allowing them so much space in my head?

I could hear the hum of a nearby bird's wings; feel the air around me being jostled by the dragons playing in the valley below. I opened my eyes and focused on the mountains on the far side of the valley. The rocks and blades of grass zoomed into sharp focus. I could taste scents on the wind: the forests of trees, the fertile dirt in the valley, the musky scent of Turos.

I turned my vision to the wooden pole that Turos held. I could see the wood grain along its shaft and smell the strong scent of the pine it had been carved from. I forgot about everything else as I watched it.

Turos's hands flexed and the pole flicked forwards. Shockwaves radiated through the air, rippling out from the pole as it moved. Air pushed ahead of it, showing me which way it was moving. I watched in astonishment as it got closer-and-closer, light refracting through the swirling air like a tiny fireworks display. And then it....

'Ouch.' The pain snapped me back into my body. I reached up and rubbed my shoulder.

'You didn't even try.' Turos shook his head.

'I got it.' I rushed forwards and wrapped my arms around him. 'I saw it, and I smelt it, and it was *beautiful*.' I pulled back and looked up into his face. 'I could see...*everything*.'

Turos looked down at me. 'Well then. I guess that's understandable. The first time is pretty distracting.'

I realised I was still clutching onto him, my legs threaded through his and my body pressed hard against him. Dark Sky. What would it be like to kiss him in that state of mind?

Heat infused my cheeks and I let him go. 'Distracting. That's one word for it.' I closed my eyes again, waiting till the same feeling of peace flowed over me, before opening them again.

Turos's pole whipped towards me in a blur of sparkling light. I stepped to the side, just enough to avoid it, and then ducked under it as it swung at my head. The other side flicked around, aiming for my ankles. I jumped lightly over it, a smile on my face as I landed.

'Don't get cocky,' he said.

'I'm not.' I said the words lightly, trying to keep all emotion out of them, but a little bit of pride snuck into the back of my mind. I was doing it. I was really doing it.

Thwack.

The end of the pole caught me mid-shin and pain exploded in my mind as the thin skin over the bone split apart. The other end of the pole whipped around, driving into my stomach. I wrapped myself around the pole like a pretzel, before whipping up into the air. I landed on my back a few metres away.

'Yoooowwwwwwww.' I didn't know whether to hold my leg or my stomach. They were neck-and-neck in the running for the year's most painful body part.

'Oh dear.' Isla looked down at me with cool, appraising eyes.

'It hurts.' I took shallow quick breaths as I stared up at her.

'Push the hurt away,' Turos said.

'I can't.' I let out another groan. 'It huuurrttttssss.'

'You've had worse.' Isla's voice was analytical.

'What?' I clenched my teeth. 'So all my future injuries don't count because I got gutted by Galanta?'

'Well.' She cocked her head to the side. 'It does sort of pale in comparison. I mean then there was blood everywhere. Now there's not even a drop.'

'Well, there is some coming through the leg of her pants,' Turos said. 'Now take a deep breath and push all that pain out of your mind.'

But the problem was that my leg and my stomach weren't the only things that were hurting. It appeared I hadn't done quite enough crying the night before and now my heart had joined the race. It sped past all the other body parts, a shoe-in for an easy win.

I rolled onto my side, pulled my knees up and wrapped my arms around them, and then I began to cry. I tried to stop. I mean it was so embarrassing, crying in front of Chanda. Crying in front of Turos. But I had broken up with Aethan, and I couldn't regain control.

'Oh dear,' Isla said again. But this time she knelt beside me and put her arms around me. 'This isn't about your leg, is it?'

'No...ooo...ooooohhhh,' I howled. I could feel my heart ripping into tiny pieces.

'Do you want to talk about it?'

I shook my head. The last thing I wanted was an audience to my private pain.

'So you can't heal yourself?' Turos asked.

'No.' I let go of my knees and rolled onto my back. Why wouldn't they all go away and let me cry in private?

'Are you sure?' Isla asked. 'I mean nobody else can. But you...well who knows *what* you're capable of.'

'Don't you think if I could, that Santanas would have healed himself?' I stabbed at the bloated ball of pain, deflating it enough that I could breathe again.

'You have a point.' Isla stood back up and reached a hand down to me. 'Can you stand?'

So much for my moment of self-pity. I let her help me to my feet and put my weight gingerly onto my damaged leg. It didn't hurt as much as I thought it would.

'Shall we begin again?'

I looked over to where Turos was standing. He had removed his shirt and was using both hands to twirl the pole in a circle above his head. His forearms and biceps flexed with the movement so that he was seven foot of delicious, rock-hard muscle.

Huh. Suddenly the drool threatening to escape my mouth was more of a problem than my pain. And that was as potentially as embarrassing as my crying had been. I pushed it all away until the world hummed with life around me.

The pole in Turos's hand seemed to halve, then quarter its speed. Light sprayed in its wake, cascading around him in a circle of fire. Sweat glistened on his bronzed skin, glowing like diamonds in the sun. His eyes blazed like aquamarines as he met my gaze, his lips parting into a smile. He was magnificent. He was beautiful. He was glorious in his perfection.

I walked over to where he was, holding all other thoughts at bay. There was nothing else but this moment. Nothing else but Turos. Nothing else than my need to avoid that spinning pole.

It tumbled towards me, flicking and sweeping and driving like a sword. But it didn't even come near to touching me. I knew where it was going to be before it even started moving, and it was a moment in time to remove myself from its path. I danced to the tune of the humming air, enjoying the weightlessness of my mind. I twisted and turned, ducked and jumped, until finally the pole stopped moving.

I felt the movement of the air as Isla started to clap, watched the multitude of lights blink out of existence. I heard Scruffy scratch an ear, and Chanda cough, but it all felt like it was in slow motion.

Turos walked towards me and put his hands on my shoulders. 'Izzy.' The sound was distorted by time. 'Izzy, you need to let it go.'

I shook my head. Why would I let this go? Everything was beautiful, and for the first time in a very long while, I wasn't worried about anything.

A thought tugged at the edge of my mind. There were things I *needed* to worry about. I pushed it away, instead soaking up the warmth of Turos's touch.

'You'll have to shock her out of it.' Isla's voice was even lovelier than I had realised. It rang like bells in my mind.

Turos shrugged his shoulders. 'Okay then. But only because you insist.'

One second he was holding me gently and the next he swept me up in his arms. His lips pressed down on mine, urgent and insistent. His tongue forced its way into my mouth as his hands found their way under my shirt.

A shot of hormones coursed through my body, and I found myself clinging to him, returning the kiss with as much, if not more fervour than he. Electricity danced over the surface of my skin at his touch, frazzling my nerves and jolting into my mind.

And in the wake of that jolt, a thousand thoughts returned. I shoved Turos away, curled up my fist and punched him in the nose.

He winced and clasped his hands to his face. 'What was that for?'

'Taking advantage of me.' How *dare* he kiss me like that without my permission?

'I had to do something.'

'And that was the only thing you could think of?'

'It was the most appealing of all the things that occurred to me.' He smiled at me around his hands.

I snorted and turned my back on him. Isla was doing a valiant job of controlling her smile but I could tell it was there.

'He had to do something,' she said. 'You'd gone all peace-not-war on us.' She looked over at Turos. 'How is she going to fight like that?'

'She's not.' He pulled a face as he pinched the bridge of his nose. 'She's taking it too far.'

'She always takes things too far.'

'Hello,' I said, waving a hand at her. 'I *am* here.'

She flashed me a smile before turning her attention back to Turos. 'What do you mean?'

'She's pushing her thoughts so far away that she has no focus. She needs to leave them there on the edge so that they can direct her, not totally forget about them all together.'

Well, that made sense. If I had gone up against Santanas like that I wouldn't have cared what he did to me.

'Give me a weapon,' I said.

'I don't think you're ready for that.'

'You scared I'll make you cry for your Mumma?' I put a hand on one hip and tilted my head to the side.

'Oh.' He stalked towards me till he was close enough that I had to look up to see him. 'Them's fighting words.'

I smiled and raised my eyebrows. 'Well, are you yella?'

'I don't even know what that means, but I am going to assume it was an insult.'

'Good,' I said. 'It would have been a wasted breath otherwise.'

He beckoned to Chanda, and the chuckling warrior ran forwards with two wooden, training swords. He handed one to me, and one to Turos, before backing away to stand next to Isla.

'I'll bet you this evening's dessert that she goes down,' he said.

'Do you know what we're having?'

'I went through the kitchen on the way here and they were chopping up apples and rolling pastry.'

'Apple pie?' Isla pursed her lips and she looked at Turos and then me. 'I'll take your bet,' she said, extending her hand.

Chanda shook it and said, 'Excellent. 'Cause I'm hungry.'

'That's a shame,' Isla replied. 'I'm going to give your portion to Scruffy. He likes apple pie.'

Scruffy stopped inspecting his private parts, looked up at Chanda and let out a bark.

'Let me know when you're ready,' Turos said.

I pushed everything away till Turos started to glow like a bronzed God, then I pulled it back till I could feel it fluttering around the edges of my mind. I could immediately feel the difference to last time. This time I knew what I should have been worried about. I remembered what my aim was; there were just no thoughts there to distract me from it.

'I'm ready,' I said, lifting my sword.

Turos's blade cut through the air. I moved to the side, sweeping my own weapon out to parry the blow. He twirled and swept down from the other side and I whirled and danced out of the way. He attacked again, and I stepped backwards so that I would have enough strength to block him. He closed on me and flicked the blade to the side and I stepped back to meet it.

I saw a smile flirting with the edges of his lips at the same time I heard Chanda laugh. They thought he had me at a disadvantage and I didn't mind letting them think that. It was the first time Turos and I had fought properly and this wouldn't work again. But it didn't have to. It only had to work the once.

All of that existed at the edge of my mind as I let him force me backwards across the training ground. His strikes increased in confidence and force, and I let mine lag just a tiny bit. To anyone else it would have looked like I was about to lose.

I waited for the strike I knew was coming; the one where he overextended himself just a little too much. And when it came - the master stroke designed to force me to my knees in a desperate attempt to block it, I was no longer there.

I dived forwards, rolling beneath the blade and past him, coming back to my feet with enough time to kick down into the back of his knee. He let out an 'Ooooff,' as that leg collapsed. A swift kick to the back of the other knee made sure he wouldn't recover in time. I whipped my blade around, stopping as the edge of it made contact with the side of his neck.

He froze, his hands dropping his weapon as he put them into the air.

'Well.' Isla clapped her hands together as Scruffy let out a happy bark. 'Apple pie for you tonight my boy.'

***

'They're forming up in the Gonian Crater.' Rako drew a circle on the ground in the dirt. 'So far the orcs and dwarves have joined them.'

I took a deep breath to help dispel the fear I could feel forming in my gut. It didn't work. 'The giants?'

'The giants are on the move. So are the trolls.'

'The Vulpines?' I asked, referring to people that rode the enormous eagle-like birds.

'We estimate it will take a few more weeks for them to arrive.'

'What about our side?' I looked around the group of men who had come to Trillania for the war council, avoiding eye contact with Aethan as I did. Awkward didn't even begin to describe how things were between us.

'Faeries are pouring in from around the globe,' Rako said.

I expected that. They knew that if *we* went down, *they* would be next. 'The humans? The witches?'

Rako ran his fingers down the long scar on his cheek and then pulled a face. 'They seem to be caught in debate. The lower house agrees there is a problem, the upper house seems to be blocking any attempts to do something about it.' He shrugged. 'We assume they are hoping we will sort it out.'

If it were physically possible for steam to have been coming out of my ears it would have been. 'The night faeries?' I shot Aethan a look, but glanced away again as his eyes met mine.

'Ebony says they are on their way,' Aethan said. 'It will take them a while to skirt the goblin territory.'

Rage, pure and white hot as the midday sun, scoured my brain of rational thought at his casual use of her name. It was irrational, I knew, and totally unproductive. I pushed my thoughts to the side till I could see bright lights, then I pulled everything back, except my rage. That was a useful by-product of what Turos had taught me.

'Izzy,' Rako said. 'We need you. When are you coming home?'

'Working on it.'

'And?'

I sighed. 'I don't know how to start. I know Santanas did it, but I have no idea how.' How did you create a tunnel between two worlds?

'I have a theory.' Wolfgang stepped forward. 'What if you aren't in another world? What if it is our world, but in a parallel universe?'

'Pardon?' There was a good chance I resembled a goldfish.

'You didn't study physics at school?'

I shook my head. Science and I had not gotten along.

He shook his head and mumbled something under his breath about the state of schools today. 'A parallel universe is one that lies parallel to ours.'

I pulled a face and shrugged my shoulders.

'So it is identical to ours and in fact would have branched off from ours at some point in time.'

'So...we all exist on this planet as well?'

He shook his head, a pleased smile on his face. 'That's the theory.'

'So, this is just a theory?' Aethan said.

'Well, if you look at the different planes that exist already in our reality, and the fact that Izzy can access Trillania from there, I think it's plausible.' He turned from Aethan back to me. 'Izzy. How many moons are there on this planet? And what do they look like?'

'There's just the one, and,' I stopped to think, 'it looks just like ours. I mean there's a bunny and everything.'

Aethan let out a snort of amusement.

'What?' I put my hands on my hips. 'Don't tell me you can't see the bunny?'

'And the sun?' There was excitement in Wolfgang's voice.

I nodded. 'The same as ours.' So much so that I had never even stopped to think about it. I had only even known one sun and one moon, so to me it had been a constant, not something to be questioned.

'Excellent.' He clapped his hands together.

'So...how does that help me?'

He tugged at his long, grey beard. 'I'm not sure. But perhaps you should approach it the same way you do the parting of the veil.'

Now was probably *not* a good time to mention I had only ever done that twice.

'Two nights from now?' Rako asked.

I nodded and then watched as one-by-one they flicked from view. Aethan was the last to go. For a second I thought he was going to say something, but then he shook his head and he, too, disappeared.

***

'Parallel universe.' Isla rolled the words around her tongue. 'Do you think he's correct?'

I nodded my head. 'It makes sense. The problem is that if Wolfgang is right, and I *can* open up the layers between this world and our own, we'll end up in the same spot on that world.' I'd been thinking about it since I'd woken up.

'Which could be anywhere,' she said.

'What could be anywhere?'

I let out a shriek as Turos appeared in the doorway. 'Don't you ever knock?' I threw a cushion at him.

'Sorry. Keep forgetting about little things like knocking.' The smile on his face let me know that he hadn't forgotten at all. He liked scaring the shit out of me. 'You ready?'

'For what?'

'Oh. I may have forgotten to mention it.' He sauntered into the room and plonked himself down on the couch next to Isla. I was guessing he chose her seat rather than mine because I couldn't reach him from there. The smug smile on his face had the fingers on my hand curling into a fist.

'Lance told me, that Emerald told him that she wanted to go for a ride.'

'Really?' My fingers unclenched as I sat upright. Emerald and I hadn't been for a ride since before she'd laid Arthur. And he was already seven weeks old.

'She's got cabin fever.'

I wondered if it was my mood rubbing off on her. I hoped not. I thought I'd been hiding my mounting frustration from her quite well. 'When are we going?'

'As soon as you're ready.' He gestured at my head.

I stuck my tongue out at him. There was nothing wrong with my hair and I knew it. With him dropping in randomly anytime of night or day I made sure I always looked presentable.

'Want to come?' I looked over at Isla.

'Nah. You two crazy kids go and have fun. I'm going to continue my training with Arthur.'

'Don't you let him talk you into going solo.' Turos looked like he might be considering staying.

'As if.' Isla stood up and pretended to dust off her pants. 'He's like, two months old. As if I'd let him set the ground rules.'

I gave her as steely a look as he did. Her voice sounded far too mischievous to be serious.

I'm ready.' I pushed my braid back over my shoulder and gave her another look as I followed Turos from our rooms.

'Do you trust them?' I asked.

'Not a chance. That's why I've asked Chanda to keep an eye on them.'

Emerald and Lance were waiting for us on the dragon platform. Smoke curled out of her nostrils and she shook her head from side-to-side.

Come on, she said. *Hurry up.*

What's the big rush?

I need to get back before my offspring does something stupid.

I peered into the stable in which Emerald was staying with Arthur. He lay on his back with his wings spread out and all four chubby, orange legs in the air. As I watched, he blew a smoke ring. The ring expanded slowly as it rose above his head. He waited till it was halfway to the ceiling before he snorted, blasting out a much smaller, faster ring. This one had a tail of flame as it shot after the bigger ring. He let out a fiery belch of satisfaction as the smaller ring went through the larger one.

His tongue flopped out of his mouth as he turned his head to look at me. He waved one chubby leg and Scruffy left my side and trotted over. He jumped onto the hatchling's neck, scrambling up till he was on his chest. Then he turned around a couple of times and lay down so that his head was sloping down towards Arthur's. Arthur raised his head off the ground, his tongue encompassing Scruffy's whole face as he licked it.

He's not going to eat him? I said to Emerald.

Please. He likes his meat skinned.

A quick look showed me that her mouth was open in a dragon smile. I was pretty sure she was joking.

'Let's go.' Turos was already astride Lance.

'Okay. Okay.' I strode to Emerald, jumped onto her front leg and climbed up to her neck. It felt good to be back there and I could tell by her satisfied rumble that she was happy too.

'On the count of three,' Turos said.

The two dragons positioned themselves on the edge of the platform. They curled their toes over the edge and leant forwards like Olympic swimmers about to start.

Turos looked over to see if we were ready. I nodded my head at him and he said, 'One.'

Before he even got to two, Lance lunged off the edge, his wings tucked in tightly to his body as they disappeared into the valley below.

Go. Go, I shrieked into Emerald's mind. I was going to make the cheat pay for that.

We rocked off the edge and plummeted after them, Emerald making short, sharp flaps of her wings that meant we were able to catch up with them. We hit the curve at the bottom side-by-side, gravity forcing us into our seats as the dragons banked and turned to soar back up the mountains on the other side.

I watched the luscious, fertile fields on the side of the mountain disappear beneath us and then we were up and over the next mountain and racing out to sea.

The sun glinted off the smooth glass of the ocean, showing the shadows of the two racing dragons. Lance matched his pace to ours, brushing the tips of his wings against Emerald's with each stroke.

Hang on, Emerald yelled.

I leant down low, looping my arms through the tough leather reins and gripping on tight with my thighs, and then Lance and Emerald were flying long, lazy barrel rolls around each other.

'Woohoo.' I could hear my voice echoing behind us off the surface of the water.

This was why Emerald hadn't wanted to be confined to the mating caverns. This was what she hadn't wanted to give up. The ultimate freedom of flying, doubled with the exhilaration of doing it with someone that you loved. I could feel the joy radiating off her.

The two dragons flew straight up, like two arrows firing towards the sun. They flew until the air felt thin, till each breath was less satisfying than the last. And then they flipped over and started their descent back to the sea.

If we hadn't flown so high I might not have seen it. A mast sticking up on the edge of the horizon.

'Look,' I yelled at Turos, pointing toward it.

He squinted into the sun, staring until I saw by the change in his body language that he had spotted it too.

Lance shifted his flight so that we were heading toward it. 'Don't get too close,' Turos yelled. 'Stay high.'

I drew short rapid breaths as I battled to maintain my oxygen supply. If they had looked up, we would have been specks in the sky, because to us they were a dot in the ocean. But even from that high I could tell it was the same type of ship we'd destroyed the day we'd gone swimming.

We flew over them, and then circled back around, making bigger and bigger loops as we searched the ocean for more of them.

'They're alone,' Turos shouted.

'Are we going to destroy it?'

'Not worth the risk. We'll keep an eye on them and if they are heading our way we'll deal with them then.'

The words had just cleared his mouth when we heard a deep booming noise.

'Break left,' Turos yelled as he and Lance broke to the right.

Emerald dived to the side, slicking her wings back against her sides. A large metallic ball sailed through the air we had occupied only a few seconds before. So much for our stealthy departure.

I formed a shield beneath Emerald and flew toward where Turos and Lance were zig-zagging through the sky. Every few seconds I could hear pinging noises as projectiles bounced off the bottom of my shield.

I heard Lance roar his displeasure. The shards of metal were small, but put enough of them into a dragon and they were bound to get painful. Plus, if they tore through a major artery, things were going to get messy.

Tell Lance to head back towards us.

He says we would make too big a target.

Tell him I can't shield him from all the way over there.

A few seconds later Turos and Lance's veering path headed back towards us. We raced towards them and, as soon as I was able to, I expanded the flat plane of my shield to include them as well.

'Are you okay?' I yelled to Turos.

He nodded and held up his arm for me to see. Blood dribbled from his bicep down his forearm. 'Lance wore the brunt of it. Can you heal him from there?'

I shook my head. 'Not while maintaining the shield. Do I have your permission to destroy the ship?'

He flashed me a grin. 'I think, given the circumstances, that *that* would be prudent.'

'Do you want to stay here?' I said.

'Do I look like a mummy's boy?'

'Only when I break your nose.'

He let out a laugh.

'Stay beside me,' I said. 'Otherwise it will be too hard to maintain the shield.'

I bent low over Emerald's neck as she tucked her wings in to her sides. My shield extended around us like a dome and I could see metallic objects scattering off it like insects bouncing off a windshield.

As we got closer, the figures on the ship started to take on features. Their faces were turned up to the sky as they watched us come. Two of them, one on the front and one on the back, sighted us down long barrels while they peppered us with metal. We would have to take them out first, but I was going to have to drop the shield to do it.

'Get ready,' I yelled at Turos. 'I'm going to drop the shield for a couple of seconds on the count of three.'

Emerald and Lance began to level out, dropping down and heading towards the front of the vessel so that only one weapon would have access to us at once. There was another gigantic boom, and I saw a piece of metal as big as a basketball soaring towards us. I let out a yelp as it smacked into my shield, the force driving me backwards in my seat.

'One,' I yelled. We levelled out just about the waterline and started to sprint towards the ship.

'Two.' Men pulled swords from their belts, their dark eyes burning with ferocity as they watched us come. The intensity of the attack on my shield increased as we got closer.

'Three.' I moved the angle of the shield from the front to beneath us when we were about thirty feet from the ship. I lifted a hand and, at the same time as Lance and

Emerald roared their fiery displeasure, I hurled a lightning bolt straight at the man with the weapon.

Fire caught in the sails and masts as a hole exploded in the deck of the ship. We raced over them and I shifted the shield back to cover us from behind as we climbed away from them.

A look over my shoulder showed me I had been true with my aim. There was now only one of the weapons left on the deck.

'Where did that ball come from?' I yelled at Turos.

'I saw a flash of light out of the side of the ship.'

I nodded my head to let him know I had heard him. 'Ready?'

'I was born ready.'

I flashed him a quick grin as Lance and Emerald banked in the sky. We came in the same way we had before, flying low over the water. This time I saw the flash of light that accompanied the huge boom. I reinforced the shield but it still struck with enough force to knock me backwards. My brain was going to be bruised if I went through that a few more times.

Instead of flying over the ship, we raced past it at water height. 'Go,' I shrieked as I shifted the shield.

I fired a bolt of lightning out of each hand into the side of the ship. They smashed into the wood at the waterline, huge splinters flying out in all directions. Water immediately began to pour in. Dragon's fire curled over the whole side of the deck including the area where the weapon stood. Men lowered buckets to the water but they needn't have bothered. By the time we had turned, readying ourselves for another attack, the ship was listing in the water. It wouldn't be long before it sank.

We circled far above it as we waited for the inevitable to happen. It finally submitted, rolling onto its side and disappearing into the depths to its watery grave.

'Let's go,' Turos said.

We didn't speak on the way back. I'm not sure what he was thinking about but I was wondering how many more of those ships existed. They had already proven that without a shield, destroying them was costly.

I wasn't going to be here for much longer. Santanas was coming and I was needed. I didn't know how, but I *would* find a way back home.

But it seemed I might be needed here as well.

Is that what it would come to? A choice between two worlds, both standing on the brink of war?

Chagrin painted my mind with a guilt-tipped brush, for if push came to shove, I already knew which world I would save, and which I would doom to die.

***

'The Prime Ministers have finally come to the table.'

It was the first bit of good news that Rako had given me. 'What changed their minds?'

'Vulpine attacks.'

I took a deep breath and rubbed my hands down the sides of my pants in an effort to stop them shaking. People were dying and there was nothing I could do about it. Not from where I was. 'So they've arrived?'

'Reports of Vulpine sightings started filtering through a few days ago. Then yesterday they began breaking through the veil and assaulting villages.'

'Slash-and-dash technique,' Aethan said. 'And of course, there's the fact that the army has started marching.

We estimate they should be on Isilvitania in a couple of days.'

I met his eyes for a moment before looking away. I didn't like seeing the despair in their depths.

'Izzy.' Wolfgang's voice was patient. 'How are you going?'

I shrugged a shoulder and scuffed at the dirt with a boot. 'I may have had a bit of a breakthrough.' I held a hand up. 'But I'm not sure.'

'What happened?'

'I could feel the weight of the barrier on me. Like when we open the veil. But it was gone as quickly as I sensed it.' I looked around the circle at the three of them. 'I'll keep trying.'

'Try harder,' Aethan said.

I could feel my mouth curl up with all the spiteful things I wanted to shoot back at him, but I held them all in. I knew he was under more pressure than I was. And he had a point. I did need to try harder.

'I will.' The words sounded as if I had strangled them.

He nodded the nod of a Royal to a subject and disappeared from view. That hurt far more than it should have.

'You'll work it out.' Rako smiled at me. 'You always do.' He pulled a face. 'But if you could hurry, well, that would be grand.'

He and Wolfgang also disappeared from view.

I was glad Wolfgang hadn't lingered like he often did. I knew the temptation to ask about Ebony and Aethan would be too great. And it was none of my business. I had *made* it none of my business. It was time to put on my big-girl pants and get over it.

I sighed and sank down onto the edge of a boulder. The problem was that every time I saw him, any progression I'd had in the 'getting over it' department, went out the window.

And I had all these confused emotions where Turos was involved: lust being the most prominent. But there probably weren't many women in the whole of Millenia that didn't lust after the seven-foot, muscle-bound, olive-skinned warrior. I'm sure his ice-blue eyes were able to crack through even the most prudent-of-maiden's defences. And that mischievous smile?

I let out another sigh. Every time he smiled at me like that I wanted a repeat performance of what had passed between us down on the beach.

But he had also become a friend. And friends didn't lead on friends. So, so far, even though Isla's hints had become less-and-less subtle, I was managing to keep my hormones under control. I had already hurt one friend, and I didn't want to do it to another.

I pushed my thoughts of Aethan aside and willed myself back to my room.

***

'Oh goody, you're awake.'

I let out a cry and Turos's hand clamped down on my mouth. 'Shhhhh. You'll wake up the neighbourhood.'

I glared at him over the top of his hand while I tried not to think about the feel of his chest pressed against my side. If I could just get him to replace his hand with his mouth then…

Arghhhhhh. Where Turos was concerned my body and my mind were at total odds with each other.

'What?' I hissed when he finally removed his hand.

He lifted a lock of my hair off the pillow and waved it around as he spoke. 'Isla wants to take Arthur for his first ride.'

I batted his hand away from my hair. 'That's great. But why are we whispering about it?'

'Because the Dragon Masters don't think he's ready.'

'Ahhhhh.' The Dragon Masters had been trying to get Arthur to keep to a 'normal' time frame. But there was nothing normal about Arthur. He was already a third of the size of Emerald, and he was only two and a half months old. The rest of the hatchlings his age were still up in the cavern.

'So we're going to break their rules? Again?'

'Of course.' His mouth curled up in a slow smile. 'Talking about breaking rules.'

He grabbed both my wrists and pulled my arms above my head. My breath left me as he rolled over on top of me. His eyes gazed into mine as he edged my knees apart with a leg.

'Turos.' I shook my head. 'I'm not ready for this.'

'You say that,' he murmured as his nose brushed the side of my neck, 'and yet your body tells me other things.'

I let out a little breath as his lips replaced his nose, moving slowly as they made their way to my throat.

'Yes...well...,' I managed to get out, 'my body and I will be having quite the talk later.'

Dark Sky he felt wonderful. The weight of him pushing me down made me feel powerful and helpless at the same time. And his tongue was doing things to my skin that made me want to beg him to explore my whole body like that.

But I *really* didn't know if I was ready for this. I didn't want to commit to something only to...

His lips found my mouth and I surged upwards against him, my legs wrapping around him as my hormones took over. He released my wrists and I clawed at his back, grabbing the bottom of his shirt and wrenching it upwards. He broke the kiss so I could get it over his head, but a second later his lips were back on mine.

He shivered as I ran my nails down his bare skin, and then his hands found their way up under my nightshirt and it was my turn to shudder.

'Are you two ready to…Oops.' Isla said. 'So sorry.' I could tell by the tone of her voice that she wasn't sorry at all.

Turos stayed where he was as he looked over at Isla. 'We're ready. Well, *I* am anyway.'

Tension curled in my stomach. I wanted more of him. Now. I bit down on my lips as I realised which way my thoughts had taken me. I wanted *all* of him.

His eyes were serious as he stared down into mine. 'Later my beauty,' he whispered as he ran a hand down my cheek.

And for once, I found that I couldn't argue with him.

He rolled over to the side of the bed and leapt to his feet, stretching both of his arms into the air above him. And then he scooped up his shirt and pulled it back over his head. I quelled my disappointment as his abdominal muscles disappeared from view.

Down hormones. Down!

Letting out a sigh, I crawled out of bed. I padded over to the dresser and dragged out my leather pants, a shirt, and one of the sturdy, leather vests the riders used. 'You going to come?' I said to Scruffy.

He opened one eye and looked at me from his position on the corner of the bed. Then he shut it, wiggled into the covers a little more, and let out a deep sigh. 'I guess not,' I said as I pushed past a grinning Isla to the bathroom.

I splashed some water on my fiery cheeks and pulled my hair back into a braid, and then I climbed into my clothes.

They were both waiting by the front door when I re-appeared.

'Turos,' I said, 'we need to talk.'

He glanced towards me, a perplexed look on his face as he pressed his finger to his lips. 'We need to be quiet.'

'They're coming,' I said. 'The goblins are almost on Isilvitania.'

Isla jerked her head towards me.

'The Vulpines have been attacking our villages.'

He pressed his lips together as he stared down at me. 'Okay,' he whispered. 'We'll talk. But not now. Now we need to go.'

I met his gaze for a second, saw the truth in their depths. He was willing to listen to me. I nodded and gestured toward the door. We would fly first and negotiate second. And then? Then we would deal with his father.

We walked quickly down the corridors till we emerged from the castle onto the landing platform. It was still dark, but I could see the faintest tinge of light beginning to grace the horizon through a gap in the mountains.

Emerald, Lance and Arthur were already waiting for us. Arthur hopped from foot-to-foot, his tongue hanging out in a happy grin when he saw Isla. She pranced towards him, her steps matching his.

'All right,' Turos whispered. 'No noise on take-off, and we're not going far.'

Turos and I climbed up onto our mounts as we watched Isla gather up the reins and hop onto Arthur's neck. She wiggled around till she was comfortable and then nodded her head at us. Arthur walked to the edge of the platform and braced himself while he waited for Lance and Turos to take off. Emerald and I would take up the rear.

I watched as Lance jumped lightly into the air. He flew out about two hundred feet and then turned, beating his wings to stay stationary as he waited for his son to take off.

Isla tightened her grip with her knees as Arthur leant over the edge. The little dragon opened his wings and with one little jump was gone.

Eeeeeeeeeek, I gasped into Emerald's head as he plummeted from view.

Have faith.

I tried to have faith, but I was already envisioning the tongue-lashing we would get from the Dragon Masters if news of this got out. But instead of diving after him, Emerald flew out past Lance, and I could see what she already knew.

Arthur was below us, but he was flying. Isla leant over his neck as his wings worked to bring him back up to our height. He circled up past us and Lance took the lead, guiding him toward the mountains on the other side.

We crested their peaks as the sun winked over the horizon, its light sparkling along the top of the water in a golden path. And there, flickering in and out of the path of light, were a hundred ships under sail.

As the light of the dawn lit up the sky, chasing the shadows of the night away, more ships appeared. Their black bodies scarred the ocean for as far as the eye could see.

The horror I felt was mirrored on Turos's and Isla's faces. Emerald let out a snarl and Lance bellowed his rage. But for all our anger, for all our defiance, we were helpless in the face of so many.

A forest of masts cast shadows. A plethora of men moved over the decks. A thousand ships told a story, for which there could be only one end.

Chapter Nine

Home, Sweet, Home

'What do you mean you took Arthur out flying?'

I stared at King Bladimir. If only the man would shut up for long enough for Turos to tell him what we had seen.

Turos cut his hand through the air 'Father. That is not the point.'

'You know what the Dragon Masters have said. If you push him too far, too fast, his wings may be damaged.'

'King Bladimir,' I said.

'This is none of your concern young lady.'

'Actually, Sir,' I said, 'it is. You need to listen to what we saw when we were flying.' I shook my head at Turos. I mean *really*, there had been no reason to even mention Arthur had been with us.

King Bladimir took a deep breath, his anger warring with reason. Reason finally won out. 'Fine.' He threw a hand up in the air. 'What did you see?'

'The enemy.' Turos said. 'They're here.'

'Well, we took down their ships before, we'll do it again.'

Turos shook his head. 'Their ships darken the waters. There are far too many for us. Even with....' He stopped what he was going to say, for which I was grateful.

Bladimir let out a laugh and turned to look at me. 'The witch will do anything to go home.'

'What are you talking about?' I put my hands on my hips.

He looked at Turos. 'She's obviously bewitched you; shown you your worst fear. And no doubt now she'll tell us the only way we can be saved is to follow her back to her own land.'

'It *is* the only way to be saved.' I stomped my foot like a small child.

'And then we will all help you save your own land.' He nodded his head in time with his own words. 'Clever. Very, very clever.'

I managed not to pull a face at his words. Well, almost managed. I could tell by the twitch of Turos's lips that he had seen my struggle.

'Fine.' I waved a hand magnanimously. 'Go see for yourself.' I stalked over to the chair in the corner and sat down, slinging one leg over the arm as I examined my nails.

'You,' Bladimir pointed a finger at Turos, 'watch her.' He pointed at me, sniffed, and then swept out of the room.

I maintained my relaxed position until he was gone, then I leapt up and started pacing the room. 'What are we going to do?' I ran my hands through my hair and turned to face Turos. He had taken up residence in the chair I had just vacated and was mimicking my formerly relaxed position.

'The real question is,' he said, 'what are *you* going to do?'

I put my hands on my hips as irrational rage coursed through me. 'Me? Why does it have to be *me* that does something?'

He shrugged. 'Well, there's nothing at all that we can do about it except fight to the death. And that doesn't seem like a palatable option.'

I struggled to control my breathing. There had been so many of them. And all of those ships had had the weapons that had caused so much destruction the last time they had gone up against them. I couldn't destroy all of them. Not by myself. Not without using black magic.

I paced to the window and sucked in a deep breath. We were surrounded. Totally surrounded. 'You need to open a way again.' I turned back to look at him.

'How am I going to do that?'

'The same way you did when you came and got Emerald and me. Just...' I flourished a hand in the air.

He had been sitting forwards on the chair. Now he slumped back into it and ran his hands through his hair. 'I didn't do that.'

'Well, get whoever did and do it again.'

'Impossible.' He closed his eyes and leant his head back.

'Why are you being so stubborn about this?' I strode over to him and leant down. 'Is it a pride thing? You caught us, and now you can't let us go?'

His eyes opened and I found myself caught like a moth in the glory of a sea of ice blue. 'Do you think,' he enunciated the words carefully, 'that I would let the pettiness of my own pride condemn my friends, my family, my dragon, to death?'

I stared into his soul for a moment longer before standing again. 'No. Of course not.'

He nodded once. 'The man who crafted the way for me to find you died a long time ago. When we fled through the way, one of the magic makers gave us a single glass globe. It held a spell that would allow us to re-open a passage to wherever we wanted to go.'

I stared at him as my mind tried to process what he was saying. They had lied when they had said we could go home after the egg was laid. They'd never had any intention of sending us back. But that wasn't the important thing. That wasn't what had me totally confounded.

'Why,' my words came out in a whisper, 'would you have wasted it to find me.'

'Well technically,' there was a wry smile on his face, 'we weren't trying to find you. We were trying to find Emerald.'

There was a possibility I was doing a damned fine impression of a goldfish.

He shook his head and stood, brushing past me on his way to the window. I swallowed and tried to ignore the tingles that swept down my arm where he had touched me. That *really* wasn't helping the situation.

'We have a seer.'

'Pardon?'

'A seer. You know, a fortune teller. Clairvoyant. A prophet.' He rubbed the palms of his hands over the smooth stone of the window sill. 'Most of the time she is totally crazy. But when she speaks coherently, we listen.' Something flickered over his face, too fast for me to identify it. 'She said if we *didn't* do it, we would be lost.'

'But,' I opened and closed my mouth a few more times as I worked my way through that, 'but *because* of it, we are lost.' They wouldn't have found the Millenium if not for that spell. And if they had found them, the Millenium would have had a chance to escape.

'She is never wrong.' He held himself stiff for a few moments more and then it seemed that he curled in on himself. His shoulders sagged and his face crumpled. 'Well, she has never been wrong before.' His feet dragged as he walked back to the chair. 'If she said a storm was coming, it always came. If she said we should plant more crops that year, there was always a drought the year after.'

'Izzy.' Isla's face appeared at the window for a second before disappearing again. A few seconds later it was back, and then gone again. It took me three goes to realise she was moving up-and-down in time with Arthur's wing beats.

'Are you crazy?' I hissed at her. 'If they see you we're in so much trouble.'

'Really?' Her voice carried up through the window. 'That's what you're worried about? I don't think they'll have time to deal with us before those pirates do.'

She had a valid point.

'What do you want?'

I heard her huff. 'The guards wouldn't let me up and you ran off before telling me what the plan was.'

'I don't have a plan.'

Her head appeared for a second and then was gone again. 'So, you're going to let us all die?'

I could feel pressure building in the back of my head. 'Why is this *my* responsibility?'

'Can you do anything other than shoot lightning?' Turos stood and crossed to stand beside me at the window.

'Oh, so now my lightning isn't good enough for you?'

'Of course it is. But can you do anything else?'

A small pain started up at the base of my neck. 'I can make shields. And blow things up.' And rip out people's hearts.

'You're a War Faery. Surely there are other things you can do.'

It was my turn to walk defeated to the chair. I sat and leant forward, putting my head between my legs as I fought the building pressure.

It was all up to me. It was always up to me. But this time, I didn't know if I was up to it. War was brimming at home, and if I didn't get back for it, all was lost. And I was trapped here, in a land where death seemed imminent.

'She can do anything.' Isla's head appeared for another second. 'Anything she needs to. She just has to believe in herself.'

'Can she open a way back home?'

I thought about letting them know I could hear them, but I was struggling to breathe let alone speak.

'Santanas did it. When he took Emerald.'

I put a hand in the air in an attempt to stop them. The pressure had moved from the back of my head to the front. It was throbbing and pulsing and threatening to tear me apart.

'The problem is,' Isla's voice was fainter, 'she has blocked herself.'

Turos looked over at me. 'Why would she do that?'

'To stop herself from using black magic.' Her voice was just a whisper on a breeze.

Turos leant out the window and peered down. 'Land now,' he barked.

I tried to be worried for my friend, but my head was about to burst into a million tiny pieces. One hundred goblins creeping through the forest. Coming to find us. Coming to kill us.

'Pull me up. She needs me.'

I leapt into the air and landed on the back of a goblin fighting Isla. Grasping his head, I ripped it to the side. There was a crack, and his arms fell limply. I jumped clear as he collapsed.

'Izzy?' I could feel Turos's hand on my arm, but even though I had my eyes open I could no longer see him. I was no longer in that room.

'Thanks,' Isla panted. She picked up her bow and loosed a couple of arrows at a goblin attacking Wilfred.

Whoa – Wilfred? Wilfred had gone with the Ubanty Goddess, Ulandes.

'How many more do you think there are?'

I looked around the clearing. Tiny was in the process of picking up some goblins that had popped out of the trees at his feet. One-by-one he threw them as far as he could over the top of the woods.

Wolfgang was shooting fireballs into the tree line where dark shapes dodged and weaved trying to escape a fiery death. Aethan, Brent, Luke and Wilfred were fighting two goblins each, their blades flicking through a complex pattern.

'Cover me.' I closed my eyes and reached out with my mind, pushing out through the woods. Darkness and evil swarmed around us, black hearts beating in anticipation of our death. Like homing pigeons they came.

It was too many. Too many by far.

I opened my eyes and stared at Isla, the horror must have shown on my face.

She stared back at me, her beautiful, blue eyes calm. 'You don't have to do this,' she said.

I blinked. 'That's not what you said.'

'It's what I should have said.'

I could feel her hands on my arms.

I shook my head. 'I have to. Or we'll all die.'

'There has to be another way. Think.'

The thousand hammers pounding on the inside of my skull changed to one single baseball bat bashing away at my head. 'How?'

'Oh Izzy.' I could feel her cool hands on the side of my face. 'There is always a way.'

All my friends stood frozen, swords and bows aimed at statue goblins. Easily a hundred goblins surrounded us. I couldn't kill them the way I had done. That way lead to madness. So if I couldn't kill them what could I do?

'What would Grams do?'

It was the question I least expected, but as soon as the words left her lips a picture of my scatty, brilliant, mischievous grandmother leapt to mind. 'She would make them all dance.'

The pressure moved out of my head and down my hands flowing out over the goblins. They woke a second before my spell got to them. One minute they wore snarls and grimaces, and the next they were turning to each other, taking each other in their arms, and beginning to waltz.

'Oh,' Isla clapped her hands together. 'That is perfect.'

Another goblin skipped from the trees, a small bunch of flowers in his hand. The picture it presented was ludicrous.

'I can't do this to all of them.' I could feel the smile on my face.

'You don't need to,' Isla said. 'You just need to do it to all of those blocking our exit.'

The rest of my friends fell in behind me as we moved in the direction of the waltzing goblins. I looked back over my shoulders and, at a thought, visions of each of us flickered into view right where we all had been a minute ago.

'Nice touch.' Isla's hand was on my arm. 'How long can you hold them for?'

'Long enough for us to make our escape. Is this what I should have done?'

Isla stopped walking and turned to face me. As she shrugged her shoulders, it all disappeared from view. Suddenly we were back in the King's study. 'There was no *one* right.'

'Only one wrong.'

She nodded.

'For too long now you have doubted yourself.'

It took me a second to realise that the voice did not belong to Isla. We all turned toward the door at the top of the staircase where a woman garbed in a tattered, black robe stood. She lifted a hand and pointed a finger. A manacle hung from her wrist, a broken chain dangling from it.

'The shadows of the worlds await you.' Her hair hung in matted clumps down her back to her knees. Even through the dirt smudged on her cheeks I could see a luminous beauty. 'You must tread warily least you welcome it once more.' She swayed on her feet as she took a step towards me. 'Wary, wary. The betrayer is already amongst you.' Her pitch-black eyes seemed to swirl with an alien light. 'What has been done, can not be undone.'

She turned her gaze to Turos and her face broke out into a broad smile. 'Hello son,' she said. And then she collapsed in a pile of torn fabric and dirt.

***

We were still staring at Turos's mother, when King Bladimir returned. His eyes were wild, and his face pale and blotchy. 'Gladaline.' He stood over the prone woman. 'Gladaline.' He bent and scooped her up in his arms, cradling her to his body as he walked to the thick rug in front of the fireplace. 'What is she doing here?' He looked up at Turos as he lay Gladaline down on the rug.

'She just appeared.' Turos moved to his mother's side.

'Now, of all times.' Bladimir rocked back onto his heels and let out a hard, rueful laugh. 'Well it *is* the end of the world.'

Bells started ringing, their metallic cries echoing out across the valley.

'We are all doomed.' Bladimir's face was blotchy as he looked over at us. 'I have failed us.'

Gladaline stirred, her eyes opening as she reached out a hand towards Bladimir. 'You are still as handsome as the day I first saw you,' she said staring up at him.

'I was only five. I'm not sure how handsome I was at five.' His face softened as her hand brushed his cheek.

'You were the most handsome, stubborn and rebellious five year old there was, and I knew as soon as I saw you we would be wed.'

I could hear men crying out from the dragon stables.

Gladaline pushed herself up until she was sitting. She raised a hand to her head and felt her matted locks. She pulled a face and dropped her hands as she said, 'How long?'

'You've been gone for twenty years.' Bladimir's hands trembled as he reached out and cupped her face. 'Are you back now?'

Her eyes glazed for a minute, as if she were performing an internal examination. Then she blinked and met his eyes. 'For now.'

Tears rolled down onto his cheeks as he pulled her to him and pressed a kiss to her lips. 'At least we will be together when we die.'

'Wait a minute,' I said. As touching as the lovers' reunion was, I wasn't ready just to sit there and get killed by those pirates.

'Why are you still here?' His eyes were hard, cold stones.

'So that's it. You've just given up.' I threw my hands in the air. 'We need to get everyone moving now.'

'You've seen what they can do,' he said.

'Yes.' I nodded my head. 'But you haven't seen what *I* can do.'

I turned and raised a hand toward the external wall of the room. At a thought, it exploded outwards. The noise was deafening as chunks of stone arced far out into the valley.

'My room. My *wall*,' Bladimir stuttered.

'No lightning?' Turos asked.

'That probably wouldn't have worked out so well for us.' I tried to control my pleased smile. Maybe Isla was right. Maybe I could do more than what I thought.

'My study.' Bladimir stood as he stared at where the wall had been.

'One second ago you were ready to die, now you're worried about your study?'

Gladaline let out a gentle laugh. 'She is right love.' She pushed herself up to stand beside him.

'So,' Bladimir shifted his gaze from the destruction to me. 'You think you can blow up all those ships. There must be thousands.'

I shook my head. I'd been in this situation before but now I knew what to do. 'I don't need to blow them all up. I just need to create a safe path out.'

'But there is nowhere else to go,' he said. The desperate edge was gone from his voice, quiet resignation replaced it. 'We've spent many years searching for other lands.'

'We've always had to return with enough strength in our mounts to make it home. We don't know for sure we won't reach land before we fail.' Turos walked over to his mother and took her hand. He raised it to his mouth and I thought I heard him whisper, 'I've missed you,' as he laid a gentle kiss on it.

'That won't be necessary,' Isla said, 'we won't be looking for new land. We'll be returning to old ones.'

Bladimir looked toward her for the first time since he had returned from his flight. 'What do you mean *old* lands, Princess.'

'You can't run,' she said, 'they will find you again eventually. It is time you returned home. You are needed there.'

'You want us to swap our problems for yours?'

'There is one big difference between our problem and yours.' She smiled broadly. 'Ours still has the chance of a happy ending.'

He let out a huff of air.

'Listen to her love.' Gladaline patted his arm. 'She speaks sense.'

'We have no way of returning.'

'I'm not so sure about that.' She turned her gaze onto me, and for a second I saw the same alien glow burn bright in the depths of her eyes.

'I can take us home.' My voice sounded strong even though my internal voice was babbling in fear.

'It will take us a while to gather everyone. And we need to bring in the animals and…'

I stopped him with a chop of my hand. 'You are the king. Start thinking like one. We need to go.'

His spine stiffened and his mouth worked soundlessly a few times, but then his face hardened and, for the first time since he had seen the opposing force, his demeanour returned to the strong, if not totally-rational leader I had known since I arrived. He turned to Turos and barked. 'Put as many people on each dragon as they can carry.' He turned to me. 'Where will you open the gateway?'

'Out at sea,' I said. 'I need space.' Well, I wasn't sure if that was true, but I knew I needed time. I had no idea how I was going to do it and I didn't need the pressure of being attacked while I worked it out. We would have to fight our way clear of the horde first, and then I could do what needed to be done.

Isla reached out a hand and squeezed mine. I was pleased that neither she nor Turos let on that I had no freaking idea how to do what was needed.

Bladimir nodded. 'Get each dragon airborne as soon as it is loaded. They can wait on the other side of the valley until we are all ready.'

Turos nodded his head and raced from the room. Isla and I followed right behind him.

'Scruffy,' I said. I was happy that Turos didn't point out that I had said we didn't have time to get animals. I would have had to knock him senseless and that would have stalled our departure.

'Meet you down at the stables.' He and Isla turned left as I turned right and started running down the corridors towards our rooms.

The bells continued to ring out and people bustled past me, hastily-packed bags of possessions clutched to their chest. Mothers held onto small children with one hand, while cloth carriers on their backs held their babies. Men belted swords to their waists or clutched axes in their hands. They weren't going to help them today, but they would be needed where we were going.

For a second, guilt lanced into my gut. I was taking them to a land about to be torn apart by war. And I was happy about that, because a legion of dragons and the extra warriors would mean we had a better chance of winning. I batted the guilt away. That was immaterial to what was happening here. Without the opportunity to fight for existence in another land they would all be lost anyway.

I turned a corner and sprinted up a winding staircase. Fewer and fewer people appeared in the halls and they were practically deserted by the time I got to my and Isla's rooms. I pushed open the door, expecting to find my little familiar right there.

'Scruffy,' I raced to my room. Where was he? It wasn't possible he had slept through those bells. 'Scruffy.'

'Don't move witch.' The voice was clipped.

I turned towards it. A warrior sat in one of the chairs in the corner of my bedroom. He held Scruffy, wrapped in a towel so that only his nose protruded. Scruffy's lips were curled back, his canines exposed as he let out a low, rasping growl.

'What do you want?'

Where are you? Emerald's thoughts were tense.

The man pulled a face as a foul smell washed over us. 'I've spent the last half hour smelling that. I've a mind to kill him just to make it stop.'

I have a little problem. I won't be long.

'He gets gassy when he's scared. Please don't hurt him. I'll do whatever you want.'

He blew out a big breath of air. 'That's right witch. You will at that.'

Emerald let out a huff. *Hurry. The first group of invaders has landed.*

I'll be there as soon as I deal with the man holding Scruffy hostage in my room.

I felt her alarm flow into me. *Traitor.*

Obviously. Now, if you don't mind. I'm a little busy.

I held a hand out towards the man. 'What do you want?'

He growled and pushed the tip of a knife to Scruffy's neck. 'I want you to put your hands behind your back. And then I want you to die.'

'Really?' I placed my hands behind my back. 'You think I'm just going to let you kill me?'

'If it's you or your smelly dog, I'm thinking you'll let me.'

The twitch of his wrist alerted me to what he was planning. Before he could throw the knife, I sent out a surge of will towards him, willing him to be frozen in place. I could tell by the way his eyes widened that it had worked.

I stalked towards him, balling up my fist as I did. 'Nobody, messes with my dog.'

I put all my speed into the blow I delivered. His eyes rolled back as his head rocked to the side. I plucked Scruffy from him, pulling off the towel and holding him to my chest. He wriggled in my arms till he could reach my face with his tongue.

The door flew open as Turos rushed into the room. 'You're safe?' He stared at the unconscious warrior, sitting stiffly in the chair.

I released my spell and he sagged to the side, his knife sliding from his hand to the floor.

Turos stared at him for a second. 'Kalvin,' he finally said. 'His brother was the man…' His voice trailed off.

'The man I fried in the hall that day?'

He nodded his head. 'Kalvin was a friend. Or so I thought.'

'What should we do with him?'

'We leave him. You ready?'

I nodded and followed him to the window. He pushed it further open and stepped out onto Lance's head, turning nimbly and jumping backwards so that his legs laid down on either side of the huge dragon's neck. I tucked Scruffy under one arm and stepped up to crouch on the ledge. I took Turos's outstretched hand with my free one, waiting for the next downward sweep of Lance's wings before stepping onto his head. Turos took Scruffy from me as I slid down to sit in front of him. He wedged my little familiar between us, wrapping his arms around me to hold him securely in place.

I told myself that I wasn't so much enjoying the feel of his broad chest pressed up against my back and his strong arms holding me against him, as I was the knowledge that Scruffy was safe. But my shiver gave lie to that thought, and instead, I found myself remembering the feel of him pressing me down into the mattress, and the sensations he had brought to life with his caresses.

He leant in even further and I felt his lips graze my neck, and then Lance was backing away from my window and we were flying down to the launching platform.

As we approached, three dragons took to the air. I counted ten people on each of their backs. They were held in place by a web of leather straps and harnesses that criss-crossed its way down the dragon's body. Of those ten, at least two were warriors, bows in their hands and full quivers on their backs.

Another couple of dragons crouched low while people clambered up their legs, pulling themselves up into the harnesses and strapping themselves in. Teams of riders worked together, fitting the harnesses.

'For a nation that has never known war, you certainly are prepared.' I looked over my shoulder at Turos.

'We've been practising for this day for a very long time.'

'But....' I stopped my question. Gladaline. His mother had warned them and they had listened and prepared.

Lance tucked his wings and dropped the last ten metres, landing on the only free piece of platform. I braced for the impact, but his legs took most of the force.

Emerald shook her head and did a dragon impression of an eye roll. *So nice of you to join us.*

Arthur squatted in front of her, Isla by his side.

I looked out over the valley. Dragons circled like birds of prey while others sat perched on rocky outcrops. I saw a couple of females, their offspring clasped in their front feet. They didn't have any extra riders on their backs. People queued in the entry to the platform, their bodies tense as they awaited their turn to mount a dragon. Children cried and others shrieked in excitement. Mothers shushed and harried their brood, drying eyes and runny noses.

'We should work out the best route.' I turned and walked to Emerald.

Turos stopped me with a touch on my arm. 'You're riding with me.'

'But...'

He shook his head. 'No buts. She has to carry Arthur and Isla. We don't know how far we are going to have to fly. And you have to concentrate on what you are doing. You need me to protect you.'

'I can protect myself, thank you very much.'

'Don't be stubborn.' He shook my shoulder gently. 'Isla told me you might collapse if it requires too much power.'

'That only happened once.'

He quirked an eyebrow but said nothing.

'Fine.' I turned and stalked back towards Lance, watching as his harness was fitted.

As soon as he was ready, eight black-garbed warriors scrambled onto his back. I knew Markus, Chanda and Yadler from my training sessions, but the rest were new to me.

Turos leapt up and held his arms out for Scruffy. I passed him up so he could strap him into a woven basket. He reached back down and hauled me up in front of him, settling an arm on either side of me.

'Don't go getting any ideas,' I said.

His laugh warmed the back of my neck and I tried to pretend it was that, and not anything else, that made me blush.

Emerald walked to the edge of the platform with Isla perched on her neck. Arthur leapt off in front of her and she followed, snatching him out of the air with her front legs. He wiggled around as if trying to get comfortable and I could see Isla smiling. I could imagine the whining that was going on in her head.

I braced as Lance leapt off, sweeping past other dragons as he circled up. The air vibrated with the beating of dragon wings as we dodged and swerved, finally breaking free of the maelstrom of bodies to burst up and over the line of mountains.

At least ten ships had docked and the intruders were flooding out of them and onto the beaches. The rest of the ships stood sentinel, dotted around the island as far out into the ocean as I could see.

It wouldn't be long before those pirates made their way up to the city. Half an hour at the most.

I looked out over the ocean, searching for a weak point in the layout of the ships. There was none. They were dotted with military precision. We were going to have to circle as high as we could as fast as we could, but even then, as soon as we rose above the height of the mountains they would have us in their line of fire.

As if to prove my words, there was a booming noise. A flash of light highlighted which ship had fired at us. Lance tucked his wings and dived to the right. I saw a large ball of metal flash by on our left. Another boom sounded, and was quickly followed by a third. I let Lance dodge them rather than throw a shield up against them. I was going to need all the strength I had.

I gestured to Turos to head back to the castle. He nodded once and tightened his arms around me as Lance turned a half loop and headed back over the mountains. The pirates were already high up the side of the rocky landscape. Once they got to the top, they'd start heading down into the valley. I could feel sweat starting to prickle at the base of my neck. We were cutting our departure rather fine.

Three more dragons sprung from the platform as we soared down towards it. They swept out over the valley with their civilians clinging to their harnesses. Five more adults, each holding the hand of a child, rushed to the next waiting dragon. They climbed up into the harnesses, taking the children from the outstretched arms of the warriors and securing them in front of them.

Faster. We needed to move faster.

Lance landed on a rocky outcrop off to the side of the platform. Emerald was already waiting there, Isla sitting calmly on her neck while Arthur played with a boulder. He rolled it to the edge with his front legs and then used his snout to push it over. It bounced and crashed its way through the low shrubs that grew on that part of the mountain.

Emerald let out a huff and, reaching out, seized the scruff of Arthur's neck with her teeth. She lifted him into the air and shook him gently before placing him back on the ground.

Trouble maker. She tried to sound mad, but unmistakeable pride shone through the cracks in her words.

He looked up at her and batted his ginormous golden eyes, an innocent expression on his face as he dragged a toe back and forth through the dirt.

I squashed a smile and looked back at the platform, watching as dragon-after-dragon leapt over the edge and winged their way across the sky.

I looked up the mountain's side to where I estimated the pirates would come. It was still clear, but it wouldn't be long before they started cascading down from the crest.

Dragons perched like gargoyles along the sides of the range as it curved around the valley. I could see glassy scales gleaming where the rising sun met the earth. Dragons huffed and snorted, shaking their magnificent heads as smoke coiled out of their nostrils.

The handlers' fingers flew as they buckled the harnesses. The people moved with speed and efficiency borne of long practice as they climbed onto the dragons.

But even knowing they had practised this before, even knowing they were carrying out a drill, I couldn't still the fear that was creeping up my spine. We weren't going to make it in time.

I jammed my teeth together to stop myself from screaming at them to hurry, and then looked back up the mountain.

The first of the pirates crested the top, standing silhouetted in place for a moment before scrambling down towards us. My breath caught in my throat as a dozen more followed, and then a dozen more. I lifted a shaking hand and pointed towards them.

Lance growled and Turos let out a groan. A hundred dragon heads swivelled to stare, their large cat eyes fixed on their prey.

More and more of the strangers flowed over the top, until it seemed a black shadow moved over the ground.

Lance threw his head back into the air, let out a challenging roar, and pushed himself forwards, rocketing off the side of the mountain. Emerald shot out a leg and pinned Arthur to the ground. He looked like a swatted fly with his little wings stretched out to either side as he shook his head and huffed out a little growl. Isla sat forwards in her seat, her arm stretched towards me.

Kill them. Kill them all. Emerald's orders bounced around inside my head as we sped towards our enemy.

All fear left me. All thoughts of strange weapons and the knowledge that tens of thousands more were waiting where these had come from. All I could see was the tide of the enemy flowing down to harm my charges.

Turos slithered backwards away from me, and I heard the sound of arrows being fitted to bows. The warriors behind me were ready and waiting. But I didn't need an arrow, and I *certainly* didn't need a bow.

The pirates paused as we sped towards them, raising strange metallic objects into the air. I heard a roar as they bucked in their hands and I formed a shield in front of us. But this shield was different to any I had formed before. This one wasn't solid. And it flexed as the metal hit it, pulling back towards us, before springing back out. The small shards of metal reversed their flight and whipped back towards their makers.

Several of the men shrieked in pain, and fell to the ground, others clasped at limbs with their free hands while they aimed their weapons at us.

I heard the twang of arrows being released and dropped my shield. The Border Guard had trained me, and to me they were the elite, but if we had gone up against Turos and his warriors with our bows, we all would have been dead before we'd loaded a second time.

The arrows swept past me in a nearly continuous stream as they calmed their minds and put all else aside. Pirates collapsed with the feathered end of arrows standing out from their chests. But with the arrows firing, we had no shield.

Lance let out a roar as the little metal pellets peppered into him. I could feel Emerald, twisting with frustration, her desire to join her mate warring with her need to protect her child. Her agonised bellow sounded from behind us.

I've got this, I said.

I calmed my mind, removing all thoughts, all worries, all fears, and then I swept my hands out and unleashed my fury on the enemy.

Lance's fire raked them moments before my power exploded the ground out from beneath their feet. Flaming bodies flew into the air, arcing out into the valley with rock and dirt and foliage. Men screamed and batted at themselves with frantic hands and others stood and stared at the gaping hole where their friends had been.

I unleashed my will again as we whipped past them, a spray of dust and dirt heralding where I ripped at the ground with my mind. More bodies tumbled through the air, while still others landed thirty metres away from where they had started, smacking into their brethren as if *they* had been the weapons I had unleashed.

Arrows flickered past, and more fire roared across them, and then we were past them. I threw up a shield to our rear and swivelled to observe the chaos we had reeked.

Lance banked as quickly as he could, fire belching out in front of him as he roared. His whole body shook with rage. I clutched at my harness with both hands and looked down toward the landing platform. People scurried desperately towards waiting dragons. Fear radiated from every movement, every glance over their shoulders.

I turned to look back up the mountain. A sea of black moved towards us. I heard the bellow of more dragons and two more lifted from the side of the mountain and flapped towards us. A score more warriors with calm faces placed arrows onto bow strings.

I drew air in through my nose and let it out through my mouth. A slow, measured breath. These men, they were nothing to me. Ants to be destroyed. I lifted a palm as we approached again, and fired a bolt of lightning into them. Arrows lanced down on them while more lightning followed. I peppered the ground with mini-explosions, watching impassively as bodies flew and men screamed. It meant nothing to me. The only thing that mattered, was stopping their flow down towards the innocent people waiting to escape.

Some managed, through the panic of our attack, to fire their weapons at us. It was impossible to shield while we were attacking, and I felt Lance shudder beneath us as he took the brunt of their attack.

Emerald roared in my head as she shared her mate's pain. I launched two more lightning bolts and three more explosions, and then we were past them again. We flew wide to allow the next dragons their turn at attack.

Is he okay? I sent the message to Emerald rather than risk breaking Turos's concentration.

It is the equivalent of you being stung by a bee. Many, many times. Anger and guilt danced through her thoughts.

You belong there. With Arthur.

I could feel her grinding her massive teeth.

Dragons roared and raced toward the enemy and we were forced to fly a larger loop this time. More and more dragons joined us, until there was a continual stream of attack. It meant poor Lance was not wearing the entire brunt of their attack, but it also meant more of our dragons were being weakened before our escape.

On our next pass, I perfected my ground explosions so that there was a continual detonation of the earth, exploding in perfect rhythm as we swept by. Fire covered the hill, clinging to the low-lying shrubs, and licking over many of the prone bodies of the fallen enemy. I released one perfect, three-pronged lightning bolt over my shoulder and then slammed a shield into place.

'It's done.' Turos gestured past me to the landing platform, and I saw the last few dragons lift into the air.

Emerald let out a shriek of rage and lifted into the air. She snatched Arthur up and flapped towards us, her eyes burning as she searched Lance's flanks for signs of damage. I leant sideways and looked backwards. Blood flecked his sides, and dark holes bloomed in the smoothness of his shiny, black scales.

She spat fire and turned toward the enemy, then shook her head and glanced down at Arthur. Her desire for revenge battled with her maternal instinct. She threw back her head and let out a shriek that made the hair on the back of my neck stand on end. Then she fell into formation beside us as we winged our way higher and higher.

A spiral of dragons followed us up, our shadows blotting out the mountain on the far side of the crater from the sun. The whole ground seemed to tremble beneath us with the combined might of the thrum of our wings. Roars and snorts and snarls echoed off the walls, as the dragons tried to carry their vulnerable cargo to safety.

I threw up a shield in front of the pirates who had breached the safety of our home. I wasn't going to be able to protect all of us when we left the volcano, but for now I would do what I could.

I saw Bladimir with Gladaline nestled in front of him, her long, matted locks blowing crazily around both of them. His dragon was a huge, blue beast, but none were as large as Lance. None as fierce or magnificent as Lance.

Stop that, I snapped at Emerald.

*Well, you have to admit, he **is** the most handsome of them all.*

Yes, I said, not sure if I was talking about Lance or Turos, *he is that.*

We continued circling up past the line of the mountains. The ships were still there, exactly where they had been. A minute or so after we appeared, I heard the first of the low booms. We spiralled ever higher, till the air became thin, and breathing was difficult. More booms echoed the first and I could see puffs of light and smoke coming from the ships nearest to the island.

A dragon's roar tore at the sky behind us, and I turned to see it falling; its neck bent at an impossible angle, flesh and blood spewing from the rent. People screamed and I saw a few jump, arms extended as they sought refuge. Two were snatched from the air, but a third plummeted, joining the rest of the riders as they smashed into the valley floor. I averted my eyes at the last instant, unable to watch.

Turos rested his hand on my shoulder, his fingers squeezing harder than he probably realised.

It was impossible to think that just a few hours ago, we had lain in a mess of tangled body limbs as our hands and lips explored each other. Now, an entire nation fled for their lives. And not all of us were going to make it.

I reached up and clutched his fingers, squeezing back. I would do what I could to save his people. I would. But already guilt was starting to trail its fingernails down my spine. I couldn't save us all. That much was evident. And the life of everyone I failed was going to weigh heavily on my mind.

Lance changed direction and headed out over the ships, arrowing towards the horizon. The flotilla of dragons followed, their wings rustling the thin air behind us.

I placed a disc of shield below us, broadening it as far as I could. The rat-a-tat-tat of the ship's weapons rattled below us. Most of it bounced off my shield, but some made it around. Dragons snorted as metal pounded into the softness of their underbellies.

The larger missiles I was able to stop, flexing my shield and firing them back. Most plummeted into the ocean below, large sprays of water the only sign of their passing. But some tore through the planking of a ship's deck, wood splintering and tearing in its wake.

Our arrows were useless from this height. And although I knew I would be able to strike the ships with lightning, that would mean dropping my shield. The peppering in my mind told me my shield was being harassed by a continual barrage of smaller pellets. I couldn't drop that shield, even for a few seconds.

'Tell Lance to get the group to come in closer,' I yelled over my shoulder to Turos.

'They daren't fly any lower. If they come any closer the buffeting from their wings will disturb everyone's wind stream.'

'I can't shield us all spread out like this.'

He didn't waste any more energy yelling at me, but a few moments later Lance slowed, and the dragons from the edges tucked in beneath us. I tugged at my shield, thinning it a little till all of us were covered.

Sweat trickled down my brow at the effort of holding the shield, and still I couldn't see an end to those ships. I needed to get to a clear patch of sea so I could open a way back home. And even then, I didn't know if I could do it. The closest I had gotten before, was feeling the thickness of the walls between this world and my own. I hadn't been able to draw it back. I didn't even know if I had enough power to do it.

A dragon screamed behind us, and then another roared in anger. Human screams reached my ears, panicked shouts, crying. I looked over my shoulder. A dragon was struggling to hold its height with one wing bent at an odd angle. The thin leather stretched over the bones was torn. As I watched, the tear extended, ripping through the tissue till the wing was useless.

The dragon pivoted to the side and fell from the sky, a roar of pain and anger, married with the cries of the riders, fading into the distance.

A second later the dragon smacked into my shield, its descent slowed as the flexible force field stretched down. I hardened the shield before it could fling them back into the air again. The extra weight added another layer of sweat to my forehead.

A large metal ball whizzed down past Lance's head. He snorted and started to the side.

'They're firing over us,' I screamed back at Lance.

'Can you block it?'

I shook my head. The weight of the dragon and its riders now resting on the shield was taking nearly everything I had.

Another dragon roared and a few moments later I felt the shield flex again. I gasped and grabbed at the edges of the shield trying to hold it in place. The weight of the dragons' bodies was pulling it down, turning it more into a sling than a shield. My carefully constructed edges were gone and it wouldn't be long now before the edges of the pack started to feel the brunt of the attack.

A dragon off to the side below us shuddered. It shook its head and continued flying but droplets of blood sprayed out from its side.

'Can't you attack them?' Turos yelled.

'Which ship?' We were being fired at by so many of them. And although every hundred metres we flew meant ships behind could no longer reach us, it is also meant we were now in range of the ships ahead of us. I would have to blow every single ship within a half mile radius out of the water. And I didn't know if I had the fire power for it.

Human shrieks were now added to that of the dragons and when I looked down, blood splattered the shield.

Turos let out a curse. I turned to see him clutching at his left arm. Blood dribbled out from beneath his fingers. 'I'm okay,' he shouted. 'Just a scratch.'

I stared at him for another second.

'Get down,' he said, flapping his wounded arm at me.

I ducked, crouching over Scruffy and making myself as small as possible. *How are you going?* Emerald was right behind us.

I'll be better when we get back home.

Home? I had thought she wanted to stay here.

No use crying over spilt milk.

I snorted. She'd got that saying from Grams and suddenly I missed my scatty, brilliant Grandmother with an urgency that hurt. I could almost feel her there with me, feel her reaching out towards me to wrap me in her arms.

I sat straight up in the air and Turos batted me back down.

'I've got it,' I shrieked.

'You've been hit?'

I shook my head, hugging my arms around myself. I could still feel Grams as if she were right there with me. All I had to do was hold onto that feeling for a little while longer.

'There.' Turos pointed an arm past me.

I squinted my eyes and peered at the horizon. A pure stretch of ocean had appeared. No ships stained its brilliant blue. I just had to hold it together for a little while longer.

I didn't even hear the next dragon that fell from the sky. Its body slammed into the shield and I felt a crack start in the fabric of my mind. I swayed in my harness and Turos steadied me with a hand.

'Can you hold them while you open the gate?'

'I have to.'

I looked down. Other dragons had picked up the stranded riders that were still conscious, but a few bodies lay sprawled beside those of the dragons. I didn't want to be the person who committed them to their deaths.

The strip of blue was getting wider and I heard a few cheers from behind. We had to get far enough beyond the ships that they wouldn't be able to access any gateway I opened before I closed it again. I couldn't be sure it wouldn't open up right down to the level of the ocean.

'Izzy.' Turos tapped my left shoulder and pointed past me in that direction.

A huge storm was brewing on the horizon. Sheets of lightning danced through the green-black clouds. The water beneath had changed from smooth silk to dancing whitecaps.

The storm swirled in place for a few moments before leaping forward like a frisky racehorse, running to intercept us where we would leave the flotilla behind.

It wasn't possible that it was natural. Not possible at all.

I resisted the urge to smash myself in the head. We had known from the beginning that there must be a magic maker. Known by the way they had shown up when a way had been opened by magic. Deduced and then forgotten.

Lance altered his course away from the dark storm. I didn't think it was going to make any difference though. Our new route was going to take us longer, which would give the storm time to catch us.

'Izzy.' Turos leant forward and yelled in my ear. 'How are you holding up?'

'Oh just fantastic.' I couldn't help the frustration from bubbling in my voice. I had just worked out how to open the portal and now we had the storm to contend with.

'No, I mean with holding the shield.'

'Not great,' I gritted out through clenched teeth.

As if to prove my point another dragon fell from the sky, its body joining the others a few seconds later. Pain lanced through my head as I fought to hold the shield in place.

'You need to let them go.'

'I can't.' I shook my head.

'Can't or won't?' He shook me as if trying to get me to see reason.

'Won't,' I screamed.

'You are our commander. We need you.'

I had carried them this far. I could take them the full way.

'You are our only hope. If you fail, trying to save a few of us, we *all* die.'

The storm seemed to grow as it closed in on us. The water beneath it boiled, water spouts swirling up into the sky.

Damn him to the Great Dark Sky and back.

'You need to let go of them and save your strength.'

I glanced down at the dragons. One of them shook his head as if trying to clear it. We were so close to the edge of the ships. It wouldn't be long before I didn't need the shield at all.

Wind whipped at us; a gale force that grabbed my braid and streamed it out behind me. Lightning sheets danced across the edge of my vision. Lance altered his flight a little more and suddenly the storm was behind us, racing after us.

A few more beats of the dragon's wings and we would be free of the pirates and at the mercy of the storm.

Dragons at the back of the pack began to roar and our speed as a group increased. Lightning arced overhead and I threw out a hand, my own lightning racing to meet it. The two electrical currents met in a blinding blaze of sparks as energy exploded outwards in a wave.

Air punched me in the gut and threw me back into Turos. His arms wrapped around me for a second before he pushed me upright. I pulled my feet up beneath myself and flipped around so that I was facing him. I looked past the dragons to where I could see the sky, a pot of boiling ink ready to stain us black.

'Let them go,' Turos yelled.

Another blaze of lightning streaked towards us. I threw up both hands, extending the shield up behind us to meet it. Electricity seared the edges of my mind as it roared across the surface of my shield.

'Izzy.' Turos's voice was gentle as he placed a hand on each side of my face and turned my gaze to meet his. Tears glimmered in his eyes. 'You have to let them go.'

Damn him. He was right. I couldn't hold the shield, and protect us from the storm and open a gateway. I had to let them go.

'No,' I choked out. 'I can't.'

'You have to.' He leant forwards, resting his forehead against mine. 'You have to,' he whispered again.

I held onto him, blinking tears from my eyes as I found the strength to do what I had to. He kissed me. A gentle, sweet kiss full, not of passion, but of understanding and support.

I let the shield slither from my mind. Tears, tracked down my face and sobs racked me as I felt them falling, fading away. But there was no time to mourn them, no time to feel the full depth of my failure. Now was the time to fight.

I pulled back from Turos and looked toward the storm. Wind rocked me in my seat and dragons and Millenium cried out in fear. I stared into the storm, mesmerised by the dancing darkness that was coming to claim our lives. And within that storm, darker even than the circling clouds, a figure appeared.

It soared towards us, and it was only as it got closer that I realised it wasn't flying. A dragon, larger and blacker than Lance, bore the man on its back. Swirling yellow eyes glared maleficently and, as the dragon threw back its head and roared, lightning shot from the man's hands.

'Santanas,' I gasped. 'Dark Sky, its Santanas.'

Lance turned to stare behind him as I threw back a lightning bolt. I wasn't quite fast enough and it met his at the edge of the dragon pack, the flying sparks causing shrieks of pain.

My mind flew through the possibilities of him being here until it settled on the one obvious answer. This *wasn't* the Santanas from my realm. This was the Santanas in this alternate reality.

'Granddaughter.' His voice thundered over the noise of the storm. 'I am surprised to see you here. I left you in charge of Europe.'

Another piece of the puzzle fell into place. In this alternate reality, Santanas hadn't been trapped. He had gone on to rule the world.

'Hello Grandfather,' I yelled. 'Just out for a morning flight.' We were well beyond the ships now. It was time to open the gateway. But there was no way I could risk *this* Santanas following us through to our world.

'So I can see.' His lips curled up. 'Why didn't you tell me you had found the missing dragons?'

Dark Sky, was it possible there was a tribe of dark faery/Ubanty offspring and a pack of dragons on an island in our world? My head spun as I tried to work through the implications of his words.

'I was going to surprise you.'

The storm had backed off during our conversation. 'But why would you let them attack you.' He flew a little closer. 'They follow your word as much as mine.' His eyes narrowed as he stared at me. 'Isadora, where is your scar?'

I threw up a shield at the precise moment he unleashed a wall of fire at me. It washed across my invisible barricade, gone as quickly as it appeared.

I heard the twang of bow strings and arrows raced towards Santanas.

He flicked his hand and let out a crazy laugh as the arrows flew wide. 'You are not as strong as she.'

'Maybe not.' I tossed a fireball of my own at him. 'But I'm strong enough.'

He batted the fireball out of the sky like a child batting away a tennis ball, and I used that second of distraction to concentrate on Grams again. An intense longing immediately started up in my gut.

More arrows followed my fireball as the warriors on Lance released volley after volley. When my feeling of longing was as strong as I could make it, I threw a hand out behind me. I peeled back the layers between this world and my own as my longing sought my grandmother.

Turos let out a shout and I risked a glance over my shoulder to see a crack appearing in the sky behind us.

'Go,' I screamed. *Go*, I urged Emerald.

She took off towards that rent in the world, the rest of the dragons fleeing after her. The storm exploded, fingers of black cloud roaring after the dragons, as lightning danced across the gap.

'Close your eyes,' I shouted to my companions. Then I pulled the lightning towards us, swirling it into a spinning vortex and using it as an electrical shield.

Light roared, burning through the darkness provided by my eyelids. I gathered it up, until I could feel the energy leaking though my pores. It sent little shocks over the surface of my skin and Lance grunted in discomfort as it flowed from me to him.

I could feel my hair standing away from my body as I plucked a piece from the nimbus surrounding me and threw it towards Santanas. His dragon let out a roar and I opened my eyes to see it charging towards us as Santanas seized my electrical ball and sent it back.

Lance screamed his challenge and reared back his head, getting ready to strike. Dark Sky. The last thing we needed was to get caught up in two male dragons fighting for dominance.

The strange dragon rolled to the side, squealing as the tip of its wing brushed through the edge of my electrical shield.

I plucked off two more pieces of lightning and threw them at Santanas. He laughed as he deflected them. I knew I wasn't going to hurt him. Not that easily. But while he was engaging me, the others were getting away.

Black clouds closed around us from either side as wind ripped at our clothes. Lance snorted as the cloud brushed him, and blood droplets flew from his nose as he shook his head.

'The clouds,' Turos yelled. 'They're eating his flesh.'

I threw another electrical ball at Santanas as Lance turned and fled from the storm.

'I'm disappointed,' Santanas called. 'Is that the best you've got?'

Half of the dragons were already through the gateway.

'You can't get away that easily.' Santanas' voice floated to us on the edge of the storm.

As fast as Lance was flying, the black clouds were keeping pace. They swirled and danced, occasional tendrils reaching out to brush Lance's side. With each touch, his snort was louder, more fearful. He rolled his eyes and looked over his shoulder.

'Easy boy,' Turos said, pressing his hand to the big dragon's flank. 'Easy.' He looked into my eyes and whispered, 'I hope you've got something up your sleeve.'

I nodded, tension giving the movement a mechanical feel. I hoped I did too. But the truth was I was nearing exhaustion.

Santanas's dragon was coasting behind Lance as if he were out for a casual afternoon flight. I threw the last of my stored electrical balls at Santanas and risked a look over my shoulder. We were almost there. Almost.

Santanas laughed again. 'I'm thinking I'll give you to *my* Isadora as a present. She liked dolls when she was a little girl. She's going to love you.'

I gritted my teeth, trying hard not to think about what I was like in this world. What atrocities had I committed? How many people had I harmed?

Turos squeezed my arm as he said, 'Whatever you're going to do, do it *now*.'

It was true that I couldn't harm Santanas, not exhausted as I was. But there was nothing to stop me from harming his mount.

Santanas raised a hand in the air, a triumphant look on his face. I reached out my mind and seized his dragon's wings. I wrapped air around them, and then I pulled all the moisture out of the air and I froze it onto his wings.

One second they were closing on us, Santanas about to unleash his killing blow, and the next they were falling from the sky, balls of ice wrapped around his dragon's wings.

I had no doubt he would unravel my work before they smacked into the ocean. But we only needed a little time.

Turos let out a yell of triumph as the world around us changed from dark to light. I saw the gateway from the other side, a slash in the fabric of the sky. I grasped it and heaved it shut, melding it closed in my mind. And then I turned to look over my shoulder to where we were heading.

Turos grabbed my head and pushed me down as an arrow sluiced through where I had been.

I let out a shriek and surveyed the ground below. We were in Eynsford, just as I had been hoping we would be. But it was not the Eynsford we had left.

Lance banked suddenly, and Turos wrapped an arm around me, holding me tight as we swerved and dodged around an eagle of unbelievable proportions. A masked figure sat on its back. As I watched, the figure jumped nimbly from the eagle onto Lance's back. He swept a short blade at one of the warriors there, was blocked, and then leapt back off Lance, into the air, and onto the back of the eagle.

The Vulpines were here.

I looked around, trying to take in what I was looking at. Dragons and eagles swooped and dived, involved in aerial battle. Arrows flew and civilians wielded swords and axes to prevent the Vulpine warriors landing on their dragons.

Down below, goblins swarmed over the field below my house. Border guards battled them, but from my aerial survey I could see they were badly outnumbered.

'We have to go down,' I screamed, pointing at the battle. 'They need our help.'

'Your place is with your dragon.'

He was right. Again. Damn him to hell and back.

Emerald, I called.

Jump left on my call.

I flipped back to face the front and untied Scruffy's carrier basket. I tucked him under one arm, and looked back over my shoulder. 'We'll get rid of these birds,' I said to Turos, 'and then I'll meet you on the ground.'

He pulled me towards him and pressed his lips to mine in a short, hard kiss. 'I look forward to it,' he said as he winked at me.

Now, Emerald screamed in my mind.

I winked back and then leapt off Lance. Emerald levelled out beneath me and I slid smoothly onto her neck. I grabbed onto the harness and then tied Scruffy on. He looked up at me with his huge, yellow eyes and licked my hand through the basket.

Where's Isla?

She's on Arthur. Her tone told me how much she approved of that.

I looked around and spied the little orange dragon. His size gave him an advantage over the adult dragons. He was much more nimble. As I watched, he twisted through the air to avoid the outstretched talons of an eagle.

Isla, a smile born of excitement stretching her mouth wide, released two arrows into the eagle's rider. He toppled from the bird's back and the eagle was forced to give up his pursuit of Arthur, instead racing after his master.

Everywhere I looked, dragons and eagles twisted and dodged. Fire scorched eagles' feathers and talons tore at tender snouts. Millenium released arrows and the Vulpine leapt from eagle to dragon to eagle. The white feathers of the eagles were tinged with the pink of blood.

Incoming. To our nine.

I tore my eyes back to my left, holding onto the reins with one hand and jumping to my feet. I placed my spare hand on the hilt of my sword but did not draw it.

The eagle was closing fast. Its rider wore black robes, and I could see now that it wasn't so much a mask they were wearing, but the end of a turban hooked over the lower half of their faces. He crouched on the eagle's neck, one hand holding a leather strap, the other his curved blade.

I calmed my mind, pushing out all thoughts as I waited for his attack.

The eagle peeled off to the right, slashing at Emerald's neck as the Bedouin man leapt towards me. I whipped my blade out in front of me at the last possible second and his momentum carried him onto my sword point. I staggered backwards and Emerald banked so that the force carried me into her, and not off her neck. The tip of my sword sank deep into his stomach, emerging out his back. His eyes widened, and he clutched at his chest where blood soaked through his black robes.

Then his eyes hardened and his blade swept around to meet me. I blocked his arm movement, lifted a knee between us, and kicked him off my sword. He flew backwards, arms and legs outstretched like a man floating in the ocean.

His eagle appeared beneath him, and he crashed onto it before sliding off again, leaving a large bloody smear on the creature's feathers.

Hang on. Emerald executed a perfect barrel roll, using one of her wings to snap down on an eagle. I heard the sound of bones cracking. It let out a cry, falling from the sky with one wing flapping uselessly.

I risked a glance below. More of the Guard had arrived but they were still badly outnumbered.

Emerald let out a puff of fire, and an eagle squawked and dived, the feathers on its tail lighting up like a candle. I released a couple of arrows into its rider, not even waiting to see if they had landed before looking around us.

Lance snatched at the air; his strong jaws clamping down on the eagle and rider in one bite. He shook his head like a cat with a mouse and feathers exploded in all directions. Then he spat them back out, blasting them with a stream of fire as they fell from the sky.

Behind you.

I felt the vibration even as Emerald warned me, ducking just in time to avoid having my head severed from my body. The blade whistled over my head and I kicked out behind, connecting with the knee of my attacker. There was a sickening popping noise and a screech of pain. I spun, swinging my other leg around in a swiping kick Turos had taught me. It connected with the side of my attacker's head and he flew sideways off Emerald's back.

I panted slightly as I looked around for the next eagle. But there were none. We had outnumbered them and out-fought them, and they were fleeing.

Some of the dragons, holding only warriors, chased after them; dragons nipping eagles from the air, and blasting others with flames. It wasn't turning out to be a very good day for the Vulpines.

Without me having to say anything, Emerald headed for the ground battle. Her flame would be no good, the two sides were two heavily engaged for her to be able to cook goblins without hitting any of the Guard.

I knocked an arrow to my bow and fired at a goblin. The arrow buried itself deep in the base of his neck and he toppled to the side. I fired off two more arrows before Emerald finished her first pass over them. She snatched a goblin up with each of her front legs, carrying them up high into the sky before throwing them into the trees.

I reached for another arrow, but the quiver slung on the side of Emerald's neck was empty.

Let me down, I said. Emerald could wreak havoc without me, my sword was going to be the most help now.

She didn't so much land as just skim across the top of the battle. I gave Scruffy a pat on the head, warned her to look after him, and then leapt off her neck and onto the back of a huge goblin warrior. My momentum knocked him forwards, onto his knees, and before he could recover I grasped his head in both hands and twisted it savagely to the side. It broke with a satisfying snap.

I jumped to my feet and Rako said, 'Well girl, you sure do know how to make an entrance.'

I shot him a grin, but before I could respond, a goblin holding a dagger in each hand ran at me. I cleared my mind of everything and attacked.

Every other time when I had engaged the Millenium warriors' mind technique, I had been fighting those doing the same. So I wasn't quite prepared for what happened this time.

It was as if everybody else on that field's movement dropped to half – no, a quarter - of what it had been. It was as if they moved through water. I, on the other hand, seemed to be moving at a normal speed.

I twirled with my sword and lopped off both the goblin's hands, and then I spun and took his head. I jumped over his still-falling body and engaged two goblins on the far side. They just had time to look surprised before I slashed through one's neck, severing the carotid artery. I plucked a dagger out of his hands and spun and wedged it into the other's chest.

Across the field I saw another man moving at normal speed. Turos. Fighting his way towards me through the mass of goblins.

'Winner takes all,' he yelled, an excited grin on his face.

'I've already got four,' I called back. 'Make that five.' I hamstringed a goblin and slit his throat as he fell backwards.

'Six,' Turos called.

'What?' I took a second to look over at him. He had a sword in each hand.

Emerald swooped over the battlefield again. I could feel excitement radiating out from her. She grabbed two more goblins and took them high into the air before throwing them into the trees. Lance flew through a few seconds later, repeating her performance.

I stooped and picked up a second sword from a fallen Border Guard. Jamis. I suppressed the pang of grief. He had been a good man, and I was going to put his sword to good use seeking his revenge.

'Ten,' Turos called out.

Damn him, he was pushing his lead out too far for me to catch him. I whirled my swords and ran at the nearest goblin. I leapt at him, feet first, using his body as a spring board as I bounded up into the air. As I spun, my braid whipped him in the face, and then I followed that up with my sword. I landed, pivoted, slashed at two goblins' necks, sprang into the air again over their toppling bodies and turned a full somersault before I landed.

I saluted a slow-moving Border Guard, grinning at the look of shock on his face, and then bounded up and onto a goblin's shoulder, mimicking a move I had once seen Isla do, as I ran from shoulder-to-shoulder. Where she had used arrows, I used my swords like walking sticks, plunging them down at a slightly outward angle into the goblins' throats. Their bodies gave out beneath me as I pushed off for my next victim.

Arthur fluttered into view. He hovered above the fight and I saw Isla, her face calm as she fired shots off into the melee below. At the speed she was firing it only took her a few seconds to empty her quiver. She patted Arthur on the neck, then slid off and dropped to a crouch on the ground, her sword already in her hand.

I leapt off my last goblin, landing in front of Turos. 'Twenty,' I said, giving him a grin.

'Impressive.' He gave me a mock bow, sweeping out to the side with his sword as he stood back up.

A goblin, his hand raised to strike, grunted, looking down in shock at the sword stuck in his belly. He let out a gurgle and fell to his knees.

'Twenty-two,' he said.

'Oh buzznuckle.' I turned to re-enter the fight, but there were no more goblins standing.

Isla whipped her sword off on the coat of a goblin she had just beheaded. 'Twenty-three,' she said. 'Did I win?'

Rako walked in slow motion towards me. 'Hooooowwww aaarreee yoooou doing thaaat?' Not only did it look like he was walking through water, he sounded like he was speaking under water too.

I smiled at him and released my mind control. 'How were we doing what?'

'That's what you were talking about,' he said. 'The training you were going through.'

I nodded. 'If we can train the Guard we're going to have a definite advantage.'

Rako shook his head. 'There's no time to train. Santanas's armies are pushing harder than we thought. They're almost at Isilvitania.'

'Izzy.' I turned to see Aethan striding towards us. His black hair was ruffled up and blood and grime covered one side of his stubble-coated face. He reached me and his hand moved awkwardly towards me before falling back to his side. 'Thank the Dark Sky you're back. You're safe.'

'Aethan.' I put a hand on the side of his face, brushing at the blood with my fingers. 'Are you hurt?'

He covered my hand with his and the flutter set up inside my stomach again, but *this* time it was for a very different reason. 'Not my blood.' His voice was low and husky and he got that look in his eyes that meant he was going to kiss me.

I stared mesmerised into the depths of his navy-blue eyes. I could already feel the heat from his muscled body radiating out towards me, any second now and I would feel the hardness of him wrapping around me.

Except, there was a reason I wasn't meant to kiss him. I knew it, but I was exhausted, and for the life of me I couldn't remember what it was.

I felt Aethan's fingers flex on top of mine, and knew he was about to make his move.

'Hmmmmmhmmm.' Turos cleared his throat loudly and stepped up next to me.

I saw Aethan's eyes break from mine and travel up the length of the bronzed, muscled warrior. Turos stood a good foot higher than Aethan and was at least half as wide again. I had gotten used to how massive he was, but seeing the slight shock in Aethan's eyes reminded me once again.

I pulled my hand from Aethan's face and stepped back, wobbling a little on legs made of jelly.

Ebony. He was going to marry Ebony.

Turos stepped to my side and wrapped an arm around me, steadying my wobble.

'Prince Turos of Millenia at your service.' He bowed his head to Rako and then to Aethan.

'Rako, head of the Border Guard.' Rako bowed in return.

'Prince Aethan of Isilvitania.' Aethan's voice had a hard brittle edge as his eyes travelled from Turos, along Turos's arm to me. One of his fists clenched and the muscles in his jaw bulged.

'Aethan,' Isla shrieked and threw herself into his arms. She looked over her shoulder at me and winked.

One-by-one the dragons had been landing at the far end of the field. Five hundred dragons take up quite a bit of room and it wasn't long before they were hovering over our heads, looking for space to land.

'You brought them all?' Rako asked.

'Had to. Santanas attacked.'

His eyebrows rode up his forehead and he scratched vigorously at the long scar running down his cheek.

'Not *our* Santanas. The alternate reality one.' I was tired. So bone tired. All I wanted to do was have a little lie down.

'We'd better move back.' Rako looked up at the sky where dragons flew slow circles looking for a place to land. 'Get the dead and wounded,' he called.

'Father.'

I turned at Turos's voice to see King Bladimir walking towards us. Gladaline strode by his side, her head held high. Even though her hair was dirty and matted, and her clothes covered in dirt, she looked every bit a Queen.

I heard Turos making introductions between his parents, and Rako and Aethan, as the Guard lifted their fallen comrades and started walking towards the edge of the field.

'Bring them up to the house,' a familiar voice called. 'We've gathered healers.'

I let out a gasp of delight. 'Sabby?'

At the sound of my voice, Sabby's fur scarf unravelled from her throat. It clambered up onto her head, let out a mewl and launched itself into the air.

Mia.

I held out my arms and the little monster thumped into me, wrapping her winged limbs around my neck and hanging on tight. Her whole body wriggled as she nuzzled her head up under my chin.

'Oh, Mia.' I ran my hands over her fur. 'I missed you girl.'

She mewed a few more times and then climbed up onto my shoulder to wrap around my neck.

Sabby picked her way gingerly through the field of fallen. 'About time you came back.' She put her hands on her hips but her smile told me she was pleased to see me.

'Oh Sabby.' I laughed and flung my arms around her. 'I've missed you.'

She pulled back and stared into my face. 'I should be so mad at you. I told you not to go off and have an adventure without me.' She looked around the field. 'Hubba hubba, *who* is *that*?'

I followed her eyes to see Turos watching us. When I met his gaze he smiled and sauntered towards us. Bladimir was talking fervently to Rako, waving his arms around and gesturing towards his people.

'Oh *my*,' Sabby said. 'He's even bigger close up.'

He rested an arm casually on my shoulder and held a hand out to her. 'You must be Sabby. Izzy told me all about you.'

'Well hopefully,' she threw him a stunning smile, 'she'll tell *me* all about *you*. But alas, for now I have to go and heal the wounded.'

Mia reached out her nose to sniff at Turos. She let go of my neck and scampered up his arm, running her paws over his face as she nipped at his jaw.

'Ah,' Turos peered down at Mia, 'what is it?'

'*Mia* is a narathymia. She's technically a monster.'

'A monster?' He reached out a finger and scratched her under the neck and she let out a purr. 'She's too adorable to be a monster.'

'Santanas took her baby. I promised her we'd find it.' I watched her wind herself around his neck. 'She likes you.'

'What's not to like?' He held his hands out sideways.

A smile curved my lips as I looked up into his beautiful eyes. 'Want to come and meet my Mum and Grams?'

He nodded and reached out to thread his fingers through mine. It felt very natural.

'Izzy.' Aethan stood off to the side. This time there was no mistaking how his eyes lingered on where Turos was touching me. 'Can I have a word with you?'

'Can it wait? There are wounded I should attend to.'

He nodded his head but said, 'It will only take a minute.'

I squeezed Turos's hand before letting go to walk over to where Aethan stood to the side.

He didn't talk straight away. He scratched the side of his nose and looked out towards the field at the dragons that were settling down to rest. I sighed as I realised I was going to have to heal them as well.

'You did well,' he finally said. 'We're going to need them.'

'That's not why I brought them here.' Dark Sky, I wasn't so ruthless as to potentially commit a whole nation of people to their deaths just to try and save us. 'We had to leave. This was the only safe place to come.' I let out a snort as I realised the ludicrousness of my words. I had taken them from the frying pan to the fire. 'Is that what you wanted to talk about?'

'I missed you.' He took my hand. 'I *miss* you.'

I pulled my hand back. 'We've had this conversation. It didn't end well last time either.' A wave of exhaustion rolled over me.

'Yes well….' He stopped and stared at me intently. 'You told me you hadn't met anyone else.'

'I hadn't.' I looked over my shoulder at Turos. He stood facing us, his enormous frame tense as if he was about to explode into action. Oh great. That was the last thing I needed. 'He's a friend. A good friend.' I decided now was not the time to mention that there had been kissing involved.

Aethan looked over at Turos. His eyes narrowed and then he nodded his head. 'You may think that, but I know a possessive male when I see one. Well, I'm throwing my hat in the ring.' He looked back at me and this time when he grabbed my hand I didn't shake him off.

'I'm not letting you go that easily. I'm going to fight for you.'

'But Ebony....'

'Ebony be damned. It's *you* I love.' The intensity of his words hammered into my heart.

I could feel my breathing coming in short, ragged bursts. It was too overwhelming. All too much. The political ramification of what Aethan was suggesting was disastrous. But I knew I wanted him to try. And that fact – the fact I wanted him to *try*, made me realise that Turos had become more than just a friend. My feelings for him were no longer just my hormones calling. Somewhere along the way he had stolen a piece of my heart. And now I didn't know who owned the biggest piece.

The last of my strength gave out. A wave of nausea rolled over me. I heard Aethan call my name as my sight disappeared and my knees buckled. I felt hands catching me and lowering me to the ground. I heard Sabby speaking urgently, calling my name. Felt the sharp snap of a palm connecting with my cheek.

I felt big, gentle hands cradling my head while still others held my hands. And then I escaped to the blissfulness of darkness, and the comforting buzz of white noise.

Chapter Ten

Do or Die

Galanta was waiting for me in Trillania. Time hadn't improved her wardrobe. She still wore the same black leather outfit, decorated with human teeth and bones that she had worn the entire time I had known her.

She stood with her back to a tree, her dreadlocks pulled over one shoulder as she watched. When she saw me, she straightened, pushing away from the tree to stride towards me.

'I come in peace.' She held her hands in the air as if to convince me she was unarmed.

I snorted. In Trillania, a weapon was only a thought away. It didn't matter though. Once upon a time she was my better, but I knew that I had surpassed her in strength, speed and power a while ago. And I knew that she knew it too.

'Give me one good reason why I shouldn't gut you right now.'

'Curiosity killed the cattle. If you kill me, you'll never know what I had to say.' Her accent was thick and foreign.

'Honestly Galanta, repeat after me. Curiosity killed the *cat*.'

She snarled and worked her jaw from side-to-side, her eyes burning with hatred.

'What *you* had to say? Or what Santanas had to say?'

Her lips pulled back to reveal her pointed teeth. 'You never were stupid.'

'I know if you had *your* way, I would be dead.'

'No.' She shook her head. 'If I had *my* way, you would be tied to a stake for me to torture.' Her eyes gleamed like black stones as she ran her tongue over her lips. 'I would eat a little bit of you every day. The tip of a finger, your earlobe, your little toe. I'm betting you would be delicious.' She let out a laugh. 'I would keep you alive for a very long time.'

I couldn't suppress the shudder that ran down my spine. 'Well, this has been a *real* pleasure. I can't thank you enough for dropping by.'

'But that is not what Santanas wants.' She spat on the ground at her feet. 'He won't even let me have a little nibble.'

'For once he and I see eye-to-eye.' We stood a few metres apart, our hands on our hips, glaring at each other. 'You've got ten seconds to give me the message. After that, I kill you.'

She spat on the ground again. 'He will call off the army if you join him.'

'Pardon?'

She shook her head, her face contorting as if the words tasted bad. 'Join him, and he will call off the army.'

'So he won't attack. Now or ever?'

'I have given you the message.'

She turned as if to leave and I said, 'Ten.' I whipped a loaded crossbow up in front of me and released the shaft.

Her laugh echoed back to me as she disappeared from view. The shaft flew through where she had been. I bit back an oath and willed myself after her.

'Wait.' It was Aethan.

I spun to look over my shoulder.

'I knew you'd be here.'

'That was fast.'

'Sabby helped me get to sleep.'

I nodded my head. 'Are you coming?'

He disappeared and reappeared by my side a second later. Then he grasped my hand and said, 'Always.'

I closed my eyes to will us after her but before I could, I heard Isla call out, 'Wait.'

I sighed and opened my eyes again. 'I don't want to sound ungrateful for the help,' I said, 'but we have totally lost the element of surprise.'

Isla smiled as she pranced up to me and took my other hand. Wilfred's wrist band was back on her slender arm. 'No we haven't. She's only expecting you. There are three of us now.'

'That's true,' I said. 'Come on.' I willed myself to where I could feel Galanta, knowing that she could feel me coming too. Isla was right. Probably the only element of surprise I had was the two of them.

We were in an empty cave. I blinked, and it was full of goblin warriors.

'Not again.' I let out a sigh and pulled two short swords out of the air.

'Do you think it will work here?' Isla asked.

I didn't need to ask what she was talking about. 'Only one way to find out.'

I cleared my mind and attacked, but unlike the previous fight, everybody else was moving at the same speed as me.

'Oh poo,' Isla said as she fired off a couple of arrows.

'Too much to hope for.' I used a shield to block a dagger thrust and then hurled an axe at my attacker. The head of the axe lodged in his chest.

'What are you two talking about?' Sweat gleamed enticingly on the part of Aethan's chest I could see in the V of his leather vest.

I spent a little too much time watching it roll over the edge of his pectoral muscle and didn't dodge quite fast enough when a goblin threw a dagger at me. It lodged in my bicep and quivered as the tip bit deep into the bone.

'Garrrrrrr,' I said, staring at the evil-looking blade. I plucked it out and threw it back at him, managing to land it in the soft part of his throat between his clavicle bones. It sunk to its hilt and he let out a gasp as he clutched at the dagger.

Blood trailed down my bicep and dripped onto the ground.

'That's it.' Aethan scooped me up. 'I'm calling it.'

Isla bounded towards us and the second her hand touched Aethan he took us back to where we had started.

'And I was having so much fun.' Isla threw her arms in the air and whirled on the spot.

I expected Aethan to put me down but he didn't. 'What were you thinking?' he shook me gently.

'I was thinking "Owwwwww".' I frowned up at him.

'No. To get hit. That was a rookie error.'

His chest was right there at eye level, and it looked just as delicious as it had before. Come to think of it his arms felt pretty damn fine wrapped around me. Maybe this wasn't a total disaster.

Isla let out another laugh. 'I think I know what she was thinking.' She plucked a flower out of the air and then she disappeared.

I tried to school a look of neutrality as Aethan looked down into my eyes, but my hormones, running riot through my body, had taken my mind hostage. My heart was ruling with an iron fist, demanding I take back what was mine.

'Oh.' Aethan's voice was husky. His pupils widened and I felt his chest move against me as he sucked in a deep breath of air.

He had no memory of the times we had spent here together, but I remembered each and every one of them. They started playing through my head like a slideshow; from the hesitancy of our first kiss, through to the raw power of him pinning me down and ravishing my mouth and my mind. Wild nights of passion, when time had had no meaning and all I had known was the feel of his skin moving against mine.

My breathing increased at the memory, and suddenly I wanted to finish what we had always started. Finish it in a way we never had. With him possessing me totally. I wanted to have him, before Ebony did. Suddenly the thought of being the other woman didn't seem quite so bad.

He let me slip out of his arms so that we were facing each other. We stared into each other's eyes, each of us seeing a mirror of what was on our own face.

My hands reached out to rest against his chest. He stepped closer, grasping the nape of my neck with one hand, and then he pulled my head to his. His lips closed on mine with a hunger, a ferocity that sucked the breath right out of me.

Every single cell in my body stood to attention as an electric shock coursed through me. I ran my hands under the edges of his vest and he moaned and clasped my buttocks, jamming me in against the hardness of him.

It was my turn to moan against his mouth as I jumped up, wrapping my legs around him. We were so close to where I wanted to be. Just a couple of layers of clothes in the way, but it would be a matter of seconds to discard those.

A bucket of icy, cold water hit me from the side. I opened my eyes and…

We were back in the cave, and it was empty except for Isla, who still held the bucket she had used to sluice us.

'What the?' I slid my legs down from Aethan's waist and stepped away from him. The remnants of the lust still remained but it was one tenth of what it had been a second ago.

I looked down at my arm where the dagger had lodged. Smooth, whole skin encased the area.

He looked around the cave, shook his head and then looked at Isla. 'What happened?'

'One minute you were standing there, and the next you were going for it like a couple of horny teenagers. I tried talking to you but it was as if you couldn't hear me.' She held up the bucket. 'This was the only thing that worked.' She tossed the bucket into the air and it disappeared before it landed. 'Can you still feel her?' she asked me.

I nodded my head. 'She's that way.' I pointed through an opening in the cave wall.

'Well, come on then.' Isla took three steps and then froze.

'What is it?' I started to step towards her but Aethan grabbed my arm.

'Stop,' he said. 'There's something going on here.'

'You think?'

Isla now had her arms held up in front of her as if she held a parcel. She started to rock them from side-to-side as she sung a soft lullaby.

'Isla,' I called.

She ignored me and kept singing.

'Isla,' I yelled a little louder.

'What is she doing?' Aethan's voice was amused.

I turned to look at Aethan. 'Haven't you ever seen someone rock a baby?'

'I'm normally out killing things. I don't have time for babies.'

I snorted. 'Do you think we should try the cold water trick?'

He nodded. 'And then we should get out of this cave.'

'She spelled it and then lured us here.' I kicked at the ground. One of these days I was going to outsmart Galanta. It hadn't happened yet, but I had high hopes.

'Oh Wilfred,' Isla said when she was finished with the song. 'She's going to have your hair.'

I turned to Aethan. 'It's possible she's nursing a baby orangutan.'

One corner of his lip curved up and a bucket appeared in his hands. 'Do you want to do the honours or should I?'

'You go,' I said.

The water from the bucket sliced through the air and smacked into Isla's head.

She spluttered and coughed and then her arms fell to her side as she looked around. 'Oh,' she said. 'Oh.' Tears welled in her eyes. 'It wasn't real.'

'Not yet,' I said. 'But it will be.'

'Do you think?' Her beautiful face crumpled a little more.

'I have no doubt that you and he will be reunited and that the two of you will have a bunch of furry children.'

Her puckered mouth spread into a smile. 'And you will be their godmother so you had better start saying nice things about them.'

'We need to go,' Aethan said. 'If all three of us get caught up in a spell we'll never get out of here.'

He was right. It had been her intention to snare me in a spell. I was lucky that both of them had come with me. A shiver ran down my spine at the thought of what would have happened if Isla hadn't come as well.

We transported back to our starting spot individually. None of us willing to move in the cave unless we triggered the spell again.

'What do you think it was?' I asked.

Isla sighed. 'Well, for a few seconds there I had everything I wanted.'

I reached out and squeezed her arm. I hadn't given enough consideration to how much she must be missing Wilfred.

'So,' she continued, 'I'm guessing it was a spell that invoked your greatest desire.'

My eyes darted guiltily towards Aethan, as I said, 'But my greatest desire is to end this damned war and send Santanas back where he came from.'

She pursed her lips and tapped a finger against them. 'Well the two of you got caught in the same spell. So I'm guessing it was a culmination of your greatest desire where each other was concerned.'

I was grateful Aethan didn't say anything. I would have had to break his nose. I didn't want my greatest wish where he was concerned to be all about sex. I wanted it to be about more than just that. Why hadn't I found myself nursing his child? That might have given me the answer I needed.

'You able to go back yet?' Isla asked.

I concentrated on being back in my body. Nothing happened. I shook my head. 'Still unconscious.'

'You should be up at the house by now. I'll get your dreamcatcher and put it under your pillow.' Isla disappeared, leaving Aethan and me alone.

'So,' he took a step towards me, 'want to take up where we left off.'

Oh great. I was going to have to break his nose after all.

'I thought I made myself clear on how things stood between us.' It was hard to keep a stern voice when he was so close. The hair on my arms was standing on end and little tingles ran across my skin as if he were already stroking me.

'Oh, I thought you had as well.' He took a step closer. 'But now I'm not so sure.' His lips curved up in a cheeky grin and a dimple appeared on his cheek as he closed the space between us.

'That was a spell. It meant nothing.' I took a step backwards and slammed into a tree.

He stepped forwards, so close now that I had to look up at him. He lifted a hand and tucked a stray piece of hair behind my ear. 'Ah Izzy,' he said as he trailed his fingers down my cheek. 'When are you going to realise?'

'Realise what?' My traitorous voice caught in a hitch.

'That you're the only woman for me.'

My fist was clenched and I knew I should have been doing something with it, but the depth of his eyes blazed all rational thoughts from my mind. I was frozen in place as his mouth moved closer to mine.

His hands settled onto my waist and he pushed me back onto the tree as he closed the last few inches between us.

My head was screaming no, but my heart was clambering for what he was offering. The memory of the moments in the spell wiped away all self-restraint and I was powerless to resist the lure of him any more.

One second I was sighing as his lips melted onto mine, and then I was gone, fading from Trillania into a blissful state of unconsciousness.

***

Ice-blue eyes stared into mine. I blinked a couple of times and my vision expanded to encompass the whole of Turos's face. I was in my room, on my bed, and Turos sat next to me with Scruffy curled up on his lap and Mia hugging his neck. Her little eyes were closed and contented snores rumbled out of her.

I raised a hand to my head. Someone had undone my braid and brushed out my hair. I suspected that someone may have been Turos. Thankfully, I still wore the same clothes I had been in.

'Sabby,' he called out. 'She's awake.'

Scruffy stretched and yawned and then leaned over to lick my face. His tail thumped against Turos's chest a few times.

'Well, it's about time.' Sabby appeared at the top of the stairs, and Phantom, her huge, black cat, appeared a few seconds later. She strode into the room and placed her hand on my head, closing her eyes as she did. I felt a tingle where her hand touched me. 'You can get up Little Miss

Lazy Bones,' she said as she opened her eyes. She softened the words with a smile. 'There're people waiting to see you.'

'Sabby, where do you want these...Oh she's awake.' My old friend Thomas stood in the doorway. His arms were loaded with a huge pile of towels.

'Thomas?' I sat up in bed and stared at my friend. I hadn't seen him in months. 'What are you doing home?'

He shrugged a shoulder. 'The School of Witching Administration has shut down. Well, to be quite honest, what with the imminent threat of war and everything, *all* of London has shut down.' He had gotten taller, and broader as well. And he had stubble on his face.

'You've grown up.' I swung my legs over the side of the bed and stood up, brushing away Turos's supporting hand as I did.

'*I've* grown up.' He let out a chuckle as he placed the towels on my couch. 'Says the village girl who just rode into Eynsford on a dragon's back, fought a pack of goblins, and saved the day.'

I laughed. 'And then passed out.'

'Yes.' He nodded his head. 'That did kind of ruin the effect.'

'I've missed you,' I said, pulling him into a hug.

'I'm surprised you've had time.' He squeezed me tight before releasing me. 'Sabby's been filling me in on everything that's been happening.' He shot a shy smile over his shoulder at Sabina. She blushed and returned the smile.

Oh. So *that's* how things stood.

'I see all those fencing classes paid off.'

I shrugged. 'Yeah. They've been kind of useful the last year.'

'Perhaps...,' he scuffed the tip of his boot against the carpet, 'I could train with you,' he said. 'You know, to sharpen my skills.'

'You're not going to fight, are you?' My voice rose up an octave.

'Izzy, *everyone's* going to fight.'

'I'd be happy to train you.' Turos stood and stretched. 'There's not much else for me to do.'

Thomas's eyes widened as they travelled up the length of Turos's body. 'Th th, thanks,' he stammered. 'I think.'

I laughed. 'He won't hurt you. In fact,' I looked to Turos for confirmation and he nodded once, 'he's going to teach you a mind technique that may just save your life.' I reached out and squeezed Turos's hand. It didn't feel so awful knowing Thomas would be fighting if he had the advantage of speed.

'I'd like to learn that technique too.' I hadn't heard Aethan come up the stairs. He entered the room, his gaze pointedly on Turos and my clasped hands.

Turos's grip tightened to an almost painful level. 'It would be a pleasure,' he said. 'But I thought Head Guard Rako said that we wouldn't have time to train.'

'The latest scouts report that the enemy advance has stopped.'

'When did you want to start?' Turos let go of my hand and wrapped an arm around me. He tucked me in close to his side.

I pasted a smile on my face to try and hide how awkward I felt. All the testosterone zinging around the room was making it hard to breathe.

'No time like the present.' Aethan's smile told me I hadn't fooled him. 'Izzy, Rako and Wolfgang are waiting to debrief you in the kitchen.'

'Mum? Grams?' I resisted the urge to add lemon cake to my list of questions.

'They are both there as well.'

'Excuse me.' I ducked out from under Turos's arm and trotted out of the room, in a hurry to put as much distance between myself and the two alpha males. I didn't want to be there if push came to shove because I wasn't sure which side I would come down on.

'That was awkward,' Sabby said as she followed me down the stairs. She let out a sigh. 'Still, it must be nice to have two gorgeous hunks fighting for your affections.'

'I'd rather fight a pack of goblins, blind-folded,' I said. I reached the bottom of the stairs and headed for the kitchen, my nostrils flaring as they picked up the scent of...lemon cake. Yes!

'Well, young lady.' Mum's foot was tapping. That was never a good sign. 'What do you have to say for yourself?'

'Ummmm.' My thoughts flitted through the many different answers to that question, trying to work out which one would be the most likely to earn me an extra slice of cake. 'I'm really sorry we left like that, and I missed you so much.'

I crossed the room and wrapped my arms around her, waiting till I felt her body soften before letting go of her. 'Honestly I am,' I said. 'And I did.' I risked a glance over my shoulder at the table. There was half a cake left, but Radismus was reaching for another piece. The man was a lemon-cake-eating machine.

She let out a rueful laugh and ruffled my hair. 'Don't worry. There's two more in the oven.'

I took that as my get-out-of-jail-free card and took a seat at the table next to Grams, smiling at Rako, Wolfgang, Lionel and Radismus.

Grams handed me a plate with a giant piece of cake on it. 'I think you've earnt that,' she said. 'But we haven't had *our* conversation yet.' Cyril, draped around Gram's neck like a scarf, lifted his head and hissed in my direction.

Scruffy, who had been sitting at my feet staring intently at the table, looked up at Cyril and barked. Cyril flicked his tongue once and then nestled his face back into Grams.

'It was all very boring,' I said to her as I picked up the piece of cake. 'You would have hated it.' The last sentence was a bit muffled, due to the cakey goodness that I had wedged into my mouth. I let out a moan as the sugar in the icing rolled over my tastebuds. It had been a long time between sugar hits for me.

I may have been a War Faery, but at heart I was just a girl.

The men waited politely for me to finish my first piece. Radismus, very nobly, pushed the platter towards me so I could take another.

When I had finished, I sighed and leant back in my chair, resisting the urge to unbutton my leather pants. 'So Aethan says the advance has stopped.'

Rako nodded. 'They must be resting their troops.'

'You don't think it's because we just whipped their butts?'

A small smile tugged at the corners of his mouth but his eyes stayed sombre. 'That was a tiny piece of their force. A drop in the ocean.'

'Even the Vulpines?'

He nodded.

'Oh.' I played with the handle on my tea cup.

'Ahhhhh.' King Bladimir stood in the doorway to the kitchen. His nose twitched a few times and his gaze locked onto the cake. 'They told me the council was being held in here.'

'King Bladimir.' I jumped out of my seat and bobbed my head.

A plate smashed behind me. 'Sorry, sorry, your Highness.' Mum swept into a low curtsy.

'Fair lady, there is nothing to be sorry for.' His nose crinkled again. 'Does that taste as good as it smells?' He pointed at the cake.

'Please.' I held my seat out for him and then retrieved another for myself from the next room.

By the time I got back, he had taken my seat, helped himself to the cake, and Rako was doing the introductions. Mum had spelled the broken plate off the floor and it sat shiny and new on the kitchen bench. I placed my chair on the other side of Grams, between her and Lionel.

'Do you know why my son and Prince Aethan are out the back wrestling?' King Bladimir said to me.

I could feel a wash of red creeping up my face. 'No.' My squeaky voice didn't lend much weight to the word.

'Well, not that it matters I am sure, but my son seems to be winning.'

'Okay. Thanks.' I nodded much too rapidly, and hid my face behind my teacup.

'Ahhhhh. If I had known there was cake, I would have come sooner.' King Arwyn stood where King Bladimir had a few moments before.

'King Arwyn.' I jumped back to my feet and gestured to my new chair.

Mum let out a squeak and knocked the plate off the bench again. Grams shot her an amused look and shook her head.

'Young Isadora,' Arwyn said as I brought in another seat. 'Do you know why my son is fighting that big, blond fellow?'

'No.' If I shook my head any harder, it was going to fall off.

'Well,' he said, 'I'm sure it isn't important, but it looks like Aethan has just given him a black eye.'

I slid further down into the chair and let my hair fall over the side of my face.

Grams let out a chuckle and elbowed me in the ribs. 'You were a late starter,' she whispered, 'but you seem to have it sorted out now.'

'That big, blond fellow is my son.' Bladimir held out his hand. 'Bladimir of Millenia.'

'Ahhhhh.' Arwyn nodded his head and looked at me again. 'That makes a bit more sense now.' He reached out and shook Bladimir's hand. 'Arwyn of Isilvitania. So you're responsible for the dragons. I hear your people saved the day. I thank you for that.'

Bladimir nodded his head. 'You are most welcome.'

Aethan and Turos appeared in the doorway. Grass and leaves clung to their clothes, bits of which were ripped. One of Turos's eyes was already swelling shut and both had broken skin on their knuckles. I couldn't be totally sure, because it was so messy, but it looked like Aethan was missing a clump of hair.

'Grab a chair boys.' Grams gestured to the lounge room as she said to me, 'And to think I always said this table was too big.'

They reappeared a few seconds later and wedged into the doorway, both trying to be the first into the kitchen. I slid even further down my chair.

Aethan managed to wiggle through first. 'Excuse me,' he said to Grams.

'Oh be my guest.' I didn't need to look at her to know she was grinning as she shuffled her chair over.

'Do you mind?' Turos said to Lionel.

'Not at all young man,' Lionel said in his huge, booming voice.

Both Aethan and Turos placed their chairs as close to me as possible. Their girths meaning their arms were touching mine.

'Awkward,' Grams stage-whispered in a sing-song voice.

There was no way I could sit here like this and discuss how we were going to win an unwinnable war. I need to be playing my A game, and at the moment I didn't even feel capable of an F.

'Right.' I stood up. 'That's quite enough. You,' I pointed at Turos, 'sit over there.'

Aethan let out a snort and I rounded on him. 'And you,' I pointed at him, 'sit over there.'

The two of them glared at each other as they shuffled around to sit at my three and nine.

I sat back down and turned my attention to Rako. 'Have you briefed King Arwyn on my situation?'

'Child, I don't *need* to know about your love life,' King Arwyn said.

I leant forwards and put my head on my hands while Grams chuckled and rubbed my back. 'Not *that* situation,' I said through my fingers.

'Isadora has been living in an alternate reality,' Rako said. 'King Bladimir was the monarch of that land.' He went on to explain where they had originally come from. 'That's as much as I know,' he said. 'I'm not sure why they have all returned.'

I sat back up as Bladimir explained about the pirates and how they had forced us to flee.

'I don't know if this is important,' I said. 'But it was Santanas. It seems that in that world he didn't get imprisoned in stone, but went on to rule.'

They were all silent for a while as they digested that bit of news.

Finally Rako said, 'I don't think it's going to affect the outcome of the next few days.' He turned to Bladimir, 'How much assistance are you willing to give us?'

Bladimir popped some cake into his mouth as he considered the question. 'Well, it appears, if we do not want to find ourselves in the same situation again, that we must support you whole-heartedly. My warriors are yours to command. We will need to ask the dragons if they will also help. They are our allies, not our pets.'

Turos got that faraway look in his eyes that meant he was talking to Lance. A second later he stiffened. His fingers gripped the chair arms and his nostrils flared. His blue eyes bored into mine, burning with a fire, an intensity that sent a jolt of electricity through me.

I sent my mind out to Emerald and instantly regretted it. Lust slammed into me like a high-speed train and it took every ounce of concentration not to leap over the table and take Turos to the floor. It appeared Emerald and Lance were having some 'alone' time.

Bladimir didn't seem to be having the same trouble with his dragon. I gripped the edge of the table with my fingers while I waited for the lust to fade away, but it didn't.

Finally, Bladimir's eyes refocused and he said, 'Reech will ask the others and they will hold a vote. Some of the dragons are busy, so he should have an answer in an hour or two.'

Against my will I met Turos's eyes. Emerald's emotions were so strong, her pleasure so great, I was having trouble severing the link I had created. An hour or two of this? I'd probably be pregnant by the time it was over.

'Water?' Grams handed me a glass.

I took it from her hand, using the coolness of the glass as a distraction. Condensation rolled down the outside, and suddenly I found myself remembering the way water droplets had danced on Turos's skin the day we had gone swimming together. I risked a glance up at him. His hands trembled where he gripped the chair and sweat had formed on his perfect brow. Aethan looking between the two of us, and I knew that that should make me feel something, but it didn't. My mind was too full of the want, of the need, of Turos.

I gripped the glass harder. Perhaps the water would be more affective if I tipped it over my head.

I lifted my hand and Isla appeared in the doorway, Mia curled around her neck.

'Izzy.' Her eyes studied my face, no doubt taking in my dilated pupils and shallow breathing. 'Some of the dragons need healing.'

The dragons! I leapt to my feet. Dark Sky. I had totally forgotten about them, what with passing out and chasing Galanta and now my problems with Turos and Aethan. It was no excuse though. They deserved better than that.

'I'm sorry.' I looked around the table. 'I need to go.' My eyes settled on Turos and I licked my lips.

'I'll come too.' Turos started to stand but Bladimir clamped a hand over his arm. 'No son, you will stay. Isadora will look after the dragons far better than you could.'

The muscles on Turos's face bulged as he clenched his teeth and for a second I thought he would disobey his father. I was toast for sure if he did. I wanted to use my teeth to rip off his clothes and my tongue to bathe him. Then he nodded stiffly and Aethan, who had also risen, relaxed back into his seat.

I dragged my gaze away from Turos and followed Isla from the room. Scruffy let out a sigh as he dragged *his* gaze from the lemon cake, and trotted after me.

'Looks like I got there in time to stop you making an idiot of yourself,' Isla said.

'Huh?' An image of Turos, stripping off his trousers and striding into the ocean, was taking up all my concentration. If I could only go back in time, I would make *much* better use of *that* situation.

Isla stopped, turned to face me, and slapped me hard on the cheek.

'Ooooowww.' I clutched my face. 'What was *that* for?'

'Trying to break you from your lust bubble.' A grin appeared on her face. 'I seem to be doing that a lot lately.'

'What are you....' I pulled a face. 'How did you know?'

'Lance and Emerald have been making cow eyes at each other since we got here. An hour ago they flew off, leaving Arthur in my care. I figured it could only mean one thing.'

'No, I mean how did you know about that?' I waved a hand back towards the house. 'About what happened to us?'

'I wasn't totally sure. It was just a hunch I had that Lance and Emerald's relationship might be influencing your and Turos's feelings for each other.'

I stopped walking and stared at her. She was the most astute person I knew. I shook my head and hurried to catch up. That was food for thought for a later time. I had work to do now.

We reached the top of the windy track down to the field below the house. Ahead, I could see Arthur. Well most of Arthur. He stood upright behind a large oak, but the bulge of his body and his tail stuck out on either side.

'What is he doing?' I asked.

Isla let out a little laugh and whispered. 'He's hiding from us.' She laughed again. 'He's so adorable. Pretend you can't see him.'

'Okaaaaay.'

We made heaps of noise as we progressed down the path. Just before we got to Arthur he leapt out from behind the tree, waving his front feet on either side of his head as he roared. We both let out terrified shrieks and Isla even went as far as to stumble backwards, landing on the ground with her legs up in the air.

Arthur let out a delighted gurgle and clapped his front feet together. Then he reached forwards and slapped Isla in the face with his huge tongue. When he had finished licking her, he grabbed the neck of her shirt with his teeth and lifted her back to her feet.

'You are so *naughty*,' she said, her huge smile belying her words. 'We had no idea you were there.'

Arthur let out another gurgle then turned, leapt into the air and floated down to the field. Little puffs of smoke came from his nose as he went.

Isla shook his head. 'I started playing peek-a-boo with him when he was in his egg. Now it's his favourite game.'

I shook my head and laughed as I followed her down the track. I wish a playful dragon was the top of my problem list.

It took us another five minutes to reach the injured dragons. I could see Sabby and her mother Grindella with some of the Guard healers.

'They can't get the metal out,' Isla said. 'They can heal all the other wounds, just not those ones.'

'So if I draw out the metal?'

She nodded. 'They should be able to finish the job.'

Well, that was a relief, because half of the dragons seemed to be in the injured area. I felt a flash of guilt. It was my fault they were hurt. If I had been stronger I could have held a bigger shield.

She punched me in the arm. 'You're such a glass-is-half-empty person.'

'What do you mean?'

'You're thinking about what you couldn't do. You should be thinking about what you did do. Without you, we'd all be dead.'

I tried to hang onto her words but the guilt still lingered. I shrugged my shoulders and strode towards the closest dragon. A particularly large surge of pleasure broke through the barrier I had erected against Emerald and I had an urge to run to Turos. I took a deep breath, squared my shoulders and placed my hands on the closest dragon.

A few moments later I felt the last of the metal balls make a sucking pop as it exited a wound. I rubbed a hand over the dragon's shiny scales and moved to the next patient.

It took the rest of the afternoon and most of the night to finish healing the dragons.

When the last one was done, I joined the other healers, flopping down with an exhausted sigh next to Sabby.

Somebody handed me a cup of broth and a chunk of bread. I looked up to see Sabby's Mum, Grindella. She looked as tired as I felt.

'You should be resting,' I said as I took the food she offered.

'I already rested. I had to stop healing a few hours ago.' She reached down and squeezed my arm before straightening back up. 'More mouths to feed.' She smiled and then turned and hurried away.

The smell of the broth assaulted my nostrils and my stomach roared in displeasure. I was suddenly, desperately hungry. I moaned as the salty broth cascaded over my taste buds. When I had finished I stood up and stretched. 'I'm going to bed.'

'Me too.' Sabby held her hand out to me.

I grabbed it and hauled her to her feet. She'd been healing all day, I didn't know how she was still able to stand.

Thomas appeared out of the shadows of the night, a sword strapped to his side. He gave Sabby a shy smile and the two of them began walking towards the village.

'I'll be your bed buddy tonight.' I hadn't even known Isla was still there.

'You don't trust me.'

She pulled a face. 'It's not *you* I don't trust. I don't want Aethan and Turos to have their next wrestling match on the floor of your bedroom.'

I let out a snort. Emerald and Lance had returned a few hours ago and I had my emotions back under control. 'Do you know what came of the War Council?'

'The rest of the army are nearly in place. We're heading out tomorrow morning to meet them.'

'Do we have a plan?'

She flashed me a grin. 'Of course we have a plan.'

'Care to expand on that?'

'And ruin all the fun?' Mia unravelled from Isla and scampered down her arm to jump over to me. She hissed down at Scruffy and then nestled into my neck, her small paws patting me as if to console me.

I sighed as I reached a hand up to smooth her pelt. 'Geographically speaking, the most tactical place for us to meet a force larger than us would be the Pass of Bones. Have the night faeries arrived?'

'No.' She pulled a face. 'Ebony says they are not far away.'

I batted down the flash of annoyance at hearing her name. 'They would have had to go around goblin territory. But still, they've had plenty of notice.'

'Apparently it takes a while to muster a full army.'

We passed a series of huge marquees that had been set up to accommodate the now homeless Milleniums. A woman sitting with her back against the wall of one of them looked up as we passed. She bowed her head to me and pressed the back of her hand to her forehead. I smiled and nodded my head woodenly. 'I'm never going to get used to that,' I said.

'You need to."

'Why?'

She quirked her head to the side and looked at me. 'Wow. You haven't worked it out yet have you?'

'Obviously not.'

'Whichever choice you make, you will end up a Queen.'

Her words took my breath away. 'But, I don't want to be a Queen,' I spluttered.

'Well, maybe you should stop making out with the heirs to the thrones.'

She had a point.

'I can't help it.' I raised both my hands in the air.

'You're going to have to choose.'

'I know, I know.' We reached the bottom of the track leading up to my house. 'It's just....'

'You're having too much fun?'

'No. Not at all.' I was appalled that she thought I was doing this for my own amusement. 'The thing is...,' I paused while I struggled to capture the vastness of my emotions and shape them into the two-dimensionality of words. 'All my life it's been Aethan.'

'But now there's Ebony.'

'Yes. But, even pretending she doesn't exist.' I stopped and turned to face her. 'I love him. You know that. But this Aethan...well, we don't have the depth, the history we should. When Galanta stole his memories, she stole our relationship. What we have now is new.'

Isla nodded as she understood. 'So what you feel for Turos, and what you feel for this Aethan is equivalent.'

I nodded, relieved she got it. 'I miss him so much.' Tears welled in my eyes. 'He was my best friend.'

'He's still there.' She grimaced. 'Well, forgetting about the whole betrothed thing.'

'It's not the same.' I started walking again. 'Don't get me wrong, I still love him. But it's like I'm loving a shadow of him, of what we had.' We walked for a while, negotiating the bumpy path in the dark. 'It's like part of him died.'

'Just as he shaped the woman you are today, you shaped the man he was. That part, the part that was because of you, it's gone.' She reached out and clasped my hand. 'It doesn't mean you can't recreate the depth in your relationship. If there was a reason to.' She shook her head slowly as if she doubted that was a possibility, and I knew what she was thinking of. *Who* she was thinking of. 'At least you've got a fall back.' She pulled a face as if to soften her words.

I felt stupidly selfish. The love of her life was off in servitude to a Goddess, and I was moaning about the hardship of having to choose between two amazing men.

'You'll see him again.' I squeezed her hand. 'You know that, right?'

She turned to face me and I could see the tears in her eyes glinting in the light of the moon. 'I know I will. I feel it here.' She beat her fist against her chest. 'And I have faith.' She nodded slowly, the wisdom of her years showing on her perfect face. 'She will return him when we need him the most.' She glanced towards the moon, a beatific look settling into a peaceful mask.

We stood like that for a while. Two friends, admiring the beauty of the moon, and hoping that we would still be here to admire it, when all was said and done.

***

I woke with a soft hand on my shoulder and a heavy lump on my chest. It turned out that the hand belonged to Isla and the lump was Scruffy. He licked my face as I opened my eyes.

I could hear a drum beat, echoing in the distance. 'Goblins? Really?' I blinked my eyes a few times and then said, 'Eric, lights please.'

The house responded by flicking on my lights.

Isla sat beside me, her long black hair tousled from sleep. 'What is she up to?' she murmured.

Mia sat up from where she was pressed against my side and shook herself.

'I never know.' I shrugged my shoulders. 'She's far too clever for me.'

Isla held her hand out to Mia and the little monster climbed over me to scramble up her arm. She let out a laugh as Mia's tongue found her cheek. 'Tickles,' she said before turning her attention back to me. 'The chess game is not won till the King is in checkmate.'

'I don't play chess.'

'Well, that's something we are going to have to fix in the future.'

A possibility of a life where there was no urgency, no need to be constantly thinking of the next attack, the next assault, came to me. I realised that there were voids in history. Times when there had been decades, no *centuries*, where the most dramatic thing to happen was a feud between two neighbours. Suddenly, the idea of being able to play a lazy game of chess was appealing.

But that time was not now.

I jumped out of bed and pulled on my fighting leathers, slapping my blades into their holsters and strapping my sword to my waist. *Emerald?*

Coming now.

I got a mental image of her, Lance and Arthur waiting for us in the field.

'Let's end this,' I said to Isla, 'before it begins.'

'My type of fight.' She grinned and hefted a bow and quiver bristling with arrows onto her shoulder.

Mum and Radismus were already in the kitchen. I couldn't help but notice Mum's nightie. Lace and skin were a predominant feature that had been lacking in her old one. I squished that thought before it could mentally scar me, and said, 'What are you doing?'

'We heard the drums.' Fear trembled in her voice.

Radismus grasped her hands. 'There now love, Izzy won't let anything happen to us.' He looked at me as if to reassure himself that that was true.

Mum pulled herself up, as if she should be the one protecting me.

'Hey.' I pulled her into my arms. 'Don't worry. I've got this.'

Isla let out a polite cough.

'Fine.' I rolled my eyes at her. '*We've* got this.'

Grams burst out of her wing of the house with Lionel right behind her. She was dressed in full camouflage gear, including her black balaclava. His striped pyjamas looked ludicrous with a sword buckled to his waist.

'Oh good.' Grams slid to a stop next to Mum. 'I thought we'd missed you.'

I let out a sigh. There would be no stopping them, and Grams had proved herself to be quite valuable in our earlier staged attacks on the field.

Banging on the door turned out to be Turos and Aethan, both with their fists raised as if competing to see who could knock the loudest.

'Rako's rallying forces down at the field,' Aethan said.

'The dragons are ready to go,' Turos said at the same time.

'Men.' Isla muttered as she shook her head.

'You're confident on Arthur?' I asked her.

She nodded, a grin spreading over her face. I knew how much she enjoyed flying.

'Grams, you and Lionel go with Turos. Aethan, you're with me.' I ignored Turos's scowl and Aethan's triumphant smile. I didn't have time for that at the moment. 'Let's go.' I hugged Mum and followed Turos and Aethan back out the door.

Our dragons were crowded onto our front lawn. We climbed onto them, even Grams scurrying up with surprising ease, and within a few seconds we were landing in the field where Rako was giving orders.

'Do we know what we're dealing with?' I asked him.

'Goblins. Lots of them.'

There was only one reason they would be attacking here. To stop us joining the rest of our forces.

'Want us to fly a reconnaissance?'

'Can you see well enough?'

I looked over at Aethan. 'He can.' I jabbed a thumb at him. 'And I can see what Emerald sees.'

'We can see as well,' Turos said, pointing between himself and Lance.

'And we can provide cover.' Grams was bouncing up and down on her toes.

Rako nodded. 'Fine. But no risky moves. I don't want you engaging the enemy.'

'What if they need to be engaged?' I said. 'If our engaging them would bite the head off the snake, so to speak.'

Rako squeezed the bridge of his nose. 'Don't do anything risky.' The six of us burst out laughing and the corners of Rako's mouth curled up. 'Fine,' he said, 'don't do anything ridiculously risky.'

The drums' beat pulsed in the cool night air. Wherever they were, they were getting closer.

We started to lift off when I remembered the cave the night before. *Stop.*

Emerald cut her wings and her legs flexed as she absorbed the force of us landing again. *What?*

I didn't answer. Instead I slid off her neck and trotted back to Rako. 'It's a trap.' It was the only thing that made sense. Always before I had fallen for her subtle manipulations, danced to her tune. But not this time.

'You're sure?'

I nodded.

He didn't question me. He just stared into my eyes for a second and then said, 'Well, you know her the best.'

When she had stolen Aethan's memories, she had kidnapped him and used a shield to manipulate the final battleground, the final players. Then she had done the same with poor Orion. Last night she had led us into a snare-filled cave. I was one hundred percent sure, that this was her attempt to control the final battle. But it wasn't happening tonight. Of that much I was also sure.

Turos strolled over to us, his long, muscular legs eating up the ground between Lance and us with ease. I tried not to think about what those legs would feel like wrapped around my body, holding me down onto the length of him. I was only partially successful and I could feel my face flush red.

'It's a trap,' I said before he could ask anything.

'What do you suggest?' Rako asked.

'We continue as planned. But we do it now.'

He nodded his head and turned away from me, whistling a high-pitched tune. The Border Guard call to arms.

Aethan hurried off in the direction of the Guard and Turos winked at me before he and Lance disappeared toward the Millenium.

It only took Isla, Grams, Lionel and me moments to get back up to the house, but Mum was already dressed. Lionel slipped off to his and Gram's quarters and returned a few minutes later clad in battle gear. Grams was opting to stick with her camouflage outfit. I suppressed a grin. It was nice that some things hadn't changed.

Sabby, Grindella and Thomas arrived not long afterwards.

'We're leaving now,' I informed them.

Sabby nodded, not at all surprised, and Thomas rested his hand on his sword as if he were readying himself to protect her.

'Did Turos get time to...?' I nodded my head at his hand.

'A little. I get the theory but I'm having trouble with the practical.'

'Well, you're doing better than I did,' I said. 'It took me ages to understand the theory.'

'She's a slow study.' Isla shuffled her arrows around in her quiver, making sure they would all pull out smoothly when she needed them. She patted her head, checking her braid was secure, then ran her hands over her fighting leathers, making sure her daggers were where they were meant to be.

I followed her example, slipping my fingers over the familiar feel of the steel blades strapped to my biceps and thighs.

There was one last thing I had to do and my heart squeezed at the thought. A war was no place for familiars. They were too easy a target, and if they were killed, the witches' powers would be neutralised. Some familiars would go. The small ones that were easily concealed on one's body. The rodents and insects. But the rest would be taken by relatives to be kept safe until the witch returned. *If* the witch returned.

Scruffy stared up at me with huge golden eyes. He stood on his hind legs and scratched at my knees with his front paws. I reached down and scooped him up, cradling him in my arms while I scratched his head. I pressed my face into his fur, breathing in his doggy smell. 'Stay with Mum,' I whispered. 'I need to know you are safe.'

'Mum.' I held Scruffy out, blinking back stupid tears as she took him from me. 'You and Radismus are to go with the civilians.' We already knew that that was the plan. That Mum and Radismus's job was to lead the civilians to London, to the barracks there. But saying it made me feel better. As if I could assure her safety by the will of my words.

Tears stood in her eyes but she nodded in acquiescence. Her magic didn't extend to anything that was going to help us this night. Nor the next few days. And I didn't want her anywhere near Santanas.

'Grindella,' I turned to Sabby's Mum, 'will you go with them? They'll need healers in case....' I didn't finish the sentence. Didn't want to think about the finish of the sentence.

Her eyes were huge and wise as she nodded her head. She turned to Sabby and held out her arms. 'Give Phantom to me,' she said. 'I'll keep him safe till you return.' Tears trembled on her lashes as she looked at her daughter.

Sabby bent and picked up her huge, black cat. She shushed him as he struggled in her arms. 'It's for the best,' she whispered. She buried her face in his fur, holding onto him as if she couldn't bear to let him go, then she took a deep breath and passed him to her Mum.

Thomas's arm crept around her shoulders and she sagged against him.

Grams unwrapped Cyril from around her shoulders. Mum took the huge python, bowing a little under his weight. He didn't look happy as he took up residence over her shoulders.

'Here.' Isla reached up and unwound Mia from her neck. She held her out to Radismus. 'Will you protect her? Where we are going is no place for her. We need to keep her safe till we can find her baby.'

At those words Mia stopped struggling. She let out a forlorn mew, and then jumped to Radismus, her body trembled as she tucked herself in against his throat.

'I'll keep her safe.' Radismus put his arm around Mum's shoulders and lifted his chin. 'I'll keep them all safe.'

'I know you will.' I had no doubt that he would fight to the death to protect them.

I hugged Mum tight, trying to pretend that that might not be the final time I got to feel the warmth of her body.

She wrapped her free arm around me, then kissed me on the cheek and pulled back till she was holding me at arm's length. 'Make me proud.'

'Have I ever not?'

'Well, there was that time....' She stopped and smiled at me, and I knew it was time to go.

A piece of my heart splintered off as I turned and walked away.

The goblin drums echoed through the night, their pace increasing, a call to action. I steeled myself to ignore it. For once, I was going to move in the opposite direction, I was no longer willing to dance to the beat of *her* drums.

***

The Guard had assembled by the time we returned to the field. The Millenium fighters scattered amongst them. Turos stood at the front, towering above them and I could see the dragons in the distance. I let out a sigh of relief. So they had agreed to help us.

The dragon handlers were busy strapping on the leather harnesses that would allow multiple people to fly at once. The Millenium civilians were filing up the path towards my house where Mum and Radismus were waiting to lead them to safety. Some of them stayed, their axes and swords clutched in their hands.

I walked over to Turos and nodded my head towards a particularly brawny looking man.

'That's the blacksmith,' Turos said.

'He's fighting?'

'Can't take away a man's right to protect his family.'

As if his word had summoned them, a group of men from Eynsford strode towards us over the field. I recognised Rowan, the Publican of The Toasted Toadstool, in the lead.

'Izzy.' He nodded his head and then turned towards Rako as he waited for the briefing.

'Right,' Rako said. 'We need to meet up with the rest of the army. And we're not going to walk. We're going to fly. Nothing else to say. Saddle up.' He crossed his arms across his chest as he waited for everyone to obey him.

Aethan appeared by my side and I smiled at him. If only Wilfred were here it would be just like old times. Except Aethan couldn't remember the old times. I stifled a sigh. Now was not the time to dwell on that.

I climbed up on Emerald's neck and waited for Grams, Lionel and more of the Border Guard to fill up Emerald's harness. Aethan climbed up, sitting snugly behind me. I could feel the warmth of his legs running alongside mine.

'Everyone grab a bridle and grip with your knees.'

Beginners. Emerald's sigh held resignation.

Lance was the first to take off, but I urged Emerald to catch up with him. He was going to need me to open up the veil. I waved an arm at Turos and saw his grin slip off his face as his eyes flicked to Aethan. I thought he was going to protest, but instead he pulled Lance back, letting Emerald take the lead. I concentrated on the feel of the veil draped over me, hoping I would be able to open it from the air. I had only ever done it a couple of times, but I figured opening a gate from an alternate universe had to be harder than this. For once, I was right.

I grasped the edges of the veil and pulled it back, the vista of Isilvitania spreading out before me. The castle was still, a silent reminder of the people that had gone to do battle with the foe.

'Is anybody still there?' I asked.

Aethan leant forwards far enough that his chest pressed against my back. I vetoed the thoughts that began dancing through my mind. Now was *not* the time to be enjoying the feel of that so much. Especially not with Turos watching like a hawk. I didn't need the two of them at each other's throats continuously.

'No. Mother and her entourage have fled to London.'

'And...,' I really didn't want to say her name, 'Ebony?'

'She has insisted she will fight. Which is ludicrous.' He let out a hard laugh. 'But she is right in the fact that we need her to be there when the night faeries finally turn up. She has gone ahead with the rest of the Guard and the human and witch army.'

I took a deep breath and dispelled the image of Ebony's perfection from my mind. I hadn't looked in a mirror for over twenty-four hours, and during that time I had flown through a storm, fought with other-world

Santanas, battled the Vulpines and the goblins, healed dragons, and slept. There was no *way* what was happening with my head at that moment was pretty.

'Where is the army?'

'At the Pass of Bones.'

The Pass of Bones was on the western border of Isilvitania. The Black Mountains and the Mountains of Doom ran together into a V, culminating at the pass. If the goblins had mustered down near the ogres' land, this would have been the only way they could come. This boded well, as the only thing stopping them from coming around the east side of the mountain ranges was the dark faeries.

I nodded. 'Perhaps that's why the dark faeries are taking their time. Because they are making sure they have to come through the pass to get to us.'

'That's what Ebony says.'

I wiggled around a little so that I could see the look on his face. I studied his expression and then said, 'But you're not so sure.'

He shrugged a shoulder. 'I'll believe it when I see it.' He was harder than he had been. Losing Orion had made him so. It saddened me and pleased me at the same time. I wished we could remain innocent, but we needed to be strong and hard if we were to have any chance of winning this war.

We didn't talk through the rest of the flight. I'm not sure what he was thinking about but I was picturing the goblin forces marching towards that pass and wondering how we were going to defeat a man that couldn't be killed.

***

Two mountain ranges loomed in front of us. The small slice of air that separated them was just visible in the early-dawn light. Fires flickered in the distance, spread out across the land like a sea of twinkling lights. Close enough to The Pass of Bones that we could defend it, yet far enough away that the camp was not immediately vulnerable. A twist in the land meant a rise hid the camp from view from the pass, and our attackers would have a ground disadvantage if we were forced back.

Guards from all around the world had come to join us, their numbers had swelled the ranks of the humans and witches.

'Rako said the training has been going well.' My voice was rough from not talking.

'Yes.' Aethan cleared his throat. 'General Tamsonite has taken control.'

'He's the head of the witch army, right?'

He nodded his head. 'And General Robertson is the head of the human army, but Tamsonite has overall command.'

The Border Guard was responsible for just that – guarding the border between the land of the Fae and that of the witches and humans. The English human-witch army was much more extensive, and used mainly in peace keeping amongst the nations.

'So, no other countries came?'

I felt Aethan move and turned to see him shaking his head.

'I suspect they're sitting back to see how this plays out.'

'Hoping we can handle it?'

'And possibly thinking about a land grab if we can't.'

That was a sombre thought. 'How can they not see that this is a threat to **ALL** of us?'

'People see what they want to see.'

I turned to look at him again, squinting suspiciously. Had there been a double meaning in that? The look on his face was pure innocence. I opened my mouth to retaliate, sighed, and then closed it again.

As we flew closer, I could make out the tents; black pyramids in the pre-dawn light. Horses stood picketed at different points, spread throughout the camp with the wagons. No need to put the supplies in one area to make it easier for the enemy to disable us.

Occasionally an ant-sized soldier could be seen, stirring pots over fires as they started the morning ritual of breakfast. Soon the rest of the soldiers would emerge and start to break up the camp. I knew we had an army, but I was gobsmacked by the size of it. Even though we were about to fly over the start of it, it disappeared into the distance.

Shouts echoed up to us and some of the soldiers on the ground began to point. I saw a few lift their bows towards us and pull back to release arrows. They paused, knowing we were too high for their arrows to do us any harm, but soon we would need to land, and then we wouldn't be so safe.

Whizbang. I hadn't even considered that they would think we were the enemy.

'Can you shield us?'

I gave him a look over my shoulder that should have made him burst into flames.

'Fine.' He rolled his eyes. 'Get Emerald to tell the others to go high. We'll land and let HQ know we're friendlies.'

I opened up my mind to Emerald and felt languid satisfaction rolling off her. Apparently last night had been more satisfying for her than it had been for me.

Already done, she said, her voice a smug sing-song.

I turned to watch the other dragons peel off and start circling upwards.

'There's the headquarters.' Aethan pointed past me to a circle of tents larger than the rest.

I wrapped a shield around us as Emerald headed for the tents.

'Helloooooo,' Grams hollered from behind me. 'Helloooo there. Oh, buzznuckle.'

'Now Bella.' I could hear Lionel's voice even at his normal tone. 'There's no need for foul language.'

'But Lionel, that was my favourite balaclava. Oh look. It's stopped.'

I heard Aethan snort, and looked down to see Gram's black balaclava sitting on my shield.

'Let me guess,' I said to Aethan. 'She was waving it at the soldiers.'

'Something like that.'

It only took us another minute to reach our destination. By then the soldiers had realised we had a shield in place and stopped shooting. Now a circle of them had drawn up around the command tents, their swords drawn, shields ready.

I'm almost tempted to fry the tents just to show them how useless that is.

Shhhhhhhh. I admonished Emerald. *They're just doing their jobs.*

She huffed out a puff of steam as the wind from her wings caused the flaps of the tents to dance in a flurry. A maelstrom of dirt swirled up into a cloud which hovered over the command post.

Dust swirled and a few tents started to collapse at the down draft we were causing. A man pushed open the flap to the largest tent, his arm held up to shield his face from flying shrapnel.

Emerald landed gracefully and folded her wings back by her sides, amusement at the mayhem she had caused brushed against my mind and I smiled in response.

Aethan leapt nimbly from her back. 'General Tamsonite,' he said.

'Prince Aethan.' He looked from Aethan to Emerald and back again. 'I see a lot has happened since we left.'

I slid down to Emerald's raised front leg. She lowered me gently and I felt that brush of amusement again. I shook my head, hid my smile and walked over to stand next to Aethan.

'Is this her?' the General said. He looked me up and down a few times. 'I thought she'd be more impressive looking. Are you sure she's up to it?'

I could feel my eyebrows rising up my forehead and I could tell Aethan was fighting a smile which only made me madder.

'I am sure she will do what needs to be done,' he said.

General Tamsonite looked back at me and nodded his head. 'Welcome Isadora Gabrielle. It is good to finally meet you.'

'Thank you,' I said.

'Athol? Is that you?' Grams pushed past me.

'Bella?' General Tamsonite blinked a few times. 'Bella?' He said again, his stony face breaking out into a huge grin. I was surprised that cracks didn't fissure across his cheeks. 'I thought you were dead.' He held his arms wide and laughed.

'Dead smed.' Grams let out a girly laugh. 'I didn't recognise you with that moustache. It's magnificent.' She trotted over to General Tamsonite and threw herself into his arms. Her black balaclava was safely tucked into the waist of her camouflage pants. 'And you're a General now too.'

It took me a few seconds to realise that the gravelly-rumbling noise that accompanied the hug was Lionel clearing his throat.

'Oh.' Grams stepped back, adjusting her uniform into place. Her cheeks held colour that hadn't been there before. 'Athol this is Sir Lionel Heartfelt.'

'Her fiancé.' Lionel emphasised the word as he held out his hand.

'Pleased to meet you.'

I suspected by the strained looks on their faces that they were both giving that handshake everything that they had.

'Aethan. Oh Aethan.'

Even though I hadn't heard it for a while, I recognised Ebony's bell-like voice.

She pushed out of the tent next to command, a vision in a pale-blue riding dress. Her dark hair flowed down her back in soft waves. Her sea-green eyes glowed with joy as they fixed on Aethan's face.

My hand went to my own hair without my permission. I snatched it back down again. I refused to apologise for how I looked. Even if there *was* still goblin blood in my hair.

She moved with a fae grace I hadn't inherited as she rushed towards Aethan and threw herself at him. 'I've been so worried. I thought, I thought....' She dashed the back of her hand across her eyes. 'Oh, it doesn't matter what I thought. You're here now.'

I resisted the urge to blast them with a lightning bolt as she pressed herself against him.

She pulled away and smoothed her riding dress down as if worrying she might have creased it. I couldn't stop the snort that escaped me. As if she ever looked anything but perfect.

'Isadora?' She spun towards me. 'Oh Darling, you found her.' She sounded genuinely pleased as she linked her arm through Aethan's and stared up at him. Her face melted into gooeyness for a second before she released him and stepped towards me, wrapping me in a hug.

Darling? The glare I gave Aethan over her shoulder drove him back a few paces.

Good. He deserved to be scared.

I dropped the glare and pasted a saccharine look on my face, smiling sweetly at her as she released me.

'Aethan said you might want to paint my nails one day.' She held her hands out in front of her face. 'Could you help me with them tonight?'

Aethan took a few more steps back, no doubt getting out of immediate range of my left hook.

'Ahhh, Ebony,' Aethan said. 'Izzy will be too busy for the next few days to paint your nails.'

'Shame.' She pushed her bottom lip out. The manoeuvre made her look even more kissable. 'Oh well. After Daddy gets here to save the day we'll have plenty of time for things like that.'

It was possible she had gotten even more annoying. I imagined Aethan having to put up with her airy prattle for the rest of his life and this time my smile was genuine.

'Sir.' Aethan seemed to be trying to pretend neither of us were there. 'We have a contingent of dragons circling a few miles from here. We also have the rest of the Guard, some civilian fighters and the dragon riders.'

General Tamsonite considered the unasked question for a few seconds, bushy, black eyebrows drawn together in concentration. 'They can land on our training ground. It's about a half mile north of here. Send the soldiers to the supply carts to the south west of the field to get tents and supplies.'

I opened my mind to Emerald. *Did you hear that?*
Yes.

A warm tingle that created a blush on my cheeks flowed back to me through our mental link. She was talking to Lance. I la-la'd in my head, trying to ignore the emotion unfurling in my stomach. Even then, I found myself anticipating Turos's arrival far too much.

A few minutes later the dragons came into view.

'Won't the soldiers try and shoot them?' Grams beat me to the question.

'Yes, we should prevent that if we can.' Tamsonite grinned at her and turned to the soldier standing to attention at the entry to his command tent. 'Roger. Sound the stand-down please.'

Roger saluted, whipped a bugle from his belt, put it to his lips and blew out an ear-piercing trill of notes. It echoed out into the dawn air, and soldiers that were starting to ready their bows immediately relaxed.

Lance led the contingent of dragons, his massive black body sparkling in the first rays of sunshine. My heart surged as I recognised Turos on his neck. Arthur flapped by his side, beating fast to keep up with his father's lazy strokes.

Emerald let out a rumble of pleasure as she saw her family drawing near. *Coming?* she asked.

I answered her by turning and trotting towards her. Within a few seconds we were on our way, both of us keen to catch up with the rest of the dragons – or with one dragon in particular.

Emerald sailed towards the group, leading them to the field General Tamsonite had mentioned. But she didn't land. She and Lance stayed aloft while the others touched down and then she turned and flew west away from the camp.

Where are we going?

I saw a meadow in the forest a few miles back. It was full of wild flowers.

Pretty.

Pretty secluded.

I liked the sound of that. A lot.

Emerald landed first and I dismounted, standing with my back leaning against her front leg.

Lance landed a few moments later. Turos swung down from Lance's neck and strode towards me. I smiled up at him, feeling shy for the first time since I'd met him.

He stopped a foot from me, his eyes searching my face. I reached out and took his hand. The callouses on his palm grated deliciously against mine as I rubbed them together. He shivered and pulled me along beside him as we walked to the nearby stand of trees. We didn't talk, an energy building between us as the shadows of the trees fell over us. He stopped and turned to face me, pushing me gently backward against a tree trunk.

I could feel the heat between our bodies, and was struck with a powerful need to be even closer. To remove the restraints our clothes were causing and to take his body with mine. Instead, I took his hand again, tracing my thumb back and forth over his skin.

'I didn't like seeing him that close to you.' He reached out his free hand and traced my bottom lip with his fingertips. 'To see him touching you.'

His hand moved to my cheek and down to my neck, his fingers leaving a trail of fire in their wake. I sighed and closed my eyes as they ran along my collar bone.

His fingers moved down my side to my waist and I let go of his other hand so that it could join its twin there. He plucked at the edge of my shirt and then suddenly both of his hands were on the soft skin of my stomach. I sucked in a sharp breath and arched toward him, urging his hands higher. He didn't disappoint.

I gasped as they grazed over the peaks of my breasts. Fire erupted in my veins and I grabbed the back of his neck with my hands and pulled his head down to mine. I bit down on his bottom lip as his hands found my breasts again. This time they stayed there, kneading the softness, rubbing over the hard peaks pressing into them through my bra. I bucked against him and wrapped a leg around his, leaning my hips into him. I moaned against his mouth, caressing his lips with mine.

Stars exploded in my head as his hands made their way under my bra, the calloused skin of his palms grazing over my erect nipples.

Dark Sky. I needed him. I needed him so badly I couldn't breathe. I needed him more than air, more than life itself. I would give anything to feel his body pressing me down underneath him. To feel the long length of his legs intertwined with mine. To feel him entering me and moving inside me.

I gasped and pushed against him, feeling the hardness of him pushing through his pants into my groin. He was so close. So close. All I had to do was....

'Ahh, Izzy.' Isla's voice intruded.

I shook my head and ignored her, revelling in the sensations he was creating within me. I kissed him deeper, grabbing his buttocks with my hands and urging him to press even harder into me. He broke the kiss and moved his mouth along my jaw and down my neck.

Oh boy, I hoped those lips were heading where I thought they were heading.

'Izzy.' Isla's voice was harder. More insistent.

His mouth was exploring the edges of my shirt, and one hand was working its way back down my stomach to the edge of my pants. The tips of his finger teased the skin under my waistband.

'Yes,' I moaned, lifting up on my toes so that his mouth was closer to my breast.

He chuckled. 'My little hell cat.' He pulled my shirt up and licked one of my nipples.

I let out a yelp and jammed his head against my chest as I raked at his hair with my hands. He licked my nipple again and then drew it into his mouth, sucking on it gently. A thousand nerves fired in an arc, radiating out over my body. It was exquisite.

I fumbled for the front of his pants, wanting to pleasure him as much as he was me. He moaned as my hand brushed over the top of his mound and suddenly I was desperate to take him in my hand. To stroke the velvety length of him.

'Don't say you didn't ask for this.'

Cold water cascaded over my head. I let out a shriek and opened my eyes, blinking in the early light of the day. The time-lust continuum I had been in disappeared and suddenly Turos and I weren't the only people in the world.

'Sorry.' Isla smiled ruefully and gestured behind her.

I could see Emerald and Lance through the trees. They were pressed up against each other. Their tails were entwined and one of Lance's wings was wrapped over Emerald's back. Her head was thrown back, her eyes closed as he bit her on the neck. He let out a low rumble, a dissatisfied animal wanting more. She shook her head and leant into him.

'Oh no.' I batted Turos's hands away from me, feeling a strange mixture of relief and disappointment when he let go. Part of me wanted to ride him to the ground and have my wicked way. The other part wanted to get as far from him as possible.

Lance snorted again and jostled Emerald, working his wing further over her back. She wiggled her haunch and urged him on. Dark Sky. If he mounted her. If he took her this close to Turos and me, I didn't know if we would be able to stop ourselves. Already my relief was fading away leaving only a desperate need for Turos.

'Izzy.' His voice was a low growl as he clasped my buttocks with both hands. 'Izzy.' He bent his head to my neck and nipped at the soft skin there.

We could stagger further into the trees, find some soft ground there and I could magic away our clothes. It would be faster that way. We could get straight to where we needed to be, him biting into my neck as he rode me like an animal.

No. I shook my head from side-to-side. I didn't want this. I didn't. I think. It was hard to see clearly through the fog of desire. Maybe I did. Maybe this *was* me. I mean his hands on me felt wonderful. Felt right.

'Fight it Izzy.'

I sucked in a deep breath, pushed him off me and turned away. He let out a growl and grabbed me from behind, pulling me back against him and wrapping his arms around me. I could feel his manhood pressing into my buttocks and suddenly I wanted it like that. On all fours.

I groaned as his hands found their way back up under my shirt, back to where they belonged on my breasts. He growled again and bit down on the back of my neck. I pushed my bottom into him, wriggling it against his hard bulge. He panted, his hands moving down to unbutton my pants.

Oh, yes. Yes. He was going to take me here. Like this. I nearly cried with the knowledge. The deliciousness of the thought of him entering me. Of sliding into me. Of pinning me against him as he did.

He let out a snarl as he wrestled with my button. A sound of feral need and desperation that matched the sounds coming out of my own throat. I needed him. I needed him now. I would go mad if I didn't have him.

Air hit the bare skin of my buttocks and his hands left me for a second as he wrestled with his own pants. His breath came in desperate rasps, and I was reaching back to find him when there was a sound similar to something hard smacking into a coconut.

Panting, I spun. He wasn't there.

Well, he was. He just wasn't standing. And he didn't appear to be conscious.

'What?' I panted a few more times, the lust leaving me like an out-going tide.

'It was the only thing I could think of.' Isla stood over him, a small branch in her hands. 'I hope I didn't hurt him too much.'

Emerald let out a bellow and I tried to avert my eyes, the view of Lance mounting her far too confrontational. But I couldn't. I could still feel it. Even though Turos was no longer pleasuring me, I was still a part of their mating ritual.

I pulled my pants back up and re-secured them, disappointment curling in my groin. I could feel Emerald's ultimate pleasure mounting. Feel her getting close to her release. And I wanted it too. I wanted my mind to be soaring toward the sun, my eyes rolling back as wave-after-wave of intense sensation rocked through me.

Lance let out a roar and flapped his wings, using the momentum to surge him forwards again-and-again. Emerald's cries matched his, each roar bellowing out around the forest. And then, a bolt of lightning rocked through me as Emerald threw back her head and let out a scream of pure, unadulterated pleasure.

Turos jerked on the ground as Lance echoed her cry. His pale-blue eyes snapped open, burning into mine. He held my gaze as the glory of their love flowed through us, both of us rocking in time with our dragons. As the last vestiges of their climaxes echoed away he said, 'You've got to admit, that would have been incredible.'

***

'Thank you.' They were the first words I had spoken since we had left the meadow half an hour ago. Now we were gathered in a loose circle around the fire near the command tent, sharpening our swords and checking our bows.

'So…you're not upset I stopped you?' Isla pulled a face and gestured towards Turos.

A bruise was starting to blossom on the side of his face. I hadn't healed him. Hadn't trusted myself to put my hands on him in case we had decided to finish off what we had started. As it was, sexual frustration was my number one emotion, but that wasn't enough for me to want to lose my virginity. Not like that. I had to know it meant something more than just raw, animal lust.

As if he knew we were talking about him, he glanced over, his eyes pinning me in place with promises of what he could do to me.

'He looks pretty frustrated.'

She was right. He did. His spiky, pale hair was even more ruffled than normal, evidence of where my fingers had curled into it, urging him on.

'I know how he feels.'

'Oh, you *are* upset with me.'

I glanced over at Aethan. He was sitting on the far side of the circle, a brooding look on his face as he glanced between Turos and me.

I let out a sigh. 'No. I'm not. I would have regretted it. After it was over.'

'I'm not sure if you would have. You looked like you were enjoying yourself. A lot.' She grinned at me and pulled another arrow out of her quiver, looking down its length before placing it in a neat pile beside her.

'What would you have regretted?' Sabby looked up from where she lay on the grass next to me.

'Oh nothing.' I pulled a face and looked toward where Thomas sat next to her. I really didn't want him overhearing that conversation.

'Oh.' She nodded wisely and closed her eyes again, no doubt making plans to pin me down for more information once we were alone.

The army around us also readied itself for the coming battle. Incoming scout reports informed us that the enemy army was still stationary on the far side of the Pass of Bones. It didn't make sense. Why would they wait while we fortified our position? My skin itched whenever I thought about it, and I was thinking about it often.

I ripped at a piece of jerky with my teeth, working it around my mouth as I tried to get enough moisture into the dried meat to allow me to swallow it. The mundane action made me miss Scruffy. If he were here he would be pawing at my leg, his eyes huge as he begged me for my share of breakfast as well as his own.

'You need to keep your strength up.' Isla handed me another piece of the hard meat.

Grams let out a laugh from the other side of the camp, beating at her leg with her hand as she chortled. Tamsonite was regaling her with a story and Lionel didn't look that pleased about it.

Isla glanced over to Grams and I stuffed the jerky into my pocket. I didn't need food. I needed sex. And lots of it. But since I wasn't going to get that I would have to get rid of my excess energy another way.

I stood up and stretched my arms above my head. Then I bent forwards and touched my toes. Perhaps I should go for a run. I hadn't done that for a while.

Before I could suggest it though, Lionel hopped to his feet. 'Izzy has the right idea. I haven't swung a sword in a while. Anyone care to train with me?'

Not surprisingly it was Tamsonite who sprung to his feet. 'I'd be delighted old chap.'

Lionel's face hardened at Tamsonite's use of the word old. He walked over to a pile of training weapons and grabbed a wooden sword, waving it from side-to-side as he warmed up his muscles.

'This should be interesting,' Isla murmured. She looked down the shaft of the last arrow in her quiver and nodded her head.

Grams clapped her hands together and said, 'You two behave yourselves. Athol, if you break any of Lionel's bones you'll have me to answer to.'

Lionel's face was a mixture of pleasure that Grams was siding with him and pain that she obviously thought

Tamsonite was better than him. He shook his head and shrugged his shoulders and then moved into an en garde position.

'Ready old man?' Tamsonite mimicked his position.

Rather than answering him, Lionel swept his sword in an arc toward him. Tamsonite blocked it, and the fight began.

'Turos,' I said, 'maybe you could continue your training with Thomas and some of the others.'

Thomas jumped to his feet. 'That would be awesome.'

Turos nodded and climbed to his feet. 'Grab a wooden sword,' he said.

I winced on Thomas's behalf. I knew from first-hand experience that that lesson was going to hurt.

'I think they may be an even match,' Isla said, pointing her sword toward Lionel and Tamsonite. She looked down its gleaming length and then took the sharpening stone to an almost invisible nick on its surface.

I sat down and picked my sword back up. She was right. Lionel was holding his own as he dodged, parried and attacked. He held his wand in his left hand and every few seconds he would flick it at Tamsonite. Tamsonite would respond with a flurry of his own wand.

'Impressive,' Sabby said, putting an arm behind her head. 'Duelling and sword fighting at the same time.

It *was* impressive. I had only ever fought with the Guard, so I had never seen witches fighting in earnest. Sweat started to appear on their foreheads and their faces turned red, but still they battled on.

Grams had her hands pressed to her mouth, a look of delight on her face. She let out a gasp as Lionel stumbled over a rock. It was only a small movement but it was enough to give Tamsonite the edge he needed.

He closed the gap between them, stepping inside Lionel's guard to crack him over the head with his wooden sword. There was a resounding crack and Lionel dropped to his knees, both hands pressed to his head.

'Lionel.' Grams let out a terrified shriek and launched herself at him. His eyes rolled back in his head as he toppled to the side. 'Izzy,' she yelled as she clutched at his hands.

I leapt to my feet and raced to his side, laying my hands on him to feel for his injury. I closed my eyes and kept them closed, fighting to keep the smile off my face.

He wasn't hurt badly at all. A little bump on his head which would be sore tomorrow.

I was tempted to leave it, to teach him a lesson for scaring Grams like that. But then I figured that she probably deserved it, what with how she had been flirting with Tamsonite. And then that made me wonder what sort of fright I deserved for leaving my heart hanging between two men.

I let out a sigh as I healed him.

'What is it?' Grams tugged at my shoulder. 'Is he going to be okay?'

'I got it in time,' I said. 'But he's going to need some rest and perhaps some extra care.'

Lionel let out a groan and opened an eye.

'I'm sure I didn't hit him that hard,' Tamsonite said.

Grams hopped up and waved a finger at him. 'You did too, you bully. I heard it from all the way over there.'

Lionel winked at me and I winked back, then I helped him into a seated position. 'Grams. We'd better get Lionel into a bed. General Tamsonite, may we use your tent?'

'What?' Tamsonite rubbed his moustache with his hand and Grams glared at him with her hands on her hips. 'Yes, of course,' he said quickly. 'Be my guest.'

Aethan helped me get Lionel up and we supported most of his weight as he staggered towards the tent.

'Don't lay it on too thick,' I murmured out of the corner of my mouth.

Aethan shot me a quick look and then understanding creased the corners of his eyes.

Grams rushed ahead of us, opening the tent flap and then fussing around the bed, straightening the sheets and plumping the pillow.

'You sure he's going to be all right?' she asked me.

'I'm quite sure.'

Aethan placed his hand on my arm as he exited the tent, stopping me from heading back to the others. 'Is that what I need to do?' he asked.

'What do you mean?'

'To get you to admit that you love me still. Do I need to fake an injury?'

'Shhhhh,' I said. 'She'll hear you.' I gestured at the tent opening. I didn't want Lionel getting sprung. And there was also Ebony to consider. She had said she was going to wash her hair but she could burst from her tent at any moment.

He took my hand, his beautiful eyes serious as they stared into mine. 'Is that what it will take?'

I pulled my hand away, guilt warring with indignation. Why couldn't I just choose Turos? Why couldn't I set Aethan free? He wasn't mine any more, and giving him any sort of hope was a cruel joke. *Especially* with Ebony actually there in the camp. The woman he was being forced to marry.

The truth swam up from the depths of my subconscious. It wasn't this Aethan I was holding out for. It was *my* Aethan. I couldn't let go because if he ever got his memories back I knew I would do whatever it took to have him.

'No.' I shook my head. 'You don't have to do that.' I gazed into his eyes, searching for the man I grew up with. The man who had crafted me into the woman I was today. But he wasn't there.

I blinked back tears and squeezed his hand, suddenly drained of all my excess energy. 'I need to get some sleep,' I said. A smile flickered over his face and I shook my head. 'Can we make each other a deal?'

'It depends what it is.' His face became wary.

'The next few days are going to be intense enough without all of this.' I waved a hand between us. 'I need my friend, not my jealous ex-boyfriend.'

His face distorted at my use of the word ex-boyfriend. 'So Turos, he is your boyfriend now?'

'This,' I poked him in the chest, 'is exactly the sort of thing I am talking about. No. He is *not* my *boyfriend*. But seeing as how you are betrothed, neither are you.'

He sucked in a big breath of air, letting it puff out his cheeks before releasing it. 'Okay,' he said. 'I'll make that deal. As long as you promise me that the minute this is all over, you'll let me do whatever I need to, to make you mine.'

Thoughts of dark-faery wrath flashed through my head but I was too tired to be responsible. Too exhausted to try to fight him any more.

'Deal.' I stuck my hand out and he grabbed it, spun me into his arms and lowered his mouth to possess mine.

Part of the kiss was like coming home to a warm fire and a hot meal, and climbing into my pyjamas and fluffy slippers, but the rest of it? Dark Sky help me, the rest of it was fire and ice shooting through my veins.

His breath mingled with mine as I curled my fingers into his back and tried to remember exactly why we shouldn't be doing this very thing.

'Hey,' I said, when I finally came up for air. 'That wasn't the deal.'

He shrugged. 'It's only fair that I get to give you a bit of me to think about.' His eyes glanced over to where Turos had disappeared with Thomas and the remaining Guard.

I tried to control my expression but I could feel a blush start up on my cheeks.

He looked back at me, tilting his head as he examined my face. 'I thought so,' he said. 'So I'll keep my bargain if you keep to your end. But I'll not stand back and watch him take what I can't have. Not unless you declare yourself for him that is.' A look of pain flashed across his face. 'If that happens, I will bow out of the competition. Maybe.'

I felt a flash of irritation, but not at him. At myself. He was right. I couldn't stand there insisting that I needed friends, not emotional turmoil, while there was a possibility I would make out with Turos. If I was going to draw a line in the sand, that line had to be long enough to contain them both.

I nodded, too ashamed and exhausted to speak. I swayed on my feet and put a hand onto the tent to support myself.

'Sleep,' he ordered. 'You're right. The next few days are going to be strenuous enough without entering them exhausted.'

Isla appeared beside us, tucking my arm through hers. 'Come on sleepy head,' she said. 'Our weapons are ready, our dragons are asleep. There is nothing more for us to do. General Tamsonite has said we can use the next tent down.'

I saw Sabby staggering towards us rubbing her eyes. I followed her to the next tent and a few seconds later was sinking gratefully onto a camp stretcher. A piece of tight fabric had never felt so good.

'Here.' Isla dumped a bag on the ground and rifled through it until she pulled out our dream catchers.

'Oh.' I hadn't thought about packing anything when we had left.

'Yes, you're hopeless,' she said. 'Lucky you have me and Sabby to look out for you.'

I saw Sabby shoot her a grateful look at being included in the statement and I made a mental note to include her more. It had been Isla and me against the rest of the world for so long now that I had to remember there were others in my life. That knowledge, along with the conversation I had just had with Aethan pressed down on me and suddenly I felt so selfish I couldn't breathe.

'Hey.' Sabby was at my side pressing a hand to my head. 'Stop it. Everything is going to be just fine. Here. Lie down.' She pressed me back down onto the pillow and picked the dream catcher up. 'What do I do with this?'

'Just tuck it under her pillow.'

'Okay then.' Her voice said that she had no idea why, but she would do it anyway.

I felt her hand moving underneath the pillow and then she rested one hand on my forehead. 'You need to get some sleep, and I'm going to help you.'

'No I need to....' What did I need to do? Apologise to Turos for leading him on. Apologise to Aethan for same. Apologise to Grams for not spending enough time with her. Apologise to Mum for never being there any more.

Apologise to Isla for Wilfred not being there with her. Apologise to the whole wide world for releasing Santanas's soul, and for not being strong enough, or fast enough, or smart enough...

Sabby released her will into me and sleep flowed up over me like a warm, thick blanket protecting me from my thoughts, and from the outside world.

Chapter Eleven

Gods and Giants

When I opened my eyes again, I was no longer in the tent.

'What?' I stared around in bewilderment. I should have been deep in a dreamless sleep, finally getting the rest my body needed. Not standing near a sandy beach, under a clear blue sky, staring up at a...what *was* that?

I walked towards the stairs that led up, up, up to the snowy-marble tower. White robes flowed around my legs, distracting me from my original focus. I spread my arms wide, gaping at the material draped over my body.

My hair flowed over one shoulder, clean and smelling like roses, and gold sandals graced my feet. I felt graceful and feminine, an unusual and not entirely comfortable experience.

I turned my attention back to the stairs. There were an awful lot of them. Perhaps I could just go and sit on the beach. I was about to do just that when a bear-like figure appeared at the top of the stairs and a familiar voice called out, 'Well, don't just stand there.'

'Wilfred?' My gasp turned to a squeal and suddenly my feet were flying up the stairs. 'Wilfred.' I laughed as I threw myself into his arms. 'I like your outfit.' He was wearing a white toga with a braided gold belt and sandals similar to mine.

He swung me around in the air, and then deposited me back on the ground. 'Ahh Izzy.' His bushy, red beard scratched against my face as he planted a kiss on my cheek. 'It's been too long.'

'Far too long.' I held his hands and pulled back so that I could see him properly. The tattoos Ulandes had given him when she had chosen him, entwined around his arms and up over his collar bones. I let go of a hand so I could trace the pattern with a finger. 'How's things?'

He shrugged and pulled a face. 'Apart from missing you guys like crazy, pretty good.'

'So,' I looked around, 'what do you crazy Demi-Gods get up to.'

He burst out laughing. 'Demi-Gods?'

'Well, you did come back from the dead. And now you live in heaven, that at *least* makes you a Demi-God.' I looked around again. 'Is this heaven?' Green grass flowed out from the tower in every direction. 'Hey. Where'd the beach go?'

'Same place this did.' He waved a hand and all of a sudden we were in a busy marketplace. People moved through the crowded mayhem with ease, some stopping to barter with store holders in a language I couldn't understand. A man pushing a small cart, sold mugs of a steaming beverage which smelt of spices.

I breathed in the heavy scent coming from the mugs. 'That smells delicious.'

'Chai tea? It is.'

Everywhere I looked there was colour and light and movement. I backed up against a wall as a mule loaded with bolts of cloth pushed toward us.

'Willy,' one of the shop holders called out in a foreign accent. 'I have that *thing* you ordered.'

'Perfect.' Wilfred slapped his hands together. 'Come on,' he said, grabbing my hand. 'I need your opinion on something.'

We followed the wiry shop holder through the crowd, turning down a series of alleys until I was totally disorientated. 'Where are we?'

'The City of Ulandes.'

'Of course we are.' I rolled my eyes. 'And where exactly is that.'

He turned to me with seriousness imprinted on his face. 'I could tell you, but I'd have to kill you.' He waited a beat, studying my expression, and then he burst out laughing. 'As far as I can tell,' he said when he could talk again. 'We're on a plane of existence halfway to heaven.'

'Really?' Wow. I hadn't really believed in the whole heaven and hell thing.

'No.' He let go of my hand to punch me on the shoulder. 'We're in India.'

'Oh.' Well that would explain why everyone but us had dark skin, shiny black hair and soulful brown eyes. 'So...you've been in India the whole time?' I heard the pain in my voice.

'What?' His head swung toward me. 'No. No.' He put a hand on my arm. 'We live....' He waved a hand in the air. 'But we can access here because Ulandes is worshipped openly here.'

'So the reason you haven't come home is because you can't.'

He ignored the impatient gestures of the wiry, little shop keeper and turned fully toward me. Putting his hands on my shoulders+ he peered into my face and said,

'Do you really believe I wouldn't have come home if I could?'

I shrugged. I knew I was being petulant, but if a girl couldn't be petulant with her big brother then who could she be petulant with?

'Ahhh Izzy.' He pulled me into a rough hug. 'Have things been that bad?'

'I....' I stopped and sighed. 'Nothing I haven't been able to handle. But I've missed you.' The last bit came out in a wail. 'And Isla. Isla misses you so much. She puts a brave face on but...well, you know how she is.'

'Yes.' He nodded, a wistful look on his bearded face. 'I know how she is.'

'Willy.' The little shopkeeper was at Wilfred's side, tugging on his arm.

We started walking again. 'We need to hurry,' Wilfred said. 'Ulandes wants to speak to you.' He shot me a cheeky grin. 'She's expecting me to bring you straight to her.'

We followed the shopkeeper again as he navigated the maze-like markets with ease. Finally, he stopped outside a small booth. He pulled a key out of his pocket and unlocked the door. 'Come.' He gestured to us and darted to the back of the room, waiting till we were inside and had shut and locked the door again before pressing some numbers into a keypad. There was a click, and the next door swung open.

'Wow.' I stopped in the doorway to take in what I was seeing. Jewellery, no artworks – each piece so exquisite and unique that they were more than mere items of jewellery, lay in velvet-lined display boxes.

'Here.' The man pulled a box off one of the many shelves lining the walls.

Wilfred took it and placed it on a table in the middle of the room. He stared at the lid for a few seconds before finally lifting it off.

Inside the box was a silver sculpture. Metal danced in an intricate weaving of scrolls, the solid lace making a long tube that was narrower at one end than the other. Wilfred picked it up and held it in his hands, a look of reverence on his face.

'Do you think she'll like it?' He held it out to me.

I took it from him carefully, but I needn't have bothered, because for all its visual delicacy, it was as strong as a metal rod. 'Isla?'

He nodded.

'What is it?'

He barked out a laugh. 'It's an armlet.'

'Oh.' I looked from the armlet to his arms and back again. It was an exact imitation of the tattoos he wore. 'May I?' I held it in front of my hand, waiting for his nod of assertion before I slipped it on.

The metal rippled as it contacted my skin, becoming light and elastic. I gasped as it moved with my flexing wrist. 'It's amazing.' I swirled my arm as if I were wielding a sword, the armlet did not interfere with my movement at all. 'Like it? She's going to *adore* it.'

His eyes shone as I slipped it back off and handed it to him. The shopkeeper wobbled his head from side-to-side, obviously pleased with my compliments. He placed it back in the box and handed it to Wilfred. The two men shook hands and then Wilfred led me back out into the lane.

'We'd better get going.' He grasped my hand and the lane disappeared, and we were back at the grassy beach with the marble tower.

'So you *do* live here?'

'Nah.' He laughed. 'But it is a portal to where I live.'

I expected him to lead me up the stairs, but instead he took me around to the back of the tower. He placed his hand on a wooden door - the hinges rusted with age, the wood splintered and worn - and he pushed. It creaked as it swung inwards. I followed him through the door into the darkness.

'You live in a closet,' I said into the inky blackness.

His laugh echoed as if we were in a small room. 'Here,' he said. 'Help me shut it.'

I turned and put my hands on the edge of the old door, watching the green grass disappear as we managed to heave it shut. It slid into place with the click of a smoothly-oiled lock, and light illuminated the room.

The door wasn't old and splintered from this side. The grain of the wood glowed in the light, oiled till it gleamed. An ornate handle, that I was guessing was solid gold, and two metal bands, also gold, decorated the surface. The metal bands were decorated with the same design that Wilfred wore on his arms.

I gasped as I turned back from the door. We were no longer in a closet. Instead, massive arches curved above us, mosaic tiles glittering in the light. The arches swept up so high I had to crane my head back to see them meet. They supported the ceiling of the hall that opened up in front of us.

'Come on.' Wilfred started walking. 'She's waiting for us in the ornate garden.'

I followed him, trying not to trip over my feet as I gawked at the beauty of our surroundings. We walked for a few minutes before I realised that there was no way we were within the tower.

'What is this?'

'It's Ulandes' residence.'

'No. I mean how can this be inside that tower?'

'Do you really think you'd understand the answer even if I knew it?'

He had a point. I had chosen not to do science at school for a very good reason.

We walked for a few minutes more before the passageway we were on opened up onto a balcony. A sweeping staircase curved around the balcony as it descended to a massive garden full of fountains and flowers.

I followed Wilfred down the stairs, looking around for Ulandes as I did. A woman, garbed in white robes as we were, but also wearing a broad-brimmed hat, bent over a small shrub, hacking away at a dying limb with a small saw.

Wilfred walked up to the gardener and said, 'Got her.'

The woman sighed, putting down the saw as she turned towards us. 'Really?' she said. 'After all this time, no grovelling in my presence, no bowing, not even a polite nod of your head?' She took off her hat and ruffled up her hair and I was surprised to recognise the Goddess who had floated out of the statue and brought Wilfred back to life.

I dropped to my knees and bowed my head.

'See,' Ulandes said, '*she* gets it.' But there was merriment in her voice, and I could tell that *this* was a conversation they had had many times.

I felt her fingertips brush my hair as she said, 'Rise child.'

I rose back to my feet and met her sombre expression. So many questions flooded into me, but none of them seemed important enough to disturb a deity with.

'Come,' she said. 'Let's sit.' She turned and walked – not floated – down a path in the garden, navigating several turns before I could see what she was heading for. It took several more minutes to reach the pagoda and its low slung couches. Pools of water ran on three sides of it, the sounds of fountains instantly unwinding the tension in my shoulders. Flashes of bright colours turned out to be fish, but not like any fish I had seen before. These were all the colours of the rainbow. Brilliant golds and reds like other goldfish, but also green and blue and purple. Some had stripes and some were perfectly polka-dotted.

Ulandes saw me staring at them. 'I find normal goldfish so boring,' she said as she sat gracefully onto one of the couches.

A bird flew down and perched on her shoulder. As she raised a hand to scratch its neck, her robe slipped up her arm revealing a twirling, dancing tattoo the same as Wilfred's. But where his was black, hers looked like she'd been gilded with 24 carat gold.

I sank onto a couch opposite her, and Wilfred slumped onto a third. He surreptitiously placed the box, holding Isla's gift, behind a cushion.

'Really?' Ulandes said. 'Like I wouldn't notice.' She held her hand out and he puffed out a sigh, reminding me of a naughty boy caught with his hand in the cookie jar. With a burst of intuition, I realised that it was all an act for her amusement.

He pulled the box back out and handed it to her, a small smile playing at the corners of his mouth. 'I thought, maybe, Izzy could take it back to her for me.' He didn't have to say who 'her' was.

She took the lid off the box and viewed the armlet inside. 'I don't think so,' she said.

Wilfred's shoulders slumped in defeat.

'Not like this anyway.' She pulled it out of the box and held it up, turning it from side-to-side as she examined it. 'I mean it's very nice and everything, but do you think it's good enough for *her*?' There was an almost reverent quality to the way she said 'her'.

He shuffled his feet. 'It was all I could afford. You don't pay well you know.' He flashed a quick smile at her.

'I suppose I don't.' She tilted her head to the side as she continued her examination. 'Well, perhaps this will make up for that.' She placed the fingertip of her free hand to the armlet and a faint glow started at the point of contact. It flowed out over the piece of jewellery till the whole thing was glowing in her hand.' She took her finger away and re-examined it. 'And I think some bling,' she said. 'What girl doesn't like a little bling in her life?' She touched her finger quickly to several points over the armlet. 'There.' She nodded her head in satisfaction. 'That's better. Except...I think she needs two. One for each arm.' She waved her free hand and a second one, a mirror image of the first, appeared.

She passed them back to Wilfred. He took them, staring at them with wide, astonished eyes. I leant closer to affirm what I was looking at.

The armlet was no longer silver, now it was solid gold. And set into that gold at the points she had touched, gigantic diamonds sparkled. Before it had been beautiful, now it was magnificent. *They*, were magnificent.

'Thank you,' he whispered, tears glistened in the corners of her eyes. 'I've never been able to give her a gift worthy of her.'

'There is no gift worthy of her,' Ulandes said. 'But they will suffice.' She turned her pleased look from Wilfred to me. 'How are you?'

The question I'd heard a million times, held so much more weight coming from her. I opened my mouth to give her my rote answer of 'fine', but under the sombre eyes of the Goddess I found, instead, the truth tumbling out.

'I'm scared,' I said. 'I'm so scared that if I concentrate on it at all I think I'll start screaming and won't be able to stop.' I paused while I sorted through my emotions, looking for the next most important. 'I'm terrified of Santanas, and to be perfectly honest Galanta isn't too much further behind. But the worst of it all is that I'm scared I'm going to let everyone down.'

Now that the words had started I couldn't seem to stem their flow. 'I don't know what to do. I don't know what they expect of me. I know I have all this power,' I flapped my hands at my chest, '*inside* me, but I don't think it will be enough. He's got so much more experience, and she's so cunning.' My voice gained speed as it rose in timbre. 'And then there's all their warriors. Even *with* the dark faeries, we're grossly outnumbered. And people are going to *die*. I mean thousands. Tens of thousands.' I waved my arms around wildly. 'And their families are going to be without them. Children without fathers. Wives without husbands, and it's all because of me.'

Tears stung the corners of my eyes and then broke over the wall of my lower lid. 'I'm not enough.' I shook my head. 'And everybody thinks I am going to be their saviour, but all I am is a fraud.' A hiccupped sob escaped with the word fraud.

Wilfred scooted over onto the couch beside me and pulled me into him. It felt so good to have his brotherly arms wrapped around me. I had missed his calm, optimistic presence more than I had realised. I buried my head into his chest and let all the emotions I had been suppressing out.

It felt like I was deflating. The terror, the shame, the confusion, all draining out of me with my tears. And at the end of my crying torrent, all that was left was me. I felt smaller, and still fragile, but somehow, more resolute. As if, somehow, facing my fears and releasing them, had made me stronger.

I sat back up and wiped the backs of my hands across my eyes, sniffling as I did. Wilfred waved his hand in a flourish and a handkerchief appeared in his fingers.

'Show off,' Ulandes sighed as he handed it to me.

I stared at it for a second before taking it and blowing my nose noisily. 'I hope they have a good laundry wherever this came from,' I said.

'It is just ethereal matter,' Ulandes said. 'My disciples,' she shook her head at the word as if unbelieving that Wilfred was her disciple, 'can manipulate it while we are here. It will disappear as soon as you leave. My gifts, on the other hand, will stay.' She nodded her head at the armlets.

'Is it going to be all right?' I asked.

She smiled. 'Child, even I don't know that. I do know that you have a chance of succeeding.'

'Where there's a will there's a way,' Wilfred said, leaning back and crossing his arms behind his head.

'Something like that.' Her smile was wistful.

'Will you help us?' My voice held a pleading quality.

'I will do what I can. But you have to understand, I can only intervene in world events if my followers are directly threatened.'

'But, the Ubanty are coming.' I crossed my fingers. I hoped they were coming. I couldn't see the dark faeries leaving their servants behind. I mean who would put up their tents and cook their meals?

'Yes, they are. But at the moment, they are not my followers. They need to choose me again. Then, and only then, will I be able to help.'

'Where's Samuel?' Thinking of her people made me think of my one-time saviour.

She smiled. 'I may have sent him back to be with his own people.'

A wave of understanding washed over me and relief quickly followed. She couldn't act directly, but she was manipulating the situation to her advantage. She had sent her loyal disciple back to walk with his people and to show them the way.

She sat up straight and cocked her head to the side as if listening to something. 'We don't have much time,' she said. 'There is something you need to know.'

'What?' I was desperately hoping she was going to show me how to destroy Santanas.

'The battle that is about to begin, will not determine the outcome of the war.' She stood and crossed to stand in front of me. 'The real battle is in here.' She reached out and put her hand on my chest over my heart. 'This is where victory or defeat is going to occur.'

My confusion must have been evident for she said, 'I wish I could just give you the answer you seek, but that is not allowed. All through time, evil has clashed with all that is good. The people involved are just instruments, the outcome based on their purity. All I can tell you is that you must not let hate shadow your heart, for if you do, you will become an agent of the dark. And then the dark will triumph over the light. Always, always, the answer is to be found in love.'

She cocked her head again and said, 'It is time. The battle is to be joined. Wilfred, you must take her back, but you must return.' Her voice was cold stone as she said the last words. In *this*, she would not tolerate disobedience.

He nodded his head and took my hand, and suddenly we were back on the grass beside the sandy beach. 'Will you give these to her?' he asked, holding out the armbands to me.

'Of course.' I took them from him and then threw my arms around him. 'I'll see you soon?'

He nodded and rubbed his hands together. 'As soon as I can, I'll be there.' He let out a laugh. 'I've got a thing or two to show you.'

I smiled back, thinking about the mind trick Turos had taught me. 'Oh good,' I said. 'Cause I've got a thing or two to show *you*.'

He rubbed has hands again, laughing as he said, 'Game on,' and then he was gone. Well, I guess it was *me* that was gone.

I could feel someone shaking my shoulder and could hear a bugle's shrill notes echoing. Something had happened while I was sleeping. It was time to return to the real world.

***

'Wake up.' Isla gave me one more big shake and I opened my eyes. 'Oh. Thank the Dark Sky. You gave me a fright. I thought something had...where did *they* come from?' Her blue eyes, round with astonishment, were staring down at my hands.

I sat up and held the armlets out to her. 'They're for you. From Wilfred.' I thought about it. 'Well this one is from Wilfred,' I shook the one in my right hand, 'and this one is from Ulandes.' I shook my left hand.

'Wilfred?' Her voice was a hushed whisper. 'You saw him? You saw *her*?' She said 'her' the same way that Ulandes had.

I stared at her while several pieces of a puzzle tumbled into place. 'Oh Dark Sky,' I said. 'You've been praying to her.'

I'd never seen Isla blush before. She made up for that now. 'She's a *Goddess*.' She shrugged her shoulders, and grimaced. 'How could I *not* worship her?'

So not just praying. Worshipping. 'Well, she seems to really like you,' I said.

Her blush brightened and she ducked her head, a pleased smile on her face. 'How is he?'

'Same old,' I said. 'Giving poor Ulandes a run for her money. You should try them on. They made them for you.'

She looked at them properly for the first time, her eyes widening at their splendour. 'Oh.' It was a soft gasp. 'They're...they're perfect.' She slipped her arm into one and it rippled as it had when I had tried it on, moulding itself to her forearms. Her mouth made a silent 'O' and then she slipped on the second one. This time though, a blast of energy exploded from them, knocking Isla onto the floor and me back onto the bed.

'Buzznuckle,' I shrieked, throwing my hands up to shield my face. 'Isla. Isla.' I threw myself off the bed onto the floor beside her, expecting the worst. But her arms were still intact.

She held them above her face, turning them from side-to-side as she stared at them. The armlets were no longer there. Instead, golden tattoos, the same as Ulandes, graced her arms. The diamonds seemed to have been set into her skin, but when I reached out and ran a finger over them they were soft.

'Great Dark Sky.' I breathed out the words.

She sat up slowly, still staring at her arms. Tears trickled down her cheeks, but I could tell by the look on her face they were tears of joy. She didn't say anything, and she didn't have to. I knew why she was crying.

Most of her life she had been an outcast; the faery who had shamed the nation. Never to be married, never to be loved, she had thrown herself not into bitterness, but into servitude. Protecting those who scorned her, fighting for their lives and their freedom. And through all of that, she was barely even accepted by her own mother.

For the first time since Arracon had raped her, she had been judged and found worthy. And by the look of her forearms, not just worthy. It seemed she had been placed on a pedestal of her own. I could feel the joy bursting out of me as I placed my arms around her.

The bugle cried out again, and this time I could hear men shouting.

'What's happening?' I asked.

'They've started coming through the pass.'

They were coming. It was happening. It was time.

I pushed myself back to my feet and rubbed my hands nervously on the outside of my pants. I wasn't ready for this. Would never be ready for this. I patted my hands over my arms and legs, the feel of the cold steel strapped there calming my mind. 'Where's Sabby?'

'She went to find Thomas.'

'Izzy?' Aethan's head appeared in the tent flap. 'We need to go. Now.'

Isla grabbed the dreamcatcher out from underneath my pillow and tucked it back in the bag, then she followed me out of the tent. Emerald, Lance and Arthur were waiting for us beyond the campfire. A group of Millenium stood off to the side.

Grams and Lionel, well recovered from his head injury, waited with Turos. General Tamsonite strode backwards and forwards, giving orders in a calmly-authorative voice. If he was worried, it didn't show. I was happy he was in charge. I knew my voice would be quavering if I tried to talk at all. The thought of meeting my grandfather again was not filling me with any joy.

The three of us joined them, waiting for Tamsonite to give us his attention.

He finished yelling orders and turned to us. 'We need to hold them off until the night faeries arrive. Can you bring down the pass?' He directed the last question to Aethan.

Aethan scratched at his cheek while he considered the question. 'There's a constriction about half way down,' he said. 'It would be the best place to block it.' He looked at me. 'Could you do it?'

'Do what?' I had no idea what he was talking about.

'Cause a landslide.'

'Oh.' I would do anything if it meant putting off a confrontation with Santanas for a little longer. 'What would I be dealing with?'

'Sheer cliffs standing about 50 yards apart.'

It was my turn to look thoughtful. 'If I threw enough power at it I'd be able to take bites out of it. Even if the whole thing didn't give, it would be enough rubble to make getting through difficult.'

'Excellent.' Tamsonite clapped his hands together. 'Take who you need to get it done.'

'Turos,' Aethan said. 'We'll need you and your men to provide cover for us. If they've made it as far as the pass we'll be under fire.' He ran a hand through his hair and stared off to where the pass waited. 'Just you and us,' he said when he turned back to Turos. 'If we come in force they'll know we are attacking. If it's just us, they may think we're on their side.'

'May think?' Turos raised one eyebrow.

A grin flashed across Aethan's face. 'No guts no glory.'

Turos gave me a long look before he nodded and strode off towards Lance. The Millenium followed in his wake.

'We're coming,' Grams said.

'I don't think so.' I didn't like the thought of her being anywhere near a goblin, let alone an army of them.

'Think stink,' she said. 'Lionel and I will be able to deflect enemy fire. You won't be able to hold a shield *and* bring down a mountain.'

'She's right.' Aethan's voice brooked no argument. 'We need them.'

'What about us?' Isla had her gleaming forearms crossed across her chest.

Aethan turned to her, opened his mouth, and then stopped to stare at her arms. 'Where did that come from?' He reached out a finger to touch her skin but she slapped his hand away.

'They were a present.' She quirked an eyebrow at him as if daring him to ask more. 'You were saying?'

It will be too dangerous for Arthur and Isla.

'Emerald said it will be too dangerous for Arthur,' I said.

She turned her steely gaze on me.

'Hey. Don't shoot the messenger.' I raised my hands in the air.

'You're probably right.' She shrugged her shoulders.

I stared at her suspiciously. 'That's it? No argument?'

'No need to argue when you are right.' She gave me her lightest, airiest smile and then walked over to Arthur, throwing her arms around his neck and rubbing at the nose he offered her. She showed him her arms and he sniffed at them a few times before letting out a pleased chuffing sound. She scrambled up and secured the bag to the harness behind her. 'I'll go join the rest of the dragons.' They lifted into the air and disappeared in the direction of the field they had landed on.

'You thinking what I'm thinking?' I said to Aethan.

'Yup. That was *way* too easy.' He touched my arm lightly and I followed him over to Emerald.

Sabby and Thomas were waiting there with a half dozen Border Guard. I waved at the Guards, a couple of whom I recognised.

'We're not coming, are we?' Sabby said.

I shook my head. 'You're too valuable to risk on this mission.'

She smiled as she shoved my shoulder. 'You mean I'd be of no use.'

I pulled a face. 'Healing on dragon back might be a tad difficult.'

She threw her arms around me. 'Stay safe,' she said.

I held onto her for a few moments, savouring the feel of my oldest, dearest friend. Then I gave Thomas a quick hug and scrambled up onto Emerald's neck. Aethan was behind me a heartbeat later, keeping a respectable distance this time when he strapped himself in. I flashed him a smile, pleased he was taking our deal seriously.

I'm not going to be able to shield us, I said to Emerald. *Not while I'm trying to cause a landslide.*

Their spears and arrows will not harm Lance or me. Arthur would be another matter. His belly scales are still soft.

He shouldn't even be flying yet. Her words were tinged with a mixture of fear and pride.

He's growing so quickly.

It is unprecedented. Now, just pride.

Lance threw back his head and took a couple of hopping steps, thrusting his enormous wings out to the side in a giant sweep. He jumped into the air as his wings pushed down again, and then he was flapping up into the sky, away from us.

It is so much easier to take off from a mountain top, Emerald said, a wistful sigh in her thoughts. Then she followed Lance's example, running forwards as she gained speed and momentum before finally becoming airborne.

I spent the rest of the trip worrying. If they had already made it far enough down the pass it would be two dragons and a collection of twenty witches, faeries and Milleniums taking on the whole damned goblin army. I wondered if the Giants would be there. Because that would seriously affect how low we could fly if we were having to worry about Giants. An adult giant could possibly grab the foot of a low flying dragon, causing it to crash into the sides of the pass.

The looming mountains changed from a gloomy darkness in the distance to large sentinels rearing ahead of us. Lance altered direction, heading toward the break in the long line of peaks. The air grew colder and I wrapped my arms around myself to try and hold in some body heat.

And then we were close enough to see them; a black stain on the earth ahead, flowing out of the mouth of the pass like a putrid tidal wave. I heard Aethan swear behind me. They were even further ahead than we had thought. They had already cleared the pass. This was going to be dangerous.

Turos wants to link, Emerald said. *It will make communicating easier.*

I knew he was right, but I reached out towards him and Lance with trepidation. Our minds touched and then flowed together and all of a sudden I had four wings, four arms, twelve legs and scales.

Why do you always go too far? I could feel Turos sighing. *Pull back a little. If you're this deep you won't be able to concentrate on what you need to do.*

I pulled back into my own body as Emerald said, *She can't help it. She's an overachiever.*

Obviously. I felt rather than heard Turos chuckle. *We need to stay high for as long as possible. Gives them less chance to attack us.*

I nodded, realised he couldn't see me and then said, *Let's do it.*

The warriors on Lance's back readied their bows as we sped towards the beginning of the pass. Goblins pointed and turned to watch us go, but none of them raised weapons in our direction. It seemed Aethan's gamble had paid off. I wasn't that surprised. Dragons did look pretty bad-ass, and all the other bad-ass creatures were already working with Santanas.

We sped through the pass, my enjoyment of the trip blending with Emerald's, Lance's and Turos's. It required steep navigation in parts but it had nothing on the entry to the breeding caves.

'Woo hoo,' Grams hollered behind me.

After a few minutes, my enjoyment was dulled by what I saw below. Goblins jammed the pass beneath us, their bodies pressing forwards in a tide of death towards our army. I gritted my teeth and narrowed my eyes. We had to stop them. We had to give the night faeries time to get to us.

It took us about five minutes to reach the constriction in the pass. A fifty yard section where the two mountain ranges closed on each other as if to fight or dance. Lance turned sideways to flit through the gap and then flew upwards into a loop.

'*What do you think?*' Turos and Aethan asked me the same question at once.

I turned to stare at the narrowing as we whipped through it. Two smooth walls faced each other. There were no boulders or outcrops or ledges of any kind.

'*It may take a while,*' I informed them at the same time.

I saw the warriors on Lance's back ready their bows and felt Aethan moving behind me. Emerald slowed her motion and twisted in the air, heading back towards the narrowing.

I lifted my hands and shot a blast of lightning into the mouth of the pass. Goblins were lifted from their feet, flying backwards into their brethren. Rocks exploded from the cliffs on either side of them, raining sharp shrapnel down upon them. But the cliffs themselves stood like sentinels. I fired two blasts of energy down to the right as we flew through the pass. A crack appeared in the smooth wall, fissuring upwards a few feet. It wasn't much, but it was a start.

Goblins can be stupid, but not so stupid as to not realise we were the enemy. They roared and began pulling crude bows off their backs. I could feel Lance and Turos sweeping down behind me and knew the warriors with them were laying down covering fire.

Lance flew high as Emerald turned, then he swooped in right behind us.

You can do this, Turos's voice was like smooth silk inside my head.

I concentrated on that fissure, sending blow-after-blow pounding into the rock. It widened, snaking further up the cliff, but the slab of rock stayed frustratingly intact.

The goblins' arrows started peppering upwards. They bounced off Lance's and Emerald's hard scales, but their wings were more vulnerable. I knew what could happen if too many arrows ripped into the wing membranes. But before I could worry too much, the arrows from below began deflecting before they made it to us. I turned to see Grams and Lionel hard at work. Their wands whipping side-to-side as they knocked the arrows from the air. Both had big grins on their faces and I was pretty sure Grams was cackling.

Aethan and the rest of the Border Guard returned fire, arrows whipping towards the goblins. There were so many of them that nearly every arrow found a mark, and yet there was no lessening in the attack from below. There were just too many of them for us to make a difference.

Emerald turned and we headed back to the pass. I ignored the goblins, I ignored their arrows, they weren't my problem. I concentrated on the crack, spacing each blow a few feet apart as I worked my way up the cliff. Loose rocks sprinkled down from further up the mountain, but the cliff stayed maddeningly intact.

Ahhh, Izzy. No pressure or anything, but there seems to be a giant heading our way.

I took my eyes off the mountain long enough to look down the pass toward the Gonian Crater. Not one, but two giants waded through the goblins, tossing them aside as if they were annoying insects. *Whizbang.* At the pace they were moving, we had maybe five minutes before they arrived.

Screaming in frustration, like I wanted to, was going to get me nowhere. I turned my attention back to the crack. It was traversing more quickly now, snaking up the cliff, but staying within the mountain. I needed it to exit, to break.

I didn't look at the giants. I didn't need to. I could feel where they were through my connection with Turos. They were closing, far too fast. My next pass would be my last before we had to deal with them as well.

You can do it. The warmth of Turos's faith flowed into me.

I stiffened my spine, took a huge breath and let my mind flow into the fissure. I braced within it, and then I shoved, expanding outwards, spreading the crack. I felt it give, a creaking, tearing sound rasping from the rock. My blood pounded in my ears as I took another breath and strained again. The crack ran upwards, racing away from me. I chased it, pushing as I went, my breath coming in short, sharp pants as sweat poured off me.

They're nearly here.

White lights danced in front of my eyes and I swayed in my seat. I felt Aethan's hands around my waist and heard Turos growl in my head.

'No pressure, Izzy,' Aethan said, 'but we just ran out of arrows.'

I ignored it all. Time was draining away from us. If I didn't do this before the giants got there, the army would have the whole might of Santanas's force bearing down upon us.

I flowed into it one more time, pressure building in my head as I strained against the rock. It was going to be me, or the mountain. We weren't both coming out of this in one piece.

Just when I thought it was going to be me, there was a noise like a thousand whips cracking. It reverberated out through the pass as a shudder ran through the mountain.

I pulled back into my own body, dizzy from the lack of oxygen. Cracks ran out like the roots of a tree. They sped up the mountain, wrapping around the bulge like a lover's arms.

There was a cry of triumph from behind me and I could feel Turos cheering in my head.

A slab broke away from the surface and slid to the floor of the gorge. It speared through a dozen goblins and into the ground below.

For a few, frustrating moments, I thought that *that*, was it. And then the whole side of the mountain came crashing down. Rock tore and splintered as it bounced into the pass, rebounding off the far wall and tumbling thunderously to the ground below.

'Woo hoo.' I heard Aethan's voice join with that of his men.

'Take that,' Grams shrieked.

I watched the chaos over my shoulder as Emerald winged her way down the pass. A cloud of dust swirled high in the air, masking the giants from view. When it settled, I could see chunks of rock blocking the pass way up past the giants heads.

I let out a sigh of relief and turned to the front as I sagged back against Aethan.

That ought to hold them for a while. Turos's voice was smug in my head.

I nodded wearily, too tired to respond.

Aethan's arms tightened, pulling me back against him further. 'Don't read anything into this,' he said into my ear. 'I just don't want you falling off.'

I closed my eyes and relaxed against him, preparing to sever the link in my mind. It was bad enough knowing that Turos's jealousy would be tearing him apart, I *really* didn't need to be experiencing it. A millisecond before I ended it, angered surprise raked through me. I felt Lance twist his head as the talons of a giant eagle reached for his eyes.

I snapped my eyes open and sat upright. A second Vulpine appeared above Lance. The rider leapt from the enormous eagle's back, landing like a cat behind the last Millenium warrior. Emerald roared in outrage, and Lance rolled in response to her mental cry, but it was too late. A knife slashed through the air and red sprayed from the Millenium's throat. He slumped to the side and the Vulpine leapt from Lance, back onto the neck of his eagle.

'Watch out,' Grams shrieked.

I looked up to see another eagle streaking towards us. I loosened the straps holding me in and bounced to my feet, opening myself even further to Emerald so that her every movement felt like my own.

I had only tried this once before, and then only when just she and I were bonded. This time, there were four of us. Awareness of Lance and Turos smacked into me, and suddenly, I could feel every movement of every muscle fibre. It was as if their nerves extended from their minds into mine, as if their movements were extensions of my own.

I felt Turos doing the same thing, felt him testing the boundaries of our combined awareness. I felt him nod his head in satisfaction as his lips pulled back in a satisfied smile. We were four, but we were one.

A wave of dizziness, at the vastness of my new body, swept over me and I crouched and grasped the harness for balance. It was gone in a second, leaving me only with my strange new awareness.

'What are you doing?' Aethan's voice was alarmed.

'Trust me.' I emptied my mind, pushing away my worries and my fears.

The first Vulpine landed behind Lionel. He twisted in his seat, flicking his wand but the man jumped over the spell and landed behind the last Guard.

I recognised him. Bernard. A tall, jolly fae with a wife and three children. He spun and flicked a dagger. The Vulpine dodged, but not enough to stop it catching him in the side of his thigh. It sliced through material and skin as it passed but did no real damage.

I reached down and grabbed one of the leather straps. Emerald didn't even need my command to know what to do. She started to roll to one side, and then quickly flicked the other way. The Vulpine flew off the far side from where his eagle had expected. The eagle tucked its wings in tight by its sides as it dived after him.

I didn't get to see if the eagle made it or not because three more eagles launched their attacks. One harried Emerald's head, darting in to peck at her eyes with its sharp beak. She blasted it with fire and it shrieked and fell away while the rider on its back slapped at the burning feathers.

Two more of the warriors landed, both of them behind Bernard. I leapt through the air, landing behind the furthest. He spun to face me but his movements were like a slug's. I slashed twice at him in the time it took him to lift his weapon. His eyes held mute surprise as he looked down at the blood gushing from his sliced throat. I kicked him to the side and his lifeless body tumbled from Emerald's back. An eagle's shriek of rage echoed up from below.

Bernard stood with his legs spread wide and one of the leather straps looped around his left wrist and clenched in his fist. He parried a dagger blow easily, flicking his sword first one way and then back the other. But the Vulpine had the advantage of balance and the use of both hands. I kicked my foot into the back of his knees and as he collapsed forward, Bernard's blade whipped through his wrist, severing his hand. He screamed and clutched the stump to his chest before throwing himself off Emerald's back.

We broke from the pass out onto the plain beyond, and like a flock of seagulls fighting over a scrap of bread, the Vulpine dived. The air was suddenly thick with white feathers.

If they had been able to attack us like this in the pass, where we were forced to fly single file, we would have been in a huge amount of trouble, but here, on the plain, Lance and Emerald could use each other's strengths.

They flew at each other, their fiery breaths scouring the sky of the attacking birds. And then they flew upwards into a loop, snatching birds out of the air with their front feet, and using their massive teeth to permanently disable them.

I knew where we were, but I also knew where we were all going to be. As we levelled out again, I leapt into the air, coming down on Emerald's broad back behind Bernard. Then I ran down Emerald's back, swiping at the incoming egales with my swords. I dived off the side, high into the air, turning a somersault as I whipped a blade through a Vulpine's neck before landing in a squat on Lance's back.

I knelt as Turos leapt over me, his blades flashing in the afternoon sun, and came back up to my feet as a half dozen Vulpines jumped to Lance's back. I didn't need to look to know a similar number of the enemy had just landed on Emerald. Neither did Turos.

Without arrows, we were turning into sitting ducks. We had to clear this mess up and get the hell out of there.

I took two quick steps towards him. He jammed his swords into their scabbards and bent, linking his hands together. I landed with a foot on his outstretched hands and, with a grunt of exertion, he straightened, flinging me high into the air.

I flew in a dive towards Emerald, tucking into a forward roll. She banked towards me, slowing my momentum as I came to my feet. I ball-kicked the closest Vulpine in the face, flipping into a backward somersault, up and over number two.

I was moving far faster than they expected, and as I passed over him, I saw him slash his dagger down into the space I had just vacated. I landed behind him and shoved the tip of my sword up under his ribcage. Then I kicked him forwards, using him as a springboard as I leapt back at the first one.

Grams and Lionel had managed to snare another two in a spell, and the Border Guard was battling the last two.

Turos's muscles flexed as he fought. The fierce grin on my face mirrored his. I looked over at him, just for a second, and a Vulpine landed on top of me. I dropped to Emerald's back, and he stepped onto my wrist, pinning my sword arm in place. Everything sped up as I lost my grip on my centre of calm.

I felt Turos stiffen in alarm. His cry of horror in my head, echoed Aethan's.

The Vulpine was too close to me for me to launch a lightning bolt. I would hurt all of us if I did. I raised my spare hand, trying to grab his wrist to prevent the killing blow, but I was too slow.

The light glinted off the edge of the dagger as it sped towards me. I winced, waiting for the bite of the metal, but before it found my flesh, an arrow thunked into the man's throat. He looked confused as his hand wavered up towards his neck, and then his eyes rolled back and he collapsed to the side.

I looked from the arrow to Aethan, but he wasn't looking at me. I felt Emerald huff in pride as I turned to follow his gaze.

Arthur glowed like the sun himself as the light flickered off his scales. Isla stood on his back, her knees slightly bent, her feet tucked under his scales. Almost too fast for me to see, she notched another arrow, pulled her hand back to her cheek, and released it. Four more followed just as swiftly and the eagles pulled away from us.

She looked like the Goddess of War, riding her dragon chariot as she dealt out death. Her forearms sparkled as the diamonds imbedded in her skin threw off rays of light.

Arthur was nimbler than his parents, but all his manoeuvring couldn't shake the eagle that dropped in on his tail. Isla knocked her arrow and sighted down its length, but the bird twisted in the sky so swiftly and unexpectedly that Isla didn't release. She couldn't predict where the eagle would go next. I felt my stomach clench in fear, but then Arthur looked back, his tongue hanging out in his normal goofy grin, and I realised it was all a ploy. Isla shoved her feet further under the scales and tucked her body, and then Arthur was rolling, like a swimmer performing a tumble turn.

He came out of the roll facing the unsuspecting eagle, and unleashed a gush of flames into the bird's face. Isla released three lightning quick arrows into it, and it plummeted like a stone.

I copied Isla, tucking my feet under scales as Emerald dived towards the ground. I leant forwards, thrilling in the feel of the wind roaring past me as she sped up.

The eagle she was chasing popped its wings out like a parachute and shot up above her line of descent. I fired a lightning bolt upwards and it exploded in a puff of singed, white feathers.

Then, as one, the eagles pulled away. Like a long line of geese, they formed up into a loose V and headed back towards the Gonian Crater.

My heartbeat began to slow from its frantic beat, back towards normal as I walked up Emerald's back and slid into my spot in front of Aethan.

Slowly, I withdrew my awareness, slithering back into my own body, until I could hear Emerald, but nothing else. I felt small and inconsequential in comparison to what I had. A dragon's sense of self was so much bigger, so much *more* than what I was used to. And to have been a part of two of them, well, it was like nothing else I had ever experienced.

Arthur and Isla dropped in next to us, Isla's broad smile mimicking Arthur's except for one small thing. She managed to keep her tongue inside her mouth.

'Yippeee,' Grams shouted as we banked. I pivoted my head to look at her. She had both her arms stretched out wide as she enjoyed the speed rush from our descent.

There was no need to give the enemy the exact co-ordinates of our army so we flew a wide arc back to camp. We soared down around the far side of the hills which were currently sheltering us from view and back along the edge of the forest on our left flank.

I still wasn't sure if I was sold on the idea of having a forest so close to the camp. All of my worst goblin encounters had happened in forests. And while it would stop them sweeping around the hill and coming en masse at us, it also meant danger could more easily creep up on us. In the end I had to conclude that the danger that could 'creep up on us' would do less damage than a ravaging horde of goblins and orcs.

I scanned the forest below, looking for unfriendly visitors. I could tell Turos saw it at the same time as I did, because Lance banked at the same time as Emerald.

'What is it?' Aethan leant forwards and stared out past me.

'There's something…weird,' there was no other way to describe it, 'in that stand of trees.' I pointed to an area populated by oaks. A narrow gap with a small creek, meandered through the trees. Something lumpy filled a part of the gap.

As I watched, it moved, and one of the lumps became an arm, and another a foot and I realised what it was.

A giant, lying in the forest.

Lance let out a roar and dipped in a dive towards it. Flames streaked out of his nostrils as he raced for an easy kill.

'Stop,' I yelled at the same time that I heard Isla let out a shriek, but Turos was too far ahead to hear us.

Stop him, I urged Emerald. *He's a friend.*

Well, I was assuming he was a friend. There was no other reason he would be on this side of the mountain range and not the other.

Lance pulled up at the last second, the downward draft from his wings throwing leaves and sticks into the air over the body of the giant.

Emerald and Arthur landed at the edge of the forest and a second later Isla and I took off at a run into the trees.

'Izzy, wait,' Aethan yelled. 'We can't be sure it's him.'

But I knew in my heart who it was.

Isla looked back over her shoulder at me, a smile spreading her lips wide. She dodged through the trees, heading in the direction we had seen him.

The ground shook, throwing us to our knees.

'It's him,' Isla said, pushing herself back up.

We took off at a sprint, leaves and twigs slapping our faces and arms. The ground trembled again and I heard a familiar voice say, 'Ouchy. Nasty dragon made a mess of Tiny's bed.'

I let out a laugh as I flew through the trees, matching Isla stride-for-stride as we raced each other to him.

'Tiny,' we yelled together. 'Tiny.'

The trembling stopped and his voice rumbled, 'Izzy? Isla?' We burst from the trees a hundred yards from where he sat.

'Tiny,' we both shrieked.

'Dollies?' He let out a gurgling laugh as we scrambled up onto his leg and then raced along his shin bone as if it was a bridge. He reached out a hand and we each grabbed a finger, hugging them as if they were trees.

'Dollies.' He nodded his head with satisfaction and then lifted his hand up to his mouth so that he could plant enormous kisses on our bodies.

'Tiny.' Aethan appeared in the clearing. 'It's good to see you man.' He jumped up onto Tiny's leg and trotted up till he was standing on his thigh.

Tiny examined him with one eye while the other one stared off to the side. 'Aethan.' He prodded him with the fingertips of his free hand. It was meant to be gentle I'm sure, but Aethan lost his balance and fell into a crouch. 'Where's Willy?' Tiny placed all of us on his thigh next to Aethan and then looked around the clearing.

'He's not here,' Isla said. 'But he will be. And look,' she held her arms up for Tiny to admire her shiny markings, 'he gave me these.'

'Pretty.' Tiny nodded his head.

Aethan looked at Isla's arms again. 'You saw Wilfred?'

'No.' She shook her head, her smile telling me she knew she was driving him crazy.

'But....' He stopped and shook his head. He knew Isla too well to play along with her game.

'What are you doing here?' I said. 'It's dangerous. There's going to be a war.'

Tiny's misshaped face screwed up, the tip of his tongue popping out between his teeth as he nodded his head. 'Tiny knows. Tiny came to help.'

Turos, Grams and Lionel stepped out of the trees. The rest of the Millenium hung back, spreading out in a protective fan around us.

'Blimey,' Grams said, 'that's the biggest giant I've ever seen.' She peered up at him. 'If I'm not mistaken, you must be Berdina Flatfoot's son.'

'You knew Mummy?' Tiny leant forwards and the small shift in his body threw us to our knees. 'Oops. Sorry.' He patted us roughly, each stroke forcing my head further onto my spine, and then turned his attention back to Grams.

'She was a dear friend of mine,' Grams said. 'I am so sorry. I heard about her death. She was a true hero.'

Tears welled up in Tiny's eyes and I scampered down the side of his pants onto the ground. I knew all too well what happened when Tiny started to cry and I didn't feel like dodging basketball-sized tears. Isla and Aethan landed beside me.

'I don't really remember her,' he said.

'My dear fellow.' Grams marched forwards and patted him on the leg. 'Would you like me to tell you some stories?'

Tiny nodded his head, and tears flew out in an arc, smacking into the ground around us like water bombs.

'Well,' Grams held a hand out to him, 'why don't you follow us back to camp and I'll tell you all about it?'

The ground trembled as Tiny placed his hands on the ground and pushed himself up. I widened my stance, relaxing my knees to ride it.

'May I suggest you let us get airborne first?' Lionel looked up from his position on all fours.

'Ooooopps.' A sheepish smile tugged at Tiny's lips.

He waited till we were all back on dragon back before he stood up.

'Tell Turos we'll head back and warn the army we've got a giant with us. I should also brief Tamsonite on the success of our mission as soon as possible.'

I nodded my head at Aethan's words and opened my mind to Emerald. A few seconds later I saw Turos nod his head and lift a hand in farewell. Emerald circled the odd group once before we shot off towards the army. I could tell she was uncomfortable leaving Arthur behind with a giant.

He won't hurt him, I reassured her.

It's just that he's bigger than Arthur. What if he accidentally swipes him from the air?

I didn't point out that he was bigger than her and Lance as well. *He won't.* I hoped.

She let out a small puff of smoke and kept the rest of her worries to herself.

A few minutes later we landed at the front of our troops. I watched as Tamsonite came to meet us. Rako, King Arwyn and another man accompanied him. I was guessing by the General's stripes the last man wore, that he was the human General.

'General Robertson,' Aethan said, nodding his head at the man. 'Father.' He clasped forearms with Arwyn and then pulled him into a hug. They slapped each other on the back before releasing each other again. 'Rako, Wolfgang, good to see you.'

I waved from my place next to Emerald and Wolfgang waved back. Rako wasn't the wavy type, he dipped his head in a nod instead.

'Well met, well met,' General Tamsonite said. 'How did you fare?'

'The mission was a success, Sir,' Aethan said. 'Except for one thing. A few thousand of them had already made it through the pass. If they keep moving at the same pace, they'll be here by nightfall.'

Tamsonite muttered an oath. 'Oh well. It will give the new recruits something to cut their teeth on.'

'There's a chance they may realise they've been cut off from the rest of the army and wait,' Aethan continued.

Tamsonite nodded. 'Well at least with aerial surveillance we will have some warning. Did you get a look at the rest of the army?'

Aethan shook his head. 'We couldn't see the crater from where we were.'

'We've had word from King Arracon,' King Arwyn said. 'They are a day away.'

'How is that possible?' Aethan asked what I am sure we were all wondering.

'Turns out their entire force is mounted. As are their slaves.' Arwyn shook his head at the thought of that many horses. 'They can cover in a day what it's been taking us four to do.'

Aethan looked around. 'Speaking of night faeries?'

'She's with the rear guard,' Rako said. 'It's the safest place.'

I nudged Aethan and raised my eyebrows at him when he looked at me.

He didn't miss a beat as he turned back to Tamsonite. 'Sir, on our way back to camp we came across a friendly giant. He's the son of Berdina Flatfoot. He should arrive in about thirty minutes and it would be good if our troops didn't try to kill him.'

'Berdina's son, hey?' Tamsonite nodded his head. 'She was a fine giant. One of a kind.' He turned to his personal aide. 'Roger,' he barked, 'make your way to the rear of the army and when you see a giant coming sound the stand down call. Just don't do it so loudly that the whole damned army hears you.' He shook his head and turned back to us. 'The last thing we need with a possible horde about to attack is an army taking a siesta.'

Roger saluted, turned, and ran towards a line of horses picketed to the side. He pulled the reins of a roan mare off a wooden post and jumped onto her back.

'Can you organise an air reconnaissance?' Tamsonite asked. 'I'd like to know if we are expecting an imminent attack or not.'

I nodded and closed my eyes as I opened my mind towards Emerald.

'Oh and can you see if King Bladimir is free. I think a council of war might be in order.'

I nodded again and started to close my eyes.

'And I guess we should get Prince Turos as well. He'll be heading the dragon riders.'

I closed them again.

'Tell them all to meet us at the command tent.'

I opened my eyes and stared at him. 'Is that it?'

He ignored the snippy tone in my voice. Apparently you don't get to be the General in charge of the army by being phased by temperamental eighteen year olds. 'For now.'

This time when I closed my eyes he was silent. Emerald sent the requests for reconnaissance, Turos and Bladimir out to the appropriate dragons.

'All done, Sir,' I said when she had finished. 'They are on their way.'

'Splendid. Shall we?' He held his arm out in the direction of the tent and then led the way. Arwyn, Robertson and Rako fell in beside him.

We beat King Bladimir to the tent by a few minutes. Gladaline was with him, the stately way she held herself belying her visual appearance. It seemed I wasn't the only one who hadn't had time to bathe since coming through the gateway from Millenium.

'This is my wife, Queen Gladaline.' King Bladimir had a firm grip on her hand. 'Darling, this is King Arwyn, Prince Aethan, General Tamsonite, General Robertson and the head of the fae Border Guard, Rako. And of course you have already met Isadora Gabrielle.'

Gladaline tilted her head as Rako, Aethan and the Generals bowed to her. King Arwyn gave her a nod of his own.

I started with a curtsy before realising it was hard to curtsy when wearing pants. I moved into an awkward bow and finished it up with a head tilt. I'm sure it looked more like a weird dance movement than anything else but the only person who seemed to see it was Aethan. He placed his hand over his mouth and coughed as he struggled not to laugh.

'I thought she should be here as well. She sometimes has a,' Bladimir cleared his throat, 'useful way of looking at things.'

'Of course.' Tamsonite waved a hand at the chairs that were arranged around a large table and everyone sat down. I had already done a head count and realised we were one chair short. That suited me fine. Instead, I stood to the side, leaning up against one of the tent poles. I really didn't want to be a part of the planning. In fact, I was kind of hoping they'd forget about me entirely. The last thing I wanted was a plan which involved me saving the day.

Turos's head appeared through the tent opening. He grinned when he saw there were no seats left and came over to where I was trying to blend into the tent canvas. His shoulder touched mine as he leant up against the other side of the tent pole. I saw Aethan glance towards us and stiffen.

The tent flap moved and Wolfgang appeared in the entrance. 'Ahhh. This is the right tent. Good. It's so easy to get disorientated when all the tents look the same.' He winked at me and then looked at the table.

Aethan jumped to his feet. 'Please,' he said, 'have my seat.' He moved over to stand on the other side of me.

I rolled my eyes to the ceiling and muttered, 'Men,' under my breath.

A bugle called far off in the distance. Tiny had arrived.

'Are we all here?' Tamsonite looked around the table.

My mind wandered while he filled them in on the situation at the pass. I was trying not to think about any of it. It wasn't that I was worried about facing goblins, orcs, Vulpine or dwarfs. The giants did make me pause just a little. I still hadn't worked out the logistical best way to deal with them, but I was betting if I blew out their knee caps it would pretty much be game over for them.

No, it wasn't any of them that had my stomach churning in knots. I was worried about something far more worrisome. I felt like I'd been chosen captain of a sports team when I wasn't actually up to it. If only this was as simple as something that started with a coin toss and ended with a victory lap and maybe an ale at the local pub.

Instead, soon, sooner than I cared to think about, it was going to begin. And shortly afterwards I would face Santanas again on the battlefield. Things hadn't worked out so well for us the last time that had happened. I wasn't up to it. I knew that. And I was pretty sure everybody else did as well. And that only made me feel even sicker.

A throat cleared outside the tent.

'Come in Roger,' Tamsonite called.

A hand appeared pushing back the flap and Roger's body followed his head. He looked around the circle of leaders as he threw a salute. 'The giant has arrived, Sir. And the aerial surveillance has arrived back as well.'

'Splendid.' Tamsonite struck his palm down on the table. 'Send them in.'

Isla slipped through the opening and stood in front of the table. She threw her father a smile and then turned to look at General Tamsonite and General Robertson. 'They're coming,' she said. 'I'm not even sure they realise they've been cut off from the rest of their group. I estimate they will come into view in about an hour.'

Robertson chuckled and rubbed his hands together. 'Like lambs to the slaughter.'

Isla tipped her head to the side. 'Possibly. Of course the Vulpine circling over them may make things a little more difficult.' She smiled. 'A couple of them thought it would be best if Arthur and I didn't make it back.' Her smile broadened.

Turos sucked in his breath. I felt him move and turned to see him shaking his head. I knew what he was thinking. It hadn't been Arthur and Isla that had been sent out to scout. She must have convinced the other dragonrider to escort Tiny in instead. 'We're smaller. We'll be less visible.' I could hear her persuasive voice echoing in my head. I was pretty sure her beatific smile had just got one of the dragon riders into big trouble.

She didn't seem concerned though. She took up a position behind her father's chair as if acting as his guard but I knew it was really so she had a better view of the map.

'And so it begins, again.' Wolfgang's voice was tinged with sadness.

I felt my spine stiffen as the full import of his words struck me. I was worrying about going up against my grandfather, a man I had never known. Wolfgang was about to go up against his son-in-law, a man he had known. Known and *loved*. And it wasn't the first time he had done this.

It didn't really matter whether or not we could win. What mattered was that we fought tooth and nail trying. What mattered the most was that we said **no** to a life of fear and tyranny, instead, choosing to fight for our freedom.

I took in a deep breath and let it slowly back out again. Yes, that I *could* do.

'Our main threat,' Tamsonite stated the obvious, 'will come from aerial attacks, and any spells they throw at us.

Their voices droned on while I thought about what Ulandes has said. What had she meant by any of it? And how could the real battle be in me? What did I have to do? Did I have to do it at a certain time? If I didn't, would we lose?'

'Gentlemen,' Tamsonite looked at Bladimir and Wolfgang, 'how do we stand on those fronts?'

'Our dragons will eat those mangy eagles for breakfast.'

'The spellcasters stand ready to serve.'

Tamsonite smoothed down his gigantic moustache. 'Well, I don't think there is anything else we need to discuss. Let's get moving. If we start marching now, we should be in place in time to deal with them before dark.' He pushed his chair back from the table and stood.

Dark Sky. I'd day dreamed my way through the whole briefing. 'Urrrrr,' I said. 'What do you want me to do?'

Rako scratched at the corner of his mouth. A habit I had noticed that presented when he was trying not to smile. 'May I?' He looked at Tamsonite and Robertson, waiting for them to nod before he continued. 'Izzy. You are to do whatever needs to be done. Within the limits of course.'

'That's it?' I knew what he was talking about. No black magic.

He nodded. 'That's it.'

Huh. So much for getting direction from them. I was no closer to understanding what my part in all of this was.

I traced a finger over the map while the rest of them filed from the room. I had flown over this area, so it all looked familiar. Turos stood next to me, staring intently at the map, but I had a feeling he wasn't concentrating on it.

'What's up?' I spoke softly enough that the others wouldn't hear.

'Not sure.' He traced a finger over the line of hills which currently sheltered us from view from the Pass of Bones. 'Something's not right though.'

'How so?'

'Don't know.' He turned to look at me. 'But when I figure it out, you'll be the first to know.'

'You see it too?' Aethan let the tent flap fall and walked back over to the table. The two of them faced each other, but for the first time there was no animosity in their stances.

Turos nodded. 'Things aren't what they seem.'

'They never are.' Aethan tilted his head as he scratched at the side of his face. 'Tell your men to be ready to move quickly.' He smiled at his own words.

'Agreed.' Turos held out his hand. 'We work together on this.'

'To keep her safe?' Aethan nodded. 'Always.'

'What are you two *talking* about?' Exasperation tinged my voice.

The tent flap pushed up and Isla pushed back through the opening. 'They're talking about the trap,' Isla said.

Chapter Twelve

The Beginning of the End

'A trap?' My voice rang out an octave higher than normal. How come I was the only person that didn't know about the trap?

Aethan put a hand on my arm. 'We don't know for sure there's a trap.'

Isla rolled her eyes. 'Really? How can there not be? There's *always* a trap.'

I groaned and sank back into my chair. Of course there was a trap.

'It would be gross incompetence if *this* was their only plan.' She waved a sparkly arm at the map.

I put my head on my hands. 'We're just puppets,' I mumbled through my fingers. I was officially the worst War Faery in the history of time.

'The attackers always have the advantage of surprise,' Aethan said.

'Shouldn't we tell someone? Rako? Tamsonite?'

'I'm sure Rako has worked it out. The others haven't dealt with Galanta before. They're working on the premise that goblins are stupid.' Aethan let out a snort. 'Which most of them are.'

'Come on.' Isla grabbed my hand and pulled me up. 'They're waiting for us to get airborne. They don't want the forward troops getting attacked by the Vulpine.'

I followed her to the exit, watching as she pushed open the flap and her arm emerged into the sun. Light glinted off her tattoos, the prism from one of her diamonds blinding me. I blinked and shook my head, trying to dispel the bright white light that obscured my vision.

'Down,' Isla screamed. She slammed into me, knocking me to my knees.

I peered up, saw the sword descending in an arc toward me, saw Isla position herself above, her arm held high to take the cut that was mine. I poured my magic out towards the attacker, toward the sword, but they were moving with the speed of light, and before I could stop them, the edge of the sword contacted Isla's arm.

I say contacted, rather than bit into, or severed.

Sparks flew as it met her skin, and an eerie screeching sound lifted the hairs on the back of my neck. She let out a delighted laugh, as she twisted her forearm, sending the sword flying, and then slammed her other arm into the attacker's nose.

Blood spurted and his head whipped back as if she had hit him with a baseball bat. He flew through the air with the force of it, and landed a few metres away.

I wasn't sure if he was dead or not until Aethan bent over and put his fingers to the man's throat.

'Dead,' he said, standing back up. He stared down at the attacker's face. 'One of yours I think.' He looked over his shoulder at Turos who let out a low oath before nodding his head.

'Izzy made some enemies before we came through.' He walked over and peered down at the man. 'What did you hit him with?' He had been the last one out of the tent and had missed most of the action. 'You crushed his skull.'

Isla lifted her arm and poked a finger into her own flesh. It dented like normal skin would under pressure.

'We need to change our plan,' Aethan said. 'How can we trust your men not to attack Izzy again?'

I pushed myself to my knees and up to my feet, brushing the dirt off my bottom as I did.

'This was a civilian,' Turos said. 'None of my men are stupid enough to hold a grudge against her for what she did. And besides, she's saved most of their lives a couple of times now. They owe her.'

The two men faced each other, their clenched fists causing their knuckles to whiten.

'You need us,' Turos said. 'You know we have the advantage of speed, and we have the dragons. When whatever is going to happen, happens, you're going to need us.'

They stared at each other for another few, tense seconds, then Aethan nodded once. 'Fine. But if any of your men try anything, I'm holding you personally responsible.'

'If any of my men try anything, *I'm* holding me personally responsible.'

Isla shook her head and whispered, '*Men,*' under her breath. 'Come on,' she took my hand and started walking toward where the dragons were.

I poked her arm with my free hand and she smiled at me.

'Did you know?' I asked.

'That *that* would happen? An arrow bounced off me in the Pass of Bones.' She shrugged.

'But you weren't totally sure and you did it anyway.'

She gave me her widest grin. 'I guess that makes me a hero.'

I nudged her. 'It makes you *something*, that's for sure.'

She laughed as she dropped my hand and danced off towards Arthur. His tongue hung out and he had his normal goofy smile on his face, but it intensified as she approached, and his whole body started to wiggle.

'Is he...,' a vision of Scruffy flashed into my head, 'wagging his tail?' I started to giggle. 'Does he think he's a dog?'

'Of course not.' Isla rubbed her hands up and down Arthur's neck and he danced from side-to-side. 'He thinks Scruffy is a dragon.'

I heard Emerald sigh in my mind.

'What took you so long?' Grams and Lionel stood by Emerald. 'Athol wanted us airborne five minutes ago.'

I opened my mouth to make a smart arse comment about assassins but before I could, there was a shout from the front of the army.

We paused, all of us craning our heads to see what had happened. A thought bubble floated in the air. The afternoon light glinted off it and an oily layer swam on its surface. More bubbles floated into view, spreading out and heading in different directions.

Two broke off from the pack and descended towards Isla and me. I backed up till I was standing beside her.

'This can't be good,' I muttered to her.

She raised one eyebrow and looked at me and then the bubbles broke over our heads.

'Welcome Daughter. Tomorrow we will meet on the battlefield. Many will die. You know what you need to do to stop this. Come to me. Let us be the family we were meant to be. I would prefer not to have to kill my own blood.'

The bubble burst and I was left with a slimy residue on my face. I wiped an arm across it and looked over at Isla in time to see hers pop.

'Santanas?' I asked.

She grimaced as she wiped her face. 'What did he say to you?'

'Pretty much the same thing he did the last time we met. Join me or die. You?'

'If we give you up, this will all go away.'

I pulled a face. 'Divide and conquer.'

'Something like that.'

I was silent while I thought about her words. 'Do you believe him?'

'Not for one pink second.'

The bubbles, which had been coming through in ones and twos, started thickening. They swirled in the afternoon breeze as they swooped down on the army.

I watched as a couple of soldiers' bubbles burst. They both looked towards me before meeting each other's eyes. I could just imagine what they were thinking.

'Come on.' I turned and walked back towards the front of the camp, searching for Aethan and Rako. They stood with their heads close together. Aethan was talking urgently, waving his arms around as he did. I could tell by the fact that the fur on the edges of their vests was damp that they had already had their bubble message.

They stopped talking as we approached. 'You two ready to move out?' Rako asked.

I glanced at the soldiers that were forming up nearby. Most had their eyes straight ahead but some watched me, thoughtful expressions on their faces.

'Yep,' I said. Their scrutiny was making the skin between my shoulder blades itch.

Turos marched towards me, a score of warriors following in his wake. His gaze scanned the surrounding soldiers. He stopped beside me while his warriors formed up on either side and behind. I realised he had just provided me with a guard.

Rako nodded once, and Aethan's shoulders lowered a fraction as he relaxed. He shared a look with Turos before turning back to me.

'Is it true?' Ebony's voice cut sharply through the relative quiet of the camp. 'Will this all end if we give Isadora up?'

Her riding skirts swirled around her legs as she made her way towards us. Her long hair shone like midnight satin as she swept it behind her shoulder. I noted that this movement accomplished two things. Firstly, it gave us all an eyeful of her cleavage, and secondly, it left the sword, strapped to her left hip, exposed. She rested her handle lightly on the pommel.

'Well? Is it?' She pursed her lips as she looked up at Aethan.

Even the soldiers that had been keeping their eyes straight ahead were now watching. Turos and his men shifted their stances, closer to outright battle than they had been a second ago.

'No,' Aethan's voice rang across the now totally still army. 'It is not true. Do you really think he would stop now?'

She tapped her finger on her bottom lip and gave me a speculative look. 'Probably not,' she said. 'But it might be worth a try.'

Several of the soldiers shifted their heads as if nodding in agreement.

'This,' Aethan waved his arm around, 'is exactly what he is trying to gain. A break in our ranks. Are we all so naïve as to believe what a murdering, madman has to say?' He turned to face the ranks of soldiers. 'Are we all so quick to sacrifice one of our own? Someone who has dedicated her life to our safety? What will he ask for next? Me? You?' He waved his hand at the men. 'Are we here to give him what he wants, or are we here to stop him for good?'

A low rumble of voices broke out around us as men debated Aethan's words.

'Well,' Ebony sniffed delicately, 'I would give myself up if that's what it took.'

'Really?' Isla let out a snort of laughter. 'I wouldn't speak too quickly Ebony. You never know what the next bubble may ask for. Your head on a stick, perhaps.'

Ebony blanched and stepped closer to Aethan, wrapping an arm around his waist.

'I think it would be a good time to leave,' Turos murmured. 'While the going is good.'

'What are we waiting for?' Tamsonite's voice boomed. 'I said form up and march out and I meant it.'

The soldiers stiffened to attention, their formerly-lax lines, straightening to resemble the edge of a ruler. The eyes of those closest to us snapped to the front and I let out a breath I hadn't realised I had been holding.

Aethan untangled himself from Ebony's arms. 'You had best take up your position near the rear,' he said to her. 'Your Father and people could arrive at any time.'

'They said they were a day out.' She stuck out her bottom lip in a pout and entwined herself around him again. 'I want to ride with you.'

'You can never be too prepared.' He unwound her arms again. 'It's where you are needed the most. And besides, I won't be riding.'

Her mouth formed a pretty O. 'You would fight on foot like a lowly soldier?'

His eyes glinted with suppressed anger. 'I would fight on foot with my men.'

'Forward march,' Tamsonite bellowed.

Ebony leant into Aethan but the immediate sound of several thousand boots striking the ground swamped what she said. I was pretty sure by the naughty curve to her lips that I hadn't wanted to hear it anyway.

'Come on.' I turned toward the dragons and Turos's warriors opened a path for me.

Isla's hadn't moved. Her head was tilted to the side and the corners of her eyes creased ever-so-slightly as she examined Ebony. She started as I touched her arm.

'What is it?' I whispered.

The shook her head. 'Just wondering how she keeps her hair so clean.'

'Really?'

'You aren't?'

The stare she levelled on me had an intensity that went way beyond the pay grade of personal hygiene. No doubt there was a hidden meaning there I wasn't clever enough to understand. I sighed and shook my head. If she wanted me to get it, she was going to have to tell me.

She shrugged a shoulder and smiled, partly amused, partly frustrated. 'Come on.' She walked ahead, leading the way back to Emerald, Lance and Arthur.

'So,' Turos fell into step beside me, 'I'm guessing that *that*, is the complication.' He looked back over his shoulder towards Ebony and Aethan.

I let out a sigh. 'They're betrothed.'

'And yet he loves you.' He was silent for a few steps. 'Remind me to send her a thank you card.'

I stopped walking and turned towards him. 'Turos....'

I didn't even get to start what I wanted to say. He clasped my forearms with his huge hands and bent down so that his head was only inches away. His ice-blue eyes bored into mine, turning me into helpless prey. 'You can't deny the attraction between us. You can't deny that your blood boils whenever I touch you.' He let the fingers of one hand trail over my collar bone and up my neck to my face.

As if he'd commanded it, my heart rate accelerated. I felt my breath hitch in my throat.

'Why do you fight it?' he whispered. 'We are perfect together.'

He was right. We *were* perfect together. He was a match for me in every way possible. And when he was this close to me, I could imagine surrendering, and making the choice that would tie our lives together. And yet something stopped me from uttering the three little words that would make him mine.

I knew that that something was standing not too far away from me.

'Izzy.' Turos shook his head. 'I know you love me.'

I pulled a face and shrank away from him, his words making the butterflies in my stomach turn into a nest of angry hornets. He tightened his grip and pulled me back.

'You do. Admit it.'

My tongue cleaved to the roof of my mouth as I struggled to generate enough saliva to swallow. 'And what if I do?' A wave of giddiness swept over me.

His eyes lit with triumph. 'Just say the words.'

I glanced sideways, my eyes searching for Aethan. He was frozen like a statue, staring at the two of us. Ebony, seemingly unaware of the drama playing out, looked up at him as she spoke.

I snatched my eyes away from Aethan. 'I don't think that now is the right time for declarations of....' I couldn't force the word love out of my mouth.

'I think now is the *perfect* time.' Turos rubbed his thumb over my bottom lip. 'We're about to risk our lives and go into battle. We're about to fight together, melded as one through our bond.'

Emerald let out a low rumble in my mind and the hard, panicked knot that was stuck in my throat melted away. He was right. What better time to declare ourselves for each other than when we were about to fight side-by-side for our freedom. There was a magnificence to the idea.

I stared even deeper into his eyes and imagined our lives intertwined. Imagined having him as my mate. Forever.

A delicious excitement unfurled inside me. I could make this decision now. I could put all the hurt and confusion behind me. I could embrace a future with this amazing man.

My heart swelled in my chest. I smiled up at a him and opened my mouth to utter the words that would change me forever.

'Izzy. Come on.' Grams prodded me in the shoulder with a bony finger. 'There'll be plenty of time for this later. I hope.' She muttered the last sentence under her breath.

As if she had poked a hole in the side of my dam, the emotion whooshed out of me. It drained away till all I was left with was my confusion. I pushed Turos's hands away from me and stepped back. 'Not now,' I said. 'Not yet.'

I looked around. The camp was a frenzy of activity, but Aethan was gone. Nausea rolled over me. What had he seen? Or more importantly, what had he thought he'd seen?

Grams tugged on my arm, 'Come on.'

I let her lead me toward Emerald while I searched for him. I knew it was fruitless. He would have deployed to the front with his men. But I tried anyway. Suddenly, my urge to see him, to touch him one last time was overwhelming.

Panic fluttered under my ribs. What if something happened to him? I closed my eyes but the picture of him, his face contorted with anguish and betrayal, danced before me.

Turos matched my steps, quiet now that Grams was within hearing distance. He reached out and squeezed my hand and then shot me a grin before trotting off towards Lance. His men were already mounted.

I waited for Grams to climb up in front of Lionel before climbing up into my seat. All of the Guard were staying on the ground but Turos had put a few of his Millenium onto Emerald.

Let's go.

Emerald didn't bother to answer. Instead, she took a few hopping steps forwards and thrust her wings down. Another stepping hop and we were airborne, soaring up to where Arthur and Isla circled. A formation of dragons flew by, the black-garbed Millenium on their backs scanning the surrounding sky for danger.

We fell in on Lance's left, flying at a pace that would not overly tax Arthur. Even then, it didn't take us long to get to the front of the army. A smudge of black darkened the land ahead of us. I felt my heart rate accelerate. The goblins were coming.

I looked back at the army, at the Border Guard lining up to lead the defence. Then I looked at the dragons circling lazily in the sky. As exhilarating as it was, being up here in the sky, it felt wrong. *I* felt wrong. I'd fought with the Guard my whole life. I belonged with the Guard, and yet I was bonded to Emerald. I knew in the Milleniums' eyes, my place was with her.

I looked back at the goblins. There were thousands of them. The Vulpines may or may not show, but if they did there were hundreds of dragons to deal with them, thousands of Millenium.

Emerald. I reached out tentatively.

You want me to land?

How did you know?

She let out a snort. *I know you. You're bonded to me, but your bond to them is just as strong.*

My place is with you. I found myself quoting Turos.

She snorted again. *We are not exactly a conventionally-bonded pair. I can fight those pesky chickens with or without you.*

What about if one of them lands on you.

Are you the only fighter on board?

I let out a sigh, fighting the surge of guilt that was warring with my need to go to the Guard. *I am not meant to leave you.*

The Millenium have lived on an island the entire time they've been bonded to my kind.

And...?

They never had a need to separate. All their training was done over water.

I glanced back down at the Guard. They had split into two groups, one each side of the main army. They were going to chop into the goblins on either side, separating the front of the goblin horde from the rest so that the army could finish them. Then they would withdraw and do the same again. That sort of tactic could elicit heavy losses. *So you're saying?*

She did the equivalent of a human sigh into my head. I didn't blame her, I was only half listening and she obviously had a point to make. I snapped my mind from the Guard back to her.

They have never been in a situation where separating might make them stronger. I am not a dumb horse that needs you to steer me.

I laughed out loud. *Tactically it seems a sound plan for us to become two separate units. You can feed me information about what you can see up here.*

The goblins had been getting ever closer. It was only a matter of minutes before they engaged the front line of our defence.

I'll let Lance know.

A few seconds later she banked and flew around to find a clear space to land. I was going to have to hustle if I was to make it back to the front before the goblins got there.

'What are you doing?'

I hadn't noticed that Lance had followed us down. Turos stood next to him with his hands on his hips.

'I'm needed down here.'

'You're needed up there.' He pointed into the sky.

'Emerald and I spoke about it. She doesn't need me.'

His mouth pressed into a thin line and his eyes tightened.

'Look.' I took a few steps towards him and took his hand. 'You've never practiced this type of warfare. All you've known is aerial fighting. And you're all very good at it. But the heaviest fighting will be down here. I'm needed where the heaviest fighting will be.'

'Who's going to save the day if you go and get yourself killed?' His face relaxed just the tiniest bit.

'Oh please.' I let out a laugh. Goblins had been slightly challenging before Turos taught me the mind trick. Now, they were chicken feed.

He cocked his head to the side and then looked over at Lance. 'Lance thinks you have a valid point,' he said.

'He does?'

'Our job is to stop the Vulpine from attacking the troops, but the main fight will be down here.' He looked thoughtful.

'I've really got to get to the front.'

'We probably don't need so many of us in the sky.' He looked back at Lance and said, 'Every second man off.'

Five Millenium slipped from Lance's back.

'Lance will spread the word. Let's go.'

They took off so quickly that I realised they had already embraced their calm. I did the same and followed, racing to try and catch up with him and his men. We slipped around the side of the army, speeding towards the front.

Men held swords ready. Some were statuesque while others jiggled from foot-to-foot as they tried to allay their nerves. Shields rested on the ground by their legs as they waited.

The rhythmical beat of the enemy drum increased its pace and the goblins moved from a march to a trot. They picked up their speed, mouths pulled back in snarling smiles, cruel daggers clenched in their fists. A tide of death flowing over the plain to meet us.

Even though this was a small piece of Santanas's army, they still covered the breadth of the land and ran one hundred deep. I estimated there were ten thousand of them. My face pulled back in a grin. Excellent. There were plenty for all of us to share.

The goblins met the might force of the allies a few seconds before we reached the front. A roar went up as the two sides clashed.

Aethan. Where was Aethan? I scoured the frontline searching for him. In the few seconds that took, Turos and his men closed on the goblins. I was there a second later.

I pushed Aethan away from my thoughts. The last thing he needed right then was me operating at less than my best. He needed me to be strong. He needed me to be powerful.

I let out a cry as I leapt into the air, landing on a goblin in the second row. His pointed teeth showed as he opened his mouth to snarl at me, and then his eyes were rolling up as he slumped to the ground. I pulled my sword out of his chest and swiped it across the throat of the goblin closest to him.

Vulpines inbound. Emerald's voice blazed in my head and for a fleeting second worries for her, and for Grams and Lionel, and all the dragons, all the Millenium, teased at the edges of my mind control. I pushed them away. I couldn't let thoughts like that distract me.

Let me know if you need help.

I could feel Emerald's wild exuberance radiating through our bond. She dodged and twisted and turned while she attacked, blowing fire and clawing birds out of the sky with her long talons. I thrust and parried, weaving through the falling bodies of the goblins.

For a fraction of a second, Turos appeared beside me, a crazy smile lighting his face as he fought. I felt my mouth stretch to match his. More and more Millenium flowed in around us as we fought beside the Guard. We were able to cut off a much larger chunk than the Guard would have first aimed for, leaving the regular army to finish them off while we turned and fought our way at a diagonal back to the side.

Arrows thudded into the necks of the goblins in front of me and I looked up to see Arthur sail by. Isla stood like a wrathful Goddess on his back, her balance perfect as she fired into the goblins below.

Arthur.

Emerald's shriek made me look back. A trio of eagles flew low and fast, their masters braced, ready to leap. I was sure they wouldn't make it, that Isla would see them and neutralise their threat with her arrows, but I couldn't be sure. I thrust my sword into a goblin's chest, felt the metal bite deep into bone, then I leapt up, using the quivering sword's handgrip to springboard me into the air. I raised my hands and fired two bolts of force at the back of the eagles. Feathers rained down on the goblins as the two birds exploded into tiny shreds of meat. The Vulpine fell from the sky. The fall wasn't high enough to kill them, but the angry goblins they hit appeared to finish the job.

Isla released three arrows into the final bird and it, too, disappeared from view, smacking into the bored, angry goblins waiting their turn to fight.

We made our way back to the edge of the army, slicing off a triangular piece of foe and then we turned and headed back toward the centre. I recognised some of the Guard I fought beside, but Aethan was nowhere to be seen. Had he fallen in the first clash? Was that possible?

I concentrated on what I was doing, on the feel of my body moving as I wielded my swords, on the familiar ache of tiring muscles, on the huge, sweat-glistened goblins with their bare chests and their loin cloths and their twisted, jagged daggers. I was like the wind that whirled around them, but instead of cooling their skin, I left death in my wake. Turos and his men raced with me, whirling and striking and tearing and shredding. Where we appeared, goblins fell. We made it back to the middle and continued, searching for our men fighting in from the other side.

A band of them had been cut off from the rest. They fought back to back, using all their skill as they fended off goblins fuelled with the knowledge of their imminent success. Aethan was amongst them. Sweat rolled off his forehead as he moved with the grace of a master swordsman, but for every enemy he felled, more pressed forward. There was nowhere for him to go, nowhere for him to seek shelter. It was only a matter of time before he was crushed beneath their numbers.

I let out a shriek of fury.

'Go.' Turos appeared beside me, holding his hands together in the same way he had when we had fought on the dragons earlier that day.

I didn't need to think about it. I sprang up into them, letting him fling me high into the air. I held my hands out to the side in a swan dive before turning a somersault that brought me down on the shoulders of a goblin two back from Aethan. I thrust my swords back into the chests of those immediately behind me and grabbed the head of the one I sat on, relishing the sound of his neck snapping as I wrenched it to the side. I rode him to the ground, retrieved my swords from the already-dead goblins and thrust them up into the backs of the two goblins facing off against Aethan. Then I jumped over them and landed beside Aethan.

'Thought you could do with some help,' I said.

'You thought right.' He flashed me a quick smile.

Incoming.

I turned my attention from the ground to the sky. Emerald was right. A score of eagles approached us. Their talons extended as they swooped down on the Guard. I imagined a wave of air roiling towards them and unleashed my will in their direction. Air distorted as it rushed back to meet them. Several of them saw the glisten of the wind stream and tried to pull up, but they were too late.

Beaks snapped and bones cracked as the eagles' bodies buckled through their necks and onto the invisible wall of air in front of them. And then all the birds behind compounded the effect. Crumpled bodies slid from the sky down the vertical wall.

I turned back to find Turos fighting toward Aethan. The two men fought like demons, but Aethan moved at a quarter of the pace that Turos did. For every goblin that Aethan downed, four or five fell at Turos's feet. I smiled as I thought about how desperate he would be for me to teach him the mind trick after the day was over.

Turos gave me a cheeky grin and a mock salute as he made it to our island of fighters. I noted that some of his men moved to the far side of the Guard, joining their group.

I could feel my blood racing through my arteries as the blood-lust sang in my veins. I parried and dodged and danced my way through the enemy. Blood dripped down my swords and up my forearms.

I stopped thinking. I stopped feeling. I saw only the goblins still standing. I laughed as I danced through them, exulting in the feeling of supremacy my skill allowed me. Twice more I struck down Vulpine. Three more times I cut through the enemy to save Aethan's group.

Yelling and cursing quietened as men concentrated on the simple act of swinging their swords, of holding their shields high enough to provide cover. The general army rotated out and fresh troops surged forwards. But still the

Guard spearhead continued its job of cutting the goblin horde into smaller manageable chunks.

The sun moved closer to the horizon and there were no more goblins ahead of me. I turned and began to fight my way back, Millenium flanking me, Turos taking my left side. We slashed our way through them until we were facing our own men. Ragged breathing hung heavy in the air as bewildered men looked around for someone to fight. But they were all dead. And then the cheering began. Slowly at first, the voices rough with exertion. Like a wave it spread, back through the army, till every man waved his sword in the air.

Something soft moved beneath me. I looked down, surprised to find I stood on a goblin's chest. Their bodies were all around us. Three deep in parts. Back the way we had come, I saw the bodies of our own men interspersed among those of the enemy, lying wounded or dead on the cold, hard ground.

I took a deep shuddering breath. Then another. All the time trying to let go of my state of mind. Finally, it shimmered to the sides and everything snapped back into place.

The cheering died off as quickly as it had begun, leaving the low moans of the wounded reverberating off the hills around us.

The survivors stood like confused cattle, shaking their heads as they surveyed the damage. It reminded me that most of these men had been the new recruits that Tamsonite was letting cut their teeth.

Healers moved amongst the battlefield, searching for people they could help. I recognised my best friend's short, curvaceous shape. She moved more quickly than the other healers, taking the time to turn the heads of those I could tell were dead, even from where I stood.

Thomas. She was searching for Thomas.

'Thomas.' I called out without thinking. 'Thomas.' My cry echoed down the valley. I moved toward Sabby, cold ice walking down my spine. He *had* to be here. He *had* to be alive.

My search felt selfish when so many around me would never open their eyes again. I pushed that thought aside. He had to be safe. He *had* to.

'Izzy.' Turos grabbed my elbow and spun me around, pointing back at his own men.

Thomas stood with the Millenium, a dazed look on his face. I knew what having that look felt like. He had embraced his centre of peace and was having trouble letting it go.

'He appeared half way through the battle,' Turos said. 'Fought like a madman the whole time.'

Relief flowed into me. Of course I was going to kill him myself for the fright he had just given me, but at least he was alive for now.

'Sabby,' I yelled. 'He's alive.'

She stopped in the act of bending over another dead soldier and looked toward me. She followed my arm with her eyes and her body sagged with relief. Turos stood beside Thomas, talking slowly to him. He was the best person to help with the problem Thomas was having. The best thing I could do now was to help with the healing.

The fit men were making their way through the field, picking up the wounded and carrying them back with them. I followed, marvelling over how few of the fallen were our own.

But it hadn't been their full force, and if we had kept fighting at that pace for much longer I know we would have started making mistakes. Tamsonite hadn't put all the army into play, and hopefully the night faeries would get here the next day. But the other side had giants, and lots of them. Plus, they had Galanta, and - I let out a deep sigh and allowed myself to think the next word – Santanas. And our army only had me. It seemed like a pretty bad deal for the allies.

I pushed that disturbing thought away, instead concentrating on the healing.

***

'We need firewood.'
I let out a sigh and pushed myself up to my feet. I was exhausted from the fighting and the healing but Grams was right. The sun had gone down and it was starting to get cold.
'Tiny help.'
I braced myself as the big giant placed a hand on the ground and pushed himself up. 'Stop.' Isla jumped up and waved an arm at him. 'We don't need *that* big a fire.'
I smiled as I thought about what sort of wood Tiny would come back with. A couple of trees, roots still intact no doubt.
'You stay here and guard the camp.' Grams patted him on the side of his leg which she was using as a back rest. 'It won't take us long.'
'And then you'll tell me about Mother?'
'Yes. And then I'll tell you about your mother.'
Tiny let out a satisfied rumble and sank back down to the ground. The resulting earthquake had me on my hands and knees again.
'For a faery,' Turos said as he pulled me up, 'you have terrible balance.'

'I'm only *three quarters* faery.' I dusted my knees off and turned towards the trees. Aethan fell into step beside me before Turos could.

'Where's Ebony?' I asked.

'At the rear. It's safer there.'

I let out a snort and nodded. We walked in silence towards the edge of the forest.

'We'll help.' Grams pushed herself away from Tiny and started to trot beside me. She reached me and sucked in a big breath of air. 'I gotta work out more.' She looked back over her shoulder to where Lionel was approaching at a more sedate pace. 'When this is all over, and you and I get married, I think we should get a gym. And maybe one of those heated pools.'

'I was thinking more a Jacuzzi.' Lionel's eyes twinkled as he reached out and pinched Grams on the bottom.

She giggled as she slapped his hand away. 'None of that now. I'm a Lieutenant you know.' But she leant closer and whispered loudly enough that I could hear, 'I've always wanted to skinny dip in a Jacuzzi.'

I heard Aethan chuckle as Grams darted off into the woods with Lionel in swift pursuit. I was doing my darnedest not to throw up.

Hrruhrmmmm. Emerald did the dragon equivalent of a throat clearing in my head. *Lance and I might take off for a while.*

I groaned. *Seriously? Now?*

You never know when it may be your last. I could feel her smiling.

Go far, far away, I ordered. *And shield your thoughts.*

I *really* didn't need the complication that she and Lance were about to give me.

A few moments later Arthur appeared fluttering above our campsite.

'Little dragon. Come sit by me.' Tiny thumped the ground with one hand and I took a staggered step forwards.

Isla shot me a meaningful look and then went to greet the hatchling.

Turos walked to the edge of the trees. He tilted his head to the side, cracked his neck, and then shook his shoulders like a boxer getting ready to fight. The look he gave me could have fried eggs.

Arthur landed near Tiny and bounced towards him on his hind legs, using his wings to give each move extra momentum. He stretched out his head and sniffed one of Tiny's feet.

Tiny let out a delighted laugh as Arthur licked his big toe.

'Shouldn't you be collecting wood?' Isla rubbed her arms with her hands. 'It's getting cold.'

It *was* getting colder. Unseasonably colder. But I wasn't feeling the cold at the moment. I could feel the fire of lust uncurling in my stomach. I stood with my fists clenched hard enough that my nails were digging into my palms. Aethan swivelled his head between Turos and me and then moved closer. I saw Turos tense, leaning towards us as if he was going to intercede.

'What's going on?' Aethan murmured in a low voice.

I was glad it was almost dark. It hid the bright red of my cheeks. 'Nothing,' I said. It was true. Kind of.

'Turos,' Isla called out. 'Firewood.'

'Yes Ma'am.' He turned away from Aethan and me, walking in the opposite direction to us into the woods.

That was good. I didn't need to be bumping into him in the growing dark.

'Come on,' Aethan said.

He stayed close to me as I gathered wood, working on his own pile. We walked back to where Tiny was sitting and deposited it. He followed me back to the trees.

When we returned, Grams was resting against Tiny again and Lionel was feeding kindling to a flame. He harrumphed in satisfaction as the fire blossomed, added a few more sticks and then sat back next to Grams. She curled her fingers into his and leant her head against his shoulder. I'm sure, if I'd been able to see her face clearly in the growing darkness, that she would have worn a dreamy look.

Turos appeared with more wood. His knuckles were white where his fingers gripped the branches. I tried to look away, but as he bent to deposit his, the firelight flickered over his body, and shadows moulded themselves to the edges of his muscles. I licked my lips and took a step towards him. He turned, as if feeling my movement, every muscle in his body tensing as our eyes met.

'Izzy.' Aethan put his hand on my shoulder. 'What's going on?'

Isla slid up next to Turos, leaning in close to murmur in his ear. He listened, a wild animal barely in control. And then something she said made him blink. He looked towards her, tilting his head to the side as he listened. Then he nodded once, closed his eyes and took a deep breath. I watched as the tension flowed out of his body and when he opened his eyes again they were calm.

'Oh,' I said. It was all so simple. The answer had been there in front of us the whole time. Of course it would be Isla who worked it out.

I pushed all thoughts away till I was a centre of calm, and then I turned to Aethan and smiled. 'Everything is okay.' I reached out, making sure that my movements were slow as I squeezed his hand.

'Now,' Grams said once we were all seated around the fire, 'where to begin?'

'Can we join you?' Even in the dim light of our fire I could see Sabby's soft, curvaceous outline. A taller figure, straight and proud, stood strong by her side. The two silhouettes were linked by their hands.

I felt a knot inside me relax. Sabby and Thomas. My last missing pieces were here.

'Sit.' I patted the ground on the far side of me and the two of them crossed to stand beside me. 'Tiny,' I said. 'These are my oldest, dearest friends, Sabby and Thomas.'

Tiny let out a contented rumble. 'Any friend of Izzy's is a friend of mine.'

In the light of the fire I could see Thomas's eyes widen as he took in the length and breadth of Tiny. 'It's our pleasure.' The words stumbled out of his mouth.

Sabby sank down beside me and I leant back against Tiny's leg, enjoying the companionship and the warmth he provided.

'I first met Berdina when she came to the castle with news of unease in the west.' Gram's voice rang out in the stillness of our camp.

Tiny let out a pleased noise at the sound of his mother's name. He reached into his bag, pulled out a chunk of bread and took a bite out of it.

I took the pieces of dried meat that Isla handed me and began the tiresome job of chewing.

'She had the most beautiful smile. Just like yours,' Grams added, patting Tiny on the leg.

I wiggled further down Tiny's leg till I was lying with my back against him. The warmth from the fire settled onto my skin.

'She told me all about you. About how you started whittling wood when you were only three years old. She said that the first animal you ever carved was so lifelike that she thought it was going to get up and walk around.'

I felt my eyelids flutter shut. It had been too long since I had had a good night's sleep. Here, within the calm of my mind, there was nothing left to prevent that. No worries, no fears.

'She loved you more than life itself. And what she did, she did to keep you safe.'

Something moved beneath my head and I opened my eyes far enough to see Isla standing back up. 'Sleep well Izzy,' she whispered.

And I did.

Chapter Thirteen

The Trap

I awoke to the cold predawn light. Sabby lay on her side next to me. Thomas had one arm flung over her as he curved protectively around her. My heart clenched and tears pricked my eyes at the view.

Aethan squatted beside me as he leant over the remnants of the fire and blew onto some glowing embers. He fed leaves and twigs into it, gently coaxing it back to life, then he placed a pot on top and sat back on his haunches. Everybody else lay motionless around us.

I had come out of my trance while I slept, but peace still draped me like a heavy blanket as I watched his silhouette. It had been so long since I'd watched him like this. Alone in his thoughts while he carried out a mundane duty. I squashed a pang of loss. Things had been so simple once.

'How are you feeling?' His voice was low, designed to reach my ears only.

'I feel good,' I whispered back.

I reached out and placed my fingertips on the back of his hand and he turned it over so that our fingers entwined. He let out a low sigh and sat back till he was leaning against Tiny's leg beside me.

'I feel....' He stopped and turned to meet my eyes. 'I feel like we've done this before. By ourselves.' His eyes flicked down to our hands. 'Am I right?'

Memories of nights we'd spent in Trillania beside fires flooded me.

I wanted to tell him, but if Rako was right, there was a chance he may never regain those memories if I did. I looked at our fingers, feeling the warmth of his companionship flowing into me through the contact. He had done it for me, back before I could remember. He had kept our secrets safe so that when the time came, the memories were still mine. I could do the same for him.

I shifted, wiggling up so that I sat beside him. 'Somewhere in here,' I reached out and touched the fingers of my free hand to his head, 'and in here,' I laid my palm against his chest, 'lives the memories of a friendship deep and true.' I refused to believe it wasn't in there somewhere.

'Just a friendship?' His voice was almost too low for me to hear it.

I shook my head. 'Never *just* a friendship.' From the first time I had laid eyes on him, friendship alone had been an impossibility. Even if it had been one-sided, love would have been involved. 'But I think that that is what I miss the most.' I shook my head, struggling to explain what I meant. 'You see our love, it grew from that friendship.'

He was silent for a few moments. 'So what you're saying,' he finally said, 'is that our relationship had substance. It wasn't a superficial affair.' His eyes flickered to where Turos lay further down the clearing next to Arthur and Isla.

I traced my free hand down the side of his face, pulling his eyes back to mine. 'Yes,' I said. 'That's *exactly* what I'm saying.'

He leant towards me, an intent look on his face. I moved my hand so that my fingers were splayed across his face, smiling as I pushed his face away.

'I know. The treaty.' A mischievous glint sparked in his eyes as one side of his mouth pulled up into my favourite, lopsided smile. 'Can't blame a guy for trying.'

'What's for breakfast?' Grams sat up and ruffled up her hair with her hands.

Lionel stretched his arms above his head, 'My first choice would be bacon and eggs on pancakes with maple syrup.'

'What's your second choice?' Grams rustled around in the bag lying next to her.

'Dried meat.'

'Oh look.' She pulled some jerky out and held it out to him. 'You're in luck.'

Aethan squeezed my hand before letting it go. He reached into a bag sitting next to the fire and sprinkled a handful of tea leaves into the boiling water.

'And look,' Grams pointed at Aethan, 'we've even got room service. I'll have mine black, thank you kind Sir.'

We continued the jovial bantering throughout breakfast, not speaking about the dark cloud that hung over our heads. Sometime today, we would be joined in war with Santanas's army.

I didn't want to think about it; was trying *not* to think about the screams of war, or a battlefield covered with broken bodies. I should have been pleased I could review those things with the cold logic that distance bequeathed me. But I knew that as soon as I drew my sword and threw myself into the battle, I would be filled with a fierce exhilaration and an unquenchable thirst for my enemies' blood. I didn't like what that said about me.

But what I was really trying not to think about was what would happen the next time Santanas and I went toe-to-toe. Even with my improved ability to control my powers I knew I was no match for him. And where did that leave the rest of the army?

I felt a tree trunk push me in the back and turned to see one of Tiny's fingers lingering there. 'Tiny see Izzy again?' Tears were collecting in the corners of his eyes.

I wrapped my arms around his finger. 'I will see you tonight.' I hoped. I was trying not to think about him going up against his brethren. I'd seen him stomping on goblins as if they were annoying insects, but this was different. Did he even know how to fight?

He nodded solemnly, the tears mercifully staying intact in his eyes, and then he leant forwards to push himself up off the ground.

'Whoa, big boy.' Aethan spread his legs to balance on the trembling ground. 'Why don't you wait till we're a little further away?'

Tiny smiled sheepishly as he froze in place.

'Stay safe,' I said as I pulled Isla into a hug.

'I'd say the same to you, but safe is boring.' She pulled a face at me and then laughed as she pulled herself up onto Arthur's neck.

I wanted to ask her to stay with us. To fight with us. But my reasons were entirely selfish. I felt as if my heart were being torn into tiny pieces, each piece attaching itself to those that I loved. Grams, Lionel, Sabby, Will, Isla, Aethan, Turos, my friends in the Guard and the Millenium. There were too many of them. Too many for me to keep safe. It was possible some bits of my heart wouldn't return to me that night, and that knowledge was almost too much to bear.

I had to work out how to defeat them. How to defeat him.

Isla waved as she and Arthur took off. I knew Emerald and Lance were already aloft with another half score of dragons. They would fly over the Pass and see if the rubble from my landslide still protected us from attack.

'Might go see where Athol wants the witches.' Grams pulled me into a quick hug then she and Lionel trotted out of the camp.

'I'd better go find the healers,' Sabby said.

'See you later.' I said it as casually as I could manage, but my voice still caught on the last syllable.

'Of course.' She pulled a face at me, her mouth smiling a smile that didn't chase the clouds from her eyes. Then she crossed to Thomas and took his hands with hers. They stared into each other's faces with such intensity that I cleared my throat and turned away.

More pain blossomed in my heart. Their love was so new, so fragile. All it would take was a mistimed stroke or an errant arrow and all of it, all that hope, all that joy, all that promise, would be turned to ash. My throat thickened at the thought of them having to live without each other.

'I'm going to fight with Turos.' Thomas said the words and then darted a glance at Turos, the crease between his eyebrows telling me he wasn't sure if Turos would want him or not.

'It would be my pleasure to share the enemy with you.' Turos flashed him a bright white smile. There was no doubt in *his* eyes. His muscles flexed as he thought about the battle that would begin sometime that day.

I tore my eyes away from the sight of Turos's biceps flexing and looked over at Aethan. 'How far away do you think the night faeries are?' I hated the fact that we needed their help.

'Today. They'll arrive sometime today.' His mouth pulled back into a grimace and I could tell he liked the thought of their help even less than I did.

It didn't surprise me, but it did make me smile.

They're gone. All gone.

I froze, my mind reaching towards Emerald. A vision filled my head. The enormous basin opening off the Pass of Bones, empty except for the dragons that soared over it. We flew into the narrow opening, dropping in behind Lance as we navigated the tight bends. The avalanche rubble hadn't been touched. The stretch beyond it deserted. Through the pass and out into the other side. Here there were signs of occupation. Trampled grass and still-smoking fire pits. But the entire area was empty of foe.

Cold ice walked down my spine. I clutched at Aethan's arm as my knees started to tremble.

'Izzy.' He shook my shoulder. 'What is it?'

'They're gone.' My voice came out in a whisper.

I looked over at Turos. His face held the shock I felt. 'Where?' he asked. 'Where could they be?'

'Izzy.' Aethan's voice held an edge of command.

I looked up into his face. 'They're all gone,' I said.

'Hidden by a shield?'

I shook my head. 'There's no sign of their passage this end of the pass.'

Surely they hadn't doubled back because of a little landslide. Their giants could have dealt with that. The next quickest route around to where we were was a week's hard march.

I walked to the other side of our little camp while I turned it over-and-over in my head. It didn't make sense.

'What are they up to?' Aethan scrubbed a hand through his hair.

Unless...unless they *weren't* making their way around to us. I mean...why would they? We had come to stop them. They had come to conquer. They were playing by a different set of rules.

'Oh no.' I could feel the blood flowing out of my head. 'Oh no.' My voice trembled with the fear my certainty had brought.

'What is it?' Both Turos and Aethan took a step towards me. Thomas left off his contemplation of Sabby's retreating form and turned back to watch me.

'They haven't gone the other way.' My voice came out on ragged breaths. 'They've gone through us. They're not going to engage us. They're marching on the capital. They're heading for London.'

Turos tilted his head to the side while he contemplated my words. 'But...'

'They went through the veil.' Aethan got there first. 'They went through the veil and are already beyond us.' His hands clenched into fists by his side.

Turos let out a long low whistle. 'It was a decoy. The fight last night, just a decoy.'

'Wait,' Aethan said. 'We need to make sure that *this* is not the trap.'

Hide behind a shield until half our number left and then attack. I nodded. Yes. We needed to make sure that was not the plan.

I held my hands up in front of me and pinched the veil with my fingertips. I pulled my hands apart, opening a peep hole from Isilvitania through to my world. I felt a flash of pride that something that had once taken up so much of my concentration now was as natural as breathing, and then I looked through my hole.

What was a grassy valley in this world, housed a sealed tarmac road in mine. I sucked in a breath. The road was no longer one smooth piece. Crevices snaked through it, breaking it up into chunks which tilted at crazy angles. Stepping stones for giants.

A four wheel drive lay on its side. The windows smashed in. Blood smeared the driver's door and lay in a pool around the body that had been dragged from it.

I sucked in a breath. This man was dead because of us. Because of our lack of foresight. While we had slept soundly he had been murdered.

I let go of the veil and pressed a hand to my stomach. 'We need to get ahead of them.' Mum, Scruffy, Radismus. I had sent them to London to keep them safe. They were there with all the fae court. All of the non-fighters. All of our familiars. The politicians, the royals, the general populace. Totally undefended except for a token Guard left to keep watch.

Aethan nodded his head. 'We need to tell Tamsonite.'

'I'll gather our fighters and call in the dragons.' Turos's face told me he was already talking to Lance.

'We'll need to send word to the dark faeries as well,' I said, trotting by Aethan's side towards the command tent.

He nodded but didn't say anything. I could tell by the way his jaw muscles tensed that he had his teeth clenched.

I couldn't believe it. They had outsmarted us again. 'I hate this.' I spat the words out.

Aethan looked sideways at me but still didn't say anything.

'I hate that we're always reacting to them.'

This time he nodded.

'It's like they had this whole thing planned out before we even knew any of it was going to happen.'

'They probably did.'

I felt like a pawn in a chess match, powerless as I tried to kill their King. I had to find a way to turn it around. I had to find a way to be the knight or the queen, but I was running out of time.

'Tamsonite,' Aethan's voice sounded out in the early morning air.

'Prince Aethan.' We rounded a tent to find Tamsonite standing with his hands stretched out towards a fire. 'Have they broken through the landslide?'

'Worse. They went through the veil during the night. I'm guessing they're marching towards London.'

'The scouts.' Tamsonite's fingers clenched and unclenched slowly.

Aethan shook his head. 'They were watching the pass. Waiting for when they broke through. We never thought...' He smacked his fist into his open palm. 'Never even thought of them doing this. We've been so preoccupied with fighting them, I never considered the option they wouldn't be doing the same.'

Tamsonite's eyes looked haunted as he processed the information. The corners of his eyes tightened as the horror of the truth settled over him. London.

'Go,' he said. 'Take the Guard, take the Millenium. Get ahead of them and hold them as long as you can. We'll come at them from behind and then as soon as the dark faeries catch up we will crush them.'

I could feel my mouth pull back into a feral grin. I liked the idea of crushing them. I liked it a lot.

Emerald. We're coming.

Here. She put a picture of a field into my head.

'Supply tent.' Aethan took off at a sprint, weaving throughout the tents. He put his fingers to his lips and let out a long whistle followed by three shorts one. The Border Guard signal to muster.

The bugle's call-to-arms tore through the morning air, followed by another signal I hadn't heard before. Men, going about their morning preparations, snapped to attention. Within seconds, the camp began to dissolve around us as men pulled tent posts from the ground.

By the time we found the supply tent, Guard were already forming up around us. I could hear others mimicking Aethan's whistle throughout the camp.

'Take as much as you can carry,' Aethan said.

I already had my swords crossed across my back and my daggers strapped to my biceps and thighs, but I grabbed a bow and slung two quivers of arrows over each shoulder. At least one hundred Guard followed us as we headed towards the field.

Turos appeared off to my left, Millenium swarming behind him as he ran. Thomas was with them, running on Turos's right.

'Izzy.' Grams and Lionel were waiting at the edge of the camp. 'What is it?'

'They went through the veil,' I said. 'We need to get ahead of them.'

'You'll need witches,' she said.

'We don't have time.'

'Make time. They'll have their magic makers with them. You can't do it all by yourself.'

'Bella's right,' Aethan said. 'You'll be exhausted if you have to block their magic by yourself.'

I nodded. 'Find Wolfgang as well. And hurry. We'll be in the field on the far side of these trees.'

More Guard were converging on us every second. I recognised about half of them.

'What's happened?' Bernard asked as he fell in beside Aethan.

'I'll brief you at the field.' Aethan nodded in the direction we were running.

I saw Emerald and Lance fluttering down to land behind the trees. Other dragons followed. I looked over my shoulder as we entered the tree line. The Guard flowed behind us. They brushed shoulders with the Millenium who followed Turos. We would have thousands of fighters, the dragons, and some witches. Thousands to stop their tens of thousands. It would have to be enough.

The dragons were waiting for us when we emerged from the trees. Isla's arms sparkled in the early morning sun as she strode towards us. 'You saw?'

I nodded.

'We will stop them, Izzy.'

I bit my lip and nodded again.

'We will.' She reached out and pushed my shoulder. 'Say it.' There was a desperate edge to her voice. '*Say* it.'

I couldn't lie. Not to her. 'How?' I whispered.

'We will do what needs to be done.'

'How am I meant to stop *him*?'

Her smile was as hard as the granite in her eyes. 'Necessity is the mother of invention Izzy. You will find a way.'

'Everyone keeps saying that.' I tried to keep the whine out of my voice. 'Turos, Aethan, you, Ulandes.'

Her fingers were digging into my bicep before I had even finished saying the word. 'Ulandes said you would find a way?'

I winced as I nodded. She was really strong.

'Well then.' This time her smile held warmth. She let go of me and dusted her hands together. 'If Ulandes said there is a way, there is. You just need to find it.'

She turned away from me as if it was a done deal. Happiness radiated out of every line of her body. She even skipped as she crossed to talk to Aethan.

'Izzy.' Sabby was back by Thomas's side. 'You're going to need healers.' A small band of healers spread out behind her.

'Yes,' I said. 'We will.' I could feel tears biting at the corners of my eyes. I didn't want her there with me, not where the fighting was fiercest. Not where a stray arrow could find her. I looked around the field. I didn't want any of them there with me, risking their lives to stop something I had started.

A cold certainty settled over me. It had to be me, alone, that ended this. It was the only way.

For a second, the knowledge of how it could be done teased around the edges of my mind. I tried to latch onto that thought, but it reared away like a wild cat refusing to be caught, and then it was gone.

'Izzy?' Sabby grabbed onto my hand, her fingers pressing onto the pulse point at my wrist. 'Are you feeling okay?'

Racing heart; short, quick breaths; nerves fluttering around the core of nausea in my stomach? Yep. That was about right.

I pulled my wrist from her grip and forced a smile onto my face. These people needed me to be strong. I drew on the optimism I could hear in Isla's voice as she chatted with the waiting Guard.

'I feel great.' I winced a little. That was a little *too* optimistic. 'I want your band of healers to spread out through the dragon fleet. There's a chance we'll run into Vulpine.'

She pressed her lips together and nodded, then she turned and marched back to them with purpose. I heard her starting to issue orders as I walked towards Emerald.

'Where do you want us?'

I started at Grams' voice. I hadn't realised she had returned. About half of the witches were with her.

'Wolfgang?'

'Coming. He and Rako are with Athol. He's updating the other leaders.'

I bit at my bottom lip. We needed to be in the air. Every second we wasted was a second closer they got to London.

'We need to make sure our efforts are as coordinated as possible.'

'I know, I know.' I ran my hands over my braid trying to calm their shaking. How did we not see this coming?

'All right everyone.' Aethan's voice ran out over the field. 'Gather in.'

He waited a few moments while Guard, Millenium, witches, and a handful of humans pushed in around us. Turos stood at the very front. His ice-blue eyes were serious and his biceps bulged as he crossed his arms across his broad chest.

'Some of you already know what has happened. For those of you that don't, the enemy breached the veil during the night. They have already gone past our position, and at our best guess, are heading for London.'

Several voices broke out, firing questions at Aethan. He raised a hand in the air, waiting till they had quietened before continuing.

'What the enemy doesn't realise is that they have played right into our hands.' His voice grew louder. 'The only way to London is through the Valley of the Kings. We will travel far fleeter than they will by foot and reposition there, blocking their passage. The rest of the troops will attack from the rear.' A vicious smile spread his lips. 'We will crack them like a nut between us.'

This time the voices broke out in a roar of approval. Fists pumped the air in time with the cheers.

'Mount up,' Aethan said. 'It's time to go kick some goblin butt.'

'Nicely done,' Rako said from behind us. I swivelled to find him there with Wolfgang and a group of human fighters. 'We're to take as many as we can.' He nodded back toward the humans.

Wolfgang squeezed my hand as he walked past me. His smile was grim and his eyes sad.

Fighters were spreading out over the field, checking their weapons and mounting dragons. I watched Isla, a small smile playing around her lips as she leant against Arthur. She had positioned quivers full of arrows all the way down his flank. He twisted his head back and blinked his eyes at her, smoke drifting lazily from his nostrils. Whatever he was thinking was funny because she broke out into a peel of laughter and then threw her arms around his neck.

Emerald snorted and shook her head. *You coming?*

I nodded and closed the remaining distance between us. Grams and Lionel were already on her back. Aethan broke away from his conversation with Rako and trotted towards me.

'Are we going through the veil here or at the other end?' Like a coward, I didn't want to see the destruction Santanas's army had left.

'The other end. I'd like to surprise them if we can.'

I turned that over in my mind a few times. Was it possible to surprise them?

I climbed up onto Emerald's neck and wrapped the leather straps around my wrists. A second later we were airborne, winging our way up to where Lance already circled. We tucked in on his left shoulder, flying long, lazy laps overhead as we waited for the rest of the dragon flock to join us.

I felt Aethan's hand on my shoulder. 'Does Turos know where the Valley of the Kings is?'

I glanced back at him. 'No, but Emerald will tell Lance.' I'd already showed her where we were going.

'So...no chance that we can lead?'

I let out a laugh. 'Does that bother you?'

He shrugged and shot me an impish grin. 'It would be nice to lead my people into battle.'

I reached back and patted him on the knee. 'Your ego will survive.'

We were silent for the rest of the time it took our mini-army to become airborne. I watched the rest of the army forming up below. I was impressed by the discipline Tamsonite had installed into them. They would be ready to start marching soon. I just hoped it was soon enough. Santanas's force had at least a night's march on us. I liked the fact that that meant they hadn't slept. It would make for tired fighters.

The final dragon took to the sky and Lance turned in a smooth arc and began winging his way towards the Valley of the Kings.

'Relax,' Aethan murmured in my ear. 'You're wound up so tight you'll be exhausted by the time we get there.'

I let out a big breath and began to relax my muscles one-by-one. He was right. I hadn't realised how tense I was.

I wiggled my shoulders and flexed my head from side-to-side. A few seconds later I felt his hands on my shoulders, strong and tender as his thumbs dug into the muscle knots they found there.

I let out a groan and wiggled backwards to give him better access. He might have lost his memories of me but his hands still knew what they were doing. They turned me to melted putty as they kneaded my flesh.

I closed my eyes and let my head drop forwards and suddenly I was standing in front of a pagoda in the middle of an ornate garden. I let out a yelp as my eyes flew open.

'Sorry.' Aethan's voice was a breeze on the back of my neck. 'Did I hurt you?' His fingers paused their dance across my skin.

'No.' I shook my head. 'I saw something.'

I could feel the weight of his body shifting behind me. 'Vulpines?'

'Nothing like that. I think I fell asleep for a second.'

He let out a throaty laugh and his fingers took up where they had left off. Even though they remained on my neck and shoulders I could feel the tension unwinding throughout my whole body. I let my head drop forwards again and slowly closed my eyes.

This time I didn't jump when the garden appeared before me. Two people reclined on the lounges in the shade of the pagoda.

'About time.' Wilfred pushed himself to his feet and strode towards me. 'We've been waiting for you for hours.'

My mouth flopped open as I stared at him. 'Willy?' I took a step towards him.

'The one and only.' He threw his arms out as he closed the last few steps between us, and swept me up into a hug. He spun me around before setting me back down.

I looked over to the person witnessing our reunion. 'Ulandes.' I pulled myself out of his arms so I could sink to my knees and bow my head.

'Rise, Isadora. There is no need for you to kneel in my presence. I can feel your reverence for me, that is enough.'

I let Wilfred pull me back up, but I kept my head bowed as I walked towards her. 'Isla asked me to thank you for her gifts.' I looked over at Wilfred.

'She liked them?' His mouth split into a wide grin, just visible through his shaggy, red beard.

'She loved them.' I looked back at Ulandes. 'Did you know…?'

'What would happen when she put them on?'

I nodded.

Golden light seemed to emanate from under her skin as she smiled. 'I hoped it would. It means her faith is true and deep.'

'So it wouldn't have happened if it wasn't?'

She shook her head as she rose gracefully to her feet. 'They would have remained what they appeared to be. Beautiful jewellery but nothing more.'

Wilfred looked from Ulandes to me and back again. 'They are more than that?'

'Oh.' She let out a laugh and I was reminded of bells tinkling in a light breeze. 'You have no idea how much more. You will see soon enough. But that is not what I brought Isadora here to talk about. Come child.' She took my hand and led me back to the chairs. 'Sit.'

I sat as gently as I could, but next to her grace I might as well have plonked myself down into the chair. Wilfred sat on the far side of me, leaning back with his hands clasped behind his head.

'You have questions for me?'

I let out a sigh of relief. She was going to tell me everything I needed to know. 'How do I defeat Santanas?'

She reached over and pressed the palm of her hand to my cheek. 'I told you last time, child, that is the one answer I can not give you. But that is immaterial. You already have the answer.' She tapped the side of my head. 'In here, and in here.' Her hand moved to hover over my heart.

'Arghhhhhhh.' I slumped back into the seat. 'I don't know what to do. I'm no match for him. Next to him I am a joke of a War Faery. I may as well not even be one.'

'Ahhhhh.' She cocked her head to the side as eyes, brimming with intelligence, studied me. 'I see where you get your misconception from.'

'Misconception?'

'That he is a better War Faery than you.'

'But he is.' I couldn't hide the frustration in my voice. 'He's stronger, faster, smarter, and his control of his magic far outweighs mine.'

'And those are the things that you think make a good War Faery?'

'Isn't it?' I sat forwards on my seat.

'No.' She shook her head as she rose and paced across the floor of the pagoda. 'Not at all.'

'But…he's better than me. And I don't have the time to learn how to improve.'

She leant over a rose bush and plucked a bloom from it. The white rose she held, when she walked back towards me, was perfect. I took it from her when she offered it.

'War Faeries weren't created to lead their people. They weren't created to be lethal and ruthless.'

'They weren't?' I turned the stem of the rose in my fingers, admiring each petal, each drop of dew that glistened on its snowy beauty.

'They were created to protect. They were created to love. They were created to serve.' She sat back down beside me and grasped my face between her palms. 'Your love is your greatest strength. Your compassion and empathy is what will allow you to succeed. You are,' she brushed her finger over the petals of the rose, 'the perfect War Faery. His hatred has corrupted him.'

'That's all you're going to tell me, isn't it?'

She nodded. 'You need to stop doubting yourself. You already have everything you need to get the job done.'

I bit my lip to stop myself from making a smart-arse comment. I'd leave those to Wilfred.

'It is time you returned.' Ulandes stood again and held her hand out to me.

'Already?' I feel like I just got here.' I turned to Wilfred. 'And I didn't even get to talk to you.'

He hooked an arm around and pulled me to him. 'Don't worry,' he rubbed the knuckles of one hand across the top of my head, 'if everything goes to plan, we'll be together again real soon.'

'Wilfred.' Ulandes voice held admonishment.

'What? I didn't mess her hair up too much.' He released me with a grin.

'That's not what I'm talking about and you know it.'

'Oh.' His hand flew to cover his mouth but his eyes twinkled merrily. 'Did I say too much?'

She let out a sigh and shook her head. 'I'm sure the other Gods and Goddesses don't have to put up with this.' She rose to her feet in one smooth movement.

I took her outstretched hand and stood. 'Thank you.' Her words hadn't allayed my fears, but I knew she had done her best.

'Believe,' she said. 'Believe in yourself. You are far more powerful than you know. Now,' she leaned over and kissed me on each cheek, 'it is time to wake up.'

Chapter Fourteen

The Final Battle

Aethan's arms were around me when I woke.

'Hey sleepy head.' He released me slowly, the tips of his fingers lingering on my bare skin as he slithered backwards down Emerald's neck.

I ignored the emotions his touch stirred in me, and asked, 'How long was I out?' I looked at the ground far below, trying to work out where we were.

'A couple of hours.'

Huh. It hadn't seemed that long.

'How much further?'

'We're nearly there. I was about to wake you.'

I nodded my head. I was going to have to open the veil soon.

Tell Lance we're taking the lead.

It's about time. Emerald let out a huff but I could tell she was joking. She didn't mind if her mate led and she followed.

Lance's wing strokes slowed and Emerald swooped into the lead. I heard Grams let out a squeal of delight at the increase in speed. I shook my head but could feel the smile on my face.

A look over my shoulder showed me the dragons were in tight formation. It meant that opening a big enough gate would be easier.

Turos raised his hand in a mock salute and winked. I winked back and flashed him a smile. Opening a gate was something I knew I could do.

'Do you think we're past them?' I swivelled back around to look at Aethan.

'Only one way to find out.'

I sucked in a breath. 'Oh well. No guts, no glory.'

As soon as I thought about it, I could feel the veil lying like a heavy blanket over me. I felt a thrill race through me at how easy this had become. Maybe one day, my magic would feel this natural to me too.

I grasped the veil a few hundred feet in front of me and tore it apart. Unlike when I was at ground level, this parting was almost invisible. The blue sky on the other side looked the same as it did in Isilvitania. I pulled on the edges, widening the gap till I was sure all the dragons would easily make it through.

Butterflies started rustling in my belly as Emerald approached it. I wasn't sure what we would do if Santanas's army was below us. We needed time to get set up, and we were counting on the narrowest part of the Valley to help us in our defence. I resisted the urge to shut my eyes. That was going to be about as helpful as hiding under my bed.

We swept through the veil and I scoured the ground below for signs of the enemy. It was possible they had already passed through the valley. Possible, but not probable.

All looked as it should. The long winding road was intact, the grass untrampled, the trees still rooted. I heard Aethan echo my own sigh of relief. We had made it in time.

'Tell Emerald to put us down at the end of the valley.'

'Tell her yourself.'

'She can understand English?'

I looked back over my shoulder at him. 'How do you think we communicate?'

'I didn't know.' He shrugged a shoulder and gave me a cheeky grin. 'Pictures?'

Emerald started to descend towards the mouth of the valley. *We do also communicate with pictures.*

I nodded. 'She said to tell you that we do use pictures. Sometimes it's faster that way.'

'Can you hear all the dragons?'

'The dragons can all hear each other, but I'm bonded to Emerald. So I only hear her.' I paused, wondering if I should tell him everything. 'Well, that's not entirely true. I can hear other dragons and other riders if we open our bonds to each other.'

'So…how does that work?'

'If we deem it beneficial, we can mind link.'

'So you can all hear each other?'

'Yes. But it goes much deeper than that. I don't just *hear* Emerald. We share each other's emotions as well.'

When he didn't reply, I risked a peek over my shoulder. His face was frozen as he worked his way through the ramifications of that. He looked from me back to Turos. 'So, when, Emerald and Lance…?'

I felt a rush of heat on my cheeks that could only mean one thing. I was blushing furiously. I looked straight ahead and crossed my fingers as I said, 'We can block it.'

He cleared his throat. 'Well, that explains a few things.'

I wanted to deny it all, but I wasn't sure exactly what I was denying. I decided, instead, to ignore it. 'Anyway, it means we can fight as if we are all extensions of a single unit. It's handy during aerial combat.'

Emerald stretched her wings wide and flapped backwards, slowing herself down as she reached out her taloned feet to grasp the ground. I heard Lance land behind us.

'First floor women's lingerie, manchester, glassware and crockery. And if we're very lucky later on there'll be a goblin or two.' Grams laughed like she'd cracked the funniest joke in the world.

I wished I was able to be so light-hearted about what we were doing, but I'd never found trying to save the world a laughing matter. Maybe in a hundred years or so I'd be able to be a bit more blasé about the whole thing.

'Ahhh Izzy.' Aethan's voice held a trace of awe.

I turned to look at him. 'What?'

He looked back up into the sky. 'Were you planning on closing the veil?'

'Oh, right.' I flashed an embarrassed smile as I reached out to where I had opened the veil and let the two sides slide back together.

He shook his head. 'It would take at least four faeries to open a split that big, and you forgot you were doing it. You don't realise how powerful you are.' He raised a hand and laid his palm on my cheek. 'Be careful today.'

My breath caught as his eyes blazed into mine. I nodded my head, watching mutely as he slid off Emerald's neck.

I watched as he trotted toward where Rako was issuing orders, then I slipped off Emerald and walked around to the front. She bowed her head till our eyes were level. I rested a hand on her snout and leant in till my forehead was pressed against it.

Be safe today, I urged her.

She puffed out a breath of warm air. It curled around me, swirling my braid up behind me. *You too little one.*

We stayed like that for a few more seconds before she let out a second snort.

I smiled as I backed away. I could feel her impatience to get back into the air. *Not yet,* I said. *We don't want them seeing us until it is absolutely necessary.*

And if the Vulpine come?

I nodded in concession. *Then all bets are off.*

Guard, Millenium, witches and humans hurried past us, following Aethan and Rako into the Valley. It was a few hundred metres to the constriction where we would set up our defence.

The dragons spread out onto the plain behind the valley. Some settled down to wait, while others pawed at the ground and shook their heads, impatient, like Emerald and Lance, to be off. But they all stayed where they were, so I knew Emerald had passed on the word.

'Come on.' Turos touched me on the shoulder and I looked up into his ice-blue eyes.

Fire inevitably started to curl in the pit of my stomach. It was a nice change to the butterflies, but just as counter-productive. I needed my head in the game, not in the bedroom.

Wrenching my eyes away from his, I started walking into the valley. It could all be so easy, if only I'd let it be, but the feel of Aethan's fingers still lingered on my skin.

'Izzy.'

I spun around at the familiar, unwanted voice. 'Ebony. What are you doing here?' It was the first time I had seen her wearing anything other than a skirt. The leather pants hugged her curves before pinching into her tiny waist.

'I came to fight with Aethan.' Her sea-green top perfectly matched the colour of her almond-shaped eyes, and her long hair was pulled back in a braid identical to mine.

I was pretty sure, though, that she looked far better than I did. Damn the woman. How did she do it?

'But....' I was momentarily speechless. She wanted to fight? She would be killed in the first rush of enemy.

She lifted her chin as her eyes took on a defiant look. 'I've had lessons.' She patted the hilts of the swords strapped to her back.

'Lessons are a totally different thing to real combat.' I wasn't sure why I was trying to dissuade her. If a goblin sword was to slice into her soft skin well then...no, as much as I disliked her, I didn't want that. She was annoying, and had something that, until very recently, I had considered mine, but that didn't warrant a death sentence.

'He's up the front.' I waved a hand in the direction we were heading. Let Aethan talk her out of fighting.

She sashayed off through the crowd, her hips swinging in an erotic way that drew the eye of every man she passed. I let out a sigh. It wasn't like I wanted to be looked at like that, but it might be nice to have the choice.

I looked up at Turos to see if he was also admiring the view. He had a smile on his face but he wasn't looking at her. He was looking down at me.

I sucked in a breath at the look on his face. Oh, yes, it could all be *so* easy.

'That will be an interesting conversation.'

I let out a yelp at Isla's voice in my ear.

Her laugh was a tinkle. 'For a War Faery, you sure are easy to scare.'

'Yes, but I think we have already ascertained that I'm not a very good War Faery.'

Ulandes voice sounded in my head, 'You are exactly the right type of War Faery to get the job done.'

I let out another yelp and whipped around, looking for the slight figure of the Goddess. It sounded like she had been right beside me.

'Looking for someone?' Isla's eyes looked totally innocent.

'Yes, I mean no.' I looked around one more time. Had I actually heard her? I shook my head to clear it of miscellaneous thoughts. It was no time to start hearing voices. 'Sorry, what were you saying?'

Isla gestured in the direction Ebony had gone. 'She was meant to stay behind to be there when the night faeries arrived.'

'Do you think it will be a problem?'

'No.' She broke out into a huge grin. 'It was just Aethan's way of keeping her under control. I bet she's better with those swords than she's letting on.'

We fell into step with the crowd heading into the valley.

'Do you think?' Turos wrapped his big hand around mine as we walked.

'I think there's a lot more going on in her head than that vapid smile lets on.'

She and Turos locked eyes for a moment, before he nodded. 'I'll take your word on that spymaster.'

She let out a dainty laugh and skipped ahead of us.

'Aren't you staying with Arthur for the fight?' I called after her.

'Oh yes.' Her voice sailed back to me. 'But I *really* want to hear this conversation first.'

I smiled. I wouldn't mind hearing it either, but there was also a chance I might have to witness Aethan admiring her form in those figure-hugging pants, and that was not something I was keen to do. Colour me yellow and call me a coward.

'This way.' Turos tugged on my hand, leading me to where the rest of the Millenium were gathered.

I nodded my head as I stared up the valley. There was no sign of Santanas's force yet. I plucked open a tiny gap in the veil and peered through it. It was like looking at two almost-identical paintings. The valley's walls were perfectly mirrored in each plain of existence, but where the one in Isilvitania was full of boulders, grass and wild flowers, the one in my world had a four lane highway.

'What's to stop them popping back through the veil?'

It was a throw away question from one Millenium fighter to another. I looked at Turos. He had both eyebrows raised as he waited for me to answer.

'Nothing,' I said. 'I'd better go talk to Aethan and Rako.' There were no more natural defences between here and London. Plenty of towns and villages, but it would be better if we could stop them without causing too much destruction of private property. This valley was our best bet.

I trotted towards the front, guessing that they would be on the one outcrop which offered a viewing platform. The forest flowed down the mountains, but stopped short in this area, the ground too rocky to offer any real purchase for the roots of the large oaks.

I heard Aethan before I saw him. 'You are not fighting. It's madness.'

'I'm touched you're so worried about my safety, but I am perfectly able to use these things.'

'Those *things* are going to get you killed.'

I could see Rako up on the platform. He had his back to Aethan and Ebony, his shoulders tight as he pretended to study the layout of the valley. Isla had no such compunction. There was a broad smile on her face as she watched Aethan and Ebony.

'Tell him Isla. Tell him I can look after myself.'

One delicate eyebrow arched up, but the smile didn't move. 'Sorry,' she said. 'This is between the two of you.'

Ebony stomped one foot and turned back to Aethan. She stared at him for a moment, her eyebrows pulling together as she chewed at her bottom lip. Then her expression cleared and a small smile hovered on her lips.

'Love.' She breathed the word out. 'I'll go crazy with worry if I'm not there with you.' Her hips swayed as she moved towards him, reaching up to twine her arms behind his head. My blood pressure increased as she pressed her breasts into him and laid her head against his shoulder. 'Please.'

I finished the climb up to the platform and made my way to Rako.

Isla turned away from Aethan and Ebony and slung an arm around me. Her voice was a whisper in my ear as she said, 'Funny how she didn't seem to be crazy with worry yesterday.'

'We weren't outnumbered yesterday, and *they* weren't there.' I knew saying Santanas and Galanta's names out loud didn't give them any power but I still couldn't bring myself to do it.

Isla let out a deep sigh and rolled her eyes.

'What?' I knew that look. She thought I was being particularly slow.

'Nothing love.' She pinched my cheek like I was a babe, dancing out of reach before I could retaliate.

'Rako.'

The stocky Guard cast me a sideways look. 'Have they finished yet?'

I looked back over my shoulder. Aethan had managed to get Ebony's arms from around his head. He held both her delicate wrists with one of his hands as he leant and whispered in her ear. I didn't want to know what he was saying.

'I think so.' I shifted so I was standing next to him staring out over the valley. 'It occurred to me they may use the veil to bypass us again.'

He ran his fingers down the right side of his face. I knew he was feeling the knotted scar tissue that ran in a rope there. 'They were still on this side when we flew over, but it is possible.' He let out a sigh. 'I'll send scouts out on both sides to check.'

'Arthur and I can do it,' Isla said. 'I can open a way big enough for him.'

'What about the Vulpines?' I didn't like the thought of her going up against them by herself.

She shrugged one shoulder. 'They can't open the veil.'

Rako let out a harrumph and nodded. His fingers continued their stroking while he considered her words.

'It's the fastest, easiest and safest way to see what they are up to.'

'No engaging the enemy,' Rako said.

'Only to defend myself.' She danced up and down on the spot.

'You find them and report straight back.'

'Of course. I'll follow on the opposite side of wherever they are, making sure they don't switch. Scouts honour.' She held three fingers in the air, kissed them and then laid them against her heart.

Aethan let out a snort. 'You're not a scout.'

She gave him an impish grin and then whirled and took off down the rocky path, cat-like as she leapt from boulder-to-boulder. I followed at a more sedate pace. I *really* didn't want to sprain my ankle.

'Izzy.'

I looked back up to Rako.

'Can you gather the leaders? It's time to talk strategy.'

Arthur lifted into the air before I had made it back to Turos. Isla leant forwards, both her arms wrapped around his neck. Arthur matched her look of excitement, his lips pulled back to expose his teeth in a dragon's grin.

Emerald's unhappiness seeped into me through our bond. I sent back a pulse of reassurance. It was the best I could offer her.

Turos was easy to spot. He towered over his men, his white-blond hair glowing in the sunshine. I tried not to admire his form as I strode towards him. 'Rako wants to discuss tactics. Take your squadron leaders with you.'

He nodded and turned back to his men. 'Andres, Liam, Raul, Taro, Delvin and Saul, come with me. Everyone else, get some rest.'

The men Turos had called threaded their way towards him, while the rest of the warriors slid downwards into a cross-legged position. I turned and headed for the Guard.

It took me another ten minutes to rally the leaders of the witches and humans and to find Wolfgang, and another five minutes to wind my way back to the platform where the others were gathering.

Ebony sat at the rear of the group, pulling at the end of the braid with her fingernails. It took me a moment to realise she was looking for split ends.

She looked up as I neared her, patting the bit of rock next to where she sat. 'Did you want to sit with me? These meetings get so boring.'

'Urrrr, thanks,' I said. 'But I need to hear this.'

She flashed me a smile and turned her attention from her hair to her nails. I was hoping Aethan had banned her from the frontline. She would only get in the way.

A thought bubble wobbled its way down the valley, floating down to hover in front of Rako. He closed his eyes as it flowed over his head, opening his eyes a few moments later as it popped.

'Princess Isla reports that the enemy is still on this side of the veil. She estimates at the pace they are travelling that they will be upon us in approximately an hour. Our forces are three hours behind them but having to travel more slowly. They are leaving behind ambush parties.'

We had to hold them for at least three hours. Probably more like four. I looked down at the narrowing in the valley we would be guarding. With the help of the witches it was entirely do-able. Of course, I said that without knowing what sort of magic they would throw at us. What *Santanas* would throw at us.

'Our job is to stop them getting through this part of the valley. Wolfgang, you and your magic makers will work with the witches to neutralise anything they throw at us. Are you happy being tucked in behind this outcrop? You should be well protected from their arrows.'

Wolfgang stroked his beard as he considered Rako's words. 'It is true we won't need to see to feel what they are brewing. Might I make a suggestion though?' He waited for Rako to nod before continuing. 'If you place us to the very rear we will be beyond the reach of their arrows but still able to see. We will be able to launch offensive as well as defensive strikes. The army witches are quite inventive. We will have a few surprises for the enemy.'

Rako's face broke out into a fierce grin. 'Surprises are good,' he said, 'but stay alert to enemy fire and drop back if you need to.'

My mind wandered as the meeting turned to a discussion on tactics. It wasn't that I found the planning boring, more that I found the unknown unbearable. If only I knew what they were going to throw at us I might be able to plan how to combat it. Of course, the problem with *that* was that I knew my magic worked better when I didn't plan. When, as Wolfgang had surmised, it was instinctive.

If only Isla had been born the War Faery. She would have been perfect at this.

I started as Turos's hand fell on my shoulder. 'Excellent plan,' he said. 'I particularly like the last bit. What did you think of it?'

The look I gave him must have been as blank as my mind because he burst out laughing. 'You know you really should pay attention more. It could save your life.'

'Life, smife,' I muttered as I followed him back down the rocky slope.

He waited at the bottom for me. 'Short version is that we will be at the front with the Guard and humans behind us. Our aim is to disable them and then send them back for the others to finish off.'

'Sort of like a goblin processing plant.'

His excited smile broadened. 'I like that analogy.'

'What happens when we need a rest?'

'The Guard will switch us out.'

It could work. It would have to. The speed of the Millenium fighters was our biggest asset at the moment. And we only had to hold for a couple of hours. Then the forward momentum of the enemy would slow as they defended their rear as well.

'I want to find Sabby.' I pulled my hand from his – strange, I hadn't even realised I had been holding it – and started making my way to the rear of our army. She would be back there with the other healers. I looked over my shoulder to see Turos following. 'What are you doing?'

'Looking for Thomas. He'll be fighting with us.'

I felt my shoulders stiffen as my feet started to thump a little harder into the earth.

'He's proved himself.' Turos's voice was firm. 'He's earned a place at the front.'

I nodded, my throat too thick to risk talking.

We found them five minutes later. They were together as Turos had guessed. Heads bowed, hands clasped, they spoke in low whispers. It looked like Sabby was trying not to cry.

I hesitated, not wanting to disturb their very private, public goodbye. Turos either lacked the social grace or didn't care.

'Thomas,' he called out. 'You ready man? We need you at the front.'

Sabby's head snapped around. Her cheeks flushed red and she pulled her hands from Thomas's, pushing some loose tendrils of hair back behind her ears.

'Hey.' I smiled at her. 'You guys ready back here?'

Her eyes widened. 'They're coming?'

'ETA fifty-five minutes.'

She tilted her head to the side and said, 'ETA?'

'Oh sorry. Estimated time of arrival.'

'Oh.' She glanced over to where Thomas now stood with Turos. 'Well, you had better get going.'

Thomas ducked his head and started to turn away from her, but then he stopped. He swung back around and closed the distance between them with three long strides. He swept her up and lowered his head to hers, taking her mouth with his own.

Her surprised struggle stopped as she let out a little, 'Oh,' and then she was kissing him back with a desperation born of potential loss.

I went to stand beside Turos, both of us turning our backs to give them a little privacy.

'Finally,' he said.

'What?' I looked up at him.

'He finally got the balls to kiss her.'

I glanced back over my shoulder. 'This is their first time?' That surprised me. I had assumed by their body language they had been doing a little more than just kissing.

'He was worried about the whole 'just being a human' thing.' He made little air quotes with his fingers so I knew those were Thomas's words and not his. 'I told him things like that didn't matter when love was involved, but he didn't feel he was good enough for her.'

'You....' I looked back over my shoulder and then up at Turos. 'You staged this whole thing. You're letting him fight with us so he feels *worthy*?' My fists clenched at my sides. He was going to get one of my best friends killed and break the other one's heart.

He shrugged a shoulder as he pulled a face. 'Of course not. He *does* deserve to fight with us. I just thought I'd milk it a little seeing as how *he* wasn't going to.' A wicked grin flashed onto his face. 'If you weren't fighting with me I'd be doing the same to you.'

I punched his shoulder lightly. 'Silly man.'

Thomas cleared his throat and said, 'Ahh, we're finished, I think.'

The flush on Sabby's cheeks was no longer from embarrassment. Her eyes shone bright and a satisfied smile curled her lips. 'Don't go getting him killed,' she said. 'I'd like to do that again, later.'

'Yes Ma'am.' Turos gave her a salute.

'You stay safe back here.' I hugged her, pulling away before I got teary. 'We'll share a campfire tonight.'

'Sabby, we've tapped an underground stream. Come and see if we have enough water.' I didn't recognise the young witch who stood about ten feet away.

'And now *I* must go.' Sabby reached out and squeezed my hand before letting the other healer lead her away.

'You heading to the front?' I turned back to Turos.

'Got to fill the men in on the plan.'

'I'm going to swing by the witches.'

'That's a good idea. Don't be too long.'

I nodded. It felt funny, after so many years of fighting with the Guard in Trillania, to now be working with the Millenium instead. But I knew it made sense. Fighting as a unit with our increased speed we would wreak havoc on the enemy. Working alone with the Guard I might end up stranded. Not that we were meant to be penetrating past the front line like we had yesterday. But unexpected things happened in the heat of battle.

I wound my way through the soldiers, busy with their battle preparation, until I found the witches. They sat in three loose circles, all of them looking to where

Wolfgang stood on a boulder to the side. A group of faeries clustered behind him.

'Your circle,' he pointed to the circle on the far right, 'will be responsible for holding a shield over our soldiers. Just like we practised.' He waited while they all nodded their heads before switching his attention to the middle circle. 'Your circle will hold a barrier out the front to stop the enemy engaging us. Their magic wielders will concentrate everything they can on breaking down that barrier. Hold as long as you can without doing yourself any permanent harm. We will weave our magic in to fortify you as much as we can.'

He didn't state the obvious. The longer they were able to hold them off, the less of us would die.

He turned to address the last group. I noticed Grams and Lionel sitting in this circle. 'Lieutenant Bella will be in control of this circle. You will link and lend your power to her. She will construct spells designed to frustrate the enemy.'

Grams smacked her hands together a couple of times and flexed her fingers. 'We're going to do more than just frustrate them.'

'Circle one. Link hands and set your circle. Handron,' he nodded at the witch who had taken the north arc of the circle, 'I want you to imagine the barrier but don't form it. Circles two and three, do the same. We're going to wind our magic into yours so you can feel us, just like we've practised.'

He looked over to where I stood and held a finger in the air. I waited while the witches began linking their circles. The air began to thrum, tightening like an invisible guitar string as the strength of their combined magics increased. I resisted an urge to scratch at my arms where my skin tingled. With an almost audible twang the circles snapped into place.

'Excellent.' Wolfgang clapped his hands. He turned to look at the faeries. 'One at a time, feel the circle and weave your magic in. You want to strengthen the fabric of their magic without disturbing it.'

Clever. The faeries were to be the reinforcement to the witches' magic. Holding them up while they concentrated on their tasks.

Wolfgang climbed down from his boulder and made his way around the circles to where I waited. I could feel the faeries' magic, strong yet supple as it wove through the witch circle.

'Can I help?' I asked him.

He pulled at the end of his beard, his bushy, grey eyebrows lowering while he considered my question. 'I suspect your magic might disrupt the circles.'

''Cause I have no control?'

He let out a rumbly laugh. 'It's not so much your control, more the wildness of your power. It would be like a lightning bolt striking the circle.'

I shuddered, imagining the effect that would have on the witches.

'However,' he continued, a grin of boyish delight flickering over his face, 'if you feel the goblin circles, perhaps you could try to lend *them* a hand.'

I let out a laugh. 'I'll see what I can do.'

He turned back to the circles. 'Now you, Rillania. Slowly now.'

I left them to their preparations and headed for the Guard. Aethan was briefing the men so I stood at the back, waiting for him to finish. I couldn't see Ebony anywhere so I was guessing he had won that argument.

'Right, split into two groups behind Baulda and Lingro. You two work out whose group will fight first.'

The men divided down the centre, moving out to stand behind two of the Guard. I recognised Baulda, but not Lingro.

'Paper, rock, scissors?' Lingro asked, his Italian accent letting me know why I had never met him before.

'Of course.' Baulda held his clenched fist up in front of him.

I suppressed a smile and started towards Aethan. He watched me coming, his adorable half-smile lighting up his eyes.

'Do you always settle your affairs with paper, rock, scissors?'

'It's the only way to do it without drawing blood.'

I let out a little laugh as he led me away from the men. Half of them were watching Baulda and Lingro – they had progressed to best of three – but the other half didn't try to hide their interest in Aethan and me. I waved at them, hoping to shame them into turning away, but the cheeky bastards just waved back, their smiles getting even broader.

I let out a sigh. It was to be expected. They had watched our relationship develop over the years, and Isla had told me they had a betting pool going on whether he would end up with me or Ebony. The odds were 3-to-1 against me.

'Do you mind that we are taking the lead?' It wasn't what I wanted to say but it was a safe conversation.

He shrugged and looked over to where the Millenium were warming up. 'It makes sense.'

I winced. It had to have hurt his ego admitting that. 'I wish I were fighting with *you*,' I whispered.

I wasn't sure he had heard me until the corners of his eyes crinkled as he reached out and took my hands. A couple of the Guard groaned while another couple let out whoops.

'Did money just change hands?' I asked.

He nodded. 'Ignore them.'

'What did you say to Ebony to get her to stand down?'

'I promised I'd see her every break.'

I nodded, desperately wanting to move closer, but the watching eyes stopped me. I was pretty sure that Turos's would be amongst them.

Aethan stiffened, his head swivelling to look out down the Valley.

'What is it?' I couldn't see anything.

'Can you hear it?'

I shook my head. 'No. Wait.' I craned my head to the side, concentrating harder. 'Yes. Drums,' I breathed. They were coming. 'I'd better go.'

Aethan's grips on my hand tightened. 'Be safe,' he said.

'You too.'

We stared into each other's eyes for a few more moments, then I wrenched myself away from him and headed over to where the Millenium waited. I could feel my heart beat accelerating as the drums grew louder. The ground shook slightly, the vibration running under my feet.

Oh great. Giants.

Every line on Turos's body screamed alert. He stared down the valley, eyes narrowed as his hands clenched and unclenched.

'Hey.' I touched his arm lightly.

He didn't move his eyes from the front. 'You ready?'

'Ready as I'll ever be.' I took a deep breath, forcing the air deep into my lungs. I didn't want to start hyperventilating. 'Somewhere in that army is my grandfather. My very pissed off grandfather. Did I mention that he's a little crazy? So's Galanta. You're going to love meeting her. She's a real treat. Her English isn't that great, but hey, I can't speak a second language so I shouldn't really be picky.'

He clasped my hand in his and turned me to face him.

'She hates it when I tease her.'

He let go of my hands and placed a palm on each side of my face. 'Izzy.' He looked down into my face, his eyes wide with concern.

'She never forgave me for dressing her in that bridal dress. But that's small change considering all the awful things she's done to me.' His hands constricted my movement but I tried to shake my head anyway. 'We're never going to be good friends.'

'I can slap you,' he said, 'or kiss you. Which would you prefer?'

I felt my eyebrows going up as I considered his question.

He sighed and shook his head. 'Never mind.'

His lips were on mine in half a beat of my heart. I had been going to tell him that I thought the slap might be more effective, but I knew immediately that I was wrong. The warmth of his skin, the movement of his lips, the feel of his breath mingling with mine, they were far more distracting than a slap would have been.

He pulled away far too soon and stared into my eyes. 'You all right?'

'Uh huh.'

'Going to start babbling again?'

The drum beat picked up its pace. 'Nah. I'm done.'

'Excellent.' He turned to gaze down the valley. 'Cause we've got work to do.'

I moved to stand next to him, staring down the winding ravine. Shadows were moving at the end of my vision. Big shadows.

I felt my pulse quicken as goosebumps broke out over my skin. This was it. The moment we had been working toward. We were going to walk away from this triumphant, or we weren't going to walk away at all.

Now I could feel the War Faery genes kicking in. My smile started to form as I pulled my swords from their crossed sheaths on my back.

Threaten my country? Threaten my family? Threaten my friends? That, was intolerable. I would not allow it, or I would die trying. All of a sudden I was okay with that.

I felt a pressure building far behind me. The witches' circles were starting to work.

The shadows at the end of the valley took form, becoming three dimensional as they gained features. Big, giant features.

A low hum resonated through me as the faeries linked into the circle.

The drums grew louder, their vibrations alluding that the enemy coming to meet us was feral and vicious. Even though I was no green rookie, I had never faced off against a force this size before. I could feel my muscles quivering in response to the beat. The new soldiers would be quaking in their boots.

I looked at Turos, at the wild, feral excitement in his eyes, and I felt it flow into me. This is where I belonged. Not hiding in London with the women and children, but here. Here where I could make a difference. Here where I could roar my defiance.

Giants rose above us as they rambled forwards. Goblins, orcs and ogres stretched behind, their presence shadowing the earth as far as I could see.

Where were the Vulpines? I had expected an aerial attack by now.

The power in the witches' circle grew till the hairs on the back of my arms were standing on end.

'Steady.' Rako paced along the front of the forces. 'Hold steady.'

Where was Santanas? Where was Galanta?

I could see the giants well enough to read the ugly expressions on their faces. They swung clubs that had been carved from whole trees, the branches along their lengths sharpened to points.

Two hundred metres out the drums broke from a rhythmical pulse to a frenzied beat. My heart rate accelerated with it.

The giants broke into a run, their car-sized feet splintering the road beneath them. Churned bitumen was left in their wake, their allies forced to clamber around it.

I knew Tiny was bigger than these giants, but they looked huge as they pounded towards us. I tried to count how many of them there were. Fifty? Sixty? A hundred? They would tear through our ranks.

One hundred metres out.

I was on a jumping castle, the ground writhing in agony beneath my feet. I fell to my knees, tilting my head back to stare up at the murderous faces bearing down on us. We would have to go for their achilles. That was if we could find our balance well enough to do it. It was the only way we would be able to stop them. And there would be so much collateral damage as we brought them down. But if we didn't, they would be trampling us, smashing us into the earth under the souls of their feet.

The only way for us to have a chance was to slow them down. Where was the…Oh. There.

I felt a zing as a barrier slammed into the earth fifty metres in front of us. The giants collided into it a second later and our troops let out a howl of savage delight as giant heads and giant bodies ricocheted off the invisible wall.

I tensed as more and more giants piled onto the barrier, praying to the Dark Sky that it would hold. It did.

They had lost their forward momentum. Even if that was the only thing the barrier gained us, it would be a lot.

One of the lead giants roared and beat on the shield, his fists blanching white with the force of the contact. Another kicked at it, letting out a howl of pain as he clutched his foot and hopped on the spot.

And just like that, terror turned to humour and laughter rippled across our force.

'Remain vigilant,' Rako roared as he continued his pacing. 'They could break through at any moment.'

The laughing stopped, and grips shifted on weapons as soldiers moved back into a fighting stance.

'Well met.'

Turos's arm stopped me from stepping backwards as a hooded figure walked through the giants' legs. Though much smaller, the malevolent energy radiating off him brought more terror to my heart than the charging giants had.

Santanas. I bit down on my lip to stop from whimpering.

'Now,' his face was hidden in the shadow of his hood as his gaze swept along the army, 'where is she?'

I lifted my chin as Santanas's darkened face turned toward me.

'Ahhhhh.' He stretched out his arms. 'Isadora.' My name rolled from his lips. 'Daughter, will you not join me?'

My traitorous knees trembled as I pushed away from Turos. I would have loved to have stayed there, letting his warmth give me a false sense of security, but I needed to be strong. 'If I've told you once, I've told you a thousand times,' I said, 'the answer is no.'

He reached up and pushed back his hood and I couldn't hide the shudder that ripped through me.

'What's the matter?' his voice crooned. 'Don't you think I'm handsome any more?'

Thick, red scars twisted down his cheeks. His lips stayed still as he spoke, the shiny, tight tissue incapable of movement. It added a slur to his speech where there had been none. Orion's eyes stared at me from the melted ruin of his face.

Santanas waved at the damage. 'I'm surprised you don't like it. This is *your* handiwork after all.'

Nausea twisted my stomach as he ran his hands through patchy tufts of blond hair. I let out a prayer to the Dark Sky that Orion was really gone. I didn't want to think that his soul had suffered through that. I would die from the guilt if that were the case.

I stiffened my spine. It had been Santanas or me. Anyone else would have died from what I had hit him with. It was his own stupid fault for binding his soul to his body so I hadn't been able to finish him off. But then again, I guessed that was rather the point.

'At some stage, you're going to have to take some responsibility for your actions.' I could feel the burning concentration of the thousands of people behind me, listening to every word.

He turned and walked along the front of the barrier, bumping it every few metres with his knuckles as if testing its strength. I prayed he wouldn't find a weak point.

'Whatever makes you think I don't take any responsibility?' He paused and looked back over his shoulder at me. 'I'm just asking that you do as well. After all, I was quite happy snoozing in my little rock. It was *you* who chose to wake me.' The skin around his mouth pulled tight and his eyes tensed. I guessed that was him smiling.

I let out a huff of air. We could play the blame game all day. 'This is getting us nowhere. What do you want?'

'You know what I want.' He turned so that his focus was beyond me. 'You all know what I want. Give Isadora to me and this will all go away.'

There was an angry mutter behind me. I tensed, waiting for someone to decide that it was a great idea.

Vulpine. Incoming. Emerald's thought pushed into my head.

The barrier should stop them.

They aren't coming from that side of the barrier.

I spun and stared back down the valley. White spots were speeding towards us.

Go, I shrieked. *Go.*

'Vulpine,' Turos yelled, stabbing at the sky.

I could hear the rustle from a thousand dragon wings unfurling. They had to get aloft before the Vulpine arrived.

I spun back to Santanas. His stiff smile dominated his face. Madness danced in his eyes as he laughed. 'Perhaps we should continue this conversation later,' he said. 'Looks like you'll be busy for a while.'

'Archers.' Rako voice was steady. 'Ready your arrows.'

Dragons sprung into the air, spiralling away to allow room for others to lift off. My heart was in my mouth as I measured the growing white dots and waited for the dragons to become airborne.

Emerald and Lance were up, and I held my breath, feeling useless as I watched them strike out towards the enemy. Every nerve in me cried out that it was wrong. Wrong for her to be up there without me. I knew the couple of Millenium flying with her should be enough to protect her back, but that should have been *my* job. She was my dragon, and I was her rider.

I was useless. Earth bound. Trapped.

Turos's hand clamped down on my arm and I swivelled to look up at him. His eyes were wide and he breathed slowly through his nose as if warding off panic.

'It's okay,' I said. 'They will be okay.'

Okay? Just okay? Emerald sniffed inside my head.

The white spots got close enough to be visible as eagles. I squinted into the sky, watching Emerald as she played chicken with a Vulpine. At the last second, she twisted into a barrel roll, reaching out with flexed talons to tear at the eagle. Feathers exploded as she hooked the soft body towards her, biting down on its head. She tossed the rest of the body away and I tracked its fall, watching the Bedouin rider pulling at the bridle as he tried to get the dead bird to fly.

The hair on the back of my neck stood on end as the second barrier slammed into place above us.

I had my back to the enemy, staring up into the sky like a newbie. But worse, I had put my back to Santanas. I spun around, scanning the enemy force for him, but he was gone.

You know you can get a bird's eye view of the fight if you want.

I could tell by the look on Turos's face that even though he wasn't with Lance in body, he was in spirit. But I couldn't share the feeling that this was just a distraction. Yet another trap. If they brought down the barrier while we had our backs to them it would mean death to hundreds before we got ourselves organised again.

I need to keep an eye on Santanas, I said.

That's probably for the best. He's as cunning as he is mad.

It was easy for me to forget that Emerald had spent decades bonded to him. She didn't think about it at all.

And besides, she added, *I think they may be about to try and bring down the barrier.*

What makes you think…Oh.

The giants at the front pulled to the sides giving me a view of the six holding a battering ram.

'Brace yourselves,' Wolfgang's voice rang out. 'We practiced for this.'

The giants started forwards in a shuffling run, each holding a metal ring that protruded from the side of the gigantic log. I didn't know trees grew that tall.

'Is that cherry wood?' How did they get a piece of cherry wood that big?

Turos looked down at me, a perplexed look on his face. 'How would I know?'

'Well, you're a man. Men know stuff about wood and metal and things.'

'Izzy,' he moved into a fighting stance as the giants neared the wall, 'I grew up on an island that had a total of six types of trees.'

Leather creaked and metal clanged as the men around me readied themselves. I gritted my teeth, cringing as the gigantic ram slammed into the barrier with a BOOM that almost blew me off my feet. But it held. The barrier held.

A surge of viscous triumph flowed into me from above. I could see Emerald, glittering like the stone I had named her after, as she wove through the sky. She left death and destruction in her wake. The battle waged above me, dragons snapping at eagles like dogs at a swarm of flies.

BOOM.

I flinched and pulled my attention back to the battle in front of me. The might of the giants against the resilience of the witches.

I wanted to help. I wanted to help so badly it was a burning yearning inside me. But Wolfgang was right, I'd only make things worse if I tried.

'You should see the look on your face.'

'What?' I looked up at Turos's amused smile.

'You look like the kid that didn't get picked for the sports team.'

'I do not.' I looked down to find that I had managed to cross my arms without cutting myself on my swords.

'You're sulking.'

'I'm not.' I stamped my foot, immediately feeling ridiculous. He was right. Dark Sky damn him.

'You'll get your turn, don't worry.'

I poked my tongue out at him and turned back to the barrier. The giants were making their third run. I could feel the wall of power humming in front of me.

BOOM.

The hair on the back of my head stood on end. I drove the tip of a sword into the earth and clutched at Turos's arm, my nails digging into his flesh as I fought the nausea that threatened me. A metallic taste coated my tongue.

Filth. Black, putrid filth.

Waves of it rolled over me.

'Izzy?'

'Shhhhhh.' I fought back the darkness and felt for the source. It was coming from the other side of the barrier.

'What is it?'

'I think the goblins are weaving a spell.'

It was the only thing it could be. The pressure built, expanding inside me, reaching up towards the sky, spinning as it grew. They were going to try and blow out the shield.

I reached towards it. There...behind the giants...hidden behind a line of goblin warriors.

Many practitioners working together, wove the body of the spell. It must have been a circle, the same as we were using. All of them contributing their power for a single user to wield.

Closer still, till the power hummed an inch away. A familiar presence brushed the edge of my mind and I pulled back before she felt me. At least now I knew where Galanta was. She was the one wielding the dark magic.

'What are you going to do?'

I could feel my smile pulling my face tight. 'I'm going to help them.'

BOOM.

Inky blackness coated me as I surged into the spell, joining my unpredictable power to theirs. The spell swelled, mushrooming out of control. I felt Galanta struggle to control it, a juggler throwing too many balls. For a terrifying second I thought she had managed, but then the magic overflowed.

I snapped my awareness back as the spell exploded. A visible shock-wave of energy ripped outwards from the centre of the circle. It tore through the goblin warriors, shredding flesh from limbs. A tsunami of air tumbled into the giants at knee height. Muscles tore and joints snapped as the giants roared in confusion.

They fell like a mighty forest under the death warrant of a developer. Tremors shook the earth, and I squatted with a hand on the ground to maintain my balance.

The force of the failed spell roared towards us, smacking into the barrier. I felt the wall bulge towards us, quivering for a few seconds before it firmed again. I let out a sigh of relief. I hadn't been one hundred percent sure it was going to hold.

In the space of a moment it was over. Goblins and orcs lay groaning on the ground, blood flowing from their eyes and noses. The giants clutched at their useless legs. Blood splattered the barrier like a gory, stained-glass window.

'Damn woman.' Turos's eyes were wide, his body frozen as he surveyed the damage. 'Remind me not to ask your help for anything.'

One figure stood in the centre of the remains of her circle. Galanta. She let out a howl of rage as she spun on the spot. I hadn't destroyed their whole army, but I had taken out a chunk of it. But more importantly, I had decimated their ability to use magic. I had bought us some time.

'You,' she shrieked. 'You, you, you....' She pulled a dagger from the sheath at her hip and strode towards me. 'You.' Spittle flew out of her mouth and joined the sticky, red that oozed down the shield. 'You...stupid...little...witch.'

'That's the best you can come up with?' I stalked towards her so there were only a few inches separating us.

She jammed her forehead on the barrier, blood smudging her skin. 'I will make you pay for that.' She spoke through clenched teeth. 'I will drain your blood and bathe in it. I will hunt down your loved ones and remove their intestines through their noses.' Veins bulged in her neck as her face turned purple. 'I will strip your skin from you in tiny little pieces and then I will eat the flesh from your body while you are still alive.'

This was the being who had killed Orion, stolen Aethan's memories, killed thousands of my people, and brought a madman back to life. Her threats, filled with ominous vehemence, should have invoked terror, but instead, they kindled my own snarling anger.

I slammed up against the other side of the barrier, wishing I could get my hands around her throat. Red filled my vision as my lips pulled back in a snarl. 'Bring it on, bitch,' I said.

'Ahh, Izzy.'

I ignored the familiar voice. She was right where I wanted her. I shoved at the barrier, wishing it was gone.

'Ahhh, Isadora.' It was Wolfgang. Part of me knew I should be listening, but I wanted this too much.

She shoved back, her pointed teeth gnashing together as if she were trying to rip out my throat.

'Stop.'

A hand clamped onto my shoulder, dragging me back from her. I shoved it off and leapt at her, my arms extended to rip out her throat.

'You're going to bring down the....'

Instead of the frigid hardness of the shield, cool air met my fingertips, and then the soft flesh of her neck was within my grasp. Her eyes flared wide with surprise and then the weight of my assault carried her to the ground. I landed on top of her, making sure my knee wedged into her stomach, and then I clenched my fist and pounded it into her face.

A roar went up around me and then black-garbed legs were flicking past as the Millenium warriors raced to meet the enemy.

Galanta stabbed the dagger up towards my face. I grabbed her wrist and slammed it onto the ground, throwing my weight onto my knee and grinding it into her as I shook the dagger free from her grasp.

The unmistakeable sound of metal clashing with metal echoed through the valley.

She jerked her back upwards, throwing me sideways as she rolled. I grasped her dreadlocks with both hands and pulled. She shrieked and reached for my braid, slapping me in the face with her spare hand as she tugged on it.

Men yelled battle screams around me and dragons trumpeted their rage overhead.

A scream of white-hot anger erupted from my throat. A quick death with a blade wasn't enough. I needed to feel my fists pummelling her flesh, my nails tearing at her skin, my fingers digging into her eyes. I needed to brutalise her and beat her into submission. I needed to dominate her to regain the control she had stolen from my life.

'Daughter.' A figure draped in a swirling cloak stood beside us. 'I need my lieutenant. You may not kill her.'

I grabbed an ear and pulled on it as hard as I could. Galanta shrieked and let go of my braid to stab a finger at my eye. I jerked my head to the side and pain lanced as her nail tore my cheek.

The patient voice let out a sigh and then knelt beside us. We froze, both of us reacting to the figure in different ways. Galanta let out a mewl, while I shrieked and threw myself backwards, scuttling away on my hands and feet like an upside-down crab.

Clarity swooped down on me and I looked around at what I had done.

Oh crap. I had brought down the shield. I had done their job for them.

Giants crawled across the valley as the Guard and Millenium dodged their grasp, darting in to slice open necks. A black line of Millenium danced at the new front line, the speed and grace of their movement hard to track with a normal eye.

I wrenched my gaze back to Santanas. His eyes glittered at me from under his hood.

'Never fear,' he said. 'I'll not end this now. There's still too much fun to be had.' He stood and held a hand down to Galanta.

She rose to her knees and let him haul her to her feet, a satisfied smirk on her face. She pursed her lips and spat at me, saliva flicking across my arms.

'Oh gross.' I jumped to my feet and backed up till I found my swords sticking out of the earth. I grasped them and pulled them free, feeling instantly better with their weight in my hands. 'And I didn't bring any alcohol wipes with me.' My voice didn't tremble nearly half as much as it should have.

'Till we meet again.' Santanas gave me a mocking salute. They turned together, took three steps, and disappeared from view.

'Damn.' How had he done that? Feeling like a fool I surveyed the damage I had wrought.

'I tried to warn you.' Wolfgang stood behind me.

'I just saw her there and I snapped.' I scuffed at the ground with the toe of my boot. 'I'm sorry.' It was a lame-arse apology.

He shook his head. 'Considering you took down the forward giant attack first I'm inclined to forgive you, but I'm sure Rako will have some things to say about it.' He let out a sigh as he tugged on his beard. 'However, from a strategic point of view, it was a good time to launch an attack, the enemy beyond the reach of that force field you unleashed was still stunned.'

I could see the healers' helpers carrying wounded back from the front line.

'Your grandmother is a little annoyed though.' His lips twitched into a smile. 'She was crafting a spell to bind up the giants' knees. You ruined all her fun.'

No doubt I wouldn't hear the last of that. 'I'd better go....' I nodded my head toward the battle.

He nodded and turned, stepping briskly as he headed back to the circles of witches.

I felt so stupid. I had let my temper get the best of me. That was a rookie's mistake. We could have waited on the other side of that barrier until Tamsonite showed up with our forces.

'Izzy.' Aethan trotted towards me through the dying giants. 'You okay?' He stopped a foot from me and wiped the back of his arm over his face. Dots of blood smeared his cheeks.

'Apart from an intense case of embarrassment.'

One side of his mouth pulled up into his lopsided grin. 'You certainly know how to put on a good show.'

'Aethan.' Ebony's voice was faint.

'Come on.' He nodded his head back to the fight. 'Let's go before she takes it into her head to come up here.'

I cleared my mind of my embarrassment, pushing it into a back corner where I could deal with it later. It wasn't going to do any good analysing it now. 'Good luck.' I touched his shoulder and then turned and ran to the front.

Turos was easily visible, a blond God of wrath, his swords hacking their way through the enemy. Emerald's blood lust flowed into me through our bond. The Vulpines were retreating to regroup, and she and the rest of the dragons were in pursuit.

Turos spun, his blades whipping through the air as he crossed his arms and slashed outwards. The razor sharp edges seemed to melt into the throat of the goblin he fought. He stepped to the side, kicking backwards so that the dying goblin stumbled past him and into the waiting Guard who quickly finished him off.

Slash, parry, stab, spin. Turos seemed to dance his way through the enemy, his movements fluid and elegant. I allowed myself to admire the view for a couple more seconds, and then I took three quick steps, leaping into a swan dive over the heads of the Guard.

A cheer went up from behind me as I flipped and landed, balancing on the shoulders of an ogre. A quick stab at an angle downwards, and I rode the dying man to the ground, stepping off to land beside Turos.

'Took you long enough.' He flashed me a grin. 'You're never going to catch up with my body count.'

'Oh really?' I stepped to the side and pushed an orc back towards the Guard. 'I'm claiming all the men that spell took down.'

He frowned as he dropped under the slash of a dagger, coming back up to shove the tip of his sword into the soft skin between the goblin's chin and throat. The goblin's eyes rolled back and he dropped to his knees. Turos stepped onto his back and ball-kicked an ogre in the nose. 'That's not fair.'

I barked out a laugh. 'All's fair in love and war.'

'Move back,' Rako shouted.

I glanced around. We had pressed well past the narrowing in the valley and Guard were flowing in to fill the widening gaps on either side of the Millenium. If we kept this up there would be no-one to swap in when we needed a rest.

'Drop back,' I echoed his call.

The swirling mass of goblins, orcs and ogres, pressed forwards eagerly as we backed down the valley. There were so many of them. At least twenty times our number, maybe thirty. I couldn't be sure because I couldn't see where they ended.

I can help with that.

A dragon's eye vision of the valley filled my head. Overflowing with bodies. It was full to overflowing. The ones at the rear sat while they waited for their chance to kill us. And there were more giants there as well. Great. They had kept some in reserve.

Four hours. We only had to hold for four hours. It had to have been nearly one already.

A zing of energy flew over our heads and the enemy behind the line we were currently fighting froze. Their eyes twitched from side-to-side, but the rest of their body stayed exactly as it had been when the spell had hit.

A goblin on the far-side of the spelled fighters pushed forwards in impatience and a frozen warrior toppled. It smacked into another one who flew to the side and knocked down two more. They in turn knocked down others, and suddenly, statuesque goblins and orcs were falling like dominos.

As one, Guard, Millenium and human surged forwards, the paralysed warriors little more than sacrificial lambs as swords, already covered with blood, swept down to end their lives. We met a fresh wave of goblins in the middle and the fighting renewed in force.

'Back,' Rako yelled. 'Back to the holding point.'

As we fell back, the remnants of an eagle smacked into a group of ogres in an explosion of red and white feathers. I kicked an orc off my sword and spun to find the next one had the shaft of an arrow protruding from his neck.

Orange flitted by above and arrows rained down, each finding a home in the neck of a goblin. Arthur and Isla sailed past, Isla loading and releasing three arrows in the space of each heartbeat.

My breathing came in pants. My arms felt like lead. And still the enemy came.

A dull horror hovered in the back of my thoughts. How were we going to win this? How could we defeat such a large army? And even if we managed it, Santanas would raise another one. It might not be for years, but it would happen again, and again, and again. Generations would be dedicated to the continual battle against him, until he wore us down enough to win. I couldn't let that happen. I had to find a way to end this here.

'Switch out.' Rako's call registered in my exhausted thoughts.

I felt men moving behind me, waiting till one tapped me on the shoulder, then I ducked and stepped back to allow a fresh Millenium into my space. I stumbled back a few more paces, suddenly free of the desperate struggle of life or death.

'Get some water, something to eat, and get some rest. You'll be going back in sooner than you'd like.' Rako paced along the line of exhausted soldiers, patting shoulders as he went. He paused in front of me and I stared at the blood splattering his face and chest. 'That means you as well.'

I nodded numbly, wondering if I could be bothered walking that far. Perhaps I could just lie down where I was and have a nap.

'Come on.' Turos tugged on my arm.

I turned towards the supply tent and Aethan fell in to step beside us. I looked sideways, checking him for damage. There was none.

'You're bleeding.' He lifted my arm, inspecting a cut on my bicep.

'It's nothing.' I looked up into the sky. The aerial battle continued, less fierce than before but it seemed the Vulpines had rallied.

'I was wondering,' Turos cleared his throat, 'couldn't you just?' He held his hands out, wiggling the tips of his fingers.

'Couldn't I just what?' I mimicked his gesture.

'You know, just blast into them. Like you did on the beach that day.'

I glanced guiltily at Aethan. Blasting pirates hadn't been the only thing I'd done on the beach that day. Thoughts of that spectacular kiss were still able to boil my blood. 'I could. I guess. Maybe.'

Men bustled around us, heading for the supply tent. We made a gory bunch, covered in blood and sweat.

'Why only maybe?'

I could feel Aethan watching me. I was pretty sure he already knew the answers. 'Well, it's not something I can kind of do in cold blood.'

Turos's eyebrows rose but he stayed silent, watching my face as I struggled to come up with a better way to describe it.

'It seems wrong to blast them with energy when they can't do it to me.'

'You're looking for a fair fight? Because I don't see one here.' He waved his arm back down the valley.

'Hmmmmm. Not a fair fight, no.' Dark Sky, why couldn't I just go blow holes in their lines?

'Things have to be desperate for Izzy to trigger her magic.' I looked at Aethan. He shrugged and gave me my favourite smile. 'It's just what I've observed. It seems to be connected to her fight-or-flight instinct.'

His hand lifted towards me and for a second I thought he was going to tuck my stray hair behind my ear, or touch my cheek, or something really nice like that. But then his gaze shifted to Turos and he let his hand fall back to his side.

'I think we're pretty much outnumbered.'

'We're containing it,' I said. 'And reinforcement is coming. Besides, if I start blowing holes in them, I'm sure Santanas will retaliate in kind, and I'm not sure I would be able to stop him.'

'I wonder why he isn't doing that now?'

It was a good question. Surely not because he was scared of me? I was pretty sure he knew I was no match for him. So why wasn't he?

'Aethan. Oh Aethan. I've been so worried.' Ebony rushed towards us from the supply tent. 'You promised you'd come and find me as soon as you had a break.'

Aethan's shoulders slumped as he let out a sigh. 'We've just come off the field. I need food and water.'

'Of course.' She fluttered in front of him, her green eyes wide with dismay as she ran them over him. 'Are you hurt? There's so much blood.'

'None of it's mine.'

'Come.' She reached out and took his arm. 'I've got food for you.' She looked over at Turos and me. 'There's some for all of you.'

She led us to a table near the supply tent. Three mugs, a pitcher of water, and some flat bread and dried meat were waiting. I sank onto a foldout chair with a sigh. It felt really good.

We were silent while we drank and ate, our gazes on the distant fight. There were so few of us holding them at bay. A plug in the neck of a full bottle. If they got around us, or through us...I shuddered and pushed my thoughts away from that.

Two of the circles of witches held hands, their eyes distant as they pooled their forces. Wolfgang stood up the hill, staring at the fight. 'Now,' he barked.

I saw a wicked smile form on Grams' face as she twisted the spell and sent it toward the enemy.

'What do you think she did?' Aethan nudged my leg with his knee and nodded toward Grams.

'Can't tell.' I shrugged. 'There's possibly a contingent of orcs who just decided to take up ballroom dancing.'

Rako dragged a seat over to our table and sat down. 'Princess.' He inclined his head to Ebony.

Turos stiffened and a second later Emerald howled in my mind. *I can see them.* She showed me the valley, full to overflowing. Out on the plain beyond the end of the enemy, another force marched.

'They're almost here.' I could feel relief forcing energy back into my muscles.

'How far?' Rako and Aethan sat forwards in their chairs.

'Twenty minutes. Maybe thirty.'

Rako nodded, his eyes gleaming. 'Eat up. I want you back at the front in twenty minutes. When he hits them from the rear they're going to increase their pressure on us.

I need my best fighters there.' He hopped up, looking down at me before he left. 'Any sign of the dark faeries?'

I shook my head. 'But Emerald didn't go far.'

'They'll be here.' Ebony put her hands on her hips. 'My father will be here to save the day.'

I looked around at the men, exhausted from fighting; the healers bent over the wounded; the witches and faeries, concentrating on their magic, then I looked back at Ebony, resentment making my voice hard. 'We're all saving the day, Ebony,' I said. 'We're *all* saving the day.

***

'Here they come,' I said. My initial guesstimation of thirty minutes had been overly optimistic. That had been an hour ago.

Aethan grunted and slashed his sword across a goblin's throat. I grabbed the falling creature's arm, pulling him forwards and out of our way.

We couldn't see the rest of our forces from where we were. They were still too far away. Emerald was sending me snapshots as she could. She had landed a short time ago, taking on another Millenium to replace one who had been wounded. But now I could see our army spread out along the enemy rear where it flowed back onto the plain at the beginning of the valley. They surged together as the battle was joined.

I had lost count of how many of the enemy I had killed. I was sure Turos and Aethan had as well, because the numbers they randomly called out had no relation at all to a numerical sequence. I had long since stopped trying to compete, concentrating, instead, on the movement of my arms and legs as I parried and thrust, dodged and weaved. I had never fought this hard for this long and it was beginning to show.

I'd had to drop my Millenium mind control. Moving that fast used up far more energy, and my normal speed had served me well enough before. One-by-one the other Millenium had dropped back to normal speed as well. We were in for the long haul and it was starting to show.

'What about the giants?' Sweat glistened on Aethan's body and dribbled down his forehead.

'They're using ropes. Winding them around their legs.'

'Swap.' Rako yelled.

I waited for the tap that would indicate my replacement was ready, then I kicked out at the nearest goblin and darted backwards past my replacement Guard.

'Fifteen minutes,' Rako said. 'Grab some water.'

A group of women waited about twenty metres behind the line. Ebony was amongst them, a pitcher of water and some mugs in a basket at her feet. I grabbed a mug, trying not to be bothered by her fussing over Aethan while he drank. At least she was making herself useful.

I didn't talk as I slumped down next to Turos, finishing my water and lying back, my knees up and one arm draped over my eyes. All around me men did the same.

'Is it true?' one of the Guard asked. 'Is the army here?'

I pulled my arm away from my face and looked over at him. 'Yes.' I nodded. 'They are fighting at the rear.'

His smile was weary. 'Did you hear that? We've done it. The army is here.' A ragged cheer came up from around us, cut off as they concentrated on consuming water and resting. Our fighting stints were getting shorter, but so were our rests. Most of our wounded were coming back from the healers ready to fight again, but some were not. I tried not to think about that.

'Get ready.' Rako sounded tired too.

I clambered back to my feet, stretching my head from side-to-side as I attempted to loosen up tightening muscles. I was going to pay for this tomorrow.

'Come on.' I looked from Aethan to Turos. 'Last one there is a rotten egg.'

Turos stood and pushed Aethan's shoulder. 'Come on rotten egg,' he said.

I wanted to smile, I mean the sight of the two of them coordinating rather than fighting should have sent pure joy zinging through my veins, but I didn't have enough energy to spend on a smile at that moment. I only had energy for fighting.

'Come on.' One of the Guard, young despite the years showing in his eyes, pushed despondently to his feet.

I looked over at them. They were fighting this war because of me. Because of mistakes I had made. Because of traps that had been laid because I existed. Because my blood had the power to unlock a monster.

Well, maybe I should take time for more than just fighting.

'Great work.' I reached over and touched the man on his shoulder. I'd never met him. Maybe he had just graduated from College. No doubt he had a wife and kids, or sweetheart at home. 'We're going to whip their butts.'

'Are we?' The look he shot me tore at my heart.

'I *know* so.' I smiled at him. 'There's nothing they can do that we can't.'

'You think? I mean, he's a *War Faery*.' Fear made his voice a rough whisper.

A group of them had stopped. All of them looked toward Aethan, Turos and me.

Aethan reached out and put a hand on my shoulder. 'Wayne,' he said, 'have I ever lied to you?'

'No, Sir.' Wayne bobbed his head.

'So if I tell you that this woman,' he shoved my shoulder again, 'has as much fire power in her finger tips as any War Faery, will you believe me?'

Their eyes swivelled to me. Wayne gulped, then licked his lips. 'So it's true?' he whispered. 'She's...?'

Aethan held a hand up, stopping his next words. 'She's exactly what we need her to be.'

I could feel the pressure of their hope pressing down on me as we walked back to the front. Dark Sky, I *hoped* I was what they needed. I *hoped* I was enough.

'Ready?' Turos's eyes were smiling as he looked down at me.

'Oh yeah. Bring it on.' I scuffed my feet along the tarmac surface.

'As much as I hate to admit it, he's right.'

I cocked an eyebrow at him and tilted my head.

'You're exactly what we need.'

'Do you think?' I hated the vulnerable edge in my voice, but nobody else seemed to have heard it.

'When I was growing up, I hated broccoli. Mum told me it was good for me but I thought she was crazy.' He pulled a face. Gladaline *had* been crazy.

'Pardon?'

'Hmmm. What I'm trying to say is that sometimes we don't know what's good for us.'

'Are you likening me to broccoli?'

'No. Well...maybe.' A grin flashed across his face. 'You're much prettier than broccoli.'

'Gee. Thanks.' I stuck my tongue out at him.

'And you're not nearly as green.'

I watched as an orc stumbled through a hurriedly made gap in the front. A Guard leapt forwards, slashing his sword through the back of its heels. As the creature toppled forwards, a downward strike severed its head. Blood sprayed out in an arc, splashing my arm and cheek with warm droplets.

A bolt of energy flew overhead, blasting into a group of goblins. The ground beneath their feet exploded, chunks of tarmac flinging them upwards and backwards into their brethren. I could just hear their roars of pain over the din of the battle.

'I don't get it.' Aethan shook his head. 'What is he doing? Why isn't he countering?'

I shrugged. Who knew what the mad bastard was thinking. He seemed to be content to let his army die.

'Ready,' Rako roared.

I pulled my swords back out of their scabbards and fell into the long line of fighters forming up. Aethan took my left, and Turos my right. I could feel more Millenium and Guard pressing in behind us.

'Go,' Rako said.

We moved forwards till we were behind the wall of men currently defending the narrowing in the valley. I reached out and tapped one on the shoulder. He ducked and fell back between a gap between Aethan and me. We worked our way forwards till suddenly we were facing goblins and orcs.

A dwarf bared his teeth and ran at us, a club rimmed with nails swinging wildly in his hands. I jumped back and kicked his arm to the side. He lunged again and I leapt over him, kicking back so he stumbled into the line of men behind. Let them deal with the little banshee.

'Going soft?' Turos's voice was mocking.

'It would be like killing a child.' I let out a growl as I faced off against a goblin easily seven feet tall with dreadlocks that hung to his waist. His dark skin rippled over his muscles and his pointed teeth welcomed me with a fierce grin.

I was tired. He was fresh. Excellent. I loved a fair fight.

They're coming.

I could see flickers of white – Vulpine flashing through the sky in front of Emerald. But beyond that, far in the distance, a shadow moved across the plain. It moved faster than our force had. An army on horseback coming to help us.

The goblin's blades flickered as he launched himself at me. I feinted to the left, then spun to the right, a whisper of air telling me of his dagger's passage past my cheek. He let out a grunt and leapt back, missing the death stroke I had planned. A thin, red line appeared across his rib cage.

I kicked out at an ogre beside him as it dashed forwards, trying to club me over the head. The ball of my feet hit his chest, forcing him back as I launched backwards into a spin. My blade slashed up in front of me, carving up through the goblin's stomach to lodge in the bottom of his rib cage. He let out a guttural humph of surprise and toppled forwards.

'They're coming,' I said to Aethan.

'They never stop.' Sunlight glinted off his blades as they danced in an elaborate pattern.

His swordplay had always been more beautiful than mine. I had initially tried to mimic it, a student copying her teacher, but it had never felt entirely natural. A pale copy of the original.

It wasn't till I had seen Wilfred fight, his style more bear than man, that I had realised not everybody fought the same way. My style had developed after that.

'Not them.' I ducked under an overhead strike and shoved my sword through the orc's stomach. It wasn't an immediate death stroke but there was less chance my sword would catch on something than if I went for the chest.

'The dark faeries?' A feral grin took over his mouth.

'Come to save the day,' I said.

The never-ending tide of the enemy hung before us. I found it hard to match his enthusiasm. I doubted that Galanta and Santanas would let us slaughter their whole army. They had something planned and for the life of me I couldn't work out what it might be.

A low hum of fatigue set up camp in my arms. I moved with care, broken tarmac exposing churned dirt which had mixed with blood to form mud. It was slippery, and even though they were also pulling their dead and wounded out of the way, there was always a chance I would trip over a body part.

I tried not to think about our next break, I tried not to wonder what Santanas was up to, I tried not to work out how long till the dark faeries arrived. I concentrated on killing the creatures that were trying to kill me. Do or die.

I wasn't sure how long we held for before Rako called the next change. I staggered backwards through the ranks, noticing how they had thinned. Ebony waited for us, a triumphant light in her eyes.

'Here.' She held out a mug of water. I grasped it in both hands and gulped down its contents. I could hear the others doing the same around me.

'My love.' Ebony was positively glowing with excitement.

Aethan slopped some water over his head and scrubbed at his face with both hands. 'Yes.' His voice was as tired as I felt.

'Come.' She held out her hand. 'Come see what our union has brought you.'

'Ebony,' he sloshed more water over his head and scrubbed some more, blinking at her through wet lashes, 'I'm tired, I'm hungry. It can wait.'

'No.' Her voice hardened and she flashed me an angry look. 'I want you to see what the *sacrifices* you have made have been for.'

His gaze followed hers to where I stood frozen, my mug of water hovering above my head. He sighed and shook his head, but I could see a glint of guilt in his eyes.

She knew about us. Knew that we loved each other. Knew he still wanted me. Suddenly, I felt ill. What had I been doing? He wasn't my toy to play with anymore.

'Awkwaaaard,' Turos whispered in my ear.

I flashed him an angry look and tipped the water over my head. The dried blood turned to slime as I scrubbed at it.

Where are they? I sent my mind out to Emerald. I could feel her enjoyment as she swooped and dived, chasing one of the few remaining Vulpines. Most of the dragons had landed to water and rest, but she, Lance, and Arthur and Isla were still up there.

Almost instantly, an aerial view filled my mind. A sea of dark faeries flowed over the land, their Ubanty slaves riding behind with the pack horses. In a few minutes they would join with our army.

'They're almost here.' I glanced at Aethan, trying not to notice how handsome he was with his wet hair slicked back off his brow. His dark-blue eyes met mine and I glanced away. Not mine.

'Right.' He straightened and handed one of the other water bearers his mug. 'Rako.' He beckoned to the stocky head of the Guard. 'The dark faeries are here.'

Rako smacked his hands together, a brief flicker of a smile on his face as he turned and trotted back towards the front.

Aethan turned back to Ebony and said. 'Fine. Let's go.'

She held out her hand, shaking it at him till, with a sigh, he reached out and took it. Then she turned and started walking toward the distant rocky outcrop.

I thought about following them, but guilt stopped me. Let her have her moment of triumph.

'Coming up?' Turos reached out his hand and shook it, mimicking Ebony perfectly.

I laughed and looked at the outcrop. It was a few minutes' walk away and I was exhausted. Plus, I could get a much better view than that right where I was. 'Nah. I think I'll watch it with Emerald.'

He surprised me when he said, 'I think I'll go anyway.'

Since when would he rather spend time with Aethan than me? Unless it wasn't about Aethan. Unless it was about...Ebony.

A flash of jealousy I didn't know I had the energy for, stabbed into my gut.

I blew at a stray piece of hair, annoyed at myself. Really? With everything going on, I still had time for jealousy?

Confusion battered the inside of my head as I watched him walk away. He towered above the soldiers around him, his white-blond hair glistening in the sun. His broad shoulders tapered into that narrow waist and, well, I knew how spectacular his legs were. And *that* wasn't helping at all.

I puffed out a breath of air, too tired to lift my arm to push at the piece of hair tickling my cheek.

'Isadora.' Ebony's voice echoed back to me. 'You should come too.'

'Fine.' I shook my head as I looked at the outcrop. What I wanted to do was sleep, but I told my right leg to move forwards. The left followed obediently and before I knew it I was trudging after them.

I sent my mind questing up to Emerald. The dark faeries had reached the back of the army. One rider at the front, Arracon most probably, was talking to someone at the back of the army. I was guessing Tamsonite was greeting them.

I glanced up at the outcrop. Aethan and Ebony were already there, standing on the edge. Turos was a third of the way up the path.

The entire dark faery force held frozen, their banners snapping in the breeze. Then Tamsonite turned and a minute later our army started to shuffle apart, making a pathway down the centre.

Ebony held one delicate arm in front of her, pointing down the valley. Could they even see what was happening from there? It was so far away.

I reached the bottom of the path, sighing as I looked upward. It felt like a lifetime to the top.

The dark faeries flowed into the space as it opened up even further, pressing towards where our troops met Santanas's. Their riders on their horses, towered over our soldiers.

Turos reached down and grabbed my hand, hauling me up the last few feet to the top. I gave him a tired smile and followed him to where Ebony and Aethan stood.

I squinted into the distance, huffing in surprise when the dark coats of the faeries there were visible. I really hadn't expected to be able to see them. Still, my view with Emerald was much better, I needn't have climbed all this way just to watch Ebony's smug satisfaction.

The dark faeries lifted gleaming spears into the air as they approached the front. I held my breath waiting for the first attack, the first thrust to come, but when it did, it was not what I had expected.

'No.' The shout left my throat as I froze in horror.

The dark faeries were attacking. They just weren't attacking our enemy. They were attacking us.

Treachery. Dark treachery.

The savage attack beat down on the army from three sides. They had divided them and surrounded them, and now they were slaughtering them.

Why? How? It didn't make sense. We had their Princess. Why would they risk her life like that.

I ripped my mind away from the carnage and stared at Ebony. Her hands covered her mouth, muffling her shout of horror.

'No,' she said. 'Why?' She looked up at Aethan, her huge green eyes brimming with tears. 'Why?' It came out in a whisper and I knew what she was asking. Not, 'Why would they attack their allies?', but, 'Why would they throw her life away?'.

His face contorted in rage and his hands fisted at his sides. 'It's okay.' The words made it out through his clenched teeth. 'You are safe here.' He looked back towards the other end of the valley. 'You will not be harmed.'

Turos's posture snapped, his knees and elbows bent into a predatory position. A trickle of rocks rolled down the cliff, a puff of dust rising where they landed.

Look. Look. Emerald pushed the view of the end of the valley back into my head.

The dark faeries still attacked, but something was happening at their rear. A crack of light appeared in the sky, fracturing the bright blue open and glowing as if a second sun shone there. The Ubanty thrust their arms into the air, and their slave bracelets fell off.

'They're rebelling,' I gasped. 'They're fighting back.'

'Who is?' Ebony asked.

'The Ubanty.'

'Impossible. They are bound to us.' She stalked towards me, an angry cat with a twitching tail.

'Not any more.' I pointed at the widening crack. 'Ulandes has come to claim them.'

She'd done it. Samuel had done it. They'd rallied the Ubanty and staged their rebellion for when it could help us the most.

Ebony's cheeks reddened as air hissed out from between her teeth. I would have thought she'd be pleased, but it was obviously true what they said, blood ran thicker than water.

Two people appeared within that white-hot fissure. Larger than life, they looked down on the fight below. The Ubanty pushed their brown cloaks back and pulled daggers from their belts. Their mouths opened in screams I couldn't hear as they hurtled towards their masters.

'No,' Ebony screamed. 'This can *not* be happening.'

A ramp appeared in the sky, lowering till it touched the ground. I let out a laugh as Wilfred, it could *only* be Wilfred, jumped onto the shiny slope and surfed his way to the bottom. I saw Ulandes shaking her head as she followed him at a stately pace. A blade of shining light appeared in her hand as she reached the bottom.

'Uhhh, Izzy.' Turos pulled his swords free, whirling them to warm up his wrists.

I brought my awareness back, turning towards him. The trickle of rocks became a stream, and then a river, till rocks the size of my hand were bouncing off the top of the outcrop.

'Incoming.' Turos danced back a few steps.

My eyes flew up the cliffs, following the slide until I saw the group of goblins riding it down. Galanta balanced in the middle of the pack, her face lit with a triumphant smile as she landed like a cat.

I was surprised to see my swords in my hands. I hadn't realised I had drawn them. But then Galanta had that effect on me. I suspected if she passed within one hundred feet of me while I slept, I would wake to find my blades in my hands. I wanted to kill her *that* badly.

'Ahhh, Aethan.' I backed back from Galanta's razor-sharp smile.

'Surprise killed the cat,' she crooned.

'It was curiosity,' I snarled. 'Curiosity killed the cat.'

'What-ev-er.' She looked way too cocky. She had to know the ten warriors with her were no match for Turos, Aethan and me. 'You ready?'

I thought she was talking to me, until I heard Ebony's cold voice from behind me. 'Let's finish this and get the hell out of here.'

I swung around. Ebony had one arm snaked around Aethan's waist. The other held the tip of a dagger to his throat. His eyes bulged with anger as he stared down at her.

'You little snake,' he hissed. 'You will die for this.'

'Oh phooey.' She pursed her lips. 'Does this mean the wedding's off?'

'You bitch.' I raised an arm and pointed a finger at her. I was almost sure my aim would be good enough to take out her and not harm Aethan. *Almost* sure.

She let out a triumphant laugh as I shook my head and lowered my arm.

'Shall we make this an even fight?' Galanta cocked her head to the side. 'We all know that these won't even dent you.' She waved the tip of her dagger at the warriors.

'Who did you have in mind?' I wasn't sure how Turos could make his voice sound so nonchalant.

A tear appeared in the veil revealing the twisted, scarred face that would haunt me forever.

'Me,' Santanas said as he pulled the way open further and stepped through.

I swallowed the lump wedged in the back of my throat. 'You just *had* to go and ask, didn't you,' I hissed at Turos.

'Forewarned is forearmed.' He backed up till he was standing next to me.

'Daughter, fancy meeting you here.' Santanas brushed at the front of his tunic as he glanced out over the battlefield.

No one had noticed what was happening on the outcrop. They were either fighting or staring at the far end of the valley. Communication bubbles wobbled their way up and down the valley.

I shot a look over my shoulder at Aethan. He had relaxed in Ebony's grip. As I watched, he blinked his eyes. Once…twice…

'Go,' I shouted as he blinked the third time. I spun and threw a fireball at Santanas as Aethan dropped low, twisting backwards out of Ebony's grasp.

She let out a yelp of pain, and then I could hear metal clashing behind me.

Turos and Galanta leapt at each other, her dagger flashing up to deflect his sword. The rest of the goblins moved to the top of the path, taking up sentry there.

Great. Even if somebody did realise our plight, they would have to fight uphill through a wall of goblin muscle to get to us.

Santanas flicked my fireball to the side, the corners of his twisted lips pulling till his face was even more grotesquely deformed. I was going to go with *happy*, in the guess-the-mood competition.

He held both his hands together till a ball of black energy filled them up. Then he plucked a piece off and blew on it. It rose into the air and floated towards me, all the more ominous for its lack of speed.

I felt my shield firm in front of me, my eyes widening with horror as the black smudge boiled on the surface like a patch of burning tar.

'You know what I want, daughter.' He blew on another piece of black energy. 'Give it to me and this will all go away.'

'Me?' I watched the second ball join the first.

'You are my family.' His voice shook with emotion. 'I want my family back.'

For a brief flicker of time, I saw reality from his point of view.

He was alone. All alone. His wife and unborn children ripped from him by the very creatures he now aligned himself with. His desperate need had warped him, twisting him into what he had once despised. If I would concede, then all of it, every terrible thing he had done, would have been worth it. To be loved again, that's all he wanted.

And for that brief flicker of time, pity touched my soul. I heard a sigh in my head and then Ulandes' voice whispered, 'You are exactly what we need.' They were both gone as quickly as they had come, leaving me with a lingering sadness and an unborn idea.

'Sorry.' I flipped my braid back over my shoulder. 'I'm a bit full up in the family department at the moment. But I'll pencil you into my diary and let you know if a position comes up.'

'You will see things my way, eventually.' He shook his hands and the black ball disappeared. 'But for now, It looks like we have to do this the hard way.' He flicked his fingers and the ground beneath my feet exploded.

I shot up into the air, shrapnel slapping into my legs and tearing at my arms. Sharp stings told me that blood had been drawn.

I had time for a quick glance at Aethan before I landed again. Sweat beaded on his forehead as he traded blows with Ebony. She hadn't been lying when she'd said she could look after herself. She was trained. But she wasn't a match for Aethan. Not on a good day. But he had been fighting for hours and she was still fresh. The life-and-death contest was closer than I would have liked.

I landed in a squat, rolling to the side to avoid a bolt of flame. I grasped at the air with my two hands, slamming them together. The air around Santanas mimicked me. He winced at the crushing force, gritting his teeth as he forced his hands out, grabbing at the air and slamming it back.

It smacked into me, lifting me up and throwing me backwards. I landed with an, 'Ooooof,' letting the momentum roll me over and back onto my feet.

Where was everybody? Couldn't they hear what was going on up here?

Turos circled Galanta warily. Blood streaked his biceps, showing where she had gotten inside his guard with her daggers. Her smile was crazy, her eyes wide with battle lust. She stalked him even as he stalked her.

I stabbed my fingers at Santanas. Air, hardened to spikes, jabbed into his flesh before he realised what I was doing. He flicked a hand downwards locking my wrists in place as he threw a lightning bolt at me. I deflected it, batting it towards the group of goblins guarding the path. Surprised screams echoed as it tore through flesh and bone.

Ebony shrieked in fury as a thin trail of blood blossomed on her cheek. It welled and trickled slowly, making its way down her previously perfect skin.

'That's going to scar,' she hissed.

'No, it won't.' Aethan waited, his blade held ready to attack.

'You think?' For one second she was the vulnerable, defenceless girl again.

'It's not going to get a chance to. You'll be dead long before that.'

I heard her snarl as she threw herself at him, her swords whistled as her rapid attack forced Aethan back.

'Isadora, you can not win.' Santanas sent a wall of fire rolling toward me.

Turos dived sideways as the flame whistled past. I held my hands up, halting its progress. Heat radiated towards me, lifting loose bits of hair to dance around my face.

I grunted as I forced it back toward Santanas inch-by-inch. Rocks popped and cracked, and leaves burst into flames.

Galanta dodged to the side, sweeping her leg out and thrusting a dagger at Turos. He jumped nimbly over her leg and grasped her wrist, blocking her free hand as it gouged at his eyes. He palmed her in the face and then swept his blade up, but she was already gone. Blood dribbled from her nose to her top lip as she grinned at him.

'Dark Sky, it's goblins.' Voices rose from below.

'Prince Aethan's up there.'

'What are you waiting for? Get up there.'

I tried not to feel relief. I tried not to feel anything as I struggled against Santanas. I traded blow-for-blow, and to anyone watching, it would have looked like an even fight. But I knew it wasn't. He was playing with me. Letting me think I might win.

'Finish him,' Galanta snarled.

'I'm trying.' Ebony's hissing reply was followed by a grunt of exertion.

Fear fluttered under my rib cage. All it would take was one wrong move and Turos or Aethan would die. I didn't know if I was equipped to deal with that. Didn't know if I would survive that level of pain.

Galanta twisted and turned, her foot knocking a stone as she stabbed upwards. It rolled, dribbling forwards till it stopped right where Turos's foot came down. His ankle twisted, throwing him onto one knee.

Galanta leapt. She grabbed his hair and twisted his head back, her dagger flicking towards his throat.

'No,' I shrieked, sending the spell I had prepared for Santanas at her instead

It smacked into her as the tip of her knife bit into his smooth skin. She flew through the air and smashed into a boulder. Her body wrapped around it, the back of her head connecting with a crack.

A wall of air smacked into me, throwing me backwards. Stones ripped at my arms and back as I tumbled over the rough ground. My breath left me in a whoosh as I crashed into a boulder. Pain lanced through my ribs as I struggled to refill my lungs. I took a short breath and then another, but it didn't seem to be enough to satisfy my body's screaming need for oxygen.

Turos pushed to his feet, a wash of blood running down his neck as he stumbled towards Galanta. He raised his sword above his head and chopped it down into the soft flesh of her throat.

Blood sprayed, and I stared as her head bounced down the side of the boulder and rolled towards me across the ground. It came to a stop, her black dreadlocks lying like octopus tentacles around her skull. Her eyes, wide with astonishment, blinked once before the light inside them died.

Santanas let out an annoyed sigh, shaking his head as he looked at Galanta.

Shouts came from the top of the path. I lay limp, unable to summon energy back into my limbs, trying to remember how to breathe. I knew I had to get up. Or shield myself. Or do something. But the rocky terrain felt blissful under my body. I was done. I had nothing left to give.

'Aghhhhhhhh.' Aethan clutched at his head with his hands. His swords fell from his fingers as he dug at his temples. 'Garghhhhhh.' He slumped to his knees and toppled slowly to the side, convulsing as his body collapsed to the dirt.

Ebony planted one of her swords into the dirt as she stepped forwards. Grasping the hilt of the other in both hands she lifted it above her head. Her arms held straight, she aimed the tip at Aethan.

Aethan screamed again, the agony ripping my heart out of my chest and tearing it into tiny pieces. My fingers curled into fists as I drew in a ragged breath and forced myself up onto an elbow. Pain lanced through my side as I lifted my hand and aimed at Ebony.

She let out a delighted laugh as she arched backwards to gain momentum for her killing strike.

My lightning bolt struck her between the shoulder blades. The blast sent her tumbling like a limp doll in a gale-force wind; a large hole visible where her sternum had been.

Santanas shook his head. 'If you want something done,' he said.

'No,' I gasped. 'Please, Father. No.' My side screamed in agony as I crawled to Aethan.

Turos slumped to the ground. He sat propped against the boulder, Galanta's body lying beside him. Blood washed down his throat onto his shirt. His eyes were glazed as he stared at me, but even then, I saw him struggle to rise.

'Don't,' I choked out, shaking my head at him. *Live. Please live.*

He nodded, defeat in his eyes as he slumped back. He lifted a hand and pressed his palm to the wound in his neck.

'You can't save them both.' Santanas wiggled his fingers at me. 'Which one is it going to be? Which Prince will you save?' He waved his hand between Aethan and Turos.

Tears tracked down my cheeks. He was right. I couldn't save them both.

Aethan shuddered on the ground, his body convulsing as I reached him. I dragged myself on top of him. I knew it was useless, that I couldn't shield him if Santanas decided to kill him, but I had to try.

Is that your final choice?' Santanas cocked his head to this side.

'Kill me,' I whispered. 'Take me. Not them.'

I heard a shout and Rako kicked the dead body of the last goblin out of the way. A flow of Guard followed him onto the outcrop.

'Over there.' Turos's voice rasped as he pointed toward me. 'She's over there.'

I stared in horror at him. So much blood. It bubbled through his fingers and ran like a river down his body.

He was dying. The vitality leaching out of him. And all he was worried about was me.

I had to heal him. I knew it. But Aethan let out another moan as he writhed in pain beneath me.

'This is most inconvenient.' Santanas shook his head. 'Till next time, Isadora.' He flicked back the veil and vanished.

'Turos,' Rako barked. 'Stay still, man. Dantus, get a healer. Now.'

That's what we needed. A healer. Sabby. We needed Sabby.

My face was slick with tears as I clambered off Aethan. How had this happened? One minute they had both been gloriously alive. And now...now I might lose them both.

Aethan moaned and jammed his fingers into his eyelids. I pulled his hands from his head.

'Izzy.'

I ignored the voice as I sent myself into Aethan, searching for something to heal. There was nothing. Nothing that I could detect.

'Izzy.' This time a shoulder shake accompanied the snappy voice. 'What's wrong with him?'

Pain radiated out from my rib cage and I struggled to catch my breath. 'I don't know,' I gasped.

What had she done to him?

I pulled him up onto my lap and wrapped my arms around him. I smoothed back his hair as I stared at his white face. Pain pulled his lips into a grimace but this time no sound emerged. Was he getting better, or worse?

'Dark Sky. What happened here? Turos. Turos, look at me.' A small slapping noise accompanied Sabby's voice. 'Stay with me,' she ordered. 'Don't you dare leave me. You stay with me you hear.'

'Everything's going to be okay,' I whispered into Aethan's hair. *Please don't let him die.* 'You're going to be fine,' I crooned, my lips brushing across his forehead. *Great Dark Sky, please don't take him. Please let him live.*

I needed him. He had always been there for me. Ever since I was a small child. He had been my first love.

My true love...

And just like that, not as a bolt of lightning, but as the quiet rush of a warm summer breeze, the answer I had been searching for flowed into me.

I bent my head over him as I wept. *Please don't take him. Please. Take me instead.*

I loved him. And it didn't matter that he might not remember me as he once had. The foundation for our love was still there. Time would bring new stories. Time would make new memories. If we had any time.

His body relaxed in my arms, the racking spasms of pain leaching away till he was still.

'Noooooo.' My sobs wracked my body and pain lanced through my rib cage. But it didn't matter. My physical pain didn't matter. My emotional pain had seen to that. It tore through me, ripping at the edges of my sanity. 'Please. No.' My hands trembled as I smoothed his hair back.

He looked so peaceful. So young with his face empty of pain.

Tears trickled off the end of my nose and splashed onto his cheek. 'I love you,' I whispered. 'Don't leave me.'

His eyelashes fluttered like a butterfly's wings as his eyes slowly opened. I stared into the depths of his glorious eyes, too stunned to speak, too scared to believe it was real.

'Correct me if I'm wrong,' he said, his voice low and husky, 'but aren't you meant to be kissing me?'

'What?' I blinked rapidly as unshed tears blinded me.

'Well, I was unconscious, and now I'm not. Normally when I wake up from being unconscious it's to find you kissing me.'

'Oh,' I said. 'You're alive.'

He reached up a hand and trailed his fingers down my cheek. 'I'm better than alive,' he whispered. His other hand rose so that he was cradling my face. 'Izzy,' his voice held the warmth of an old, deep love, 'I remember. I remember everything.'

'Oh.' My voice came out in a whisper. 'So, if you remember, why aren't you kissing me?'

His hands slid up around my neck as he pulled my head down towards him. His lips met mine in a fury of white hot heat as his soul seared itself to mine. I lost myself within him. My lips tasting the salt on his skin, my tongue feeling the warmth of his breath, my heart racing to keep up with the joy that fluttered through my veins.

I could feel him. Feel his energy mingling with mine as his arms wrapped around me. One hand moved to the nape of my neck, burrowing into my hair, while the other wrapped low around me, pulling me into him as he sat up. Suddenly I was on his lap, cradled in the certainty of him.

He knew everything about me, all my flaws, all my childish tendencies, and he still wanted me. His love filled me to overflowing, and the bud of an idea that had lodged in my mind, burst; the petals unfolding till it was a fully-blown flower.

And there, in the safety of his body, in the hunger of his lips, in the power of his love, I found my other answer.

He was alive. He remembered me. And I knew what I had to do.

The circle was complete.

Chapter Fifteen

Endings

'They're retreating.' Rako nodded in satisfaction.

'About time.' Aethan squeezed my hand before letting it go. He walked over to stand beside Rako, staring out over the scene of carnage below.

I remained where I was, sitting next to Turos as I let Sabby fuss over me. She had healed my broken ribs, but one of the shards had pierced a lung and she was worried there might still be internal bleeding.

Thomas stood next to Sabby, staring down at the supine Turos with a worried expression.

'He's fine, Thomas,' Sabby snapped for the third time.

'He's so white.'

'He lost a lot of blood. He'll be weak for a while.'

'I'm healthy as a horse.' Turos opened one eye and peered up at Thomas.

I winced at the lack of emotion in his voice.

A bubble wobbled up to Rako, encompassing his head and then popping a few second later. 'Tamsonite reports they're retreating down the valley towards us.' A grin flashed over his face as he looked at me. 'Your Goddess and the Ubanty are making them run for their lives.'

'What about Wilfred? Did he mention Wilfred at all?' Aethan put a hand up over his eyes as he stared at the end of the valley trying to see his best friend.

'There *was* something about a red-haired berserker.' Rako scratched at his cheek. 'He could have been talking about Wilfred.'

I let out a snort, pushing out my mind to watch the fight from Emerald's point of view.

Ulandes glowed like a beacon as she led the attack against the dark faeries. Wilfred and Samuel stood on either side of her, their tattoos lit up like cracks of lava as they slashed and stabbed. Wilfred was howling with laughter.

'Oh yeah.' I nodded my head. 'It's Wilfred all right.'

Aethan bounced up and down on his toes, staring into the distance. 'So the question is,' he said, 'if they are retreating at both ends, where are they going?'

'Through the veil.' Rako scratched at his scar.

'Dark Sky.' Turos pushed himself up to a sitting position.

'Relax Prince. They're not making a run on London. Isla and Arthur are watching. They're heading back home.'

'Till next time.' Aethan let out a growl and smacked a fist into his other hand.

'We have earned some breathing space,' Rako said. 'The goblins have lost their leader. It will take a while for them to choose another.'

'And then Santanas will need to persuade them to help again.' Aethan nodded in satisfaction. 'We have six months, a year tops to prepare.'

I was silent during their political discussion. I wasn't going to let it go six months. I was going to finish it that night.

Just me and Santanas.

It was the only way. It had *always* been the only way. I was embarrassed it had taken me this long to work it out.

Of course if any of them knew what I was planning they'd try to stop me. Or come with me. And while the thought of having support was seductive, I knew I would only risk losing someone I loved.

Turos stood up and flexed his head slowly from side-to-side.

'Are you okay?' I put a hand on his arm and peered up into his eyes.

'My neck is fully healed. Tell her Sabby.'

'Oh sure. Your *neck* is fine.' She stressed the word neck as her eyes darted from Aethan to me.

'Oh, ahhh, I, ahhh….' I looked up at him.

'So it's not true what they say.' His eyes also flickered over to Aethan before coming back to rest on me. He reached out and touched my shoulder. 'The best man doesn't always win.' He smiled, but it didn't make it to his eyes.

'Ahhhhh.' Dark Sky I felt awful. Only hours ago I had been considering the possibility of a life with him. But that was before, well, it was before *everything*.

It was almost inconceivable how far I was emotionally from where I'd been then.

'I'm sorry.' I pulled a face. It didn't really cut it.

'I'd like to say you are forgiven,' he shrugged a shoulder, 'but firstly, I'm not that nice, and secondly,' he let out a sigh, 'there's nothing to forgive. You told me from the beginning how things were for you.'

'Yes, but, then I….' I could feel a blush start up on my cheeks. Dark Skies. The *things* I had done with him.

He shook his head. 'It wasn't you. Not really. It might have become if....' He shrugged again. 'It's a moot point now. If wishes were fishes.'

'I do love you,' I whispered. I knew that much was true. 'It's just....' Different? Not enough? Too late?

He smiled and reached out to brush his fingers down my cheek. 'I know. I'll be waiting,' he raised his voice as he looked over to where Aethan stood, 'just in case he screws up.'

I glanced over at Aethan, worried about how he might have taken that. But Aethan chuckled and shook his head. 'That won't be happening.'

'You never know,' Turos's voice was conversational, 'she may not want to be Queen.'

'She'd be a Queen with you as well.'

'Yes, but the Queen of a people with no lands has a lot less pressure on her.'

'Izzy,' Sabby pulled on my hand, 'have Isla and Wilfred reunited yet?'

I closed my mouth and turned to face her. *Queen?* 'Huh?'

'Isla and Wilfred. Have they found each other yet?'

'What?' My mind was still whirling.

'Isla and Wilfred.' She put her hands on her hips and stamped her foot.

'Oh. No. They haven't.' I turned and looked down the valley. Emerald and Lance circled lazily overhead but I couldn't see Arthur anywhere. 'They're on the other side of the veil.'

'All right people.' Rako clapped his hands together. 'It's time to get camp sorted out.'

'Do you want us back on the front?' Aethan asked.

'I think I've risked the heirs to the thrones enough for one day. Let's not push it.'

I followed Thomas and Sabby back down the path, their hands linked as firmly as Aethan's and mine. Turos walked ahead with Rako. As soon as we got to the bottom, Turos trotted off towards the dragons.

'I'll be with Sabby,' I told Aethan.

'I'll be at the supply tent.' He kissed me on the nose and then turned and followed Rako.

I saw Lance coming into land just before I reached the healers. Turos sat on his neck with Gladaline right behind him. She had a hand resting on his shoulder as she leant forwards to talk to him. I pushed away the guilt threatening to overwhelm me.

There was a flash of gold near them and then Arthur and Isla slid back into our plane of existence.

'Sabby.' I looked over to where Sabby was healing a human with a leg wound. 'Isla's back.'

'Oooooh.'

The man whose leg she was probing said, 'Who's Isla?'

'The Faery Princess. Can you bend it?'

He flexed his leg and straightened it again. 'The one that looks like her sister?' He nodded his head at me.

'That's the one. She's in love with one of the Guards.'

He sat up and put some weight onto his leg. 'That's a bit beneath her isn't it?'

Sabby pursed her lips while she watched him walk back and forth. 'I don't think so. Anyway he died and....'

'Oh, so it's a *sad* story.' The soldier put his hands on his hips. 'Do you think after a day like today we need a sad story?'

A couple of the soldiers waiting to be healed let out a, 'Here, here.'

Sabby sighed. 'Of course it's not a sad story. If you shut up for a minute I'll tell you.'

I took my hands off the Guard I was working on. He took a deep breath and rolled his shoulder. 'Oh that feels better. What'd you do?'

'Put your clavicle back together.'

'So he died,' Sabby continued, 'but a Goddess brought him back to life and took him to be her personal soldier.'

The soldier barked out a laugh. 'Now you're pulling my leg.'

'I'm not.' Sabby moved down the row to the next in line. 'Tell him Izzy.'

'She's not.' I also moved onto the next waiting in my line. 'We were on a mission to bring home the dark faery Princess.'

The soldier turned and spat onto the ground. 'Dirty traitors.'

I nodded as I continued. 'Anyway, there were some pretty nasty monsters after us and one of them ripped out Wilfred's throat.' I paused while I regained control of myself. It had been one of the darkest moments of my life. 'But we were in Ulandes' sanctuary, and the Ubanty we were with was one of her worshippers.'

'Wait,' the Guard I had healed put his hand up, 'the Ubanty are the ones who rebelled?'

'The dark faeries had turned them into slaves. Anyway Samuel called Ulandes and she healed Wilfred and then claimed him.'

'So, where is he now?' the man I was working on asked. He winced as I probed his broken arm.

'He's over there.' I nodded down the valley. 'He, Samuel and Ulandes are leading the revolt. They've beaten the dark faeries.'

'So…you're telling me there's a freakin' Goddess down there?' The first soldier turned and pointed.

'Yes. And she's glowing like the sun.' I opened my eyes and released the previously broken arm.

'And this Wilfred? Has he seen the Princess yet?' The man I'd healed flexed his arm slowly.

'Exactly,' Sabby said. 'That's *exactly* what I've been trying to find out.'

All of a sudden, every person within hearing distance turned towards me. 'So what happens?' The first soldier said.

'It hasn't happened yet.'

'But, how will we know?'

A wave of energy flowed over me. Hope glowed in the tent. The indomitable human spirit. You hold it down under water, and it pops right back up again.

'Well…,' I looked around the tent, 'I might be able to see.'

There was dead silence for a few beats and then cheering broke out in the tent. 'Go on love,' the Guard I sat in front of said, 'I can wait.'

I closed my eyes and reached for Emerald, seeing the ground below as she did.

The dark faeries had given up fighting. Now they scrambled forwards, pulling each other back in their attempt to get away. The Ubanty still pursued them, but their efforts were half-hearted. There's no sport in killing a fleeing foe.

Ulandes' swords were gone. She walked amongst her people, touching a hand here, a cheek there. They knelt before her with heads bowed.

Samuel walked by her right hand side, but Wilfred wasn't there. Where was he?

Where's Wilfred?

Emerald's head pivoted as she searched for him.

I let out a laugh as her search showed me Tiny. He was alive and unharmed, and walking behind the fleeing foe, shushing them forwards with his hands. I saw him bend and upright a fallen dark faery.

Finally, Emerald found Wilfred. He was pushing through his army, his head pivoted up as he stared at the sky.

'Oh,' I said. 'He sees her.'

Arthur broke off from circling above him, flapping ahead to open ground.

I could almost see the frustration on Wilfred's face. He wanted to push through the Ubanty but when they saw him, they bowed their heads and reached out their hands.

I let out a giggle.

'What?' Sabby said.

'Nothing. Just the Ubanty are making Wilfred's progress hard.'

'They're trying to stop him getting to her?' The soldier's hand strayed to his empty scabbard, as if he would take up arms to rush to Wilfred's aid.

I laughed again. 'It's not deliberate.' I was silent for a moment while I watched. 'She's landed. Isla is off her dragon.'

A cheer echoed around the tent.

'And Wilfred's nearly there. Just a few more Ubanty to get past. Oh...he's there.' I could feel tears forming in my eyes.

'What's happening,' Sabby squealed.

'He's running. She's running. They're running,' I said.

'So they're running?'

'Shush.' I batted at my latest patient. 'They're running towards each other. And...oh...they've met.

They're hugging.' The tears broke over their barrier and started running down my cheeks. 'They're kissing. He's lifted her up and he's swinging her around.'

Cheering broke out again and I heard Sabby let out a choked sob.

'Wait.' I could see a glow at the edge of the Ubanty line. 'Ulandes is coming.'

'Will she stop them?'

A debate broke out around me.

'She's a Goddess, she can do what she wants.'

'It's not right to stop true love.'

'She's walking towards them,' I said.

Walking was a trite word for what Ulandes was doing. Gliding maybe? Flowing?

Wilfred broke off from his latest kiss and faced Ulandes, his gigantic hand dwarfing Isla's as he linked fingers with her.

'What's happening?' Somebody shook my shoulder.

'They're facing Her. Isla is kneeling, and so is her dragon, Arthur, and…and…' my voice trailed off. It didn't feel right to broadcast what I was seeing now.

Ulandes knelt before Isla. She reached out a hand and cupped Isla's chin, bringing Isla's face up till it was level with her own.

The two women stared into each other's eyes. Ulandes' lips were moving and Isla tilted her head to the side as she listened.

What's she saying?

I can't tell. Arthur's blocked me. I could feel Emerald swishing her tail in frustration.

Wilfred backed away, standing off to Isla's side with his hands folded in front of him. Isla shook her head and looked as if she would stand, but Ulandes' lips kept moving and Isla stilled.

I could see how wide Isla's eyes were, how white her face. She appeared to be protesting. She bowed her head, clasping Ulandes' hands.

'What's happening?' Sabby asked.

I could feel her hand on my back. 'I don't know. Ulandes and Isla are talking. She doesn't look happy.'

'Ulandes?'

'No. Isla.'

Not happy was an understatement. She looked miserable as she cast a look over her shoulder at Wilfred. His lips were pressed into a tight line, his body coiled tight.

And then Isla's argument seemed to fade. Her shoulders sagged in defeat. I couldn't believe that Ulandes would prevent Isla and Wilfred from being together. Why would she give Isla the jewellery, her tattoos, if she was going to reject her?

And then Isla reached out toward Ulandes. She placed her hands on either side of the Goddess's face. I could see her mouth moving. Could see the frantic look in her eyes.

In comparison, Ulandes looked peaceful, accepting. She mimicked Isla, raising her hands to place one on each side of Isla's face.

The two of them knelt like that, staring into each other's eyes, cradling each other's faces, and then Ulandes leant forwards. She pulled Isla towards her and kissed her.

Ulandes' glow grew, expanding out to encompass both of them. It brightened as it spread till it blazed like a newborn star.

Wilfred held his arm in front of his face, watching, but it seemed also that he waited. That he knew there was more to come.

A random arrow soared through the sky. I let out a garbled yell as it thunked into Ulandes' back, quivering with its excess force. She sagged forwards into Isla's arms, breaking the kiss.

Isla's face already held tears. She cradled the Goddess to her chest, rocking her backwards and forwards. Wilfred knelt beside them. Bowing his head he placed his arms around both of them. Arthur threw his head back, roaring a blaze of fire into the sky.

The glow burst out to encompass all of them, pulsing in time with a dying heartbeat. Once, twice...three times...

Like a dying sun, the blaze exploded before shrinking back in on itself. But when it coalesced, it didn't formate onto Ulandes, it slammed into Isla, whirling around her, forcing her head to go back as she gasped.

Wilfred supported them both, his head bowed in grief as he helped Isla lower Ulandes' body to the ground.

Samuel burst from the line of Ubanty. He paused as he watched, confusion written over his face. He walked towards them, tears tracking his cheeks. He knelt by Ulandes' side.

Her body limp, her eyes closed, her chest still, he held her hand as he cried.

And then he backed away, wiping the back of his arm across his face as he turned to Isla.

Isla sat up, the glow pulsing around her in time with her heart. Wilfred supported her as she climbed to her feet. Her gold tattoos now ran past her forearms, snaking their way up her biceps and across her shoulders.

Samuel stood, moving to stand in front of her, and then he sank to his knees and bowed. It wasn't till Isla reached out her hand and placed it onto Samuel's head that I realised what had happened.

Ulandes wasn't dead. Just her body was. Her spirit now resided in Isla.

***

I was silent while I worked, trying to come to grips with what I had witnessed. Was Isla now Ulandes or Ulandes now Isla? Was my best friend gone? And if she was, did I have a right to be upset about it if it meant a Goddess lived?

The afternoon shadows grew longer, merging into darkness, and still the wounded lay. I worked without pause, feeling that if I could heal the wounded, then the fact that they were hurt because of me, ceased to matter. My guilt doubled, tripled, halved, depending on how I was feeling.

I took my hands from my latest patient, returning his smile as he sat up and stretched.

'That's it.'

I turned to look at the familiar voice. Sabby. Her eyes looked as hollow as mine felt.

'We're finished.'

I looked around. I had reached the end of the queue of wounded.

'The enemy has gone. Let's get some food.'

I let Sabby pull me up, leaning against her for a moment while my equilibrium stabilised. I was tired. So very tired.

'Here.' Aethan's voice flowed over me even as his arms wrapped around me.

I saw Thomas hovering behind Sabby.

They led us through the newly erected tents to a fire. Grams and Lionel sat beside it.

'Izzy.' Grams rose when she saw me, coming forward to help lead me to a seat.

I collapsed into it and leant forwards so my elbows were resting on my knees. Sabby took the seat to my right.

'I tried to make her stop,' she said.

'She never knows when to stop.'

I started at Turos's voice, searching until I met his eyes over the glow of the fire. 'You're here.' A tiny sliver of guilt slid away. If he was here, surely he couldn't hate me too much.

'I wanted to make sure you were all right. Now that I know you are, I'll go back to my own people.'

'We *are* your people,' I said. Did I have the right to make that claim, after the choice I'd made?

His tense smile relaxed into something more normal.

'That's what I've been trying to tell him,' Grams said. Her eyes widened as she saw Aethan's hand snake into mine. She stared for a second and then nodded. 'It doesn't matter Turos,' she said. 'You don't need to marry into our family to be a part of it. As far as I'm concerned, you already are.'

'Grams,' I hissed. Who was talking marriage?

Turos smirked at my discomfort. 'Thank you Bella,' he stood, 'but my mother is waiting for me.' He looked at Aethan and me. 'Is Isla safe?'

I nodded. 'She's better than ever.' I didn't clarify that statement.

'Ahhhh, she's with Wilfred.' Turos stood. 'Hopefully tomorrow I'll get to meet the infamous Wilfred.' He waved a hand. 'Sleep well all of you.'

'Say hello to your Mum for me,' I said.

He barked out a laugh. 'Not Father?'

'He hates me.'

Aethan pulled me onto his lap as Turos walked chuckling away from the fire. It was weird how I could feel so empty and yet so complete at the same time. I pushed the thought away, concentrating instead, on the feel of Aethan's warmth wrapping me up.

'Anyone hungry?' Grams asked. 'The supply tent was cooking up a mean stew this afternoon. It should be ready by now.'

She and Lionel headed off, returning a short time later with a pot of the thick stew. The smell of the meat hit my nostrils and suddenly I was wide awake and ravenous.

I listened while the others chatted, too busy shovelling food into my mouth to join in on the conversation totally. They were piecing together the events of the day. I stopped chewing long enough to add a few bits and pieces, but Aethan pretty much knew everything I did. Except about Isla. I hadn't told anybody about that.

I was pleased to hear that Tiny was safe and with the dragons. We were going to have to find him a home in Isilvitania. Somewhere with plenty of wildlife and lots of wood for sculpting. He couldn't return home. He'd be killed.

When we had finished eating, Aethan stood, letting out a sigh as he bent to kiss me on the top of the head. 'I want to talk to Wolfgang. I couldn't find him this afternoon.' He stretched his arms above his head. 'And I'd better go see the men.'

'What's happening tomorrow?'

'We need to decide whether or not to pursue them.'

'We should get them while we've got them on the run.' Grams punched her hand into the air.

'Those goblins are totally demoralised. It would be a good opportunity to end this threat for all time,' Lionel said.

I wiggled, not comfortable with the idea of genocide. Sabby reached over and patted my hand. I could tell by the look on her face that she felt the same way. Maybe it was because we were too young to have seen the circle of time repeat?

The fire burned lower and still Aethan hadn't returned. Grams stood and stretched. 'Take me to bed lover.' Her face held a naughty grin as she looked down at Lionel.

'I thought you'd never ask.' He stood and wrapped an arm over her shoulders as they drifted off through the tents.

'Uhhh,' I called after them. 'Do you know where I'm sleeping?'

Grams looked back over her shoulder and pointed to the tent directly behind me. 'At a guess, I'd say you're in there.'

At a guess? What did that mean?

Thomas stood and extended his hand to Sabby. 'Would you like me to walk you to your tent?'

She bit her lip and looked at the fire for long enough to let me know she was considering implications far beyond that of the simple question. She squared her shoulders and took his hand. 'Please,' she said.

And just like that I was alone by the fire. Evening sounds echoed across the camp. Zips being undone and redone. The occasional shout of laughter from a rowdier campfire. A dragon stamping at the ground as it settled down to sleep.

It would be a while before the entire camp slept. A while before I could put my plan into play.

I let it loose to run around my head while I examined its weaknesses. I had to have a plausible excuse for what I was doing, especially after we had won the day.

That would be my main weakness. If I couldn't convince him of my sincerity it wasn't going to work.

Butterflies started to flit around in my stomach and I pushed the plan away. Nerves weren't going to help.

Aethan reappeared on the other side of the fire, a silent figure in the semi-darkness. Light flickered over him, the shadows it cast emphasising the perfection of his body. Dark eyes met mine, silent and intense, and chills crawled down my spine.

Fatigue fled, and suddenly, every cell in my body was alive with a fire of its own. He was beautiful. So very beautiful. And he was mine.

I stood as he crossed the space between us, looking at his outstretched hand. My heart beats slowed, shuddering through my body. I reached out, pressing my fingers into his.

He stared down at me, his face stunning in its angular perfection. The depth of his need evident in his eyes. Anticipation unfurled, reaching out though me, stretching like a cat.

This wasn't be the first night we'd spent together. But it *was* the first night when we had no reason to stop.

We didn't speak as he led me to the tent Grams had pointed out. We didn't speak as we entered the dark space. We didn't speak as he re-zipped the doorway, or as I examined the large bed.

His hand trailed down my arm, leaving goosebumps in its wake. I felt his fingers undoing the straps that held my daggers in place. I shivered and turned back to him as he pulled them from my body and let them fall to the floor.

There was just enough light to see his outline. Just enough to see his hands rise to my face. And then I closed my eyes, surrendering myself to the feel of his calloused palms sliding over my skin.

His breath shuddered as I ran my fingertips down his chest, undoing the leather ties of his vest. I let out a sigh as I undid the last one, dizzy with desire as I trailed my hands over his sculpted muscles.

And then his lips were on my neck, nuzzling and nipping as he worked his way up to my jaw. His body tensed as he fought to control his urgency. To go slow. To take his time. To make every moment the most delicious of our existence.

Every sensation was tenfold what I had felt before. Every stroke, every touch, a glorious assault on my mind.

His arms wrapped around me, pulling me up tight against him and then his mouth was on mine. The darkness wrapped us in its magic as my hands roved over his bare back.

I couldn't think. I couldn't breathe. His kisses stole my sanity.

Finally his hand found the edge of my vest, his fingers sliding beneath it as they started to lift it up. He paused and broke our kiss, his mouth just inches from mine as he whispered, 'Are you sure?'

'Don't stop.' My voice was rough. 'I've never been this sure of anything.'

He paused for one more second, his eyes, almost invisible in the dark, searching my face for any indecision. I grasped his head and pulled it back down, fastening my lips to his. I wrapped my arms around him so he couldn't escape.

He groaned as I rubbed against him, my movements sinuous and hypnotic. He felt so good. So damned good. I couldn't have made myself stop even if I'd wanted to.

Fire trailed over my skin as he pulled my vest above my head. His lips found mine again, frantic with need as his hands fumbled with the strap of my bra. He grunted with frustration and I laughed against his mouth as I slipped my hands under his and undid the clasp.

My nipples hardened at the cool air, and he let out a groan as his hands brushed over them. I gasped, throwing my head back as a shudder rippled through me.

Dark Sky. I felt like my nerves were hot-wired to my groin. Already I was aching to feel him inside me.

He swept me up in his arms and deposited me on the bed. I wriggled backwards, undoing my leather pants and arching up to let him pull them off. Within seconds, his trousers were on the floor and he was crawling onto the bed to lie beside me.

'Ahhh Izzy,' he breathed, lowering his head to nuzzle my breasts.

I grabbed him and twisted so that his body was on top, his weight pushing me down, his skin rubbing against mine.

'Aethan. Dark Sky, Aethan,' I whimpered as his knee nudged my legs apart.

His tongue ran rough and wet across my nipples, as I ran my hands through his hair. I arched up and wrapped my legs around him, feeling the hardness of his manhood pressing into me.

I wanted to make this last; our first real time together, but he was driving me wild with his mouth and his hands. Always before we'd maintained a reserve, a safety net to stop us pushing over the edge. Tonight that safety net was gone.

I pulled his head up to mine, deepening our kiss even further. I breathed him in as my hands ran down his back. Hooking my hands in his underwear, I pushed them down past his buttocks.

He stopped and I thought he was going to ask me again. Ask me if this was what I wanted. Like there was any possible way that I didn't. But instead, he wiggled backwards, pulling my underwear down past my ankles and snagging them off my feet. His followed mine on a pile on the floor and he stood before me, glorious in his nakedness as he ran worshipping eyes over my body.

'Come here,' I whispered, holding my arms open.

'You're so beautiful.' He trailed a finger over my ankle. 'So very beautiful.' His fingers ran up the side of my calf as he crawled on top of me. They ran round till they were teasing the inside of my thigh.

'Oh…Dark…Sky….' I threw my head back against the pillow. 'Please,' I whimpered. 'Please Aethan. I love you. Oh, I need you. Now.' My whimpers became more frantic as his fingers whispered circles on my skin. I reached down till my hand found him, hard and soft velvet.

He let out a groan as I stroked him, and then he reared up over me, leaning down to press a kiss to my lips. 'Tell me if I hurt you,' he whispered.

I opened myself to him, gasping at the glory of him sliding deep inside. I convulsed up against him, wrapping my legs around him.

'Izzy. Oh, Izzy,' he moaned into my neck.

'Aethan,' I cried out as he moved inside me. 'I love you. Don't stop. I love you.'

I had no control over my body any more. It was moving by itself. Primal instinct pushing me harder and faster, as my body tightened and sensation rushed over me, flying me up away from that time, that place, till there was just us two, and no-one else in the world.

His breath became mine. His body, mine. Our love combining and hurtling us forward, till our bodies spasmed as we teetered on the edge of something bigger than us both, and suddenly, suddenly, I became undone, my mind exploding into glorious pieces that slowly rained down around us.

We clutched each other as we lay panting, our sweat mingling, our limbs entwined.

'So tell me,' I said, when I could construct sentences again, 'why haven't we done that before?'

Aethan's chuckle echoed through my chest. 'Believe me,' he said, 'if I had realised it was going to be anything like that, we would have.'

We lay in each other's arms, too exultant to move, too exhausted to speak. His hands traced patterns on my back, as mine played with his hair. My eyelids grew heavier as I fought off sleep.

I didn't want this to ever end. Didn't want the sun to rise. I wanted to exist forever in that moment. Perfectly happy. Perfectly sated.

But in the end I lost the battle, and as my body floated weightless in Aethan's arms, I drifted off to sleep.

***

It was the glow that woke me. Soft warmth oozing into the tent. It's epicentre stood at the tent flap.

Isla.

I lifted Aethan's arm from over my waist and wiggled out of bed, scrambling around till I found my clothes. It took me longer than normal to get into them, hopping around on one foot, while the other caught in the soft leather of my pants. I crawled around on the floor till my hands brushed one of my daggers. I buckled it around the top of my left bicep and then, with a last glance at Aethan, I unzipped the tent flap and pushed out into the night.

'Isla,' I said, squinting into the light, 'is it...is it you?' I still wasn't sure exactly what I had seen.

'It's me.' She flashed me a grin. 'And then some.'

'So, you're a Goddess now?'

'Is it wrong to be happy about that?' She tilted her head to the side. 'I keep waiting to go all holier than nought, but I still feel normal.'

'You're *glowing*. It's not normal to glow.'

'I do seem to be having some trouble controlling that.' The impish grin was back. 'Oh well, I'm sure I'll get the hang of it. But...not until after I see mother. I'd like to be glowing when I see her again.'

I barked out a laugh and then slammed my hand over my mouth, looking over my shoulder at the tent. I didn't want to wake Aethan and have to explain where I was going.

'He won't wake. Nobody will wake.' She wiggled the tips of her fingers at me.

'Niiiicccc.' I nodded my head. 'So, why are you here? I thought you'd be with Wilfred.'

'He's asleep. And besides, why does there have to be a reason. Can't I just want to see my best friend?' She hooked her arm through mine and patted my hand as she started walking.

I let out a snort as I fell into step beside her.

'Oh fine,' she said. 'Someone had to make sure you woke up in time.'

'So is this part of the deal?' I asked. 'Omnipotence and all that? Do you know everything that people are thinking?'

'Not unless I concentrate on them.' She stuck out her bottom lip. 'I'm not sure if I'm happy about that.'

'Why on earth not?'

'It was much more fun when I had to use more devious methods to find out what I wanted to know.'

I laughed and squeezed her hand. She was still the same old Isla, even if it *was* hard to look directly at her.

'So,' she said, 'how are you going to get to Santanas?'

'You already know the answer to that.'

'Humour me.'

'A gateway. Like when we came home.'

'It should work. I'm not sure about the rest of the plan.'

'No words of wisdom?'

She stopped walking and turned to face me. 'Dear Isadora.' She raised a hand to my cheek, a shock of electricity flowing into me at her touch. 'You need to look inside yourself and find that which none others find when they look at him.'

'You know I hate riddles.'

'I know you can do this.'

'If…urhmmmm,' I cleared my throat, 'If I don't make it back, will you tell him I love him.'

'I think he already knows that.' She smiled. 'I think half the camp knows that.'

The heat of a fiery blush burnt into my cheeks. 'You were eavesdropping,' I gasped.

'Dark Sky,' she said. 'I was only a couple of hundred feet away. I didn't need to eavesdrop.'

I dropped my head into my hands as she let out a throaty chuckle. Oh, the shame.

She laughed again as she tugged on my arm. 'Come on.'

We walked in silence for a while, enjoying the comfort from each other's presence, as we wove through the trees. When we got to a clearing she stopped and turned to face me.

'It is time,' she said.

'Isla.' Tears filled my eyes. 'Why did she do it? Why did Ulandes choose to die?' There was no doubt that she had known what was going to happen.

Isla's face contorted as grief rippled through her. 'She took it as a punishment.'

'But she wasn't interfering.' She had been very clever about that.

'It was for taking dark faeries' lives. That's what she said.' She looked at the ground, scuffing at a leaf with the tip of her boot. 'But I think it was so Wilfred and I could be together. Because, you know, he's a Demi-God now.' The last came out in a garbled whisper.

'So he can't be with a mortal?'

'He can't live here, not permanently, and I couldn't live there.' She was silent while she stared into the distance. 'She's not really dead,' she said. 'I can feel her in here.' She pressed her hand to her heart.

I reached out and put my hand over hers, not knowing what to say. How do you console someone for this? It was unprecedented. 'You won't let her sacrifice go to waste,' I said. 'She knew that. I don't know anyone else who lives life the way you do. So fully.'

'Thank you.' Her eyes were solemn as she tilted her head to the side and repeated her earlier words, 'It is time.'

'Time for...Oh.' I had forgotten. For a few glorious moments I had totally forgotten what I was about to do. Now that I remembered though, I could feel butterflies starting a lazy circuit around my stomach. 'Right.'

I closed my eyes, thinking about Santanas. Pushing out my awareness towards him. Unlike when I had focused on Grams, I felt nothing.

'It's not working.' I opened my eyes again and stared at Isla.

'What are you concentrating on?'

'Santanas.' I managed to stop myself from adding the word stupid at the end of the sentence. I mean she *was* a Goddess after all.

'That's your problem.' She held a hand up as I opened my mouth to protest. 'You're thinking about Santanas, *not* your grandfather.'

'Oh.' I slammed my mouth shut and closed my eyes. This time I concentrated on the man whose blood I shared, not the enemy I wanted to defeat. I reached out, questing for my kin.

There. A faint tug. A brush of recognition. 'I've got him,' I said.

'Well, what are you waiting for? Go get that sucker.'

I cracked one eye open. 'That's not very Goddessy.'

'Who's the Goddess here?'

'You.'

She crossed her arms over her chest and raised an eyebrow. 'Right. And don't you forget it. If I want to say sucker, I can.' She flashed me a grin and then waved her hands at me.

I smiled back, keeping my eye open just long enough to press the memory of her, how she looked as she glowed amongst the trees, into my mind. If I was going to die, I wanted to die looking at her, not him.

'Hey.' My eyes flew back open. 'If I die, can I come live with you?'

'You're not going to die.'

'Really?' The hope in my voice was palpable.

She let out a sigh. 'Yes, if you die you can come live with me. Now will you please go and finish this.'

'Thank you.' I closed my eyes for the last time and searched for the tenuous connection. When I found it, I pulled back the layers of reality between me and Santanas, and stepped through the gateway.

Chapter Sixteen

Betrayed

'There you go Wolfie, I told you she would come.'

'Don't call me Wolfie.'

It was dark. Too dark to see. I blinked my eyes a few times, squinting towards the voices, waiting for my eyes to adjust. It seemed looking at Isla had ruined my night vision.

'Ahhh. Would some light help?'

'Please.' I hated being this vulnerable.

A second later a lit lantern threw light out over a meadow. I looked around. Grass cloaked the ground and oaks stood as sentinels around the edge.

Santanas stood by the lantern, his head up, his shoulders back. I stifled my fear as he watched me through eyes alight with madness.

Wolfgang didn't look at me as he sat slumped in a chair, instead, he stared at the grass between his feet.

Santanas's face pulled into a shiny, tight mask as the red, twisted scarring allowed his lips to move up just marginally.

'Father.' I walked towards them.

'Daughter. You are reconsidering?'

The grass was soft under my feet. 'This will all go away?'

'Everything you know will change.'

I paused. 'How will it change?'

'For the better.' The twisted smile was back. 'Together, we could accomplish so much.'

I risked a glance at Wolfgang. He continued to stare at the ground.

'We will be a family again.'

Wolfgang looked up at me, his eyes full of pain. He stood slowly, stooping as if a weight hung from his neck as he walked toward me. 'I didn't have a choice,' he said.

'Wolfgang.' I reached a hand out to him. 'Everything's going to be fine.'

'You don't understand.' His head wobbled from side-to-side.

'What don't I understand?'

'I miss her so much.'

I let my hand fall back to my side. This wasn't the Wolfgang I knew. This man was broken.

'Too much,' he whispered.

I didn't see it coming, so focused on his pain I didn't feel the spell swirling.

My eyes bulged as my breath caught in my throat. I couldn't move. Couldn't lift my arms. Couldn't run.

I scrabbled at the edges of the spell, trying to find a weak point. There was none.

My lungs burned as my need for air intensified. Black spots appeared in my vision.

'Wolfie.' Santanas sounded like a father rebuking a favoured child. 'Let her breathe. We need her alive. For now.'

The metal bands around me loosened just enough to allow a puff of air into my lungs. The black spots dancing in front of my eyes vanished.

I watched Santanas as he walked to a pile of wood. He pointed at it, and flames burst from the centre. 'I had a lot of time to think while I was trapped in that cursed bit of stone,' he said. 'We were doing it wrong before.'

'*You* were doing it wrong,' Wolfgang said. 'I had nothing to do with it.'

Santanas's face twisted. He turned to look at Wolfgang. 'Yes, I remember. You wouldn't help. You betrayed her.' He turned back to the fire and held his hands out. 'So tell me, why is it that you are helping me now?'

I rotated my eyes back to Wolfgang. He had his back to me.

'I...,' His head bent even further as he rung his hands. 'It never stopped hurting.'

'She was special.' Santanas walked to a lone stone, standing in the middle of the meadow. 'She *is* special.' He bent and pressed a palm to it. 'Not long now, my love. Not long now.'

I shuddered. His words were laced with a deeper meaning my brain was trying not to understand.

'So what were you doing wrong?'

'Using children.'

Wolfgang nodded his head, a look of professional interest on his face. 'You think an adult female will make the difference?'

'This one will.' Santanas crossed back to where I stood, frozen like a statue. He reached out and grasped my chin. 'And Littiana will have her powers. We will be equals.'

'She will be powerful all right.' Wolfgang tugged on his beard. 'So you are going to use her blood and her body?'

Santanas nodded. 'It will work. What could be a more powerful sacrifice than one's own daughter?'

He still didn't know I wasn't his daughter. My eyes flicked back to Wolfgang as a wave of panic washed over me. He knew. He knew about Mum, but he didn't say anything as he walked to the fire.

Instead, he looked up at the moon. 'It's nearly time.'

My pulse sped up as Santanas wrapped an arm around my waist. My body stayed stiff as he carried me across the meadow to the stone. He set me down facing it. My breathing rasped laboriously as I read the carvings on it.

Littiana Gabrielle
Daughter, Wife
I Will Not Rest
Till I Am With You Again

Claustrophobic panic raced through my veins. I clawed at the inside of my mind, my body a prison that held me trapped.

Dark Sky. It was all my childhood nightmares come true. They were going to sacrifice me.

I could feel tears trailing down my face. I didn't want to die. Not like this. Helpless. It went against every grain in my body.

'Don't worry.' Santanas rested a hand on my face. 'I will make sure it is quick.'

'Not too quick,' Wolfgang said. 'You need her to bleed out.'

'Well, not quick, but as painless as possible.'

I think he meant it. I think he was trying to soothe me. But my eyes bulged as I fought against the spell. I wanted to scream in fury.

Dead was dead, no matter how slowly or painlessly it came. This wasn't what I had planned. I had come here to kill him.

Terror replaced panic as Santanas pulled a knife from his belt.

My eyes swivelled to Wolfgang. I couldn't believe he was doing this. Couldn't believe he would let this happen. But she was his daughter. What father wouldn't want his daughter back?

Wolfgang's eyes were steady as they met mine. And then he winked, and the bindings holding me in place disappeared.

I felt my eyes widen but I managed not to move. Relief made my knees weak but I held steady. I would only have one chance. One chance to end this.

Santanas looked up, the knife rising toward me as he stared at the moon.

'Not too soon,' Wolfgang warned him.

I dug deep into my heart, searching for my greatest weapon. Searching for the one thing which would allow me to kill Santanas. I thought about how he must have felt to have come home and found Littiana dead. How much sorrow he must have felt, how alone he must have been to have gone mad with his grief.

Compassion drifted up, but that wasn't enough. I needed more.

I forced myself to relax as Santanas tensed. To think about how he was my grandfather. To wonder how differently things might have been if Grams hadn't fled when she'd realised she was pregnant. Perhaps having had a daughter would have brought him back.

'Grandfather,' I thought, as the tip of his knife rested on my throat. '*My* Grandfather.' And with that, as I finally accepted the bond between us, love poured into my heart.

He wasn't really a monster. He just had different priorities. But like a rabid dog, he needed to die.

He glanced back up to the sky and I embraced my centre of peace. Holding onto my love, I struck like a snake. Too fast for him to see. Too fast for him to stop me, I unsheathed my dagger and shoved it up under his rib cage and into his heart.

His eyes widened with pain as he stared down at me.

'I love you, Grandfather.' Tears choked my voice. 'I *love* you.'

He looked down at the dagger and then back up at me.

Tears cascaded down my face. 'I'm sorry. It was the only way.' Blood flowed down over my hand. 'I love you,' I said again. It was important that he knew that. That he died knowing that.

'Granddaughter?' His hand dropped the knife and fluttered towards my face. 'Granddaughter?' He coughed and blood dribbled out of the corner of his mouth.

He sagged in my arms and I lowered him to the ground next to his wife's grave. My arms were slick with his blood as I raised my hand and pushed his hair back from his face.

'I'm sorry,' I said, pulling out my dagger.

Blood flowed out of the wound, pooling on his chest and running down the side. He dabbed his fingers into it and then held them up in front of his face, staring at the sticky red.

'I'm dying.' His head swivelled so he could look at me. 'You love me?'

'I do, Grandfather.'

His eyes changed, madness fleeing. He looked over at Wolfgang. 'Father,' he said, 'will you sit by me as I die.'

Wolfgang moved to Santanas's other side, lowering himself to sit beside him. 'I'm sorry son.' He picked up Santanas's hand. 'I miss her too, but what you were doing was wrong.'

Santanas nodded. 'It doesn't matter now.' His eyes were fervent as he stared into mine, as if he could hold onto his life with sheer effort of will. But more blood pulsed out of his wound, and with each beat, his heart became weaker.

His eyes shifted from mine to stare past my head. They widened and then he reached a hand up, stretching his fingers towards something only he could see.

'Littiana?' His voice held wonder. 'Litty, is that you?'

The skin on the back of my neck tingled and the hair there stood on end. Santanas's fingers curled as if holding onto something and his mouth pulled into a smile.

'You're so beautiful,' he whispered. 'So very beautiful.' Tears leaked from the corners of his eyes. 'I've missed you so much. I've done things. Terrible things.'

It felt as if fabric brushed the skin on my arm. Goosebumps followed in the wake of the invisible touch.

Wolfgang stared past me, his face desperate with hope. 'Is she here?' he asked. 'Is my Litty here?'

'Yes.' Santanas didn't take his eyes off the ghost. 'She's here. She says she was always here. She loves you, but she wants you to be happy. For her,' he turned his head toward Wolfgang, 'you have to be happy for her.'

Wolfgang bowed his head, sobs shuddering through his body.

Santanas turned back to where his wife stood. His face held peace as he smiled up at her. Then, like a puppet whose strings had been cut, his arm fell to his side and dull eyes stared at the stars.

***

We stayed like that as the moon crept towards the horizon and the first blush of morning appeared above the trees. Neither of us talking. Both following the path of our own thoughts.

Santanas's body cooled as we sat beside it and I struggled to come to terms with all that had happened. In the end, he had gotten the very thing he had wanted, but he had sacrificed all other love along the way.

I sighed and put my palms on the ground, groaning as I pushed myself up to my feet. I was stiff and sore and cold.

'What should we do with him?' I asked.

Wolfgang started as if he had forgotten I was there. He stared at me for a moment before his eyes refocused. 'We should take him back.' He also groaned as he pushed himself up. 'I am guessing you can get us back?'

'Yes.' I bent to help him lift Santanas's body.

'I've got him,' he said, repositioning one arm under Santanas's shoulders and the other under his knees. 'You concentrate on getting us home.'

I closed my eyes and thought of Aethan, my sudden urge to be safely cocooned in his arms almost overwhelming. The connection was immediate. I reached out for him, pushing back the fabric of reality and opened my eyes.

'Dark Sky help me Isla.' Aethan's back was to us as he waved his arms in the air.

Isla looked beatific in a white robe as she faced him, a smug smile appearing on her lips as she shifted her eyes from him to us. Wilfred's smile, as he stood at her side with his arms crossed, was broader. They were in a tent. *Their* tent I was guessing by the flowing fabric draping the roof.

'I don't care who or what you are, if you don't tell me where she is I'll...I'll....' He froze with his arms in the air. 'She's behind me isn't she?'

He spun around and I launched myself through the gateway and into his arms. He pulled me to him, burying his face in my hair. Then he pushed me back till he was holding me at arms' length. 'Whose blood is this?' His eyes searched me, looking for injuries.

'Santanas's.' Sorrow shook my voice as I turned and beckoned to Wolfgang.

He stepped through the gateway, his face solemn as he viewed Isla and Wilfred.

'What? Who? How?' Aethan's voice stuttered to a stop as he stared at Santanas. His head spun to stare at me. 'You killed him?'

I took a step back at the accusation in his voice. 'Urrrr. I kind of thought that was the aim of all this.'

His nostrils flared and he took a deep breath, running both hands through his hair. 'Not by yourself it wasn't. You could have been killed. Dark Sky, Izzy. I only just got you back.'

'It had to be her,' Isla said. 'She was the only one with the power to do it.' She glided forward to Wolfgang and pressed her fingertips to Santanas's cheek. 'She was the only one who could break the curse.' The glow around her intensified as she stared down into his face.

'Uhh, babe.' Wilfred threw a hand up in front of his face. 'You're doing it again.'

Isla looked down at herself and tutted in disgust. Her wattage dimmed till it was barely visible.

'She's like a firefly,' Wilfred said. 'You should see what happens when she gets really excited.'

'Wilfred.' Her voice held admonishment, but the smile she shot him spoke of other things. She turned back to Santanas and sighed. 'It had to be. He saw to that.' She sighed again. 'Come. We should take his body to Tamsonite. He will need to see it so he can officially call an end to this war.' She turned and pushed out through the tent flap, holding it to the side so that Wolfgang, still cradling his son-in-law's body, could fit through.

Aethan and Wilfred led the way as we threaded our way through the tents. I fell into step next to Isla, while Wolfgang took up the rear.

'Where's Samuel?' I wouldn't have thought he would let her out of his sight.

'He's with the Ubanty. He has chosen to stay with them and train my new priests and priestesses.'

I saw Aethan's eyebrows raise as he looked over his shoulder. It would take him a while to get used to Isla's new status. He turned back to Wilfred and shoved him in the shoulder. 'Never thought I'd see you as a priest.'

'Priest?' Wilfred let out a huff and smoothed his palms down the front of his vest. 'My official title is Demi-God, thank you very much. The way I hear it, that out-ranks Heir to The Throne any day.'

I rolled my eyes as I shared a look with Isla. Some things never changed.

Tamsonite was out the front of his tent issuing orders. He turned when he heard Aethan call his name.

'Prince Aethan. Just the man I was looking for.' He turned back to a table he was standing in front of. Books held down the corners of a large sheet of paper that was covered in scribbles. ' I've been going over some plans and I'd like your opinion. I think we should extinguish the goblins first before they can regroup. Then we can go after the dark faeries.'

'General Tamsonite.' Isla's voice rang like a bell. 'It is over.'

He started in surprise when Isla pushed through between Aethan and Wilfred. She was doing the high-wattage glow again.

'Over? My dear, Princess,' he said the word uncertainly, 'the threat is still out there. We must strike while we have the upper hand.'

'The threat has been eliminated.' She waved her hand and Wolfgang walked forwards and lay Santanas's body down at Tamsonite's feet.

You had to give him credit. He kept his cool as he stared at Santanas's body. 'How?' was all he said.

'Isadora broke the spell that bound his soul to his body. She killed him.'

His gaze moved from the body to me and back to the body. He nodded a couple of times and then smoothed his moustache down with his fingertips. 'Right, he said. 'Well that answers *that* question. It will take the goblins a while to regroup after losing their Queen and their battle leader. We'll go after the dark faeries first, then swing back for the goblins.'

'Nooooo.' Isla's voice sounded as if a universe of people were crying out in agony. 'Enough pain. Enough death. This ends now.' Her glow flared to dying-star brilliance as the earth shook beneath our feet.

I clamped my eyes shut and then wrapped my arms over my face.

My admiration for Tamsonite increased as he continued his argument. He was either the most brave, or the most stupid man in the world. 'They will come again. It may not be for years, but they will come.'

'Yes, they will come again one day. And we will respond. That is the difference between good and evil. We respond to violence and death. We defend our lands and our homes. We do not start it.'

I cracked an eyelid, slamming it shut again when pain pierced my eyeball.

I heard Tamsonite sigh and then he said, 'You are right. I apologise. Thank you for reminding me of who I am.'

My next experimental peak revealed Isla had returned to normal. Well, *her* version of normal.

'Athol, is that Santanas?' Grams and Lionel stood a few metres away, a crowd of soldiers behind them.

I swivelled to see that we were surrounded by our army.

'Yes.' Tamsonite nodded. 'He is dead.'

Sorrow filled Gram's face. The last time she'd seen him would have been when she had been pregnant with Mum.

'Might I make a suggestion?' I said. I blushed when hundreds of eyes swivelled to look at me. Up until then they had either been staring at Isla or Santanas. 'I think we should bury him with his wife, Littiana.'

Isla clapped her hands together, looking for all the world like a six year old just advised there was to be a party. 'That's a wonderful idea,' she said. 'I will oversee the burial.'

Tamsonite shot her a nervous look and then nodded. 'It seems the best option. How far away is it?'

'I can take us straight there.'

He pulled himself upright and brushed at his moustache again. 'Let us gather the Heads of State and then we will see him buried.'

It took another twenty minutes before King Arwyn, King Bladimir, Queen Gladaline, and Turos were gathered in front of the tent with Rako.

I used that time to wash off the dried blood and change into a dress that Isla supplied me. She also brushed my hair and redid my braid but I couldn't remember the last time I had washed it, so I was glad we didn't have a mirror big enough to see my whole head at once. I must have been a mess.

Aethan's eyes said he didn't think I was a mess when I reappeared. I blushed and looked at my slippered feet.

It was only when they were all watching me, waiting for me to open the gateway that I realised my mistake. Always before I had used a connection to someone I knew to direct me.

'Uhhh, Isla,' I whispered out of the corner of my mouth. 'I've got nobody to concentrate on.'

'Santanas,' she whispered back. 'His soul is still there.'

I nodded and closed my eyes, praying to, well to Isla I guessed, that it would work. My shoulders relaxed as I felt a connection, and then my gateway opened up onto the meadow with Littiana's headstone.

I left it open so everybody who wanted to watch this phase of history unfold, could. It seemed that the whole army poured through, standing at a distance as Aethan and Wilfred started to dig a grave next to Littiana's. The sun rose over the tips of the oaks and the heat in the meadow increased.

Sweat formed on Aethan and Wilfred's brows and they stopped to undo and remove their vests. Turos joined them, pulling his shirt off over his head and taking up a spade.

I stared at the three sweating, half-naked men as their muscles flexed in rhythm with the movement of the spades. It looked like a cover for a Mills and Boon novel.

Grams sidled up beside us and nodded her head at Isla. 'Unseasonably warm for this time of day,' she noted.

Isla flashed her a smile.

'I like your work.' Grams chuckled and rubbed her hands together as she turned to her fiancée. 'Lionel. Why don't you help them.'

She waited till Lionel was picking up a spade before calling out, 'Don't you dare get dirt on that shirt.'

Lionel sighed as he put the spade down and pulled his shirt off over his head.

I felt my eyes widened as I viewed his muscled torso. I raised my eyebrows and turned to look at Grams.

'I know, right.' She chuckled and rubbed her hands together. 'So Isla,' she said, 'do you do weddings?' She blinked and put her hands over her mouth as she giggled. 'I do apologise. That didn't come out quite the way I meant it.' She cleared her throat looking almost nervous as she said, 'Lionel and I were wondering if you would marry us?'

'Well,' Isla said, with a deadpan face, 'that's an awfully kind offer, but I was kind of thinking I might marry Wilfred.'

'Oh no, no,' Grams stammered, 'I mean would you be the one who….' Her eyebrows lowered as she stopped talking. 'You're teasing me.'

I burst out laughing. It was the first time I had ever seen Grams blush.

Isla reached out and took one of Gram's hands. 'I would love to be the one who joins you and Lionel in matrimony.'

Is it true? It was the first I had heard from Emerald since the day before. She and Lance had been off having some 'adult time'. I had been pleasantly surprised to find it didn't affect me any more. I was guessing it was because I was totally committed to Aethan now.

Is what true? I turned to find her head poking through the gateway. I could see Tiny's legs beside her.

Is he dead?

I winced. It was information I should have given her. After what he had put her through she deserved to know. *Yes. I followed him last night and killed him.*

She huffed in my mind.

Would you like to come and see his body?

She huffed again, too annoyed with me, and too proud to admit it. *No,* she said, *I can see him in your thoughts. That is enough.*

I pulled at the gateway, opening it up to allow her to come through if she wanted to but only Tiny pushed through. He waved at me, but moved very slowly to the back of the meadow. It seemed he was finally learning how to walk without causing a minor earthquake.

Aethan and Wilfred climbed out of the hole and stood to the side while Turos and Lionel lifted Santanas and lowered him into his grave. It seemed a bit undignified when they began dumping dirt on him straight away.

Nobody spoke words over him, nobody cried for his loss. But then what did I expect? The man had terrorised the country for years and was responsible for the loss of tens of thousands of lives. Why would anybody be anything but elated to witness his burial? It was a surprise nobody was trying to spit on his grave.

Finally, it was done. They beat down the dirt with the backs of their spades till only a slight hump showed.

Isla drifted forwards, bending to run her hand over the stone marking the grave. When she stood back up I saw that Santanas's details had appeared under Littiana's.

I waited while the spectators filed back through the gateway, then I crossed to stand by the freshly-turned dirt. I had to say something. I didn't know why. It just seemed wrong not to.

'Goodbye Grandfather,' I whispered. 'I wish I could have known you in a better time.'

Grams patted my arm as she moved to stand beside me. 'Goodbye Santanas,' she said. 'I'm sorry you never knew your daughter. I'm sorry I couldn't find it in my heart to trust you. For whatever it's worth, I did love you.'

'And so we enter a new age,' Isla murmured. She bent and picked up a handful of dirt, letting it flow down over the grave. 'An age of peace and love, when all things prosper.'

As she spoke she walked around the grave, a seemingly endless supply of dirt snowing out of her hand. And where that dirt landed, green began to grow. Wildflowers wriggled up out of the earth. They climbed up the side of the stone and cascaded down it, a waterfall of colour.

'There.' She stopped and dusted her hands together and a rose bush pushed up towards the sky. Buds swelled and burst open, red roses releasing the heady scent of Turkish delight.

'Thank you.' I squeezed Isla's hand. 'It's perfect.'

Grams took my other hand and the three of us stood like that, each with our thoughts, each with our memories, that if woven together, might manage to capture the complexity of the man that had been Santanas.

Chapter Seventeen

Mia

'I don't know Sabby, it's going to be dangerous.' I twisted my head to better look at the buckle I was tightening on my bicep. 'We may have beaten them, but it doesn't mean they won't attack when we enter their territory.' I picked the next sheath up off the dining room table.

'I'm coming. And that's, that.' She put her hands on her hips as she glared at me.

'Sabby.'

'No.' She held a hand up. 'You've had too many adventures without me. Unless....' She paused and tears flooded into her beautiful green eyes. 'You just don't want me to come?' The last was said in a horrified whisper.

'Dark Sky, no.' I let go of the dagger I was about to strap to my calf and crossed the room to her. 'Of course that's not it. I worry about you.'

'So I can come?' She looked up at me though tear-drenched lashes.

I bit my lip. I really didn't want her to come. There could be fighting. Lots of it. What if something happened to her?

'Please.'

'Okay. Okay.' I took a deep breath. 'You can come.'

A chuckle came from the arm chair behind us. 'Works every time,' Thomas said.

Sabby threw me a broad grin as she ran across the room to jump into Thomas's lap. 'Did you hear that? I can come.' She planted a kiss firmly on his lips. 'Finally. An adventure.'

'She's right though, love. It might be dangerous.'

'You'll look after me.'

'You know I will.'

I turned away as the love birds' words turned to whispers and then kisses. I was quite sure that Aethan and I weren't *that* bad.

'Ready.' Grams and Lionel emerged from her wing. I wasn't surprised to see that she had on her customary camouflage pants and military issue boots, I *was* surprised to see that Lionel was dressed to match. 'Shall I brew us a pot of tea while we wait?'

'I'll do it.' Mum appeared in the doorway. 'It's the least I can do.'

'I think all the food you've packed for us to take is more than enough,' I said. 'We'll probably only be a few hours.'

Mum sniffed. 'The last time you told me you were just going for a little dragon ride you came back months later.'

'She's got you there.' Grams shoved my shoulder. 'When are the others arriving?'

'Any minute now.' I looked at the clock over the fireplace. They were late. By a minute. Not that I was counting, but I hadn't seen Aethan for a week now and I was starting to feel the strain.

Scruffy let out a happy bark and raced to the door, scrabbling at it with his front paws. A second later there was a knock.

I tried to remain calm, but I found myself running to open it. I turned the lock and threw back the door and there he was. Isla and Wilfred were there with him, but if it wasn't for the fact that Isla was still glowing, I probably wouldn't have noticed them. Aethan filled up my whole field of vision.

Aethan, in the flesh, and not just in my dreams.

Tension I didn't know I was holding, oozed out of my body. Relief flowed into the void left by that tension. Everything was better now. He was here.

Scruffy let out another bark and threw himself at Isla. She scooped him up and rubbed her fingers through the fur on his belly. 'Yes, he's in the field below,' she said. 'He misses you too.' She bent and placed Scruffy on the ground, and with a quick lick of Wilfred's leg he was off and running. I was guessing Arthur was waiting for him.

I gazed up at Aethan. Was it possible he was even better looking than he had been? He looked utterly biteable.

I didn't know if I was ever going to get used to how perfect he was. Didn't know if I was ever going to get used to the fact that he was mine.

'Can we come in?' Isla asked.

'Of course.' I stepped back, my eyes glued to Aethan's face as they entered.

Navy-blue eyes, crinkled at the corner with amusement, met mine. 'Hey, beautiful.' He stepped close enough that I could feel the warmth of his body, but it wasn't close enough by far.

'Oh good. Just in time.' Grams grabbed Aethan's hand and dragged him into the lounge room. 'What do you think? The black one, or the khaki one?' She held up two balaclavas.

'The khaki,' he said. 'It looks better with your shirt.'

'See.' She turned to Lionel and stuck out her tongue. 'I told you the khaki looked better.'

I shook my head, smiling as I finished with my last dagger. My bag sat packed ready to go and my swords were...I looked around for them before remembering. They were still in my room. I trotted up the stairs and found them exactly where I had left them the night before when I had finished sharpening them. The battle the week before had left some serious nicks in them.

'Happy birthday, Izzy.' Strong hands grasped my waist and spun me. My breath left me as Aethan covered my mouth with his and slammed me up against the wall. Fingers, frantic with need, moved expertly over my skin leaving a fiery trail in their wake.

Happy birthday, indeed. I closed my eyes and breathed him in, revelling in the feel of our kiss. My hands moved over his back, kneading the muscles through his leather vest. It would be a matter of seconds to have that off.

He broke the kiss before I could start to shed his clothing, and instead, pressed his forehead to mine. 'I missed you,' he murmured. He pulled back and gazed into my eyes. 'I missed you *too* much. I couldn't concentrate on anything.'

'Good.' I trailed my fingers up and down his arms. 'I've been totally useless.'

'You could *never* be useless.'

I let out a chuckle. 'I think Mum might disagree.'

We were silent for a minute while we soaked each other up. But all too soon, the questions that had been chasing each other around in my head demanded attention.

'So,' I looked down at my boots, 'how did it go?'

He placed his hand under my chin and drew my head back up, tracing my lips with his fingertip as he replied. 'Well.'

He bent to kiss me again but I put a hand on his chest.

'Well?' I arched an eyebrows at him and he let out a rueful chuckle. 'You didn't really think that would cut it did you?' I asked.

'Not with you.' His finger recommenced its pattern on my lips. 'She didn't like it at first, but then Isla burst into flames and did that multiple voice thing. That pretty much settled it.'

I grimaced. I hadn't really expected Aethan's mother, Queen Eloise, to take the news of our relationship well. But a tiny part of me had been hoping, that after everything that had gone down, she might be receptive to something that made her son happy.

'On the other hand, father was most supportive.' He cleared his throat, his face suddenly not as confident as it had been. 'He gave me something to give you.'

'Really? What is it? Swords? I could do with a couple of new ones.'

'Nothing like that.' He shook his head, his eyes serious as they stared into mine. 'I wanted to get you something nice for your birthday, and I still will. I just haven't had time. I really wanted to make you something.'

'Stop.' I put a hand on his chest. 'I don't need a birthday present. I have *you*.' That was the only thing I was ever going to need.

'Still.' He reached down and pulled a small box out of his pocket. 'Isadora Scrumpleton,' his voice was serious as he sunk to one knee in front of me, 'will you do me the very great honour of becoming my wife.' He flicked open the lid of the little box. A ring, with the largest diamond I had ever seen, sat nestled within a fold of velvet. 'It's the Gabrielle House ring.'

'Wife?' I choked out the word. It really was a *very* large diamond. I reached out a finger and poked it.

'Yes, wife.' Aethan stood up and pulled the ring from the box. 'Izzy, I love you. I don't want to spend another minute without you by my side. Say you'll marry me. Please.'

My eyes flew to his face. 'I love you too. More than anything in the world. I can't imagine life without you.'

'Then marry me.'

'I'm only nineteen.'

'Think you're going to change your mind about me?'

'Never.' I shook my head frantically.

'Then marry me.' His voice had a pleading quality. 'Say you'll be mine.'

'I *am* yours.'

'Say it in front of everyone.' He paused as his eyes dropped. 'Say it in front of the royal court.'

'Oh. Is that the deal?' One second I had been resisting the idea of marriage, but now? Now that I knew it was to pacify his parents? Now I was disappointed.

He bent to capture my mouth again. 'No,' he murmured against my lips. 'If I had my way, we would go far away. We would make a cottage in the woods somewhere, and we would live there forever. And you would be my wife, no matter what anybody else thought or said.'

I sagged against him, giving into his kiss.

'Turos is here.'

I let out a squeal and spun toward Isla. Aethan snapped the ring box shut and stuffed it back into his pocket. I couldn't see it any more, but I could feel its presence. An ominous pressure starting to pound away at the back of my head.

Married?

'Don't you ever knock?' Aethan asked his sister.

'Don't need to. I always know what's going on anyway.' She let out a laugh and prodded him in the chest. 'You will have plenty of time to finish your *conversation* later.'

A fiery warmth spread up my cheeks as I cringed.

I was blushing. Great. Now everyone would think we'd been caught doing something we shouldn't. It was the last thing I needed Turos to see.

'Come on Izzy.' Isla grabbed my hand and dragged me from the room.

I looked back at Aethan as he picked up my swords and followed us.

Husband? I was still getting used to *boyfriend*.

Turos stood in the door to the kitchen talking to Mum. Mia was curled around his neck. At the sound of our footsteps she turned bright, blinking eyes toward us. She let out a mewl and stood up on her rear legs, reaching towards me with her front paws.

'Hey, girl.' I scooped her off Turos's neck. 'Hey, Turos.'

'Hey, Izzy.' He turned to face me, his eyes softening as they rested on my face. They hardened again as Aethan appeared at my side.

'Turos.' He nodded his head as he slipped an arm around my waist.

Ahhhh. Awkward. That was really awkward.

Turos nodded stiffly and turned back towards Mum. 'Thank you Prunella. When we get back I'd love that,' he said.

'Love what?' I stroked Mia's belly as I wiggled out from Aethan's arm and moved to Turos's side.

'Your Mum offered to teach me to bake.'

'Oh.' There was nothing much else I could say to that.

'Let's get this show on the road,' Grams said. 'I'd like to be home in time for dinner.'

A nervous flutter started in my belly as I passed Mia back to Turos. I was going to try and open a gateway to Mia's baby. It was a snatch and grab mission, and we really didn't need this many people involved, but I hadn't been able to say no.

Grams, Lionel, Thomas, Sabby, Isla, Wilfred, Aethan and Turos all moved to stand behind me. I took a deep breath and reached out toward Mia with my senses. If I could tap into her baby through her...

'Please tell me you are not trying to open up a gateway in my kitchen.'

I opened my eyes and looked back at Mum. Technically, I was in the lounge, but I was guessing that *now* was not the time to quibble over *that* small detail.

'Of course not. We're going down to the field.' I pulled a face at my friends and beckoned to the front door.

'Really Prunella,' Grams said, 'as if we would do something like that.'

I was guessing by the look on Mum's face, and the tapping of her left foot, that she wasn't falling for it.

I took my swords from Aethan and slid them into the sheaths on my back, then I followed Grams out the front door.

Isla took the lead, skipping ahead of us to the path leading down to the meadow. She plucked a couple of flowers and pranced back to Wilfred, reaching up to thread them into his beard. He stood dutifully, still managing to look manly as she worked.

'There,' she said, 'now you look like the proper consort for the Goddess of Love.'

'So you've decided on love?' Sabby asked.

'I think so.'

'Not too narrow a field?' I asked.

She shook her head. 'We're not just talking about sexual love,' she said. 'It's much broader than that. Love between friends, spouses, families,' she looked at me and winked, 'nations.'

I felt my mouth shape a soundless 'Oh'. She was positioning herself to be a political force. *The* political force really. Who would say no to a Goddess? She outranked everyone.

She looked at Aethan and blew him a kiss. 'So just you mind your p's and q's baby brother. I'll be watching.'

Wilfred let out a booming chuckle, clasping her hand as he pulled her into him. He planted a kiss on her nose before spinning and sprinting off down the path. 'Last one there's a rotten egg,' he yelled.

Isla let out a delighted laugh and raced off after him. By the time the rest of us reached them in the field she was threading more flowers into his beard.

'Okay.' I took a deep breath. 'Everyone ready?'

I waited for them all to fall in behind me before sending my senses out to Mia. I brushed against her mind and she let out a chirrup, standing up on her hind legs and patting Turos's face with her little paws.

'It's okay, girl,' he said, stroking her back. 'It's just Izzy.'

She looked toward me and I nodded my head. 'I need to use your connection to your baby so we can find her.' I was guessing it was a girl.

She squatted back down, wrapping her tail more firmly around Turos's neck.

This time when I connected, she sat still, her eyes fixed firmly on my face. I flowed into her and quested through her mind, reaching out for her child.

The trail was faint, a tenuous tug on my mind. I turned so it felt like a thread pulling from the middle of my chest, and then I rolled back the layers of reality between me and it.

We rushed through the gateway, spreading out with weapons ready to secure the area. Thomas ushered Sabby behind him with one arm as he fell in beside Turos.

A female goblin turned towards us. Her eyes were calm and her hands continued their task of pushing the needle and thread through the garment she was mending.

Apart from Galanta, I had never seen a female goblin. I had assumed they were all as fierce as she had been. I had been wrong.

This female wore a skirt and blouse and had her long, lustrous hair pulled up in a bun on the top of her head. She stood gracefully, turning to place her sewing on the chair. Then she beckoned and crossed the room to a hall that opened off it.

I looked at Isla as I chewed on my bottom lip. Was it a trap?

Isla nodded her head and gestured for me to follow. I sheathed one of my swords, I wasn't trusting enough to sheath both, and followed her down the narrow hall. I could hear the others behind me.

The floors and walls of the structure were made of packed earth. Tree limbs supported a roof that also seemed to be made of dirt, but roots wound through this earth holding it all together. Lamps lit the room and hall.

I followed her down the hallway and then left into a room filled with natural light. On one side of the room, stairs led upwards. I followed the female up, my head swivelling from side-to-side as I searched for danger. She waited up the top, watching me with an amused look on her face.

Vines wound their way up wooden archways and flowers cascaded from above. Small vegetable patches were dotted throughout.

Mia let out a chitter. I turned to see her standing on her rear legs, one paw resting on Turos's head. She bounced up and down and pointed with her free paw as she let out a mewing cry.

'What is it, girl?' he asked.

There was an answering mew from a stand of trees about a hundred feet away. Mia clambered up onto Turos's head, a somewhat painful procedure for him I knew from experience. But he stood still as she propelled herself off, stretching her limbs out so her skin wings ballooned with air. She glided the distance to the trees, landing on a trunk and then scurrying up into the branches.

I tucked my remaining sword into its scabbard as we followed her. Aethan, Turos, Thomas, Lionel and Wilfred spread out around us, while Sabby, Grams, Isla and I peered up into the tree.

Mia clasped a half-grown narathymia to her side. She nuzzled the babe, snuffling all over its body as if searching for damage. Her child had its paws wrapped around her neck as it made little chuffing noises.

'Oh,' Sabby choked out. 'That's adorable.'

'Cutest thing I ever saw,' Grams agreed.

'I looked after him as best I could.'

I spun to face the female goblin. She held a basket out towards me.

'Just in case the mother can not produce milk. This will feed him for a few days until you can get more.' Her accent was thick and her words clipped, but she spoke far better English than Galanta.

'Thank you.' I stepped forwards and took the basket from her. It held a dozen bottles of white liquid.

'Sheep milk,' she said. 'Don't give him cow's. It will make him ill.'

'Where did you get him from?'

'My daughter. She had him in a cage. I asked her for him. A daughter should do what a mother asks.' She shook her head. 'That was the only thing I ever asked of her that she did.'

My eyes grew wide as I fought the urge to reach for my swords. 'Your name?' I whispered.

'Brushenta. Mother of Galanta.' Her eyes were solemn as they bore into mine. 'I can not thank you for killing my daughter,' she said, 'but I *can* thank you for ending this war. We are not so different, your people and mine. Some of us thirst for violence, some of us want only peace.'

I opened my mouth to argue but shut it again. We had killed her daughter. Quibbling would have been callous.

'She was not prophesised to be the great chief. Her child was.' Brushenta sighed and shook her head. 'She could not accept that *that* glory was not hers. And then *He* came, whispering dark thoughts into her mind.'

Isla's glow increased as she drifted forwards. 'We are sorry for your loss. Would you show us the child? I would like to bless him.'

I looked back at where Mia and her babe now sat on Turos's shoulder. We already had the child.

Brushenta stared at Isla, uncertain for the first time since we had arrived, but she nodded once and turned back towards the staircase into her home.

We trailed behind her, following her back to where our gateway still stood open.

'You must promise you will not harm him.'

'We promise,' Isla said. 'We would not harm a babe.'

Brushenta hesitated. She clenched and unclenched her fists as she ran her eyes over us. '*She* must also bless him.' She pointed a finger at me. 'He is of her blood.'

Isla nodded. 'It will be done.'

The women nodded back and then darted into the hallway, in a hurry now that her mind was made up.

'What in the Great Dark Sky is going on?' I turned to Isla.

'You're about to meet your Uncle.'

When the female returned she held a wrapped bundle in her arms. Two little feet stuck out from the end of the swaddling.

A baby. She was holding a baby.

My mouth opened and closed but no sound came out.

Galanta had had a son. More importantly Galanta and Santanas had had a son.

I could hear the collective intake of breaths around me as everybody else finally caught up. This was the real reason Isla had come. To bless the baby. To hopefully sway him to a path of good and not evil.

'May I?' Isla held her hands out.

Brushenta nodded and placed the babe into Isla's cradled arms.

Isla tucked the swaddling down till we could see his face. A strange mixture of blunt goblin and dainty faery features. 'His name?'

'Bulldar.'

Isla licked the base of her thumb and pressed it to Bulldar's forehead. 'I, Isla, Goddess of Love, anoint you and bless you, Bulldar. I will be watching over you as you grow, guiding you to a life filled with compassion and grace.' She met my eyes, raising her eyebrows as she jerked her head.

I walked to her side, licked my thumb and pressed it to his forehead. 'I, Isadora, War Faery and niece, anoint you and bless you, Bulldar. I will be watching over you as you grow, guiding you to a life filled with compassion and grace.'

I turned to find a queue forming behind me. One-by-one, the rest of our group took turns in blessing Bulldar.

When it was done, Isla handed him back to Brushenta. 'You will allow me to visit?'

'I would like that.' The grandmother bowed her head. 'It would be good for him to have wise council as he grows.'

The sound of feet slapping dirt echoed down the corridor. 'You must go,' Brushenta waved her hands at us. 'They will not be happy if they know you were here.'

'Quick,' I said. 'Through the gate.' I didn't want to shed blood in Brushenta's house.

My friends dashed through the gateway and I followed them. I spun, raising my arms to close it, and a goblin warrior burst into the room. I pressed the two sides of the gate together as he roared and hefted a spear.

I wasn't fast enough.

It hit me like a truck. Slamming into me. Through me.

I looked down at the quivering shaft of wood where it extended from my stomach. I heard Sabby's scream and Aethan calling my name.

There wasn't much blood. Not considering the width of the spear. And how far it had gone in. The blood would no doubt start soon.

'Isla.' I held my hand up.

'Shhhhh.' She took it. 'Don't talk. Sabby is going to heal you.'

'Will you take me back with you?'

'You're not going to die.'

'Really?' It felt like it. The pain had taken a few more seconds to get there than the spear had, but it was operating in full force now.

Hands under my arms lowered me to my knees. I looked up into Aethan's face. So glorious. So worried.

'Don't frown,' I slurred. 'You'll get a line.' I rubbed at the skin between my eyebrows. 'Right here.'

'We have to get the spear out before I can heal her.' Sabby sounded like she was just managing to remain calm. Little skips of hysteria tainted her syllables.

'I'll do it.'

Turos. Dear Turos. I would have been happy with him if it weren't for Aethan. But having known Aethan, I could never have been happy with anybody else.

It was a moot point now. I was dying. I knew it. Already I was starting to feel myself disconnecting from my body.

'Isla.' The pain wasn't so bad any more. And the fact that Isla was there meant I wasn't scared. She would take me home.

'Izzy,' Grams' voice barked at me. 'You stay with us. Don't you go getting any stupid ideas about going off on an adventure by yourself.'

'Lie her on her side.'

Strong arms lay me down.

'Now brace her.'

Hands held my shoulders and hips.

I looked up at Aethan. I wanted my last vision to be of him. What a shame I wasn't going to get to marry him. It seemed so stupid now to have been so against it. I mean all I had ever wanted was to be with him. Why had I been so stubborn? Because it hadn't been my idea?

'Love you,' I whispered. I tried to reach a hand towards him but I had no control over my limbs.

'Now.' Sabby's voice was like a whip cracking, and all of a sudden the pain was back.

It ripped through me, tearing a scream from deep within. Blood gushed out of the hole the spear had exited.

I drew a ragged breath, trying to bring in more air so I could scream it back out. But I couldn't get any. My lungs were full, but not with air. I coughed and blood flowed from my mouth.

I scrabbled at my mouth, trying to force air in. The blood flowed freely. There was no room for air.

And then the healing began. Fire raked me from the inside, arching my body back like a bow. I wanted to beg her to stop. This was not how I wanted to die. Drowning in a pool of my own blood. I wanted time to perfect my memory of Aethan's face.

My eyes closed. I struggled to open them. To see Aethan one last time.

'Izzy.' There was a stinging slap on my face. Just one more pain. Not a bad one. More like an insect bite. An annoyance. 'Stay with me Izzy.'

I wanted to. I really did. But even his voice was getting faint. An echo. Not real. Just a memory.

Then light. Sparkly lights dancing before me. They spun as they lifted into the air. A whirlpool. I followed them up. Chasing after them. If I could just catch them. Just see what they were. Fireflies? Sparks?

'Isadora.' This time the blow to my face hurt.

'Owwwww.' I rubbed at my cheek as I opened my eyes. 'What did you do that for?'

'If you had touched one of them, I wouldn't have been able to bring you back.' Isla laid her palm on my cheek.

'Don't follow the lights,' Wilfred said.

'I died?' I sat up. 'You brought me back? So I'm, what, like Wilfred now?'

'You wish.' Wilfred let out a laugh.

'Sabby saved you.' Aethan's eyes were wet as he squatted in front of me.

'Hey,' I reached out a hand and took his. 'Aren't you meant to be kissing me?'

He smiled his crooked smile as he said, 'I would, but I don't like the taste of blood.'

'Oh.' I pulled my hand from his and put it over my mouth. I must have looked hideous.

'Stop moving.' Sabby's hands moved over my back. 'I'm checking I got everything.'

'Thank you.' I turned my head toward her.

'I said stop moving.' I could hear the smile in her voice. 'You're welcome. Aren't you glad you brought me with you?'

'Yes.' My voice was rough from trying to scream. 'Never going anywhere without you again.'

She chuckled. 'You're healed. Can you stand?'

I pulled my feet up underneath me and pushed myself up. A small bundle of fur leapt at me, scrabbling up my body to my arms. I scratched Scruffy under the chin. 'It's okay boy. I'm okay.'

You sure know how to make an entrance. I could feel the relief in Emerald's voice.

I concentrated on putting one foot in front of the other as we made our way up the path. The healing process had sucked my energy from me.

'How did it go?' The scent of lemon cake accompanied Mum's voice from the kitchen as we opened the front door.

'Successful mission,' Grams yelled back. 'Go and get cleaned up,' she hissed at me. 'She'll have kittens if she sees you like that.'

'I'll help her.' Isla took my arm and led me up to my room.

She chatted to me as I sat on the floor in the shower, watching the blood run off me. Then she handed me a towel and watched as I dried myself and dressed.

'Feeling better?' she asked me.

'Getting there.'

'Good. 'Cause you have a conversation to finish.' She gave me a cheeky grin as she danced from the bathroom.

By the time I followed her she was gone. But my bedroom wasn't empty. Aethan stood near the foot of my bed. He looked nervous as he played with the lid of the ring box. When he noticed me, he slammed the lid shut.

'Yes,' I said.

'Yes, what?' His face was still strained.

I crossed to stand before him. 'Yes, I will marry you.' I held my hand out and wiggled my fingers.

His face relaxed, but he didn't open the box. 'You sure? I don't want you making any rash decisions just 'cause you had a near-death experience.'

'I can be a bit thick,' I said. 'Apparently it takes a near-death experience to make me see sense.'

He still didn't open the box.

'Oh, Aethan.' I stepped into his arms. 'I'm sorry. I didn't mean to make you doubt this. I love you. I want to be with you. I want to marry you.'

'You're sure?'

'I'm totally sure.' I smiled up at him. 'Now kiss me before I get mad. It *is* my birthday after all.'

Finally, a true smile graced his lips. He pulled me into his arms and gave me the kiss I was craving. But better still, I heard the sound of the ring box opening and then felt the cool metal band being slipped over the fourth finger of my left hand.

'Mine.' I breathed against his mouth. 'You are mine.'

'Forever,' he murmured. 'I am yours, forever.'

Chapter Eighteen

Happily Ever After

The bride looked radiant in a full-length dress of sunset orange. Cyril, draped around her shoulders like a smooth feather boa, as her new husband spun and dipped her on the dance floor.

I rubbed my thumb against the inside of the ring that adorned the fourth finger of my left hand. My finger ached but I couldn't complain about its ridiculous weight without risking offence to my future mother-in-law. Not that the thought of Eloise not talking to me worried me that much, it actually sounded quite nice, but I didn't want to make things any more difficult for Aethan than they had been. She hadn't warmed to me at all.

Anyway, wearing the Gabrielle House ring was not something one complained about. Not even when its massive diamond got in the way of one's swordplay.

I looked down at it and sighed.

'Having second thoughts?' Aethan's voice sent a thrill running down my spine.

'Never.' I looked up at him through my lashes. He looked divine in a black suit and bow tie. His hair, even though he had tried to tame it, was ruffled up on top, and for a second I remembered the night before and flames burst into my cheeks.

Aethan's pupils widened as his midnight-blue eyes met mine. 'Dance with me.' His voice was husky.

I didn't answer. I didn't protest that I didn't know how to dance, even though it was true. His eyes held me in a trance as I placed my hand in his.

Garden faeries drifted through the trees surrounding the dance floor, little lights that bobbed and glowed in time with the music. Aethan had generously let Grams and Lionel have their wedding at the castle, and between that, and the fact that a deity had married them, Grams was satisfied that all her friends were green with envy.

I relaxed into Aethan's arms, trying not to concentrate *too* much on the feel of him, lest I wrestle him off into the trees to have my wicked way with him. Instead, I examined the faces of the people dancing around us.

Grams and Lionel – well ecstatic, that went without saying.

Radismus and Mum rocked on the spot, their eyes closed, bliss on their faces. Radismus had moved in as soon as they had gotten back from London and it was nice to have a male around the house. Not that I was there that much. Although Aethan and I did split our time between Isilvitania, the barracks, and home.

I was pleased when Turos had turned up to the wedding with a leggy, blonde faery called Priscilla. Watching him mourn me had been almost more than I could bear. She seemed perfect, and if the look he was giving her as they swept past on the dance floor was any indication, she was going to be around long enough for me to get to know her. There was that look, and the fact that while Mia sat on Turos's neck, Rupert, her baby, sat on Priscilla's.

Turos's mother, Gladaline, danced with exuberance, her head thrown back and her arms in the air while Bladimir struggled to catch her. The two of them had moved into a cottage near the castle and Bladimir seemed to feel that the trade-off of his crown for his wife was worth it.

Wilfred spun Isla under his arm and out to the extent of his reach before snatching her back into the safety of his embrace. He held her as tightly as he could considering her expanding girth. She only had three months left till their triplets were born. Well, she told me she was having triplets, two boys and a girl, and whatever Isla said, I believed. She *was* the Goddess after all.

Thomas led Sabina in an awkward march across the floor. She rolled her eyes at me and smiled. She didn't care if he could dance or not, he was always going to be her hero. He had joined the Millenium fighting force for real and she had become one of their healers. Emerald and Lance were expecting another egg soon and we were hoping that it would choose Thomas.

A puff of flame drew my eyes out past the dance floor. Arthur was there, sitting with Tiny. I could see a dot of white on Tiny's leg. Scruffy. I should have known he would be with them. The three were inseparable when they were all in the same plane of existence.

'Do you think it was right?'

I started at Isla's voice in my ear. 'You two getting married without us there to witness it?' I waved my finger between her and Wilfred. 'How was that *ever* going to be right?'

She pulled a face at me. 'I told you, Gods only.'

'Oh please. Like rules ever stopped you before.'

She let out a laugh. 'I wasn't talking about that.' She nodded her head toward Tiny.

'Oh…that.' The giant now wore tattoos that wound their way up his arms and across his shoulders. 'Making him your disciple?'

She nodded, a frown of uncertainty creasing her brow.

'Honestly, Isla. It was perfect.'

'Really?'

I shook my head. For a Goddess she sure was uncertain sometimes. I was putting it down to the pregnancy hormones. 'He was peopleless. You gave him a home, but more importantly, you gave him a purpose.'

Her face switched from forlorn to radiant. Yep, it was the hormones for sure.

'Thank you,' she said.

'You're welcome, your Deity.' I poked my tongue out at her.

'I love you sister,' Aethan said, 'but if you don't mind, I'd like some alone time with my soon-to-be wife.'

My stomach did a flip at his words.

Wife. *Eeekkkkk*. I was still getting used to the weight of the engagement ring, let alone the word wife.

He spun me around and danced me backwards across the floor. And all the time his gaze mesmerised me so I was unaware of what my feet were doing. We could have been floating for all I knew.

Suddenly, there were trees around us and just the light from the garden faeries to guide our way. He backed me up a few more steps till my back was against an oak.

'Isadora Scrumpleton,' he growled, 'you are far too ravishing to appear in public. If I'd had to fight every man looking at you inappropriately, well, I wouldn't have had time to do this to you.'

My knees went weak as he traced the length of my neck with his lips, the warmth of his breath caressing my skin. I tightened my arms around him, pulling his lips towards mine.

I stopped when his lips were mere millimetres away. 'Do you think it was worth it?'

He looked out amongst the trees to where our friends and family danced. 'Definitely,' he said. 'This was worth fighting for.' He grazed my lips with his and whispered against my mouth, 'I can't wait to grow old with you.'

The right to love, the right to live, the right to grow old together, *this* is what we had fought for. This is what we had *all* fought for.

We knew they might come again one day. We knew that war might once again shadow the land. And we would be ready. But until that day, we would rejoice in our love and live every day as if it were our last.

I smiled against his lips as I wrapped my arms around him, letting his kiss carry me far, far, away.

THE END

Did you enjoy the War Faery Trilogy? Want to find out when my books are released?

Sign up to my Fantasy Book Club to find out.

You can find the sign up button on the top right of my website www.donnajoyusher.com on any page BUT the home page, or go to http://eepurl.com/2IMcT to go straight to the sign up page.

If you enjoyed this book, I ask that you give me the gift of a review on the site that you bought it. Reviews are the lifeblood of any author. It doesn't have to be long or flowery, I just ask that it is honest. Without those reviews the task of marketing becomes a lot harder so I thank you in advance for your time and effort.

About Donna Joy Usher

Hi there. I'm Donna Joy Usher. I started writing my first novel when I was seven. With no idea about plot or character development (I mean I *was* only seven) my storyline quickly disintegrated into a muddled jumble of boring dialogue between two horses. Disillusioned, I gave up writing stories for quite a while after that. Instead, I concentrated on my studies, eventually graduating as a dentist.

After many years of 'drilling and filling' I turned to writing in an effort to escape the seriousness of my day job. During that time I created my first book, *The Seven Steps to Closure*, and discovered that I love nothing more than making other people laugh. Well that, and my husband and two miniature schnauzers, Chloe and Xena.

I currently live near the river in beautiful Perth. When I am not working or writing, I love to paddle board, walk on the beach and sip chai lattes at the local cafe.

You can connect with me on my website site (www.donnajoyusher.com), Facebook, Goodreads, or LinkedIn.

Here's a couple of my other books. They're all available for sale in print form on Amazon, CreateSpace, and other online distributors. It is also available as an eBook on Amazon, Nook, Kobo, iBooks, Page Foundry, Scribd and Tolino.

Cocoa and Chanel

Book One in The Chanel Series

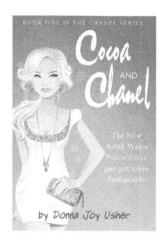

by Donna Joy Usher

Winner of the 2014 Next Generation Indie Book Awards - Ebook Fiction Category.

Winner of the 2014 National Indie Excellence Awards - Humor Category.

Faced with the unattractive options of an affair with her boss's husband or the unknown, Chanel Smith chooses the unknown and unwittingly traps herself into joining the New South Wales Police Force. More interested in fashion than felony, Chanel staggers through training and finds herself posted to the forces most notorious crime hot spot: Kings Cross. Against her wishes she becomes entangled in a case of the worst kind, a serial killer targeting young women in The Cross.

 As she is drawn further into the seedy underworld of The Cross in her attempt to unravel the truth, Chanel makes new friends, new enemies and draws the attention of the killer. Can she solve the case in time, or will she become the killer's next victim?

Goons 'n' Roses

Book Two in the Chanel Series

by Donna Joy Usher

Finalist in the 2015 Indi Excellence Awards Humor Category

It's been 3 months since Chanel's world fell apart and now she's ready for a vacation. Unfortunately, her all-expenses-paid trip to Las Vegas is not turning out as she had hoped. Within hours of arriving, her mum, Lorraine, is kidnapped. Then Trent, her boss and Lorraine's boyfriend, disappears; but not before he imparts information about an Interpol investigation into missing girls in Las Vegas.

When Chanel hooks up with local bad boy, the seriously sexy Billy, in a bid to get information, things only start to get worse. As she and Martine search for answers they are thwarted by obstacles and pursued by ruthless killers.

Who really kidnapped Lorraine? What happened to the missing girls? Can the delicious Billy be trusted? These are all questions that she needs to find the answers to, before the answers find her.

The Seven Steps to Closure

Winner of the 2012 elit Publishing Award Humor Category.

Honourable mention in the London Book Festival.

Tara Babcock awakes the morning after her 30th birthday with a hangover that could kill an elephant - and the knowledge she is still no closer to achieving closure on her marriage breakup. Things go from bad to worse when she discovers that, not only is her ex-husband engaged to her cousin - Tash, the woman he left her for - but that Jake is also running for Lord Major of Sydney.

Desperate to leave the destructive relationship behind and with nothing to lose, she decides - with encouragement from her three best friends - to follow the dubious advice from a magazine article, *Closure in Seven Easy Steps*.

The Seven Steps to Closure follows Tara on her sometimes disastrous - always hilarious - path to achieve the seemingly impossible.

CPSIA information can be obtained
at www.ICGtesting.com
Printed in the USA
LVOW01s2253130317
527109LV00008B/110/P